The Gown of Glory

Novels by
Agnes Sligh Turnbull

THE ROLLING YEARS

REMEMBER THE END

THE DAY MUST DAWN

THE BISHOP'S MANTLE

THE GOWN OF GLORY

The Gown of Glory

Agnes Sligh Turnbull

HOUGHTON MIFFLIN COMPANY BOSTON

The Riverside Press Cambridge

FIRST PRINTING, DECEMBER, 1951
SECOND PRINTING, FEBRUARY, 1952
THIRD PRINTING, MARCH, 1952
FOURTH PRINTING, MAY, 1952

The Riverside Press
CAMBRIDGE · MASSACHUSETTS
PRINTED IN THE U.S.A.

To my sister
JANET GUTHRIE SLIGH

*"Happy is he to whom God has given,
with sparing hand, as much as is enough."*

— HORACE

The Gown of Glory

Prologue

ON A GUSTY March afternoon in the year eighteen and eighty-one, a battered black hack drawn by two gray horses appeared on the top of Haldeman's Hill, swayed for a moment as the wind from the high ground struck it, and then lurched forward in the hub-deep mud almost upon the horses' haunches as the down grade sharply began.

Josiah Hunt, the driver, sat on the front seat, the reins secure in his bare, red hands, his felt boots braced against the dashboard, a quid of tobacco in his cheek, and the mailbag beside him. Once a day, except Sundays, he made the three-mile trip from the little town of Ladykirk to Thornton, the nearest railroad junction, to convey travelers and mail to and from that point.

At intervals now, out of the tail of his eye, he glanced at his only passengers. They sat very close together on one of the lengthwise seats that faced each other in the back of the hack. Josiah couldn't be certain (as he reported around the post-office stove that night), but he was under the impression that the two were holding hands under cover of the folds of the lady's skirt.

The young man was tall and slender with a very stiff white collar and a black, clerical-looking hat. The young woman was small, sweetly plump and pretty, and clad in a fringed gray dolman and a boat-shaped little bonnet with a bluebird's wing at the side. It was quite apparent that they were both trying hard to be dignified.

As the hack strained suddenly around a curve, the two pitched forward to the seat opposite, righted themselves, replaced their hats, looked at each other and laughed. It was a pleasant sound and Josiah turned clear about then to look at them.

"All right?" he inquired. "These here March roads are rough enough to pull the tail feathers out of a turkey gobbler. First time you've been here, ain't it, Missus? 'Course we've sort of got to know the Reverend."

The young woman smiled at him and at once the dull day became brighter. Josiah didn't know that she smiled partly because of the *Missus*. She was not used to it yet for she had been married only a week.

"Yes, it is the first time and I'm very eager to see Ladykirk."

The hack pitched violently again, but this time her husband held her firmly. "Is . . . is it very much farther?" she asked somewhat breathlessly.

"No," Josiah reassured her. "Just about a quarter of a mile. I'll throw off the mailbag at the post office an' drive you right up to the manse, like you said you wanted. Guess the Blackburns are expectin' you at the hotel for overnight. City girl, ain't you?" he added.

The young woman flushed a little as though admitting a fault.

"Well, yes, I've always lived in the city, but I know I'm going to love Ladykirk. Mr. Lyall," she added, looking up with shameless pride at the tall young man, "has told me so much about it."

"I guess your flittin's here already," Josiah informed them

The young people looked blankly at each other.

"I . . . I beg your pardon?" said Mr. Lyall.

"Your *flittin'*, I said. It come through yesterday. Women hardly got any work done for lookin'. They all say you've got an awful lot of furniture for a young couple. Well, them rooms are pretty big. Can take it all, I guess. Look yon-away," he added suddenly. "Nice view if you care for it."

Mary Lyall followed the direction of his pointing whip and gave a cry of delight. To the south were spread wide, rolling fields, patched here and there with the young wheat's living green and the rich brown of the freshly turned earth. Budding woodland touched the lower hills with palest rose while far to the east stretched the smoky, misty, undulating blue of the mountain ridges. Just ahead now, too, with a sudden brightness of white against the darker surroundings, could be seen the village of Ladykirk with its long, sloping Main Street beyond the covered bridge.

Mary adjusted her dolman and gave a little shiver of nervous anticipation; David felt of his tie and settled his new black hat more firmly upon his head. They both sat up very straight indeed as the hack rolled noisily over the bridge planks and started up the street.

They were conscious of curious eyes peering from windows and doors and store steps as they proceeded, but Josiah with a magnificent flourish threw off the mailbag at the post office without stopping and hurried his horses toward the manse which stood at the end of town with an open field at either side of it.

Here, he drew the reins tightly, wrapped the ends around the whipstock, jumped out over the front wheel and waded through the mud of the street to open the back door of the hack for his passengers. When they were safely on the gravel path which led to the house, their one large bag gripped in David's hand, Josiah made his farewell.

"Well, good luck to ye. I wouldn't take to preacherin' myself, but every man to his trade. I'll bring the trunks around as soon as they come in an' you can let me know if you want me to help you get settled. I can stretch carpets with the next one. Brussels, ingrain or rag — all the same to me. Well, good day, Reverend. Good day, Missus."

The horses' hoofs sank deep, rose and plopped again as the hack made a precarious swing and plunged off down the street. Mary turned on a sudden impulse and waved to Josiah. He was watching, but upon sight of the gay hand signaling friendship he stared straight ahead of him and began chewing violently.

David and Mary stood still, just inside the white fence, their eyes fixed upon the wide-spreading ancient clapboard dwelling in front of them. Even as they looked, the winds ceased, the capricious March clouds turned to blue and in a sudden golden welcoming, the sun shone down upon the house, the pine trees, the lilac bushes, the rose hedge and the two travelers by the gate.

"Look, it's an omen!" Mary said, and catching David's hand, started for the house almost at a run.

Suddenly they both became conscious of their position and with great decorum walked the rest of the way. Once inside, however, David threw the bag in the corner of the wide hall, and then carried his bride over the sill into the big front room to the right.

"There! I didn't dare pick you up at the outside door," he said, "so this will have to do instead. How do you like it all? Is it too bad, really? The house and the town and everything? When the furniture's in place here, it ought to shape up fairly well. Look at the big grate and the bay window, too. The main thing is it's our home. *Ours!* Oh, Mary, do you think you can be happy here?"

She was standing in the middle of the room where he had gently set her down. She had caught off her bonnet and without it, under the soft, wavy brown hair, her face looked younger and more eager than ever.

"You know I'll be happy! And the house is quaint and sweet. I'll do wonders with it. Just you wait and see. And we've got to be so grateful to Grandmother for willing me the furniture. Don't look like that, David. The money doesn't matter. Let Cousin Annabelle have it. I don't care a fig. Truly!"

"If it hadn't been for me . . ."

"Nonsense! Look who Annabelle's got for a husband. That fat old banker. Oh, David, how can you think I mind about anything else in the world when I have you? It's almost better having the furniture anyway, for it will just suit these rooms and we never could have bought anything like it even if we had gotten some of the money. Come on, let's go all over the house."

They went from room to room, dodging the heavy crates, exclaiming, planning, pretending not to notice the faded wallpaper, the too wide cracks in the ceiling and the evident leaks under the eaves. It was a big house with odd little halls and storage spaces upstairs where one would least expect them. The main rooms, however, were large and square. Downstairs there was one of these on either side of the hall, a dining room behind, somewhat darkened by one of the pine trees, and a kitchen back of that within which the two young people, having reached it last, stood silent. There was an ancient wooden sink, an oil-cloth-covered table, an ill-tempered-looking coal range, bare, uneven boards below and dark, smudged walls and woodwork above. As they stood there speechless, motionless, a mouse came out from under the sink and scurried across the floor in front of them.

Mary screamed and threw herself upon her husband, shaken with sudden sobs.

"I c . . . couldn't, Davy! I really c . . . couldn't stand *mice*. I don't mind anything else but I c . . . couldn't . . ."

He held her close and patted her gently. "You won't have to, darling. You'll see. I'll stop up all the holes and set traps. I'll absolutely take care of everything. There won't be a single one left to trouble you. Why, I know what! I'll get you a cat!"

Mary raised her head, light slowly breaking over her countenance.

"A cat!" she echoed. "Could you really? Why, I'd love that. I've never had a pet. You know Grandmother wouldn't tolerate them. Do you think you *could* get one, David?"

"Of course. People in places like this always have extra cats. I'll inquire right away. I think I'd like one myself."

All at once he grinned, struck an oratorical pose, one hand beneath the buttons of his coat and declaimed in a deep voice:

> *"A cat*
> *I keep, that plays about my house,*
> *Grown fat*
> *With eating many a miching mouse.*

That's Herrick. Doesn't it just fit the case, though? Miching means thieving. Quaint old word. Shakespeare used it too." He snapped his fingers. "Avaunt, I say, you little miching mouse!"

Mary giggled a bit shakily and stroked his black coat lapel.

"You're so clever. You know so much. Taking all those honors in college and the Seminary and everything. You know what, David? You won't stay long in Ladykirk. In a very short time some big city church will call you. Don't you honestly think so, yourself?"

He smiled back at her with the complete confidence of youth, fingered his stiff white collar and tried hard to look humble.

"Well, of course I do feel this is just the beginning. But one never knows. Maybe I won't be a success at all."

Mary laughed happily then at the sheer absurdity of the

statement and they went back, arms entwined, for a last look at the front room to the left which was going to be the study. They planned where the book cases would go and the big desk. There must be several easy chairs near the fire, also, to accommodate callers. "And perhaps here, in front of the window, the small sofa where I can sit and sew sometimes. I'll never say a word," Mary added, "to disturb you."

David viewed the room tenderly. "We must leave now," he said, "or we'll catch our deaths of cold. Tomorrow I'll get all the fires going and get Josiah to help uncrate the furniture and when it's warm enough you can come up and boss us around. We'll have this place looking like home in no time."

He walked over to the window and stood with an odd little smile on his face as he looked off toward the far blue ridges.

"I may even have a chance here to do a little scribbling on the side if I'm not too busy. I've always wanted to write a book." He tried to say it carelessly but Mary's eyes grew large with amazement and worship.

"You never told me," she breathed, "that you were going to be an author too! I can't believe it. Oh, Davy, the thing is, will I be smart enough to keep up with you? It worries me all at once."

He took her round, rosy face between his hands, which trembled.

"I'm not worthy to touch one of your little shoes," he said. "I don't know how you ever came to marry me. You're my darling bride and I love you more than the world and all that's in it."

When she could speak again, she made a small, solemn pronouncement.

"I'll tell you, Davy, just how it's going to be. We'll be here in Ladykirk about five years, no longer."

Those words had been spoken twenty-five years ago.

Chapter One

T HE VILLAGE of Ladykirk lay in the eastern end of the county like a pretty brooch on a fair lady's bosom. The name had a British ring and rightly so, for the first settlement had been made in colonial times and it is probable that the christening had been done by a homesick young Scot or Englishman in memory of his native town back home. Even in those early days when the surrounding hills were dark and heavy with forests, tradition had it that there were sunny meadows beside the stream where the pioneers had been able to build their first cabins and raise their crops of corn without the preliminary labor of swinging an ax.

The stream, also called Ladykirk on deeds and county maps, but which was known simply as *The Crick* to the villagers, had through the years dug its way deeper and deeper into the rich soil and now flowed between banks. During the spring rains, however, and even sometimes of a calm summer evening, its low, throaty ripple could be heard in the town. A pleasant hay meadow, designated somewhat ambiguously as "Aunt Betsy Wade's Bottom," still bordered it on the yonder side.

The village itself had for many years possessed a serenely static quality. Once in a while a farmer, feeling the ripeness of old age and a modest bank account pressing upon him, sold his farm and built a house in town in which to end his days. But even with these additions the village could never be said actually to grow; rather it absorbed anything new with such leisurely assurance that changes only made it more than ever the same.

There was a long, sloping main thoroughfare with the business affairs of the town in the middle of it; and two parallel side streets reached on dark nights by aid of kerosene lanterns and an intuitive knowledge of paving pitfalls. There was a flourishing blacksmith shop, a large general store in which could be purchased carriages, corsets or coffee according to desire; an apothecary's combined, as the Spoils System permitted, with the post office; a livery stable, large, sprawling and richly odorous, which served also as club for the male population; a two-story frame schoolhouse on The Green, as one of the side streets was still familiarly called; and three churches representing as many variations of Calvinism, set so closely together on Ash Street that, as Josiah Hunt, the hack driver, said, "You could stand in the Covenanter graveyard and spit on a Presbyterian if you had a mind to." There was nothing of dogmatic prejudice in this statement. It was purely descriptive.

The fact that Josiah was still known as the hack driver, was a concrete evidence of the villagers' ability to incorporate the new within the framework of the old. When a branch railroad finally ran from Thornton to Ladykirk through thickets of laurel and May-apples, it stopped short of the town on the other side of the Crick. Josiah continued to meet the train with his battered black hack. He received the mailbag, such luggage as was too heavy to carry by hand, and passengers who, owing to the infirmities of age or the lack of a vehicle of their own to meet them, eschewed the long walk through the covered bridge and up the sloping main street and rode for the sum of ten cents with Josiah.

In twenty-five years, then, since the Lyalls had been set down from the hack at the old manse gate, the physical aspects of the town had changed surprisingly little. As to population, many new lives had been born, many older ones had closed, but a general nucleus had remained the same, touched, of course, by the years.

The manse itself seemed smaller than it had on that first day, because there were now more people in it. In addition to David and Mary there was Faith, the eldest, a tall, pretty girl of twenty-four, with blonde braids, her father's thoughtful gray eyes, a gentle wit and a shy smile. She gave piano lessons to all the children of Ladykirk who could afford them, and to some who couldn't, and went once a week to the city, spending all she had made and a little more, to continue her own studies. There was Jeremy, a charmingly irrepressible youth of twenty who, by dint of selling books in summer and teaching in little red country schoolhouses in winter, was earning money to help him through college. There was Lucy at eighteen, blue-eyed, curly-haired, impulsive and lovely, who, having graduated at a little seminary in Woodstock over the hills, was being "finished" by her father at home since the family funds simply couldn't be stretched for a woman's college. And there was in the cemetery back of the town a small grave with a little gray lamb asleep upon the headstone. When Mary slipped off on a summer's evening saying simply that she was going for a walk, no one ever questioned her about her destination. They all knew.

On this warm June afternoon, Lucy sat under the apple tree in the side yard applying black paint to a high-backed wooden rocker. A large, checked gingham apron was tied around her waist, a white sunbonnet dangled by its strings on her shoulders where it had slipped during her quick movements, a tiny daub of paint chased a freckle on her tilted nose and she sang softly to herself out of her deep contentment with life in general. She had chosen this spot in which to work, not only because of the apple tree's shade but because it commanded a view of the front street. For since this thoroughfare, after modestly passing through Ladykirk, became both to east and west the big Turnpike which arrived at length in larger towns, it was exciting to watch the equipages pass by. Most of them, of course, were only the familiar rigs of the farmers of the community, but once in a while a strange buggy or surrey passed and one was left with a delightful sense of conjecture.

It was nearing four o'clock and the shadow from the biggest pine tree was slanting across the front lawn when Lucy, glancing up, saw a strange young man walking slowly up the other side of the street. In a second she had tossed down her paintbrush and stood with quick beating heart watching him. By every outward and visible sign, by every bitter reality of past experience, she recognized what his errand must be. In only a few more moments he would cross to the manse gate, come up the gravel path, find Father in his study and then — it would be too late. No one else was at home. She must act and act quickly, if she were to avert calamity.

She ran down the path, crossed the street and appeared flushed and breathless before the stranger. She saw that he was tall, taller even than Jeremy, with a thin face and dark eyes. He looked tired but, while Lucy's heart smote her, she was not deterred.

"I'm so dreadfully sorry to do this," she began to the astonished young man, "but would you mind too much not stopping at our house? To see Father, that is. You see we're trying so hard just now to save up for a special purpose and Father just can't resist books. They're his weakness. And now, especially since Jeremy, my brother, is out selling *The Volume of*

Golden Deeds, Father feels he must buy from every other agent who comes. And of course since he's a minister they all come to him!"

"You thought I was a book agent?" the young man asked, his tired face smiling a little.

"I knew it the minute I laid eyes on you!" Lucy replied triumphantly. "You're just the right age — they're all working their way through college. And I knew why you hadn't a satchel, for Jeremy has learned that new trick too. He just carries a *Prospectus* in the inside of his coat. Mother made him a big pocket though she wasn't sure it was quite *ethical.* He says it works wonderfully though, for when he stops at houses they don't know he's selling books until he's inside, and then he's got such a way with him . . . "

She stopped embarrassed. As the young man said nothing, she eyed him sympathetically.

"Will it matter to you too much if you don't make a sale with Father? Will it?"

"Not at all."

"You truly mean it?"

"Truly."

"Have you had a good day, then?"

"The latter part has been wonderful. Quite amazing, in fact."

Lucy drew a breath of relief. "I'm so glad! Would you care to come in anyway? Jeremy says he gets awfully tired. It will make me feel easier in my conscience if you come in and rest a little at least."

The young man brightened visibly.

"Thank you. I'd like to very much. I promise you I won't produce a *Prospectus* from the inside of my coat or try to sell anybody a book!"

"You're very kind," Lucy said gratefully, leading the way around to the back porch. "This is our coolest spot and we practically live here in summer. I would call Father right away, but . . ." She eyed him with a shy dubiety.

"You still don't entirely trust me?" he asked laughing.

"Well," Lucy said hesitantly, "of course after all you are only human."

He looked at her steadily then and his eyes were very dark and intense even as he smiled.

"I'm afraid very much so," he answered.

Lucy felt herself coloring under his gaze. It was embarrassing but not altogether unpleasant for a feeling of warmth and excitement went through her whole body. She had been thinking so intently before about the miracle of salvation she had just wrought for her family and also her pity for her victim that she had paid scant attention to the stranger as an attractive young man. Now she was acutely aware of it.

"I hope you won't think me rude and of course I'll trust you. It's just that we are trying so hard to save for Mother's birthday gift in the fall. It's a very big present and if we have too many book agents or missionaries between now and then we're lost."

"*Missionaries?*" the young man repeated in surprise. "Are you afraid of them too?"

"Oh, they're the worst of all. I mean having them come here is awful because most of them are so good themselves and they make such a plea for the poor heathen that Father gives more than he can afford and so does Mother. We children are just *praying* we won't have a missionary between now and September. That's when the birthday is. Did I tell you what the present is to be? A kitchen cabinet! Mother wants that more than anything else in the world. Does your mother have one?"

The young man looked bewildered.

"I . . . I really don't know," he stammered.

"You don't *know!*" Lucy repeated in amazement.

"Well," he hedged, "I'm not very observant about things in

the house. But I . . . I'm quite sure, come to think of it, that she has."

"They're wonderful!" Lucy went on. "Our kitchen is the worst feature of the house. Mother said when she first saw it she thought she'd really just have to leave Father and go away. She was joking, of course. But she does *so* want the cabinet. It's not actually a surprise, for she knows we're getting it. Would you like a drink?"

"I beg your pardon?" he asked quickly.

"It's so hot I thought you might care for a glass of lemonade. It won't take but a minute."

"Thank you. I'd like it very much. And I should introduce myself. I'm Ninian Ross."

"I'm Lucy — from Wordsworth, you know, one of Father's favorites. And I suppose you got our last name, Lyall, from someone downtown. That's the way the other agents do."

"It's a beautiful name," he said slowly. "Lucy Lyall."

"I like yours, too, though I've never known a *Ninian* before."

Then for a long moment the two young people regarded each other as though at the sound of their names for the first time upon each other's lips, a door had opened and they had passed through together.

Lucy spoke quickly to break the spell. "And Jeremy is named for Jeremy Taylor the great preacher. He lived a long time ago and he wrote *Holy Living* and *Holy Dying*. I never read them, but Father knows them nearly by heart. And Faith, my sister, was called that because Mother said it really took a lot of faith for her to come to live in Ladykirk after being brought up in the city. Has your name a story?"

"It's just a family one. Though I believe there was a Saint Ninian whom the Scotch claim. I don't think I should mention it in connection with my own name, though."

"Oh, but that's lovely, I think. I must tell Father." She

sobered. "I don't think I was quite fair to Father when I talked about his weakness, for I truly think he's the best man in the world. It's just that we all have weaknesses and books are his. I've got one. It's *dreadful*. It's stereopticon views. When the last agent came selling them I hid and never came out till he was gone. I didn't *dare!*"

"You enjoy them so much?"

"I *revel* in them," said Lucy, throwing out her hands in an unconscious gesture of abandon. "That's the way I travel. Under the pine tree. The ones I want next are the *Fountains at Versailles* and the *Hall of Mirrors*, but I have to wait. Do rest yourself now while I make the lemonade."

When she was gone, Ninian sank down on one of the high-backed wooden rockers and looked about him. The porch was large and low, shaded at the eastern end by a thick grapevine. There was a large drop-leaf table at the other end littered with books and papers, with round-armed wooden chairs and more rockers near it. A few gardening tools and a pair of work gloves lay tossed in a corner and some odd-looking boxes stood along the side wall which he felt vaguely might have something to do with bees. Sure enough, as his eyes wandered across the back lawn and down through the long garden, he saw a row of beehives along the fence with blooming hollyhocks behind them.

There was somethng indescribably soothing in the sight and in the faint, soft sound of accompanying wings. The warm afternoon air held in it the pines, the young green grapes, the sweet peas and stocks in the garden and the freshly cut hay in the neighboring field. The young man leaned his head against the back of the rocker and closed his eyes. His drawn face relaxed. When Lucy came out without her apron and sunbonnet, carrying the glasses on great-grandmother's silver tray, she saw that he was fast asleep.

She set the tray down softly and went through the house to the study. The door was ajar and she slipped in to stand beside her father's desk until he would look up.

The room itself would have seemed beautiful to any student the world over, even though the Brussels carpet was worn threadbare in spots, the curtains many times mended and the chairs shabby, for there were books on three walls rising from floor to ceiling, a fine print of Magdalen tower over the mantel, and above the big desk by the window a far view of blue hills to rest a tired reader's eye.

Lucy coughed softly and her father, until then absorbed in his work, looked up. Although David Lyall was past fifty and his temples gray, he was still slender which gave to his appearance an illusion of youth. He no longer struggled as he once did to keep from looking proud. When he considered himself now at all it was with deep humility.

"Hello, Lucy," he said, smiling up at his youngest daughter, "did you want something?"

She leaned over the piled books on the desk.

"There's a young man sound asleep on the back porch," she whispered.

"Is he a tramp?"

"Good gracious, *no!*" Lucy returned emphatically. Then under her father's gaze a rosy color grew and spread until her face was suffused with it. At the sight the man's eyes narrowed slightly but he waited for her to go on.

"He's a book agent, but he's not interested in selling to you . . . I mean not since I . . . he was really so kind about it when . . . "

"Lucy," her father said gently, "you can't dissemble worth a cent. You'd better tell it straight."

"I know," she sighed ruefully. "I never can keep anything to myself. Well, I saw him coming and I knew how dangerous it would be if he was selling Encyclopedias or anything expensive like that. It might be a . . . a temptation so I asked him not to sell to you and then I invited him in to rest and he's gone asleep. Should I wake him?"

David Lyall looked at the flushed young face above him.

"No," he said slowly. "I wouldn't if I were you. If a young man under the present circumstances *falls asleep*, I should think he needed the rest. Don't disturb him until your mother comes, anyway."

"That's what I thought," said Lucy. "And please don't open up the subject of books to him, Father, for he said it didn't matter in the slightest whether you bought or not. He said he'd had a wonderful day, especially the latter part!"

"Oh, he did, did he?" David said, a small smile on his lips. "All right, I'll be good. Do you know what book he's selling?"

"There you go!" Lucy exclaimed. "I'm afraid to trust either of you. But you promised, Father."

"Right and I'll keep it. Run along, now. I have a little more to do here."

At a few minutes before five, Lucy, moving quietly about the kitchen, heard sounds which indicated that the rest of the family had returned. First, the buckboard rattled along the drive toward the stable at the back of the lot with Jeremy standing up precariously, slapping the reins over Prince's back and shouting, "Hail, the conquering hero comes! I sold four books! Hip, Hooray!"

Next came voices in the front hall, Faith's quiet as usual but Mother's eager and excited. Whenever Mary entered the house or even a room it was as though a pleasant little breeze had sprung up.

Lucy hurried to the porch to find the young man on his feet, looking dazedly about him. His face was scarlet.

"I'm so ashamed," he said, "I don't know what to do. I don't deserve to have you even speak to me! How could I possibly have been so rude?"

"You were tired," Lucy said, "and it's perfectly all right. The sleep would do you good."

"You're not angry?"

"Why should I be angry?" Lucy asked in surprise.

"Most girls would be, I think. I guess you're different. I must go now but could I . . . would you . . . will you be home this evening if I should drop in?"

"Of course. We're nearly always at home. Wouldn't you like to meet the others now? They've just come."

"I think I'd rather wait until later if you'll excuse me. I still feel pretty embarrassed over what I did."

In another minute he was gone before Jeremy had come from the stable or the rest from the study.

"I know you all think I dreamed him up," Lucy kept repeating to the banter over the supper table, "but he was really here and he's coming back tonight."

"But to go asleep, dear, while you were making the lemonade! How very odd! And Lucy, remember if you should ever be here alone, never, *never* ask any man to come in, young or old. There are so many tramps and peddlers abroad this summer," her mother admonished.

David smiled mischievously.

> *"Oh, sleep it is a gentle thing*
> *Beloved from pole to pole;*
> *She sent the gentle sleep from heaven*
> *That slid into his soul,"*

he quoted.

"If you ask me," Jeremy predicted after the laughter had subsided, "he's probably off by now on the evening train. None

of the agents ever stay around here over Sunday. I think, Lucy
my lass, you have, in the language of the day, *been buncoed!*"

"Unless he isn't a book agent at all," Faith said thoughtfully.
"He never actually *said* he was, did he? Maybe he's a surveyor
or something like that. You know there were some at the hotel
a few weeks ago.

"Well," Mary said brightly, "while you girls do the dishes
I'll stir up a spice cake in case he does come. Oh, David, what
an afternoon I had. I made six calls. Actually. That takes care
of the shut-ins for another month. The town ones. Do you
know, I think we should start country calling next week before
harvest really gets started. We could do up the sick and the
old at least," she urged.

"Mother talks about them as if they were preserves," Jeremy
chuckled.

"Oh, you know I don't mean to sound casual or . . . or busi-
nesslike about it," Mary said anxiously, "it's just that it's part
of our work and people get offended if we don't call on them
often enough. Besides," she added with her quick smile, "I love
to go calling in the country in summer!"

"We'll start then, next week," David said. "You're usually
right. Meanwhile, I'm quite curious to see Lucy's young man, if
he turns up."

"He won't," said Jeremy.

But he did. Not before nine o'clock, however, when the
golden cloud of fireflies in the field next door had grown dim
and when even Lucy had given him up with a small desolation in
her heart. The house, after supper, had been hastily tidied, the
cake baked, the back porch rearranged with fresh flowers on the
table and the corners cleared of tools and bee boxes. There had
been a last flurry of pressing lawn dresses and then the family
had seated themselves to wait. At eight-thirty David had quietly
started a song, and the others, even Lucy, had joined in. This

singing was a habit with the Lyalls. Often in winter in front of the grate fire with Faith at the piano, and more often still on quiet summer evenings on the back porch, they sang, David leading with his fine tenor, the girls carrying the soprano, Mary the contralto and Jeremy an unsteady but developing bass. Many families in that end of town sitting on their own porches stopped talking to listen when the Lyalls began to sing.

They were in the midst of "Come Where My Love Lies Dreaming," when Jeremy saw a tall, hesitant shadow by the grapevine. He jumped up at once and in a few minutes Ninian was introduced and welcomed.

"Won't you please go on singing," he begged eagerly. "It sounded wonderful. I'm very fond of music myself."

"Will you join us?" Jeremy asked.

"I'd like to."

So they sang on, and as the newcomer's voice blended with the others, the gap of strangeness seemed more quickly bridged, so, than by conversation. A delicate accord of spirit moved itself into the concord of sound.

Soft o'er the fountain
Lingering falls the southern moon. . . .

David spoke when the last harmony died away. "Fine, Ninian! That's the best we've ever sung it. You see what you did for us. We'd better stop now, though. We don't want to bore you."

"Bore me!" the young man repeated. "I've never known such a delightful evening . . . "

"Except," Jeremy broke in abruptly, "that it is *very warm*."

"Oh, extremely hot," Lucy echoed eagerly.

"And humid," said Faith.

"Almost stifling," Mary added.

"One might even say torrid," David finished.

"It's unanimous!" Jeremy shouted, jumping to his feet. "We've got to hurry, though, or the store will be closed. I'll give fifteen cents since I had such a big day."

"Ten from me," Faith said quickly.

Mary began to laugh. "I found a dime in the old blue teapot yesterday. I must have put it there once and forgotten it. I'll give that."

"Here's one from me," David said, fishing it from his pocket.

"I've only got an extra nickel," Lucy said mournfully, "but . . ."

"That does it!" Jeremy cried in triumph. "That makes fifty and we can get more than a quart. What shall it be, Mother, chocolate or vanilla?"

"I believe vanilla with the spice cake, and hurry, dear. We should explain to you, Ninian, that this is just a silly way we have of voting whether we can get ice cream or not."

"Where's your dime, Mother?" Lucy called from the hall.

"It's still in the teapot. I thought I'd told you."

The guest sat silent during the flurry of collecting the money, his face a strange study. His offer of a contribution had been firmly refused, but he went along with Jeremy to purchase the ice cream. When they returned Jeremy gave Ninian the precious package to convey to the kitchen where the girls were cutting the cake, while he, alone then with his parents, lowered his voice and spoke excitedly.

"What do you think! Ninian says that two men drove up to the hotel tonight before supper and got rooms. He says he doesn't know where they're from. He says he heard one of the men asking just where the Presbyterian church was as they expected to attend service there tomorrow!"

"David!" Mary breathed, "could it possibly be . . ."

"That's what I thought," Jeremy hurried on. "Of course Ninian just mentioned it casually but I got all the details from him that I could for it did look so . . . *suspicious!*"

"We're not considering a murder," David said, making his voice as casual as he could.

"No, but you see what I mean! It does look like a visiting committee, Father, doesn't it?"

"Oh, David, how's your sermon? Is it specially good? Couldn't you preach your 'Where are the Nine?' again? The one you gave that time at Presbytery? I really think it's your best, and nobody would know the difference!"

David was still outwardly calm though his voice sounded a trifle husky.

"The sermon for tomorrow is no better nor worse than usual, I guess. Just about average, so if these men are coming to hear me preach they can make a fair decision."

"But Davy," Mary pleaded with some asperity. "There's no sin in putting your best foot forward."

David's dark brows puckered as they always did when he was considering.

"No sin, but I always think 'best feet' are likely to trip you. I will preach the sermon I've prepared and do my best with it. I'll go over it again very carefully before I go to bed. But please don't go getting excited, Mary, and expecting things. We've been through all this before."

"Not for a long time."

"No," David echoed so low it could scarcely be heard, "not for a long time."

Then the other young people came out, the big kerosene lamp on the table was lighted, its high, rounded glass globe protecting the flame, the plates were passed, the talking and laughter went on apace, with Jeremy even more exuberant than usual and Mary herself nervously gay. Of them all only David remained silent.

Suddenly they all stopped to listen. From the hall came three long rings from the telephone, repeated insistently.

"I thought that was us," Jeremy said, getting to his feet. "I wonder who wants us at this hour."

David rose too and motioned him back. "I'll answer it," he said. "It's probably for me."

"It must be nearly eleven," Mary said anxiously. "I hope nothing serious has happened."

They waited, a lull falling upon the group until David returned.

"It's old Mrs. Wesley," he said quietly. "She's having another bad spell and wants me to go out."

"Oh, no," Mary cried, jumping up to face him. "Oh, David, you can't. You can't lose sleep tonight! You know what that does to you. Think of tomorrow and all it might mean."

She was close to him now, her hand on his arm.

"Call the Wesleys back. Tell them you can't come tonight. Tell them you'll go right after church tomorrow."

"It might be too late then."

"Oh, nonsense. You know she's been dying in these attacks for two years now and she never does. She's always better in the morning, and you're the one who's worn out. Oh, Davy, please don't go tonight!"

"Why, I have to, dear. I couldn't fail her. You know that. Tomorrow will have to take care of itself."

She stood very still for a moment and the others saw him put his hand over hers. Ninian watching, scarcely breathing, sensed drama though its essence was hidden from him.

"Of course," Mary said quietly, "you'll have to go, but try to come back as soon as you can. You will do that, won't you?"

David nodded and then turned to Ninian with an air of apology.

"This old woman lives out in the country. She gets frightened in these attacks. It's rather pitiful — at her age. I'm sorry to leave so abruptly and I hope you'll drop in again while you're in town."

"Thank you, sir. I'll be happy to."

"I'll hitch up for you," Jeremy broke in, vaulting over the low porch rail. "Just a minute, Father."

Ninian waited until the buggy had driven off, then he took his leave. He said good-bye to Lucy last of all. She walked with him to the step and stood there on the soft edge of the night with the pale gold lamplight behind her. He crossed the lawn instead of going by the path so that he might look back at her and she waited until he was finally lost to sight.

When he had gone, Mary and Jeremy told the others the news.

"Of course we're not *sure* that's what they're after, but it certainly looks like it," Mary kept repeating.

"Plain as the nose on your face!" Jeremy pronounced excitedly. "Why else would they be so particular to ask where the church was?"

"If only they don't run into Mr. Dilling at the hotel . . . and they're almost sure to," Mary's voice was anxious.

"But Mr. Dilling *loves* Father," Lucy said quickly.

"I know he does, that's the trouble. He's such a close friend of your father and yet he holds such queer views on all sorts of subjects. He might say something to the strange men that would seem to compromise . . . Oh, well, we'll just have to hope and pray that all will go smoothly. Get on to bed, children. It's late and I'd like you all to look your best tomorrow."

"And what about you?" Jeremy asked.

"I'm going to press Father's black suit. It's needed it this good while, and I must check on his shirt, too. Some of the cuffs are fraying and I've been too busy lately to turn them."

"I'll bring the clothes down, Mother," Faith said, starting for the stairs.

"And his black necktie," Mary called after her, "I'll press that, too."

Jeremy set up the ironing board in the kitchen, placed the lamp where it would shed the best light and poked up the fire.

"I wouldn't fuss too much, Mother. You know Father looks distinguished even in his nightshirt. It's going to take a while for these things to get hot," he added as he set the heavy flat-irons on the range.

"That's all right," Mary said cheerfully. "I'd rather have something to occupy me just now than not. I never can sleep till Father gets home. But go on to bed, the rest of you. You look dead tired, Jeremy."

"I could court repose on a brick," he grinned, "but I had a fine day. What did you all think of Ninian?"

Mary turned to bid her youngest daughter good night as she answered. She had seen an odd brightness in Lucy's eyes and noted that she watched the departing figure out of sight. A strange young man of whom they knew nothing, here today, and gone tomorrow. . . . Lucy must not think too much about him.

"He seems a very nice boy, indeed. I'm glad he came up and didn't spend a lonely evening at the hotel. We never asked him about his own sales today!"

"I did," Jeremy said, giving an odd glance at Lucy. "Well, I'm going on up."

Some time after the girls had followed him, Mary stopped short in her work, hurried to the foot of the stairs and called Faith.

"The music," she said breathlessly, "for tomorrow! I never thought of it till now. How is it?"

Faith leaned over the banister in the hall above. A blonde braid hung down on either side over her white nightgown, giving her the appearance of a gentle Marguerite.

"It's not too bad," she said, "provided Miss Minnie shows up. She's been undependable lately. If she doesn't come I'll just have to play a Voluntary while the collection's being taken."

"Oh, I hope she comes tomorrow. If she doesn't, then play something pretty like the Nocturne from *Martha*. That's about the best for the old organ."

"All right. I'll play that. And don't worry too much, Mother. Good night."

Mary returned to the kitchen. It was already nearing midnight. She went on with her pressing, sponging a small spot here and there, holding the garments up to the lamplight, then patiently doing over what seemed less than perfect. At last she had done all she could. She banked the fire so there would be heat enough for a glass of warm milk for David when he returned, then softly went upstairs, carrying the freshened clothes with her.

She undressed in the big square chamber over the study which had been hers and David's all these years. Even now the massive four-poster and bureaus, once grandmother's, gave the room an air of elegance in spite of the other worn appointments.

Mary watched the clock in the pale lamplight until one, and then went over to kneel by the south window. The little town was asleep. Below, the garden was fragrant in the darkness; the bees were quiet in their hives. There was no sound except the faint murmur of Ladykirk Creek and the indescribable breathing of the June night which made her feel that the earth itself was listening and aware.

Mary knelt, her heart beating heavily. There would be no chance now for David to look over his sermon again, and the hard, sleepless hours would leave him wan and weakened in spite of his efforts to do his best. She knew! There came back to her vividly now each time through the years that a visiting committee had come to hear David preach. The memory of the first was the most poignant. They — she and David — had been so assured, so happily confident in their expectations. David had laughed gleefully as he had told her the news after church that day.

"Guess what? Spies in the land of Canaan! Did you see those two strange men at service? They sat behind the Woods."

"Yes, but I. . . . Oh, David, you mean they've come for you? Just like I said they would! And the five years not even up yet."

"Looks that way. They're from Moreswell. Just the place I'd like to go to next! I really couldn't be more pleased."

"Davy, I'm so happy and so proud of you! I love Ladykirk but I do want you to have a bigger opportunity. And Moreswell! The county seat! Oh, that will be wonderful. Is it all settled?"

"Well, no," David admitted, "but they seemed very much interested and asked a great many questions. I imagine they mean business. The one man said I would probably hear something further soon."

They had watched the mails then, full of excited plans. The days passed. What were days? The weeks passed. It would take time, wouldn't it? The months passed. And the first small question showed in their eager young eyes. They lay close in the big four-poster at night, cheering each other with brave philosophy.

How foolish he had been, David said over and over, to imagine that the very first time a committee came it meant *a call*. Never again would he make that mistake? If another committee should come some time they must pay no attention to the incident — never give it a thought until — that is, *unless* something really came of it.

They were able soon to laugh at their over-confidence and pride and settle again into the pleasant routine of Ladykirk days. As time went on they twitted each other gaily about Moreswell. It became a pleasant mirage. But occasionally a tiny doubt arose to stab Mary's heart. David was primarily a student. His sermons were quiet, couched in that deceptively simple language which is the result of clear and logical thought. He quoted frequently from his beloved poets, but unlike the visiting ministers who came to preach for him during Week of Prayer or Revival Services, he did not besprinkle his sermons with colorful, illustrative stories; he never shouted or pounded the pulpit, and he *never* ended with a dramatic hell-fire climax. What, Mary asked herself with a little shudder, what if he never got another call? What if most congregations wanted more excitement in their preaching than David could or would give them? But she always flung this thought from her with violence when it returned as though it were blasphemy.

Ladykirk, meanwhile, was more than content. The people liked David. They liked Mary. They sat, like many more intellectual congregations, hearing the preaching vaguely through a gentle veil of their own private thoughts. None of their former ministers had been Sons of Thunder, but good, simple men, kindly pastors, satisfied, apparently, with the small rural world which contained them. It would have struck Ladykirk as extremely odd if David had been known to have any larger ambition, what with a good manse and eight hundred dollars a year! Indeed, a sort of tradition, the Lyalls discovered, went with the church. The ministers who came there, remained.

And so it had been with David. There had been through the years other occasional visiting committees who came, listened, spoke to him after the service, often with a show of interest, then disappeared into silence. And a certain patience had finally fallen upon his sensitive face. The burning expectations of the first years receded; Ladykirk made him her own. It was Mary to whom resignation was a stranger. It was not that she herself was unhappy; quite the contrary. Life was to her a constant delight. But with it all she clung fiercely to her first ambitions for David, intensified these latter years by the needs of her children.

She turned now to look back at the bureau. She had meant, when she knelt down, to pray, but her thoughts were so turbulent at first that the petitions grew confused.

She prayed now, however, with all the intensity of her soul, for it was two of the clock and David was still out on his unfortunate, useless errand, and the men who were come to judge him were calmly asleep in their hotel beds not knowing.

She prayed that he might return soon; that he might not be too tired tomorrow to do his best; that A Call would at last come so that David's years might be crowned with honor and that the children might have the opportunities they needed. Jeremy his college without more delay, Faith her music and congenial friends, and Lucy. . . .

Mary smiled up, as it were, into the very face of God. No one could help smiling at the thought of Lucy. Sweet, impetuous, unpredictable child, who should, as David had once remarked, have remained a gentle thing out of Wordsworth but who had at once jumped over into Browning and become a creature of "spirit, fire, and dew."

Mary finished her petitions and walked over to the bureau. On it, carefully placed, lay a blue volume lettered in gilt, still unworn though it was not new. Mary lifted it reverently as she always did, and held it close to the lamp, smoothing the binding as one might caress the face of a child. She read the title for the thousandth time: *Religious Aspects of the Greater Poets* by David Lyall.

She leafed it slowly, remembering the days, the years of its writing. For David with his meticulous conscience had been careful to steal no hours from his regular duties to put upon this substance of his dream. Even so, the book had slowly and secretly developed under his painstaking student's care. In one sense he had been glad to be unhurried, to see the fulfillment always in the future. The hope, then, could be kept undiminished and bright to cheer them on dark days. He and Mary both held the innocent beliefs of the uninitiated in regard to authorship. Anyone who published a book must of necessity make money from it . . . perhaps a great deal. So as the years passed each time they had felt the economic pinch too keenly Mary was sure to say, "When your book is done, Davy, we'll have more to do with!" And David, himself, remarked more and more often as the chapters grew, "Of course if this book of mine ever amounts to anything . . . "

At last it was finished, corrected, laboriously recopied. On a never to be forgotten evening David had discussed with Mary the dedication.

"Which would you like better: *To My Wife:* or *To Mary?*"

She had looked up at him in ecstatic amazement and then thrown herself, with tears, into his arms.

"Oh, David, you never told me I was to be in it! I'm so pleased I just have to cry! You see I always thought when the whole thing was to be a surprise to Mr. Dilling, you'd dedicate it to him!"

"No," David answered, "I've got that worked out another way. I'm going to have him on the next page like this: *The author wishes to acknowledge the invaluable stimulus and inspiration of his friend, Horace P. Dilling* — something like that. And won't he open his eyes! I think I've done pretty well never once to let slip the fact that I was working on the thing. I've always set my heart so on surprising him at the last. But the dedication, darling, is for you alone. Which form do you like best?"

"Oh, it doesn't matter which! It will be so wonderful either way. I'm so proud of you and so thrilled I can hardly bear it."

She woke him in the middle of the night by leaning over to kiss his cheek.

"You know, Davy, it's funny, but I never even once thought I'd be in the book! Never, all this time. I was so sure it was to be only Mr. Dilling. And I've just decided I want: *To My Wife*, for *To Mary* could sound as if it were someone else. To the general public, that is. Don't you think so?"

They had lain talking in their naïve delight, time and sleep being negligible in the face of the coming possibilities.

"There's another thing in addition to the money," David confessed in the darkness. "There is a certain prestige about having written a book. I don't want to sound egotistical — you know that — but if it comes out I imagine people will know about it even at a distance. I mean it really might lead to something."

"It will!" Mary was positive. "You know what I think? I believe when it's published it will cause such a stir that you'll be called to the *Old First* in the city. I do, Davy. Doctor Mott there is seventy."

"Oh, not that!" David disclaimed the idea with pleasure in his tone. "Oh, I couldn't jump from Ladykirk to the Old First. But it might be a steppingstone. You never can tell. It might mean Moreswell, for instance. They seem to have a vacancy every few years. Their ministers always keep moving up. Well, it will be interesting to see what happens. But of course, the first thing is to get the thing printed now that it's done."

They spent long evenings weighing with complete ignorance the respective merits of various publishers. Since the content of the volume was not actually secular, David leaned to a religious publishing house. He pointed out that as a minister it would look better for him to ally himself with such a firm rather than one which published more profane material. Mary happily agreed.

On a blustery March day very like the one on which they had first arrived, Josiah Hunt was called upon to collect the heavy package and take it to the express office. He received it in his big bony hands and with the privilege of the years, stopped to read the address aloud.

The John Knox Publishing Co.
181 Fourth Ave., New York City
Manuscript

He shifted his tobacco and raised his shrewd eyes inquiringly.

"What you been up to, Reverend, writin' a book or something?"

"Oh, doing a little scribbling in my spare time, Josiah. Nothing to *mention*."

"Sure," Josiah nodded eagerly, "no call to tell the mice where you keep the cheese. *I* understand. One thing I will say for you, Reverend, is that you're smart as the next one and if you took it in your head to write a book, I'll bet, by gum, you could do it!"

The waiting had been intolerable. After the first perfunctory card acknowledging the manuscript's arrival, the John Knox Company had been veiled in silence. Three long months of it. David grew thin and Mary nervous as a witch. They died a hundred deaths of disappointment and despair between their little spasms of hope. The book was so poor the publishers hadn't even troubled to read it. (No, No, from Mary.) It had been lost in the publisher's office. It had been stolen by a wicked and jealous reader to be printed later under his own name. (Oh, no, this surely could not be, from David!) It had been received and they thought it was so wonderful they were just waiting — just waiting — Mary always floundered at this point, but stuck staunchly to her statement as far as it went.

When the letter came at last Mary had been swept by a sudden wave of nausea as she watched David's fingers draw the missive shakily from its envelope. She leaned against him to read. The John Knox Publishing Company wished to inform Mr. Lyall that his manuscript had been carefully read by their editorial staff and they all agreed that it was an excellent, even scholarly piece of work.

At this point Mary threw herself into a chair. "I knew it! I knew it, Davy! Didn't I tell you so? Oh, what a relief to have the suspense over!"

"Wait," David cautioned. "There's a *but* coming."

But — the publishers went on — owing to the nature of the material they feared the book would appeal only to a rather limited audience. They might be mistaken in this opinion, as they had occasionally been before. But, basing their present judgment upon long experience, they now felt they could not assume the entire financial risk of publishing the book. If the author would assist in this to the amount of $500, they would feel justified in going ahead, bringing the book out in the late fall. Otherwise, they must regretfully return the manuscript. Hoping to hear favorably from him and congratulating him upon the superior quality of his writing, they remained very truly his.

David had sunk down, still clutching the letter.

"Five hundred dollars," he repeated through stiff lips. "That ends it."

"It does nothing of the kind," Mary cried, though her eyes had a woeful hurt in them. "They may be all wrong. They even say so. You've got to publish it and it's bound to sell. You'll get all the money back and more. It will be just . . . just an investment, don't you see, Davy?"

They read the letter threadbare, slowly rebuilding their confidence upon the pleasant parts of it. There was a little nest egg in the savings bank. If they sent the $500, it would all but wipe it out. David resisted, his conscience raw and torn between his longing and what he feared was his duty. But as Mary constantly pointed out, how could he be sure it was not his duty to invest the money in the book? Suppose he made only one hundred dollars over and above what he put into it? They would be ahead, wouldn't they? And of course they would make much more than that. It stood to reason!

After wrestling and prayer on David's part and a stubborn determination on Mary's, the money had been sent, the contract signed and the book published. That had been ten years ago. It had sold to date eight hundred copies, bringing to David exactly one hundred and sixty dollars. Like a small pebble in a very large pool it had dropped with the minimum ripple and was now fallen from sight. There had been one good review in *The Presbyterian Banner* and one tiny ad in the Knox catalogue. There had been seven letters in all, from across the country, commending it; but aside from the volumes purchased by Ladykirk church members, which now lay imposing and unread on parlor tables beside the big family Bibles, there had been a scarcely appreciable show of interest in the county or even in the Presbytery. A few ministers here and there had heard of the book and told David at meetings that they really must read it soon. Very clever of him to find time to work on it. As to themselves, they had always intended to write a book but just couldn't get the time, etc., etc.

The John Knox Company had been generous in one particular. Because of David's monetary assistance they had sent him fifteen free copies instead of the author's usual six. Nine of these were still stacked in a hidden corner of the study.

The effect of the book upon Mr. Dilling had been almost fatal, for his surprise and delight in the volume, coupled with his bitter chagrin that it had been wasted (as he felt) upon the John Knox Company, had brought on one of his heart attacks.

He had recovered, however, and still insisted upon discussing it with David in terms of highest praise and blasting him roundly for the hurt in his conscience which would not heal. He owed it to himself and his family, said Mr. Dilling, to have the book published, so he had nothing with which to reproach himself. It was only unfortunate that he had sent it to . . . well, no use going into that again. At least the book was still in print and selling a few copies each year. It was reaching a small circle of choice readers here and there.

Mary looked again now at the one precious review pasted in the front, at the dedication page, *To My Wife*, then closed it and with a little sigh, put it back on the bureau. She walked over to the front windows to listen, but not a sound of a horse's hoofs broke the stillness of the night. One too early rooster crowed feebly from the Carvers' barnyard across the fields. That was all.

Mary sat down on the edge of the bed, leaning her head against the tall foot post. She could not sleep if she tried, with all this anxiety and anticipation upon her. Besides she must be awake when David returned to give him a hot drink and some last advice, for there would be scant time in the morning.

Three o'clock came and here and there more faint crowing borne on the hushed air, while the tension in her own heart became unbearable. In all the night trips to old Mrs. Wesley, David had never been as late as this. Life was hard to understand sometimes . . .

It was four when she heard the sound of wheels far down the road. She flew downstairs, stirred the fire to flame, and had the milk heating when the buggy rolled along the drive. She met David on the porch in the pale, cool dawn. His face was haggard from weariness but his eyes were alight.

"Oh, Davy, whatever kept you so?"

"She died," he said simply, "just about three. She had been

restless up until an hour before. I did what I could. Suddenly, just as from one minute to the next, peace seemed to come to her. She was conscious right up to the end, but she wasn't afraid any more. I was glad I was there."

Mary dropped her head against his breast, clinging to him. When she raised her face the tears were wet on her cheeks. They kissed without speaking, then she led the way to the kitchen. She poured out the warm milk.

"You must drink this and then get quickly to bed. Don't give a thought to your sermon. I know it will be fine. Your black suit is pressed, and all your clothes laid out, ready to put on. You can sleep until nearly nine."

They went upstairs where the young light of the new day was filling the big room. Mary set the alarm clock for herself — David would not hear it — drew the shades and sank back at last against her pillow.

"Davy!"

"Yes, dear."

"I've been wondering. Wouldn't it be possible in your sermon to bring in something about your book? Couldn't you say, 'As I mention in my book, *Religious Aspects of the Greater Poets*'? Couldn't you, Davy? That would really make an impression."

"I'd rather not be reminded of my book. Please, dear, we'll let come what come may. Let's go to sleep now."

In a few minutes his breathing was regular, but Mary still lay, watching the light. There was a small stirring of the air, bringing a scent of the garden through the window and the birds were waking. I'll cut the best of the flowers, she thought, and arrange them in the brass vases. I'll use only the tallest blooms with long sprays of ribbon grass. Then I'll send Jeremy down to the church with them early so as to forestall Mrs. Crombie with her awful, chunky little bouquets. I believe I'll even do it before breakfast. That would be safest! With the grace and lightness of spirit which were part of her nature she smiled as she pillowed her head on her hand.

Wouldn't it be wonderful, she thought, if the men were from Moreswell again, after all these years!

She closed her eyes.

Chapter Two

LADYKIRK came to life slowly on a summer Sabbath morning. If the day was fine, as was usually the case, a warm hush touched with the freshness of dewy gardens first brooded over the town. Then came the leisurely opening of front doors up and down Main Street with every here and there a woman, her hair still in curling pins, briskly sweeping her porch and sidewalk. This latter exercise was one of the very few physical tasks which were deemed to be compatible with the Fourth Commandment.

There were, indeed, certain fixed and unalterable customs prevailing regarding manual labor on the first day of the week. A man did none at all besides feeding his live stock if he had any. In his stiff and unaccustomed clothes, he sat about or dozed between services. It *was* considered seemly for him to take an afternoon walk to stretch his legs and stop to converse with another man bent upon the same errand. But though his eyes might turn wistfully toward the livery stable, no man except those on the very outer fringe of godliness, as it were, ever went there on a Sunday for the bonhomie of a social hour as he would do upon a week-day.

The women in their turn prepared three meals within the strict limits of Sabbatarian custom, that is to say, only the heavier and more necessary viands. To have baked a cake or pie on Sunday would have been considered a sin to be concealed. These more frivolous articles of diet were served in great abundance but were prepared the day before. As to the Sunday making of *ice cream* in the type of heavy, hand-turned wooden freezer owned by the more prosperous families, it is quite safe to say that such a preposterously wicked notion had never entered the head of a Ladykirk inhabitant.

At a quarter to ten, as the first church bell rang out, there was from the houses a sudden disgorgement of young people of all ages, and some adults, who passed up the street, dressed in their precious best with a look of bright anticipation upon their faces. Buggies, buckboards, and occasional carriages from the country began then to roll through the heavy dust in the same direction. There was in the whole general movement toward the bell's sound a delightful alacrity, indicative of expected pleasure.

Mr. Dilling, who lived at the Stone Hotel, had made a remark twenty years before which had never been entirely forgotten nor forgiven. As he had watched for the first time this Sunday morning exodus, he had turned to Mr. Blackburn, the proprietor, in a humorous amazement.

" 'Pon my soul, the place looks like Hamelin, doesn't it?"

Just then the Newburt twins, aged fifty-odd, had passed up the street. They did cobbling and harness-making in a little house and shop next to the bridge where they kept "bach" together. Their legs had never been as long as their bodies warranted, and their duplicate faces were swarthy and sharp. As Mr. Dilling had watched them scurrying along, he had smiled sardonically, as he stroked his mustache.

"I had not originally been referring to the *rats*," he drawled, "but now . . . I'm not so sure."

Since Mr. Blackburn was not conversant with Browning he had been forced to get the sense of this from Mr. Wilson, the schoolteacher. After that the word spread all over town and it had taken many a pleasant Sabbath morning before the people of Ladykirk began to speak cordially to Mr. Dilling.

They had accepted him, however, as the years passed, even though he never went to church and was reputed to be an *Atheist*. Mr. Dilling did not take the trouble to contradict them on the latter point, although it was not true. Mr. Dilling had a God, only He was not the same as Ladykirk's God. His Deity was occupied with immutable laws which kept the swinging galaxies in their courses but He was entirely unconcerned over such matters as cake-baking on Sunday or even, indeed, over the Westminster Shorter Catechism.

This fair June Sabbath, drenched in sun and rose fragrance, had in it for Mr. Dilling anxious overtones, even as it had for the Lyall family in the manse. Mr. Dilling had talked to the strange men the night before. He knew that they really *were* a visiting committee. They had questioned him in rather direct fashion about the Presbyterian church and its pastor. Mr. Dilling had all but choked upon his reply, but he had given it like a scholar and a gentleman.

"I have never known as fine a man as David Lyall. 'But Christes lore and his apostles twelve, he taught, but first he followed it himselve.' "

Having quoted thus in his best Chaucerian accent, he bade the gentlemen good night and went up to his solitary room. He dropped heavily on the side of his bed, his hands hanging limply between his knees, his head bowed. He was wondering almost with despair how he could go on living in Ladykirk if David Lyall should leave.

This morning as was his wont, he came out of the hotel early and seated himself in one of the big round-armed chairs which stood in the courtyard along the side wall. From here he could survey the Sunday panorama which never failed to interest him. Occasionally as the procession began to pass, he raised a hand in salute; once in a great while he raised his cap; as a rule he stared, motionless. One person to whom he always doffed his cap was Minnie Masters. She lived with her three bachelor brothers in the large frame house opposite the hotel. It had a side porch and a long garden at the back and Mr. Dilling, by observing carefully, could watch Miss Minnie through the week at many of her daily tasks. It warmed his heart to do so, for from his arrival in the town when he was fifty-five and Minnie was twenty-two, he had admired her. He could still see her rosy face as she brought milk from her family's cow over to the hotel that first night. She hesitated before him, swinging the empty pail on her way back. Perhaps the blackness of his mood and his evident physical weakness compelled her.

"Are you staying long?" she queried shyly.

"I'm afraid so," he had replied with bitterness.

"Oh, don't be afraid," she said earnestly. "I think Ladykirk's a lovely place to live. Well, I'll see you tomorrow for I bring the milk every day."

She had been his first friend. He had watched her grow into riper young womanhood, noting a beauty which apparently no one else in the town appreciated. Mrs. Blackburn even said, "Minnie was odd looking, kind of."

"Yes," Mr. Dilling had agreed with his cutting sarcasm, "very odd looking, like a Rossetti angel."

Of course Mrs. Blackburn could make neither head nor tail of that nor could anybody else. It was true, however, to Mr. Dilling's keen disappointment (even though he would not have considered any of them good enough for her!) that none of the village or country swains were ever drawn to Minnie Masters' looks. So at forty-two, tall, full-bosomed, auburn-haired and to his discerning eye, beautiful, she was still unwed. Her gait especially entranced Mr. Dilling. As she moved along the street, erect, graceful, unhurrying, he could be heard to mutter to himself:

"*Incessu patuit dea.*"

Mr. Blackburn overheard this so often that he finally dared to ask its meaning. Mr. Dilling scowled. " 'The goddess is shown by her walk,' " he shouted. "Can't you see? *Minerva* has just passed by!"

This, when circulated freely through the town, was felt to be a sign that Mr. Dilling was really growing senile. His vagaries, however, made interesting conversation and lifted the quiet level of the days with small glimpses into the unknown as though the sky had been diversified with peepholes.

This morning after Mr. Dilling had watched the first passers-by on their way to Sunday School, the two strange men came out of the hotel, smoked their stogies, strolled about the courtyard, chatted a few moments with him and then, arbiters of destiny as they were, went decorously up the street. Mr. Dilling sighed heavily and watched for Miss Minnie to revive his spirits. Her brothers had already gone at ten. But the last bell rang and Miss Minnie did not emerge. Mr. Dilling sighed heavily again and tilted his chair on its hind legs, his broad shoulders settled against the cool stone of the wall. A vast empty quiet now possessed the town as though it had been deserted of all life, except that at intervals the faint echo of song was borne through the tranquil air; a soft, blurred melody from the Presbyterians who used an organ, and a sharper, more strident sound from the U.P.'s and Covenanters who believed that God should be praised by the human voice, unaccompanied.

Mr. Dilling gave a sudden quizzical thought to the dark

young chap who had been there last night but who had not been seen this morning, and then trying to forget that danger threatened, he dozed in the penetrant sun.

Meanwhile back on Ash Street, in the upper sanctuary room of the big, plain brick building which the Presbyterian fathers had built a hundred years before, David Lyall had started to preach his sermon, and Mary, sitting with Jeremy in the second pew from the front, right-hand side, held her hands so tightly together, that the bones ached. David was very pale and quieter even than usual in his delivery. Indeed, he hesitated perceptibly now and then. No one of the congregation would dream of criticizing him, for by now everybody would not only know that old Mrs. Wesley had died at three that morning; they would also know by all the past experiences of their own lives that David would have been with her to the end. But the visiting men would not know!

Nothing had been right about the whole service, except the tall flowers in the brass vases. Miss Minnie hadn't come and as Faith was playing the Nocturne as a Voluntary the high E of the organ had stuck again! That hadn't happened now in a long time. It seemed cruel that it should happen today. Then the Lamson's baby had cried all through the long, pastoral prayer practically drowning out the words, and now, oh, crown of embarrassments, out of the tail of her eye Mary could see Mr. Harmon and Mr. McKnight, both ruddy-faced farmers, sound asleep! And dear knows how many more through the congregation that she could not see! How would *that* look to the Committee? David was always very kind about this. He insisted that they were men who worked hard in the fields all week and it was natural that the sudden inactivity should make them drowsy. "They get the hymns and the prayers and the peace of God's house. Maybe that's enough without my exhortations," he always said.

Bird songs came through the tall, opened windows, and occasional neighing from the horses hitched to the long row of posts outside. Within, fans stirred the warm air gently, an infant's chatter rose and was hushed, a child's feet clattered down the stairs, and Dick Hussey in the chair yawned openly. Slow tears blurred Mary's eyes. Everything was as usual. It was like this every Sunday except for David's pallor and slower speech. But it had had for her before the comfortable harmony of the long familiar. Now, with every sense acute, and every thought keyed to the reaction of the strangers, she was sensitive and ashamed.

She glanced at the girls in the choir to the left of the pulpit. Faith sat relaxed and thoughtful, her face toward her father. Lucy's eyes roved over the congregation, came back and met hers with an impulsive smile. This too might easily be misconstrued as levity while Mary knew it was only love. What she did not know was that Lucy's bright smile was partly a mask to hide the sinking of her heart. For while she had examined face by face every human being in the church, both downstairs and in the "gallery," she had not found Ninian's. It hurt her unaccountably for she had fully expected him to be there. Her thoughts as she dressed that morning in her best flowered lawn and chip hat were not of the visiting committee, exciting as their presence seemed. She was thinking of Ninian as she brushed each curl twice over around her finger. She was thinking that he would look up at the choir and suddenly see her there and maybe their eyes would meet as they sang the hymns. The thought was very sweet, but there had been no realization of it. Ninian was not in church.

David had now picked up his small notebook, and closed the big pulpit Bible. He leaned slightly upon it and raised a slender finger, his only gesture. His quiet voice had sunk still lower and, as always at this point, a hush fell upon the congregation. For David always had something he most earnestly desired to say, and his conclusion recapitulated it. Moreover, from his wide reading and natural bent for writing, he possessed a literary sense of proportion and emphasis. Those who had dozed betimes or whose thoughts had dwelt upon private problems during the sermon always tensed, awake and aware, and listened for these last words after the big Bible was closed. They were what most people carried home with them.

They were spoken now, in the moment of deep quiet, the brief prayer was uttered, the last hymn sung, the benediction pronounced.

Mary settled her hat, held Jeremy back from bolting down the aisle as all the young men did at the end of service in order to range themselves on either side of the walk below and study the girls as they passed out. She slipped a hand through his arm and leaning gently upon it, moved toward the back of the church as fast as she could where, she felt sure, the strange men would be waiting to meet her. Her progress was retarded, however, for she had to speak to everybody as she went. Old Sarah Stowe went on endlessly about her rheumatism, and she had to pause and "make" over the Lamsons' first baby (the one that cried), but she reached the back doors at last that opened into the upper hall. Here David stood as usual greeting his flock but there were no strange men to be seen.

When the last member had left, the last horse and buggy driven away, David and Mary started in the direction of the manse, Mary all but breathless from her pent emotions.

"Davy, did they not come at all?"

"Yes, they were there. They sat just behind the Murdochs. And I somehow think they *were* a committee."

"What did they say, Davy? How did they act?"

"They were pleasant, and casual. Nothing more. There was a youngish man and an older one. I liked the older man's looks.

He told me he had been interested in the sermon and recalled hearing me preach once before. I could swear he was one of the men that came from Moreswell twenty years ago!"

"*Moreswell!*" She breathed. "And they didn't say anything else? They didn't ask . . ."

"No. They acted like any two men who happened to be in a strange church. Nothing else. One thing is sure, if that is any comfort, they behaved quite differently from any other committee that ever were here."

"Could it be a good sign, Davy?"

"I don't know. I doubt it."

They reached the manse gate and started slowly up the gravel path. Their feet dragged a little, for to their physical weariness was added the heaviness of hope deferred. They saw now sharply what they usually noted but vaguely, that the sprawling clapboard house before them needed paint. The trustees had promised it by another year. Meanwhile it bore a worn and shabby appearance which the pink rambler rose and the honeysuckle vine could not conceal.

"I think I'll give those steps a fresh coat myself," David said suddenly. "It would smarten the place up a little."

Before they entered the door, Mary turned to her husband with a familiar, quick gesture.

"Davy, if we never hear anything more from the men, don't let's be too disappointed."

"Don't let's," he agreed.

"But," she went on eagerly, "you may be right. Just because they acted differently from any of the other committees they may be all the more serious. It may really mean something. We might hear yet. Oh, don't let's give up, Davy."

"All right," he said, smiling down at her, "don't let's."

The air that afternoon was hot and still. David was never

able to sleep in the daytime, so while the others rested according to their various tastes, he took his favorite form of relaxation: he went out to the garden to watch the bees. There were four hives along the fence, in front of the hollyhocks, and any day now there was likely to be a swarm, which would make another. A new box was ready and waiting the event. David's interest in bees had grown through the years until now, day by day as time permitted, he might be said to lead a second life in the strange, waxen cities. His greatest physical treasure after his books was a glass-doored hive which Mr. Dilling had given him as a gift a year ago. The secrets of the golden citizens were now, in large part, made plain.

David sank down in one of the old chairs he kept there for the purpose and leaned forward, absorbed and motionless. It was a good day for the bees. The garden was full of flowers, many of them blue, their favorite color. Through the warm air the workers went their way, returning to the hive with their baskets of pollen on either thigh. David peered closely, all his own problems for the moment lost. He saw the gatherers of the sweets pause for a wing beat or so at the portal of the hive. He saw the young bees stationed there to greet them give a tiny wave of their antennae. He saw the workers hurry on into the hive where more young bees, waiting at their posts, received the precious burden. Then, quickly turning, the busy gatherers went out once more to do it all over again, unresting, never pausing. Never one indulgence, never even a holiday, David mused, until their one great day of all the year — the swarm. He pondered again upon the mystery of these virgins' dedicated lives. How came to them this allegiance to something greater than themselves? To their queen, to the eternally renewing life of the hive, to the future? Why was sacrifice so difficult for a human and so easy, apparently, for a bee?

Each time he sat there, fascinated, David blessed his friend for the glass box. At first Mr. Dilling had scorned the bees, contenting himself with quoting variously from the classics concerning them.

"Bees are gluttons. Virgil says so.

> *Sweet gardens full of saffron flowers invite*
> *The wandering gluttons and retard their flight."*

"But Dilling, I tell you they aren't gluttons. Look at those workers! They never take even a taste of the pollen while they gather it, and they'll starve themselves to death, if need be, for their queen."

"Well, they're all Communists. Read the *Fourth Georgic*. Even back in those days they knew it.

" 'All is the state's! The state provides for all.' And I don't like the system even in bees. Besides all that, they're treacherous. I'd as lief be mixed up with a den of rattlesnakes. For myself I shall continue my study of the stars. They don't bite."

"Sting," corrected David.

"It feels like a bite. I had one once," insisted Mr. Dilling.

But little by little, and gingerly, he had edged nearer the hives and as David had described the incredible life within, he had forgotten his fears and begun to watch, also. It was David's chance remark once that certain of the female workers used their wings as brooms to sweep out any particles of foreign material which got into the hive or upon their entrance platform which broke down Mr. Dilling's last resistance.

"No!" he said excitedly. "Even the bees? I've watched so many human females sweeping all along Main Street that I've got to see the apiarian counterpart. My God!" he added suddenly, leaning close, "that one there," indicating a worker poised on the threshold, "looks exactly like Sarah Stowe in a sunbonnet. There's more to this bee business of yours than I thought, David."

That very night he had begun upon the inquiries which led finally to the glass box. After its installation the two men did not play chess every Monday afternoon as they had been wont to do upon the ministerial holiday. They now alternated during the fine weather between chess and the bees. Tomorrow, David was now recalling, it would be chess. He leaned back in his chair and closed his eyes for a moment, thinking of his old friend.

He had first met Mr. Dilling long ago in the office of the Stone Hotel where he had gone one day to see Mr. Blackburn. No one was there except a pale, bitter-mouthed man of fifty-odd.

"I beg your pardon," David had said, "you must be the new guest. I'm David Lyall, pastor of the Presbyterian church. Mr. Blackburn has spoken of you and I'm glad to welcome you to Ladykirk. Is he around anywhere, by the way?"

His question had been ignored. "I suppose he told you that a wreck of a man with a death sentence on him had come from the tents of Sodom to this stagnant frog pond to end his days?"

"No . . ."

"And I might as well tell you, Mr. Lyall, that I don't care to be visited by the clergy. I've already had two here, like buzzards waiting for their prey. I do not intend to go to any church and I . . . don't . . . like . . . preachers."

Now David had just been through one of his periodic attempts to advance to terms of companionship with the United Presbyterian and the Covenanter ministers who were then in the town. As at other times he had met with no success. Estimable men both, but friendly to him only in a distant fashion, as across an insurmountable theological fence. No comraderie and no congenial mental spark. Out of his disappointment, he did a rarely impulsive thing. He looked around furtively, then whispered to Mr. Dilling.

"*Neither do I.*"

A tremendous change came over Mr. Dilling's features. He stared at the man before him. David's eyes were young, honest and discouraged. Mr. Dilling's were tired, cynical, but discerning.

"I think I understand perfectly. Will you come up and have a look at my diggings? I brought a few of my own things."

Surprised and pleased, David had gone with him. Mr. Dilling climbed the stairs slowly. At the top, out of breath, he apologized.

"Heart," he said, "damn it!"

He opened the door of one of the big back rooms which showed a view of Aunt Betsy Wade's Bottom and the low hills and farm fields beyond. Inside there were books everywhere, a handsome desk, a canopy bed, leather chairs, good rugs and a carved mahogany table with a chess board set out upon it. This latter so struck David that he exclaimed at once.

"You play chess?"

"Don't tell me you do!"

"Used to in college, but I've had no one here, of course, to play with."

Mr. Dilling's eyes glistened.

"Young fellow," he said. "I may put off my demise for a little while. When can we have a game?"

They had gone on from that point, until there had developed between them one of those rare men's friendships which no woman ever completely understands. Even Mary did not, although she liked Mr. Dilling in spite of his oddities, rejoiced in the fact that by rest and quiet living his battered and abused heart had not only pulsed out the span of the doctor's predictions but was still beating after all these years, and she was glad that David had someone with whom to discuss all sorts of deep verities which she could not fathom herself.

David, sitting now, listening to the soothing hum of the bees felt his body being released from the tension of the morning. The tightness went out of his muscles; his nerves gave up their strain. Only deep within him was left the dull ache of his disappointment. For his defection at the service had not been due merely to weariness; he could have surmounted that. The thing that had caught at his heart and his throat together was panic. He was on trial once again, and perhaps for the last time. For he had remained twenty-five years in a country parish and was now past fifty. If he failed this time it would surely mean failure for life. Not that the thought was new to him. He had already quietly faced and accepted it; but the possibility of advancement presented once again in the shape of a visiting committee had roused within him the old ardent hope which he had thought safely buried. He knew that his sermon that morning had been in no wise his best, and his delivery had been hampered by the very desperation of his wish to impress the strangers favorably. But back of that, even as he spoke, had been the sudden sickening fear that he himself, in spite of the constant study which was congenial to his nature, might be deteriorating. Was today's sermon any better, he wondered anxiously, than the one he had preached years ago to the guests from Moreswell? Was it as good? How could he judge? If only Dilling attended church, he would know; he would tell him the truth. But Mr. Dilling would not go to church.

" 'Excellent sermons are occasioned by men's iniquities,' " he was fond of quoting, "so my life should furnish you with plenty of material. Go right ahead. I don't mind being preached *about*, but I won't be preached *at*, even by you."

As he recalled the quotation his mind brought back to him with the tender pang of maturity one of his early dreams.

Brooding, as a young theological student, over the beauties of the great old sermonizers, he had determined to be such another. He had pictured himself preaching to great city congregations with the fire and poetic diction of a John Donne or a Jeremy Taylor. But especially of Jeremy! The world, he hoped, would hear the like again in his own sermons. How young, how very young that dream! All that was left of it now were the well-worn copies of Donne and Taylor upon his desk and the exquisite phrases that constantly rose to his mind and lips through the homely pattern of his days. They slipped through the commonplace to beautify it, as now.

"God is glorified in the Sunne and Moon, in the rare fabrick of the honey combs, in the discipline of Bees, in the economy of Pismires, in the little houses of birds . . ."

David pondered upon the words, and the dubious virtue of ambition, while the sunny Sabbath afternoon wore away. He rose at last and stood looking down at his strange golden friends.

"Perhaps," he muttered with a wry smile, "what I need is to forget myself as an individual and become lost in the spirit of the hive."

Nevertheless he knew that even as Mary, and in spite of all reason, his heart still harbored a small hope.

As Mary started off alone for church that evening, she too felt an easement from the grip of the earlier hours. She watched the last bright-colored daylight darkle slowly against the hills, as she entered the sanctuary which, for Sunday night service, was always quiet and peaceful. No babies or little children broke in then upon the worship. The congregation was smaller in the evening, for the older country folk could not drive in twice in one day, and Mary, her conscience eased by knowing it could be no other, enjoyed the restfulness of the empty spaces. There was also no compulsion then for members to sit in their stated family pews, so Mary, who endured the eye strain of looking straight up at David in the morning, dropped down where she wished at the second service and relaxed. She always chose a seat rather far back because, as she was decorously able, she liked to note the young couples who came, many of them from miles back in the country. For "to bring a girl to night church" in Ladykirk meant that the young man's intentions were becoming serious. This lent an intangible romantic aspect to the atmosphere of the worship.

David had risen to announce the opening hymn when Mary noticed someone at the end of her pew. She glanced up and saw Ninian standing there, hesitant. She smiled and moved quickly to make room for him and he smiled shyly back at her and sat down. She held out her hymnbook for him to share as they began to sing:

> "Softly now the light of day
> Fades upon the sight away."

His voice blended with hers as he carefully followed the lines. At the end of the second stanza he suddenly raised his head and the hand that held his side of the hymnal twitched. Mary, looking up also, saw Lucy in the choir, her curls soft upon her shoulders, the small chip hat on the back of her head, her expression one of unconcealed pleasure. She had doubtless seen Ninian at once, but now Ninian had seen her. He did not sing any more, his eyes were fixed upon the choir.

A small tremor touched Mary. She could feel the tension in the young man beside her. She could see the light on Lucy's face. This was troubling. A book agent who would be gone tomorrow and never heard of again! A youth from . . . why, they didn't even know where he was from. They had asked no questions and he had proffered no information. Yet there had been that quick, involuntary twitching of the hymnbook just now when he had seen Lucy; and there was that shining look upon her face. Lucy never could cover her feelings! She must talk to David. Though it was all but a day's fancy, Lucy must be in no wise hurt by it.

The hour moved on its accustomed course. A breeze rustled the catalpa leaves outside the window. As darkness came on, a faint premonitory chirring of a cricket gave soft undertone, while far below, if one listened carefully, could be heard the ripple of Ladykirk Crick.

Mary never knew just how matters got completely out of hand when the service was over. She had mentally arranged just how she would chaperon Ninian and Lucy from the moment they would now meet, until she got Lucy safely home. But the plan did not work. In less time than seemed possible after the final "*Amen*," Lucy was at the end of the pew and she and Ninian were starting for the door. Mrs. Crombie, the one woman in the congregation who had to be continually placated and mollified, had caught Mary's arm and begun on a hot tirade about the forthcoming strawberry and ice-cream festival on the U.P. church lawn. *Why*, Mrs. Crombie wished to know, had the Presbyterians allowed the U.P.'s to get ahead of them on this?

By the time Mary had explained, argued, cajoled and promised, she found herself at the outside door, with Lucy and Ninian nowhere in sight.

As a matter of fact, they were at that moment sauntering along Ash Street, both tremulously excited over their nearness to each other.

"I thought you might be at church this morning," Lucy said shyly.

"I'm ashamed. The truth is I never woke up until one o'clock. It was something new for I haven't been sleeping too well lately."

"You've been worrying?"

"Well, yes, a little."

"Oh, don't," said Lucy earnestly. "Even if you can't earn enough money this summer for college, you could maybe teach a winter the way Jeremy's doing. You mustn't ever worry. When any of us gets discouraged, Mother always says, 'Remember, the darkest hour is just before the dawn,' and it's amazing how it works! Something nice always pops up. Why don't you try saying that to yourself? It really helps."

"Thank you. I will try."

"You won't forget?"

"How could I?" said Ninian. Then he added quickly, "Isn't there a longer way back? I mean . . . it's such a beautiful evening and so pleasant walking. There's a moon and the fireflies are so pretty . . . I . . . I just wondered if there were more fields where we could see them . . .

It was all very lame, of course, but Lucy did not notice.

"We could walk just a *little* way out Paxton Road. I think it would be all right. We mustn't go far, but there is a hay field near just full of fireflies."

"We'll go," said Ninian.

As they turned into the road they found themselves on the narrow path which ran beside it. They should have gone single file by rights but Ninian held her arm firmly. The touch of his hand on her bare, soft flesh sent a little flash of fire through Lucy. No young man had ever held her arm like this before. Unconsciously she leaned close to him.

They came to the hay field, sweet-scented in the darkness and bright with a million dancing lights. Above it, rising low, the moon. They stood still without speaking.

"Do you know much poetry about the moon?" Lucy inquired at last conversationally.

"I'm afraid I don't."

"Father loves the moon poetry. He made an anthology of it. Just in a notebook, of course. When we were little he started us in with 'Lady Moon, Lady Moon, where are you roving?' I suppose you were brought up on that too. And then we sort of progressed by degrees to the real ones. We each have our favorites. Jeremy likes, 'How sweet the moon doth sleep on yonder bank,' and Faith likes, 'That orbèd maiden with white fire laden.' "

"And you?" Ninian prompted.

"I'm a little shy about my favorite. Father says it's odd that I should pick out the only really *sad* one, but I can't help it. Nothing," said Lucy earnestly, her face turned toward the shining orb, "*nothing* moves me like that one. It gives me the shivers."

"Please say it," Ninian urged.

Her voice was low and there was a breath of feeling in it more than her years would warrant as she began:

"*Ah, moon of my delight, which knows no wane,*
The moon of heaven is rising once again. . . ."

When she finished he drew her arm almost imperceptibly closer.

"You picked about the only one I do know, but I never really felt it before. . . . I mean the way you said it was so beautiful."

"Did it give you shivers?" Lucy asked eagerly, looking up at him.

"Yes, yes. Very definitely."

"I'm glad," she said, "for then we felt the same. Have you seen enough of the fireflies?"

"I could go on looking forever, I guess, but we'll go back if you think we should."

"They might wonder where we are," she said, as she turned about.

It was not until they were back at the manse gate that Ninian cleared his throat and spoke with embarrassment.

"There's something I have to tell you, Miss Lucy, and I hope you can forgive me. I'm not really what you thought I was. I just let you think it, I guess, because I wanted so much to . . . to accept your invitation to go in yesterday. You see I wanted to be with you a little longer. It was reprehensible of me, though, to go under false pretenses. I . . . I don't quite know what to say . . ."

"I don't understand what you're talking about," Lucy said, bewildered.

"Why, you see, I'm not a book agent. I'm not selling anything at all."

"You're . . . not . . . selling . . . books?" she echoed in slow amazement.

He shook his head. His face as it showed in the dim light was anxious as he waited for her anger.

Instead, Lucy suddenly threw back her head and began to laugh. She kept on laughing, a delicious sound in the quiet, before she could speak.

"Oh," she finally gasped, "that is too funny! To think that I rushed out to head you off from getting to Father and you weren't selling books at all! What must you have thought of me. I'm so ashamed, but it *is* funny, isn't it?"

"You're really not angry with me then?"

Lucy stopped laughing.

"Of course I'm not. I don't see how I could ever be angry with you, for you're so . . . so *nice!*"

It was not Ninian's fault that her face was so close to his, and that the scent of honeysuckle breathed upon the moonlight.

With a strong sweep his arms went around her and held her close while his lips, which had known other kisses but never one like this, rested hard and long upon Lucy's soft, virginal ones.

She made no move, no struggle. It even seemed that she relaxed in his arms until he released her. Then he saw that her eyes were wild and frightened. In a second she had opened the gate and was running swiftly up the gravel walk. Her little chip hat fell off as she ran, but she paid no attention. She stumbled up the front steps and through the door and there darkness swallowed her up, for the front part of the house was unlighted.

Ninian leaned his head upon the gatepost, drowned in despair. There would be no hope for him now. He, a perfect stranger, who had met Lucy for the first time only yesterday, had tonight kissed her like a lover. He had terrified her, young and unsophisticated as she was. And what would her parents think? After their courtesy, their friendliness toward him? No, he was lost again in the dark abyss, just as he had glimpsed for the first time a sweet light like that of breaking dawn.

He stood, his legs shaking beneath him, wondering what he should do. Must he turn now away from Paradise, walk back over the uneven sidewalks to the Stone Hotel, then without a word take the train back to the emptiness of the city in the morning? Perhaps that was the most honorable course he could pursue.

But as he pondered, he decided against this. He must speak to Mr. Lyall, difficult as this would be, and tell him all the truth.

He opened the gate and started slowly up the walk. When he came to Lucy's hat he picked it up tenderly by its streamers and carried it against his heart, like a shield. The front door was open, but the hall was unlighted. He rang the bell and waited, with fast-beating heart, as the loud peal shattered the stillness, hoping it would be Mr. Lyall, himself, who would answer.

It was. David came along the hall, recognized Ninian in the moonlight and looked anxious.

"Why, Ninian!" he exclaimed. "Where is Lucy?"

"Could I talk to you, sir? Lucy came in a few minutes ago. She might have gone directly to her room. I think I . . . I frightened her, sir."

David went into the study at once, struck a match and lighted the big student lamp on the desk, then he motioned Ninian to the sofa and sat down opposite him.

"You look upset, my boy," he said. "Could you tell me just what happened?"

Ninian moistened his lips. "It's all a long story and it's hard for me to tell you, but I feel honor bound to . . . only I don't know how to begin."

"Suppose," David said, "that you begin at the end and tell what frightened Lucy."

Ninian turned scarlet. "I . . . I kissed her," he said. "It was a dreadful thing to do on such short acquaintance. And without declaring myself in any way. I'm sure you couldn't ever understand that I love Lucy. You couldn't possibly believe that just from yesterday . . ."

"Oh yes," David said calmly, "I could very easily believe that."

Ninian's face was first blankly incredulous and then lighted as though the sun had burst upon it.

"You could?" he breathed. "You could actually believe that?"

"Oh, quite," said David. "That's the way it happened to me. You know what the poet said — 'He never loves who loves not at first sight.'"

Ninian still stared at him as at a creature from another world.

"I didn't know," he stammered, "that any older person ever understood how any younger person feels about . . . about things like that."

"To return to Lucy," David said, "she seemed frightened, you say."

"Yes, sir. She ran up the walk and dropped her hat." He held up the little headpiece in his hands as though he hated to let go of this physical link with his beloved and then laid it gently on the sofa beside him. "I never thought of frightening her. It was just that all at once I couldn't help it. And it was . . . I mean . . . it was . . ."

"Quite a kiss," David finished.

"My heart was in it," Ninian replied simply. Then there was a pause.

"There was something more you wished to tell me?" David said.

The light died out of Ninian's face at once.

"Yes, sir, I feel I must even if it kills me. You see, I'm afraid I'm not really a good sort. I guess I've been what you would call wild. I've just been in a scrape. A crowd of us got too much to . . . I mean after a party we were all pretty . . ."

"Intoxicated?" David prompted gravely.

"Yes, sir, and we just ran amuck of everything. We broke a lot of rather important windows and got arrested. My father fixed it up and paid the fines, but I wanted to get away from home for a few days and of course I'd often heard of Ladykirk so I came out here just sort of at random. It didn't seem to make much difference what I did or where I went." His young voice was bitter.

"How do your parents feel about all this?"

"My mother's gone away to our summer house. My father was furious, of course. He thinks I'm not much good. I . . . I really don't see him too often. He's off to the office in the mornings and has a lot of meetings and things in the evenings. We don't even eat together most of the time. I hate big houses," he ended violently.

"Who *is* your father?" David asked.

"Robert P. Ross."

David's hands gripped his chair arms.

"Not Universal Steel?" he said in a strained voice.

"Yes, sir."

There was now a much longer pause. David was so dumbfounded he could not speak and Ninian supposed he was meant to continue. He swallowed hard and went on.

"I failed college this year and didn't graduate. That didn't seem to matter then, either. In fact, nothing ever has mattered to me until I suddenly met Lucy. And now, being the kind of person I am you may not want me to see her again. But I had to tell you all this, don't you see? For I'd rather be wretched all the rest of my life than hurt Lucy. You believe me, sir?"

David smiled slowly into the stricken young face before him.

"Yes, Ninian, I believe you."

The boy leaned forward, his head in his hands.

"I don't know what to do next. I'm all at sea."

"Well, now," David said practically, "let's consider a few possibilities. If you went back to college next year and worked, could you graduate?"

"Oh, yes." Ninian almost smiled. "Books come easily to me. I guess that's been unfortunate. I could usually get through without studying much, so there was plenty of time for . . . for trouble."

"I see. Are you man enough to go back and work your hardest for top marks?"

"I think I could be," he said slowly, "especially if . . . "

"If you had an incentive?"

"That would help enormously."

"What have been your plans for this summer?" David pursued.

"Oh, about the same as usual. I had intended to go on to our summer home and — I guess loaf, mostly — but now I want to stay in Pittsburgh all summer if I can," he said eyeing David with shy uncertainty.

"What about getting a job?"

"What could I do?"

"Well you *could* sell books like Jeremy. But if I were the son of the man who owns a steel company and living in Pittsburgh, I would get a job there. I don't mean in an office. I mean down where the real work is. It would toughen you up. It would make you so dead tired you wouldn't want to do anything at night but fall into bed. I think, Ninian, it would make a man of you. And incidentally I think your father would begin to respect you."

"You mean actual laborer's work?"

"I do."

Ninian sat thoughtful.

"You may be right," he said at last. "It would be tough, but it might be what I need. I'm sure I can get the job all right. I'll start trying as soon as I get back. The thing I want to ask is whether you will let me see Lucy again."

David pondered a moment.

"Yes," he said, "of course. But I would like to make one condition. Get your job and test yourself first. It's going to be hard. Then when a month has passed, if Lucy is willing, and if you still want to come out, do so."

"*A month!*" Ninian echoed in dismay.

"Yes. I believe in love at first sight, as I've told you, but I do not think everyone who fancies himself in love all in a moment really is. Time has to prove that, and a month is very short."

Ninian rose. "I can't thank you enough, Mr. Lyall." His voice shook a little. "I've never met anyone like you, or been in a family like this before. That's why I want . . . I have to be quite honest about — well, all the wild-oats part . . . if you understand what I mean."

David held out his hand. His face was grave.

"I'm very sorry about the wild oats, Ninian, but I believe in you in spite of them. I expect to be proud of you, one day."

Ninian couldn't speak. He wrung the older man's hand and hurriedly left the house.

Jeremy had gone up to his room to read before Ninian came in, and Faith had done so in the meantime. There was only Mary waiting on the back porch when David went out. He drew his chair close to hers and she spoke at once.

"Who was in there, David?"

"Ninian."

"Mercy! What for? I've been worrying over Lucy. Do you know, she went right upstairs and was sitting all in the dark by the window when Faith went up! And she had been *crying*. We must be careful, David. I like that boy but we've no idea who he is or whether she'll ever see him again and we can't have her bothered or hurt. What did he want?"

"Well, to put it in a nutshell, I think ultimately he wants Lucy."

"Oh David! That's ridiculous. He only met her yesterday and we know nothing about him."

"I do," said David, a small relish in his tone, "and I'll tell you if you hold on to your chair with both hands. Ready? Well, he's the only son of Robert P. Ross, Universal Steel."

A queer sound issued from Mary's lips, then she sat up very straight.

"Davy, I can't believe it! He's just been making it up. But

oh, if it is true, how dreadful for us to have taken up the ice-cream collection in front of him last night! What would he ever think of us?"

"I rather think he liked us. As far as I can determine he's an honest boy with great possibilities. He's been all but ruined by too much money and no sort of home life or affection. I think with even a little direction and encouragement he'll someday be a fine fellow."

"And marry Lucy?" Mary gasped.

"Well, now, don't let us plan for that at the moment. I told him he could not come back for a month. That will give them both time to consider their feelings. He has another year in college and of course Lucy is very young. The thing to do this summer is to give him a friendly lift, as we can, for I think he needs it badly."

"But to fall in love like that the first time he met her, practically. That couldn't be real, could it?"

He looked down into her eager face.

"It was with me," he said. "Do you remember the day you stood on your grandmother's steps in the snow with the red coat and fur tippet? I knew in the moment that I loved you. It comes that way to some people. It depends on the man — and the girl too. I can see how in Lucy's case it might come to . . . well, let's say Ninian, just for illustration, in one red-hot once-and-forever flash. Now the man who falls in love with Faith will have first a feeling of interest, deepening gradually as she reveals her fine qualities. At least I imagine so."

"You know everything, Davy," she said; then in solemn awe, "I never dreamed I'd even *see* a member of a millionaire's family, let alone have one come to our house and even be interested in . . . I won't sleep a wink tonight! Do you think we've ever had as exciting a day? One good thing is that tomorrow is Monday and we can relax. We couldn't . . . hear from the Committee as early as tomorrow, could we? Even if . . . even though there might be the least chance?"

"I don't think so," said David.

"Then we'll have a quiet time and be able to rest up and collect our thoughts!" she said with relief.

David smiled quizzically as at past memories.

"I never trust Ladykirk in that regard," he said, "but we shall see."

Chapter Three

~~~~~~

Mᴏɴᴅᴀʏ was sunny and warm with a lighthearted western breeze blowing. The Lyalls slept later than usual and breakfasted in leisurely fashion on the back porch, with Lucy, rather wan and quiet, for her, wielding the paper fly brush at intervals to frighten a wasp from the jelly dish. Jeremy left promptly when the meal was finished since he could not afford to miss a book-selling day, Faith and Lucy began to tidy up the house, David elected to work in the garden for that morning, and Mary seated herself in one of the porch rockers with what was known as her "Pretty Thoughts Box" on her knee.

When she had decided long ago that she would observe Monday as a day of leisure along with David, she had to do some explaining in Ladykirk, where a wash on the line early Monday morning was considered almost as much an evidence of godly respectability as attendance upon divine worship on Sunday. But Mary had won out, even with old Brinnie Coombs who helped with the laundry. The latter had insisted dourly at first that clothes never dried well on a Tuesday and also that everybody in town would blame *her* if the preacher's wash wasn't out on the proper day. But that had been long ago and now even Brinnie accepted the odd situation, and ceased to apologize.

Mary slowly rocked back and forth in relaxed mood as she fingered the Pretty Thoughts papers in the box. It could have been a distinctly morbid pastime, but Mary's own serene and practical mind, combined with the unquenchable high humor of the family, had long since brought the box and its purpose into a cheerful perspective.

It was one of the traditions of the church that when the death of any member, old or young, occurred, "Resolutions" must be prepared which were read at public service and then given to the bereaved family. Soon after the Lyalls had come to Lady-kirk, it was discovered that Mary had a peculiar gift for this somewhat unusual and lugubrious form of composition. She had a deft way, which defied even David's analysis, of weaving together into one complimentary and consoling whole, expressions of eulogy, verses of scripture, quotations from the poets and selections culled from inspirational periodicals. So famous had her Resolutions soon become that now for many years past, the various committees appointed to this task had always mentioned Mrs. David Lyall as *chairman*, leaving the other members free from all effort, and yet pleasantly proud as they heard their vicarious work read and approved.

While the Lyalls, in the bosom of the family, had always poked quiet fun at Mary's peculiar form of literary effort, and her sudden ejaculations of pleasure as she happened upon a "pretty thought" in her reading, the climax had come one day when a wind blew some of the contents of the box over the porch. Jeremy, retrieving the papers swiftly, had for the first time noted that certain names were scrawled lightly across the margin of certain Pretty Thoughts. His hilarious yell had brought the others.

"Holy Jumping Jiminy," he had gasped, "Mother's picked

out obituaries for everybody in town before they die even!"

Mary had rescued her precious box with scarlet cheeks.

"Jeremy, that's dreadful of you! I do *not* do . . . do . . . what you said. It's only that some thoughts I read just seem so appropriate to certain . . . I mean I never know when I'll . . . or when they'll . . . I think that's a terrible thing for you to say, Jeremy. You ought to be ashamed."

And then, quite suddenly, everybody burst into laughter, Mary included. But David had told the children privately that there were to be no sly remarks made about Mary's methods with her obituaries, for he alone had noted the sudden look of hurt in her eyes at the discovery of her innocent *pre mortem* preparations. Only once in a long time the irrepressible Jeremy broke the rule.

"Oh, Mother," he would exclaim from his reading, "here's a very Pretty Thought for Sarah Stowe when you need it. Better make a note of it, she doesn't look too spry to me right now!"

But David's firm voice always silenced him.

This morning, when she had a little time of quiet, Mary thought she would try to find a few clippings suitable for old Mrs. Wesley and get the Resolutions started early, for the July rambo tree at the foot of the garden would soon keep her busy with jelly and apple butter. She read over a number of paragraphs, copied a few sentences on a sheet of paper, chewed the end of her pencil meditatively and decided that since Mrs. Wesley's only distinguishing attribute through the years had been that of a superlative pie maker, she had better stick to comfortable generalities and Bible verses. She wondered, though, if there was any possible way by which she *could* work in a veiled allusion to the pies, which until the last two years had graced every church supper and sociable in Ladykirk during David's encumbency. She murmured a few verses as possible

leads. "She looketh well to the ways of her own household."
"She brought him butter in a lordly dish." No, no help there.
But *Martha*, she thought suddenly, what about *Martha?* An
inspiration! Mary bent quickly to write a line before she forgot
it. *Like Martha of old, Mrs. Wesley offered the food which her
hands had prepared as her peculiar gift. . . .*

There was a sudden sharp repeating ringing of the telephone
in the hall. The girls were upstairs. Mary set down her box
and answered it. Dr. Faraday's voice, quick, peremptory, came
over the wire. "Is Mr. Lyall there?"

"Yes, I'll . . . "

"I must speak to him quickly."

Mary left the receiver hanging on its cord and rushed to the
garden. She called David excitedly. At the sound of her voice
he dropped his hoe and hurried to the house.

"Bad news, I'm afraid, Davy," she said. "Someone's sick.
It's Doctor Faraday on the phone."

Alas for the quiet Monday! Alas for the peaceful hours! But
that disappointment was as nothing compared to the anxious
thought of who might be in trouble. No one that she knew of at
the moment was dangerously ill. Yet Dr. Faraday had sounded
upset, his speech so unlike his usual Victorian manner.

David meanwhile had reached the phone.

"Hello."

"Mr. Lyall, I need you at once. Come to the Masters' as fast
as you can leg it."

"I'll be there," said David, and hung up the receiver.

"It's someone sick at the Masters'," he told Mary. "I don't
know which one. I can't stop to change for Doctor Faraday
was so urgent. He didn't sound like himself. Don't wait dinner
for me. I may be detained."

He washed his hands, got into his coat and started down the

street almost at a run. Mrs. Crombie, her washing always first upon the line, was now sweeping her pavement. She tried to intercept him.

"Anything the matter, Mr. Lyall? Somebody sick?"

"I'm afraid so."

"Who is it?"

"Someone at the Masters'. I don't know which one."

Mr. Shotwell on the post-office step called to him.

"Anything wrong, Reverend?"

"Someone's sick at the Masters'," he said, without pausing.

Joe Hench, the storekeeper, made a little joke.

"What's all the hurry, Mr. Lyall? I thought this was your day of rest."

David merely shook his head and went on.

He could see Mr. Dilling in the hotel courtyard as he passed, but he did not pause even to wave his hand. He stumbled up the front steps of the Masters' frame house, crossed the porch and almost fell upon Dr. Faraday who was in the front hall, waiting for him. The doctor was tall and stoutly built, with a round face, wrinkled and weathered russet red by years of hard country practice. Just now, his brow was covered with sweat and his normally steady gray eyes had a wild look in them. He clutched David by the arm, muttered, "Thank God you're here," and propelled him through the center hall to the big airy kitchen at the back. Here the three Masters' "boys," as they were still known, were waiting, distraction upon their faces. This turned to despair as they saw David enter.

"You needn't say it, Doctor." Robbie, the youngest, spoke in his sharp, quick voice. "We know now that Minnie's not going to get well. I've felt it since she was taken early this morning."

Ben, the eldest, a stone mason, stood with his great body bent forward, his face convulsed, listening to the sounds from the room above.

"Minnie! Minnie!" he kept repeating. "You can't die. You can't let her die, Doctor. Get somebody out from the city, even, to consult. Or get her to a hospital. If it takes all we have, save her! Let nothing go undone!"

Jacob, the middle brother, slow and kindly-faced, did not speak. He only looked with beseeching eyes at the doctor.

Dr. Faraday stood looking back at them as though he were dumb. Then he cleared his throat and began to speak while the sweat rolled unheeded down his face.

"Gentlemen," he said. "I can't put it off any longer. I have to tell you the truth. Minnie is not going to die, but in a few hours there is going to be a birth here."

It was as though lightning had torn through the room, searing death upon them. For a moment neither sound nor breath came from the four men who had heard the words spoken. Then Robbie, his face livid, lurched toward the doctor with his fist raised.

"Take that back, you dirty liar, or I'll kill you!"

Jacob caught his brother by the back of the neck and threw him against the wall.

"Shut up, you fool," he said, and then sank down beside the table, his head buried in his arms.

From above there came a scream and then a long, shuddering moan.

"I must get back up there," Dr. Faraday said. "It won't be for two or three more hours. Maybe longer. I need a woman. Someone must go for Becky Bates . . . perhaps you, Mr. Lyall. It would be easier, maybe, for you to go . . ."

Ben raised his head. He looked like a big wounded creature of the wilderness.

"No," he shouted in wrath. "No. We'll not have Becky Bates in this house with her tongue wagging the shame of it. We're disgraced. We're brought to the dust. Minnie's done this to us. Let her die of it if she has to," he said between his teeth. "I wish we could all die together and be done with it."

Dr. Faraday's voice cut in sharply. "Hush! This is no time to talk of shame or disgrace. The facts are before us. I've got two lives to save. I think all will go well, but Minnie's not young and the birth will be a hard one. I've got to have help and Becky is the best. Get her, Mr. Lyall, as soon as she can come. And tell her," he called over his shoulder as he started for the stairs, "that she's the only person in town outside of us who knows about this. I think that will fetch her."

When he was gone David looked at the men before him. His own countenance was as aghast as theirs. He crossed to the brothers and laid a hand on their shoulders in turn.

"Bear up," he said, "hold steady."

"Who was the man?" Robbie gritted out. "I'll kill him with my own hands. Who was the man?"

Jacob raised his head from his arms. "The surveyor," he muttered hoarsely. "The one that boarded here those weeks the hotel was full. It must have been. There's just been . . . time enough." He dropped his head again.

Ben had gone back now to his muttering of Minnie's name, the first rage spent out of him, but his face still drowned in shame.

"Hold steady," David said again, his own mouth too dry for clear speech. "Wait" — as though there was any place for them to run to for shelter from this woe — "wait right here till I come back. I'll have to get Becky. Trust me. I'll be back soon."

He left them, and went out again into the familiar Main Street overarched with maples. A farmer's wagon rattled past, Sarah Stowe with sunbonnet and market basket was just entering the General Store, Mr. Dilling still drowsed against the hotel wall and Mr. Shotwell still sat ruminant, on the post-office steps, spitting at intervals into the dust beyond the sidewalk. David saw all this dazedly as through a mist. His mind felt numb, too numb even for articulate prayer. *O God, O God, O God,* repeated itself formlessly within him like Ladykirk Crick running over its stones.

He went up to the thin frame house wedged between the barbershop and the ice-cream parlor. He could see straight through to the kitchen where the widow Bates was just entering with a basket of fresh clothes from the line. He tapped lightly and she came at once. Her angular body with its large head topped by a tight knot of gray hair blurred in David's eyes as she advanced.

"Well, Mr. Lyall! Come right in." Her nose twitched slightly as though already she smelled news.

He stood in her little front parlor under the illustrated copy of the Lord's Prayer, and spoke as one bare soul to another.

"Mrs. Bates, you are badly needed to help with a birth. It is all going to be a great shock to you . . . and to the whole town. You must prepare yourself. Minnie Masters is about to have a child."

Becky's hand flew to her lips. She moved backward with an unconscious stage-like pose of tragedy as though she might topple and fall.

"*Minnie Masters!*" It was hardly a whisper.

"Yes. We can't stop to conjecture now or to blame. Doctor Faraday wants you as soon as possible. Will you come?"

Becky quickly regained her powers of speech.

"Minnie, with her head always up and her fine airs and just last year elected secretary of the Missionary Society when there's others older deserved it more! How are the mighty fallen and the proud brought low! I've noticed these last months that she's fleshened up so, but I just thought it was her time of life. . . ."

"Mrs. Bates, will you . . ."

"Once I almost said to Mrs. Murdoch, I almost said in confidence, '*Could* anything be wrong with Minnie? *Could* such a thing be?' . . . but . . . "

"Mrs. Bates, will you come quickly?"

"And why should I go to help Minnie when she's all at once turned into a trollop? Mr. Lyall, I won't do it. Why, I'm shaking all over now just with the thought of it. If it was even a young girl who didn't half know what she was doing . . . but Minnie with her high head and forty-two years old if she's a day, for I mind the very time she was born herself. Who could the man be? Oh, this is past believing."

"Mrs. Bates, we need you in more ways than one. You are the only person who knows this, outside of the Masters boys, the doctor and myself. There's hard work ahead at the birth, but after that there's the problem of the town's reaction. You could maybe guide us a little in that. . . . "

Becky's sharp eyes glistened, and then softened.

"Nobody else knows yet?"

"You are the only one."

"Of course," Becky said slowly, "who am I to shirk my duty?"

There was slowly breaking upon her face an expression almost of eagerness.

"It'll be the worst piece of news the town's ever heard, but I'll be willing to help break it. Time enough when the child's born. You go on back, Mr. Lyall, and I'll come right away after you. I won't take my satchel. I'll put my things in my market basket. Anybody to see me will think I'm going for tomato plants, for Minnie promised me some late ones. After all, we can't judge, Mr. Lyall, and I've always been a friend of Minnie's. This has about felled me, but I'll be right down."

David turned and went back down the street, his heart lightening a little. Becky's skill at a birth approached that of a trained midwife and all of it would be needed. But over and above that, she would become an intimate part of the whole incredible scene and therefore view it subjectively. This would affect her telling of the news with moderation and even perhaps with charity.

On a sudden impulse he ducked between the barbershop and the General Store, and followed the narrow cobbled path until he reached the alley which ran at the back of the lots. This, he felt, might secure him from the questioning eyes of Main Street. As he hurried along, however, he felt he had chosen unwisely, for every here and there a woman at her clothesline or working in her garden stopped to look at him and call good morning and then stand watching until he entered the Masters' back yard by the wooden gate.

As he passed the stable he saw Jacob leaning against the horses' stall. The sick misery of his face smote David's heart as nothing so far in the day had done. He went in and threw an arm across the man's shoulder. Jacob's body was rent with great heavings which in a woman would have been sobs.

"I can't stay in the house," he said at last. "I can't stand it to hear her. I can't even get my mind used to what's befallen us. It's as though it was all a different world since yesterday."

"I know," David said. "I know, Jacob."

"We've tried so hard to be good to Minnie," he went on. "We've set such store by her; ever since Mother died we've tried to live . . . special good ourselves because of Minnie. She was just seventeen then. It don't seem as if she *could* have done this thing and yet . . ." his voice sank, "when I heard her first this morning early, I feared, I someway feared what it was."

"Why?" said David.

"It was the way she looked those weeks the surveyor was here. The other boys didn't seem to notice, but I did. It was the shine in her eyes and the way she laughed, and the talk at the table. We don't ever talk much, nor laugh. We eat and go about our business. Never seems much anyway to talk about. Minnie and this . . . man had always something to say somehow.

They'd laugh when we couldn't see anything to laugh at. Then, the shine in her eyes," he repeated. "I never forgot that, for it went away after he'd gone. So that's how I come to think of it."

"Are Ben and Robbie any calmer?" David asked.

Jacob shook his head. "They're still ravin'. That's another reason I left. They're like to kill Minnie."

"I'll go in at once," David said, and leaving the stable, started up the path. He was just in time, for Becky was about to enter the front door. He met her, saw her started up the stairs, and then came back to the kitchen to the two brothers and sat down weakly. His face was haggard and his hands worked together as they lay on the table in front of him.

"It is hard," he began, "for me to say anything that might comfort you. In a sudden blow like this, man's words are not worth much. But I do beg you to pray hard every minute for wisdom and for freedom from anger. You have all done your part as best you knew to be good brothers to Minnie through the years, haven't you?"

They burst out together, telling bitterly of their devotion.

"Very well," said David, "what about Minnie? She took the place of the woman of the house at seventeen, didn't she? Those were heavy responsibilities for a young girl. She's made a home for you three men, cared for you and waited upon you through all these years, without complaint. Has she ever failed you in any way up until now? Has she?"

"No," Ben admitted slowly.

"Not till now," said Robbie.

"Then think of that and say your prayers for her till this is safely over. Suppose we brew a pot of tea now and set out a bite to eat. The folks upstairs may need it too."

"You wont leave us, Mr. Lyall?" Ben begged tremulously.

"I'll stay right here as long as you want me," he said.

They called Jacob from the stable and all sat down at the

kitchen table to bread and apple butter and cheese. Jacob seemed to have difficulty in swallowing the bread, but he drank the hot tea with feverish eagerness. Becky came down once, declined Mr. Lyall's offer of refreshment, searched through the drawers in kitchen and dining room, then returned with her hands filled with clean cloths. She came down the back stairs again for a bucket of hot water, and withdrew without speaking, for the Masters boys would not look up to meet her eyes.

"Is everything going . . . is it all right?" David asked awkwardly.

Becky's face was flushed and anxious.

"It's been terrible," she said. "The doctor had to give her something. He thinks it won't be long now."

Robbie's sharp voice rose as she left.

"He oughtn't to have done that. Minnie ought to bear the whole of it for what she's done."

"None of us knows what the whole of it is, Robbie," David said quietly, "I think it behooves us men to be merciful."

In a short time Becky came tearing down the stairs again. Her tight knot of hair was loosened and her sleeves were rolled to the elbows.

"The clothesbasket," she burst out. "Give me the clothesbasket quick."

Jacob got it from a nail on the back porch and she rushed off with it.

"What would she want the clothesbasket for?" Ben asked sternly.

"I suppose it's to put the baby in," David said.

At his words the Masters boys turned and looked at each other, an expression of dumb amazement upon their faces. As clearly as though they had spoken, David read their thoughts. Up until this moment, so busy had they been over Minnie's unbelievable defection and their own sense of disgrace, they had never fully comprehended the fact of the *child* itself.

Even as they sat there, with that look of terrified incredulity upon their faces, there came from above a thin, strident cry which pierced to the very marrow of the listeners below.

"My God!" Ben said.

"It's alive!" Robbie whispered.

Jacob did not speak. He sat, a sudden pale shine in his own eyes, watching the stairs.

The suppressed tension above of which they had been conscious was broken. There were busy movements now: the heavy tread of the doctor and Becky's quick steps back and forth. There was more of the shrill crying. There was once, incredibly, the sound of laughter, Becky's and the doctor's. It seemed to run through all the house, jolting it back toward normal.

At last Dr. Faraday came down. His black alpaca jacket was on, his bag was firm in his hand, his face no longer streamed with sweat, his gray eyes were keen and calm as usual. Moreover, his head was high and the air of victory lay upon him.

He smiled upon the men in the kitchen.

"Well, gentlemen," he said, "it's over and I think I have never delivered as perfect a child in all my practice. It was rough going, but I'm confident Minnie will be in fair shape by to-morrow. She's still asleep and will be till toward evening likely. As soon as Becky gets the baby washed she'll bring it down for you to see." He paused for a moment, as though he felt he should add something that would break through the surface silence to the depths beneath, then with a glance at David whose peculiar business that was, he turned briskly to leave, having completed his own part in the drama.

"I'll look in again this evening, but be sure to call me if I'm needed before. Becky will stay on and look after things. Good afternoon, gentlemen. I forgot to say it's a girl," he added and was gone.

David had caught the doctor's look. He saw it repeated beseechingly on the faces of the Masters boys as they watched him. It was time, now that the harrowing vigil was past, for him, as the man of God, to speak to them, to give them fresh counsel. He had never felt less confidence in himself or his office, but he must try.

"There are times in life," he began hesitantly, "when there is only one act possible for us. That is, acceptance. And when once we have done this completely the way becomes easier. As I see it now, you must accept this strange happening without bitterness. There is in the house now a new life, a child to whom you will all have to give fatherly care. Accept this responsibility. Stop lamenting over what people will say or think. Minnie will suffer enough. Forgive her and take care of her. It's hard. I know . . . I know what you're going through! But there will arise light out of the darkness if you do your duty. If you . . ."

There was Becky's foot on the stairs. She came down, and on into the kitchen with her bundle. Her sharp face was miraculously softened, proud and smiling. She stopped first beside David. He looked at what she held, and suddenly he smiled too. It was, indeed, a perfect child. The little face was rounded, unwrinkled and fair. He noted that the features were not blurred, as often happens at birth, but firm and distinct. Minnie's own beauty, and something besides, lay upon the small girl child.

Becky went to each in turn, Robbie and Ben looked upon the baby, speechless, motionless. Jacob slowly put out one work-roughened finger and touched the soft cheek and the little sleeping hands.

"She hasn't a dress to her name, Lord love her!" Becky said. "But I'll soon get some clothes gathered up. Minnie never thought they'd come through alive, either of them, so she didn't have anything ready. But we'll fix her up, won't we, lambie! I'll take her back now to her basket and then I'll come down for some tea. I'm weak as a cat, I'll tell you!"

Robbie turned quickly and went out toward the stable. Ben blew his nose hard and followed him. Jacob filled the teakettle at the sink pump and set it on the side of the stove while he prepared to poke up the fire in the range. He paused with the poker in his hand to look at David shyly.

"I never saw one as little as that," he said, very low. "You know when I touched it, it felt as soft as . . . as . . . " Words failed him. His face colored and he began poking the fire violently. David knew that he had heard Jacob's first and perhaps only attempt at fancy.

When Becky came down she seated herself with her tea, drinking lustily, the while she steadied the teaspoon in the cup with a dexterous forefinger. Then she began to explain her plan of campaign to the men, identifying herself completely with the household as David had hoped she would.

"We'll have our hands full with the town," she said. "But I've been thinking just what I'll do. If I'm *pushed* I'll just say there's a man or two in this town that ain't any better than they ought to be — and you both know who I mean — and they march up to church every Sunday as big as life with their Bibles under their arms and who ever makes much fuss about it? Nobody. Oh, mebbe you have, Mr. Lyall, in private, but I mean they just go on the same way and I could tell you plenty if I wasn't ashamed to; well, if I'm *pushed* about this I'll just point to them and say, do something about them and let poor Minnie alone, I'll say."

She took a large bite of bread and apple butter and went on.

"Or I'll say, 'Them as are without sin can cast the first stone,' and I'll shut up like a clam. They'll think then I know more than I'm telling. But unless I'm *pushed*, I'm just going to talk about that child. I'll tell everybody it's the finest baby I've ever seen and Doctor Faraday says so too. And if I stick to that and talk hard enough, why, before long . . . well, we'll see."

It was four o'clock when David left the house. He saw a group of men in front of the livery stable a little distance down the street and shuddered. He crossed to the hotel, walked hastily past Mr. Rayburn at the desk, who he could see was bristling with questions, but keeping his own face set to preclude conversation, he proceeded as was his custom to Mr. Dilling's room. The voice that answered his knock was barely audible. Upon entering he saw the old man, very white, leaning back in one of the big leather chairs.

"How is she?" he asked weakly. "Is she safe? What of the child?"

"You *know!*" David exclaimed.

"Why wouldn't I know in this gossip-pot of a place? Mrs. Rayburn had it nosed out hours ago. Is Minnie all right?"

"She had a hard time but Doctor Faraday thinks by tomorrow she'll be doing well."

"And . . . the child?"

"A girl. A beautiful, perfect specimen." David rested himself on the edge of the table where the chessmen still stood mutely waiting.

A long, relaxed sigh escaped Mr. Dilling.

"A girl," he murmured, "a little girl. The only thing Mrs. Rayburn couldn't make out from over here was the sex," he added dryly.

"Jacob thinks the father was that surveyor that boarded with them last fall."

"Yes," Mr. Dilling said. "I knew him. Yes, it must be. I thought of that myself. An attractive fellow! But he had responsibilities of his own and is off now heaven knows where. Any thought of marriage was out of the question from the start, apparently."

He sat, his face fallen into its heaviest lines, his shoulders sagging. Then he roused suddenly.

"Will you be seeing Minnie soon?"

"I suppose so," David said. "I'd rather take a beating than face her, but I'll have to, somehow. I think I'll send Mary down tonight."

"Then tell her to tell Minnie that I sent my congratulations and not to name the child until she hears from me."

"Did you say *congratulations?*" There was horror in David's voice.

"I did! But on second thought I shall take them in person. Go along, now. You look as though you'd had the labor pains yourself. But David, remember the miracle of life deserves respect no matter how it's arrived at. A little girl," he added, as though to himself. "A daughter to the goddess, Minerva."

David walked up the street on the opposite side from the stores, the post office and Mrs. Crombie, urging his weary legs to move fast. He felt like a fugitive momentarily expecting to be stopped and called upon to stand and deliver. Not until he was safely inside the manse gate did he relax as he dragged himself up the gravel walk. Mary was on the front porch waiting to greet him. It was going to be painful to break the news to her but a relief to share the burden of it. She caught his hands and drew him into the front hall and on to the study. He could see she had been crying.

"Oh, Davy," she burst out, "I've been nearly crazy and yet I didn't dare call you up. I can't believe it! I'm still weak with the shock!"

David sank down beside her on the sofa, and eyed his wife, incredulously.

"You mean you know all about it?"

"Yes. I knew this morning. Jennie McLean came over and told me. Mrs. Crombie had told her. People saw you hurrying down to the Masters' and someone had seen the doctor go in and stay so long, and Mrs. Purdue had noticed the boys all out in the yard one time or another so she knew it was Minnie and then Mrs. Hays saw Becky Bates go in about eleven and saw her put the window down in Minnie's room. Then everybody began to think of how Minnie had gotten out of shape lately and we all just thought it was forty-ish weight, but then there was the fact she'd given up her Sunday School class last fall and wasn't regular any more in the choir — oh, I guess everyone really *knew* as early as noon only we just wouldn't let ourselves accept it. Then Mrs. Purdue heard the baby cry about three, for Becky had put the windows up again for air, I suppose. When we had to admit it, I got sick at my stomach." Mary stopped breathless, and dropped her head in her hands. Her next words were muffled through tears.

"*Minnie Masters!* Oh, Davy, it seems as though all the foundations had fallen. I can't forgive her this. I can't."

"I know," he said despairingly, "that's the way I feel, but we mustn't show it, God help us!"

The news was broken briefly and with great embarrassment to the young people of the manse after supper. Moral irregularities and the general processes of procreation were not discussed in the family so it was all distressingly awkward. The disclosure could not be postponed longer, for already the country people were calling the manse for verification, many not being able to credit the fact without it. David called Jeremy into the study and Mary tried to speak to the girls upstairs. The whole problem of sex was always covered with dignity and reserve, so she floundered and sank several times in her efforts on the one side not to minimize the enormity of the error and on the other not to leave in their minds utter condemnation of Minnie.

Faith listened in silence, but Lucy cried out impulsively.

"But Mother how could she? I mean . . . I mean, how *could* she?"

"We don't know," Mary answered and then feeling herself for the first time on the firm foundation of a definite statement, she repeated it with conviction. "That's it. We simply don't know how this could have happened. So, say as little about it as you can, and later when you have the chance, be kind."

Lucy turned suddenly and ran out. Faith waited and spoke to her mother when they were alone.

"Who is the father?" she asked shyly.

"That surveyor who boarded with them when the hotel was full last fall. At least that's what the Masters boys think."

Something woke in Faith's eyes. "Oh," she said slowly, "him! He was . . . I mean I thought he was very handsome. He had such . . . and his eyes were . . . of course I only spoke to him a few times on the street, but I thought he was very attractive."

Under her mother's gaze Faith colored slightly, and then from the annoyance of it turned scarlet. "I must go," she said hastily. "I have to practice some more for tomorrow's lesson. And it's simply dreadful about Miss Minnie!"

When she was gone, Mary stood very still for a moment. So Faith, in her innocent young heart, had felt the charm of the surveyor! Some passing feeling of romance must have touched her in those chance meetings to make her face turn crimson now. She tried to recall the man among the many who had come and gone in the last two years, surveying the countryside for the coal companies. She decided he was the tall young fellow in his late thirties who had walked in his trim boots with a faint swagger and had smiled easily behind his brown mustache. His eyes had been dark and very bright and had looked out upon the village and all within it with a quick friendly curiosity as though the setting had been novel and interesting to him.

Yes, that was the man. She remembered that David had tried to get him to come to church with the Masters but he had refused politely, and with a certain air of amusement. There was no logical reason why the sudden color in Faith's cheeks should disturb her. All young girls were romantically moved by handsome, dashing men, enough older than they to seem holders of the mystery of the unknown world beyond them. Faith's reaction had been natural, normal, something to smile over and forget! It was also, she knew, largely embarrassment. And yet in spite of reason, that little errant flush on her own daughter's cheek seemed somehow to link them all with the catastrophic event of the day. At least sympathetically. She walked slowly over to her own bedroom, wondering uneasily if the heart's armor was ever perfect. Were its defenses ever sure? Then she flung the thought from her with distaste. She must not let her emotions run riot in this fashion, just because her world for the moment had been turned upside down. It would right itself and steady values prevail again. She changed her dress, combed her hair, rubbed her nose carefully with a bit of chamois (excitement always reddened it) and then went down to receive a last word of advice from David before she set out for the Masters'. She had agreed at once to his suggestion that she be the one to go to see Minnie that evening. It was embarrassing enough in all conscience for anyone but less for a woman than a man.

She waited for first dusk and then set off, her heart beating uncomfortably. At the gate she met Mr. Woodbridge, clerk of the Session and one of David's best friends. He spoke to her most earnestly of the weather and then hurried up the path. By dint of dodging, waiting in shadows and quick movements when the way was clear, she managed to reach the Masters' house without stopping to converse along the way. Jacob met her in the hall. She saw that he was trying his best to look stricken — but found it impossible. A shameless delight shone in his eyes.

He creaked eagerly up the ingrain-carpeted stairs in his thick shoes and followed her into Minnie's room to look again upon the small occupant of the clothesbasket. Becky, now completely mistress of the unusual scene, was in her element. Elation was in her shrill stage whispers.

"Now, Mrs. Lyall, I take it very kindly of you to come, don't we, Jacob? Everything's fine and never was there as nice a baby! You can see for yourself, Mrs. Lyall. Minnie's still asleep, poor soul. She had a terrible time. The doctor had to give her something and you know he don't do that till it's pretty bad. Jacob, you go back down and watch the front door. There may be other folks coming. Ben and Robbie are no help at all, but Jacob here's my mainstay, ain't you, Jacob?"

Jacob turned crimson, looked again at the baby, bowed awkwardly and went out. The atmosphere had become intimate.

"He's daft about the child," Becky went on. "You can see that. A good thing, for the other two won't even look at it. But oh, Mrs. Lyall, I can speak free to you, isn't this the awfullest thing the town has ever seen? Who would have thought a thing like this could come to pass in Ladykirk? And what about the Missionary Society, and Minnie secretary? I'll bet the scandal of this will go all around the county, and us planning for the Presbyterial meeting here next spring!"

"Shhh!" Mary warned. She thought she heard a faint movement from the bed. As they turned, however, Minnie lay still upon her pillow. Mary watched her, seeing, with a rush of feeling, the young, defenseless quality of her beauty. It was as though suffering, like death, had brought back the illusion of youth to her whole face. Her auburn hair lay in neat braids upon the pillow, and the nightgown with its crocheted yoke rose and fell over her rounded breasts.

"I can't stay long," Mary said quietly. "I just wanted to tell

Minnie and you that if there is anything I can do, you must call on me. Has . . . anyone else been in?"

"Not a living soul! They're not over the shock yet of course, and they all know *I'm* here and can 'tend to everything. But even so, you'd think somebody might . . . I look for Maggie Hays and Lizzie Purdue tomorrow. Being neighbors and all they'll surely come. You can't tell though."

"I'll go now," Mary said, "since Minnie's asleep. Good night, Mrs. Bates. I'm glad you're here, and tell Minnie as soon as she wakes that I called. What about clothes for the baby?"

When she was at the door Mary turned to look again at the bed. She saw that Minnie's eyes were open and regarding her fixedly, but her head moved back and forth negatively upon the auburn braids. Mary accepted the sign, tried her best to smile and went out quickly.

It was a long, distressing evening at the manse. David had received his various men callers in the study; Mary had talked to the women on the back porch. The last of these to leave was her closest friend, Jennie McLean. Mary walked with her around the yard to the big pine tree. Here with their arms interlocked and their voices hushed, they went over it all again. What now, they asked each other with tears, should be done about Minnie's office as secretary of the Missionary Society? They held each other closer.

At long last David and Mary climbed the stairs. Jeremy's light was still on; Faith, from her movements, was now preparing for bed; Lucy's little room was in darkness. It came to Mary suddenly that she had not seen Lucy since she had turned and run away from the news as Mary had imparted it. She opened the door softly but there was no sound within. She could see the slim young shape on the bed, so she closed the door again and went on to her own room.

"We must not talk or think any more about it," she said to

David after their good-night kiss. She tried hard to make her voice calm and casual. "We must go to sleep, if we can. I know you're exhausted and I am too."

An hour later, sensing that David was still awake, she said, "I forgot to tell you that Jennie and I are going to get some material tomorrow morning, and run up some little dresses and things. Minnie had nothing. She was so sure they would both die."

"I thought you were going to sleep."

"I am. I mean I'm trying. It's just that . . . Oh, David, it can't be true! Surely we'll wake up tomorrow and find it's all a bad dream."

By two o'clock David got up softly and dressed. He felt smothered. He had to have air. Mary turned from her first slumber.

"I'm going out for a little walk," he whispered. "I won't be gone long."

He went down the stairs and out into the night. The little village lay sleeping upon the bosom of the moon and the stars were bright above it. He walked slowly down the street, his feet from long practice avoiding the holes in the flagstones. He noted each house as he passed and thought of the family within it. Not one but would have gone to sleep thinking of Minnie and the unbelievable thing which had occurred that day. Here and there perhaps, some couple still lay wakeful, as he and Mary had done. They would hear his step and wonder.

"Was that someone passing?"

"Who would be out walking this time of the night?"

But if, from behind a curtain, they saw him, it would be all right.

"It's Mr. Lyall," they would say, "I suppose he can't sleep either, poor man."

No one, though, not even Mary, would guess that under all

his shock and concern lay something like remorse in his own soul. How had he failed in his preaching or in his pastoral relationships that such a thing as this could happen in his congregation? What word had he not spoken, what guidance had he not given, what virtue had not gone out of him through the years that a woman like Minnie Masters in time of temptation should have been weak? The old sensation of failure rose to smite him. He walked on, communing with the sleeping houses, thinking humbly of his own omissions. The strangers from Moreswell drifted through his mind and were gone. What had he ever done to be worthy of Moreswell? There was also, though he fought against it, a feeling of bitterness and revulsion toward Minnie in his heart. It was as though she had done this thing against *him*. Easy enough to give lofty advice to the Masters boys! But what of himself?

He was passing the business section of the town now. He knew what had been discussed that evening in front of the post office, in the barbershop, on the store steps and at the livery stable. The ugly wind of scandal had blown the normal peace and quiet far away.

He kept on walking until he found himself opposite the Stone Hotel. Here he stopped short, for he saw two lighted windows, the only ones in town. One was in Mr. Dilling's room, the other across the street in Minnie Masters'. He stood there, looking from one to the other, praying for the old man whose anodyne now would be Plato or *Amiel's Journal;* praying for her who would soon awaken in the troublous new world she had made for herself and her child.

At last he turned and was starting slowly back when he stopped again, smitten by the violence of a sudden illumination. He was conscious of all the unmarried women in the town. Mary was always disturbed by this number and entering upon endless little matchmaking schemes to remedy it. He had merely smiled at her efforts and given the situation scant thought. Now he saw it with a strange emotional understanding. There were so many cheerful, busy, happy spinsters, to whom the daily round of village life with its small joys and excitements and achievements were sufficient, that he had never tried before to penetrate below the mask of those who must be hiding an unquenchable sorrow.

For as he now suddenly realized it, there must have been those through the years who, in an April night when the airs were sweet, and Ladykirk Crick could be heard running softly, leaned from their windows to drink the tender fragrance of the midnight rains, to feel again the beauty of their own unfulfilled bodies, and to pray again with hope.

And in the last of summer when the red harvest moon rode high and the hot breath came from the gardens and the nearby hay-stooks, there must have been those who confessed to God alone, upon their wet pillows, their longings and their despair.

The scrap of a translation came back dimly and then clearly to his mind. He murmured the words to himself, as he started on again over the uneven sidewalk.

> *Sunk is the moon,*
> *And the Pleiades soon*
> *Will sink in the sky;*
> *The hours go past,*
> *Midnight at last —*
> *But alone I lie.*

It was all the same, from the isles of Greece to Ladykirk! From burning Sappho to Minnie Masters! But he had never known it until now.

As he walked along, he thought deeply. The town as a whole

would take small stock in Sappho's poetry even if they were aware of it. They would stop short of any intuitive insight in connection with Minnie's strange and illicit love. And yet — he could foresee how it would be. For weeks the gossip would go on: the constant repetition of all the facts, all the surmises, all the condemnation, even that small, unconscious satisfaction on the part of some over the error of another. But through it all would be, running at first slowly and unseen but gradually strong as the tide as the days went by, that powerful urge to rally to the defense of one's own. The good mothers in Israel would recall the day when Minnie had been left motherless. Small, forgotten kindnesses from gifts of fresh bread from her oven to flowers from her garden would be recalled and counted unto Minnie for righteousness. Women would begin to appear at the Masters' kitchen door again in neighborly errands. The affectionate familiarity of a lifetime would gradually reassert itself and enfold Minnie and her child. As all the town together had shared the shock and the shame so together it would forgive and, in so far as was possible, accept. He had watched this happen before.

David was back now at the manse gate. He looked down the dark, silent street which he had walked these twenty-five years. Ladykirk, he was thinking, sleep lightly now, sleep softly, before the cares of tomorrow wake you!

His heart felt almost at peace as he opened the gate and started up the path. Tomorrow could in no wise be as hard as today. He and Mary had so often noted that a small hiatus of happiness always seemed to follow disturbance or pain. He would neglect a few regular duties and stay in the garden most of the morning. He would watch the bees for an hour in the afternoon. The small, compact mystery of the hive would give his spirit refreshment as usual, even as the star-flung heavens seemed now to throw new perspective upon the events of this troubled day.

But as he laid his head again upon his pillow his last thought was that perhaps in all the universe there was no greater mystery than that this small group of souls which men call a village, could take life in their hands like a chalice, and drain it together.

Chapter Four

~~~~~~

MARY woke next morning to find a gentle rain falling.
She drew a long breath, and closed her eyes again in relief. The
light, steady drumming of the drops was like a gift of God. If
the town had stirred to broad garish sunshine, there would have
been no place to hide from the dismaying facts of yesterday.
Now, the rain was like a curtain falling about them all, soften-
ing the harsh outline of reality, shutting Minnie away for a few
hours from the noise of tongues, and hiding them all, as it were,
each from the other.

She decided as she dressed to make life within the manse
as normal as possible, so she sang as usual as she prepared breakfast and lightened her own spirits by placing mentally, as she
had done a hundred times, the new kitchen cabinet. She tried
not to speak of it openly, for she dearly loved the mechanics of
a surprise, and while confidently anticipating the event of the
great birthday gift, intended still to play her role of excited
recipient when the time came. She even had a small hoard of
savings now amounting to nearly ten dollars which she intended
to throw into the fund surreptitiously by way of David if it
was needed at the end.

The cabinet, she decided, would stand at the right of the window and opposite the stove. Here, with all the ingredients for cookery at her very finger tips, she could then brew and bake without all the extra steps and waste motion she had been forced to exercise during the years. The cabinet she wanted would be all white rather than golden oak like Jennie McLean's. Then, if Jeremy repainted the walls and wooden sink — well, the prospect was rather intoxicating.

She sang a little more blithely as she put a pan of biscuits in the oven — luckily the coal range always heated up quickly — and then went into the hall to call the family who because of the dull morning had overslept.

"Hurry up, girls. You don't want to miss your train, Faith. Come on, Jeremy. David, are you up?"

"In a manner of speaking," he said, appearing at the top of the stairs. "I still feel a bit dazed, but my late walk last night did me good."

He leaned against the kitchen doorway sipping his first cup of coffee.

"I was thinking of Dilling as I dressed. You know, I believe he has some idea of his own about naming the child."

"Oh, I forgot to ask you how he was taking it!"

"He looked ghastly when I went in to see him, but was self-possessed of course. He said he intended going to see Minnie himself to convey his congratulations."

"Davy, he *didn't!* Oh, he is so queer! If he does that it will stir the town all up again. He's always been so fond of Minnie, they might even think he was . . ."

David smiled a bit roguishly. "You flatter my friend. I suppose his going over will give everyone more to gossip about, but perhaps that will be a help. Oh, good morning, children," he added as Jeremy and Faith appeared. "Where's Lucy?"

Faith lowered her voice. "I don't know what's wrong with her. She looked strange last night and she wouldn't talk to me this morning when I went in to wake her."

Mary hurried again to the hall.

"Lucy, dear, are you coming? Breakfast's ready."

There was a faint affirmative from above and a few minutes later Lucy slipped into her chair. She looked white and strained, had not much to say and ate little. It was the shock of the news, Mary thought as she watched her quietly. Lucy was more emotional than Faith; besides, she was younger and had always evinced a naïve attitude toward life and its mysteries. Mary wondered sometimes anxiously how much she really knew, but was loath to intrude upon her innocence.

"I'm going downtown to do a few errands," Mary said now, "and after that Mrs. McLean and I are going to sew at her house. Faith, you'd better let Jeremy drive you over to the train since it's so wet. I hope your lesson goes well today, dear. Can you manage the housework alone, Lucy?"

Lucy nodded, her eyes downcast.

"It's a bad day for my business," Jeremy announced mournfully. "Women don't like wet book agents with muddy boots, but I suppose I'd better make a try at it. Come on, Faith."

When the buggy had rattled off and David had gone into the study, Mary turned to her younger daughter.

"Lucy, dear, you mustn't think too much about . . . about what I told you last night. We must all just go on about our work as usual and not let our minds dwell upon what we can't help. You're not sick, are you?"

"No," Lucy said, "it's just that I feel . . ."

"I know," Mary returned comfortingly. "We all do, but we mustn't give way to it. Keep busy and you'll feel better."

When Mary had gone Lucy did her household chores with a hot head and a heavy heart. The night before, for the first time in all her life she had lain awake. It had been a terrifying experience, for strange noises through the old house had risen to smite her; creaks from the stairs as though someone were furtively climbing them; a click as of a latch, a muffled thud, and finally a sharp knock at her window. She had started up from a doze, trembling, only to realize it was the shutter moved by a quick breeze. Then the rain had come on and blotted out all other sounds and she had fallen into an exhausted sleep.

She pondered now as to what she should do about the problem which was racking her, and finally decided that come what might, confession was the only course. Everything was at last quiet in the house. The phone, active enough earlier, was for the moment still. Lucy, her heart thudding, went along the hall and knocked at the study door.

"It's me, Father," she called in an unsteady voice.

"Oh, come in, Lucy."

She entered, closing the door carefully behind her.

"Hello," David said smiling, "what can I do for you?" Then he added more seriously, "You look upset. What is it?"

It went through his mind that those were almost the words he had used to Ninian a short time before.

Lucy sat down beside the desk and held her hands very tightly together.

"I am upset and I'm frightened, sort of, and I don't quite know what to do. I think it's Mother I ought to ask about it all, but I hate to worry her just now and . . . do you think it would be all right and *proper* for me to tell you?"

David tried to keep his face grave.

"I feel sure it would. It's just barely possible I may know something about the thing that's on your mind."

"Oh, no, you couldn't," Lucy said earnestly, "for it happened *in the dark* Sunday night by the gate. You see, Ninian walked home with me and we went out Paxton Road first to see the fireflies in the pasture field and we talked about the moon poetry and he likes Omar too, and then we came back and just at the gate it . . . it happened."

Lucy swallowed hard and went on headlong.

"I really couldn't help it, Father, for it all came so fast. You must believe that. He just suddenly caught hold of me and . . . and held me awfully, that is . . . close. I could practically feel his heart beating, and then he . . . he kissed me, but just to say that won't make you understand in the least how it was. It was quite different . . . I can't explain it to you . . . and I ran away from him as fast as I could, but now I'm so worried about it. You know . . . with Miss Minnie and all . . ." Her voice faltered and fell as she looked up at him beseechingly, her face scarlet.

David's eyes were misty. He laid a hand on Lucy's.

"Someday soon," he said gently, "you must have a long talk with your mother. But I can assure you right now that there was nothing wrong about the strange kiss. A little matter of good taste involved, for Ninian should not have startled you or shown so much feeling himself on short acquaintance, certainly not before he knew your own. But I repeat, there was nothing . . ." he hesitated, trying not to smile, "in the least *immoral* about it if that is what is troubling you."

"You're sure?"

"Oh, absolutely. You see, Ninian came in to see me after you had left him and told me all about it in a very manly fashion. He was sorry he had frightened you, for he would like to come out again to see us if we are all agreed. He seems to like you."

"He does?"

"He said so, and I believe he meant it. He's going to get a job and so probably won't be back for a few weeks. But you might possibly hear from him in the meanwhile."

Lucy's face had undergone one of its sudden transformations. The luminous glow which was likely to rise suddenly from within her and flood her features now almost dazzled David.

"That's true. I might! Oh, I'm really so happy now I can hardly bear it. The relief and everything. Being so miserable before makes it all the more wonderful. I wouldn't have believed I could like anybody so much all at once. That night watching the fireflies it was just as if we'd known each other always. Oh, Father, I hope he comes back! I was afraid I might never see him again."

"Well, try to keep your feelings in hand, Lucy. I think Ninian means what he says, but after all he is quite a stranger. One other thing. I found out he's the son of a very rich man. That fact we'll all try to forget, for it hasn't made Ninian happy, and it has no bearing on your friendship with him."

"*Rich!*" Lucy gasped. "My goodness, I thought he was worried about money for college! I'm not sure I like that. I'd feel more comfortable, I think, if he were just selling books like Jeremy. But anyway, it doesn't change his being *nice*."

"Certainly not. Now do you think you could run along? I have to write a little sermon for old Mrs. Wesley's funeral tomorrow."

Lucy rose slowly. "Yes, I'll go. You've been *such* a comfort, Father. I believe I'll tell you something I never intended to tell anybody." Her voice grew dramatic. "I meant to carry my secret to the grave, I was so ashamed. But now that everything's all right I might as well tell you. It's about . . . you know . . . what happened at the gate."

She moved swiftly to her father and cupped his ear with her two slim hands. Then she paused.

"You think you won't be shocked?"

David shook his head. "I don't believe so."

She bent down. "I really . . . *liked* it," she whispered. And then ran from the room.

When she was gone, David had difficulty in returning to his sermon. He blew his nose hard, and then sat thinking. How strange that the human soul in any setting, no matter how outwardly simple and removed, still ran the full gamut of emotions. Here, for example, in this very house which, to the occupants of the occasional dashing city equipages passing by, must look prodigiously dull, there had occurred the full drama of life. As to Ladykirk — everything that could happen anywhere, had happened here. His mind returned to Lucy, the sweet, the innocent! That the son of one of Pittsburgh's steel barons should have kissed her with passion at the old manse gate was a crowning illustration of the fact in hand. Suppose the call to Moreswell had come to him years ago, this romantic incident would never have occurred, would it? He bent over his papers, chiding himself for straining the imaginative thread too far. The "ifs" of life were imponderable. His eyes misted again as he thought of Lucy's fears.

He was deliberately putting off his usual morning trip to the post office until noon for the sake of discipline. He would not allow himself to consider the possibility of a letter from the Committee. It was too soon, anyway. He concentrated again upon his funeral text, "There shall be no more tears, neither any more crying for the former things are passed away."

In a half-hour Lucy knocked again. "Telephone, Father," she called.

He went to the hall and picked up the receiver. It was Mr. Blackburn at the hotel with a message from Mr. Dilling who would not use the instrument himself.

"I would as lief walk up Main Street naked as talk on those damned party lines," he often said.

The message was to ask whether Mr. Lyall could come down at once. David considered a moment and promised to go.

It was a relief to get out into the freshly washed air. The rain was still falling steadily so there were few people on the street to interrupt him. He glanced across at the Masters' house, but it stood silent, with no showing of life about it. He entered the Stone Hotel and made his way to the familiar room. Mr. Dilling was not wearing his ordinary wet-weather dressing gown and slippers; he was completely dressed and meticulously groomed.

"Sit down, David. I have something very important to say to you," he began. "I've been over to see Minnie."

"You have? How . . . how are things this morning?"

"She is fairly comfortable, the infant is beautiful and that she-dragon of a Bates woman is a hellish nuisance. I had to all but knock her down before I could talk to Minnie alone. Even then I'm sure she listened at the keyhole."

"Were the boys there?"

"Fortunately not. David, I did not sleep at all last night. I spent the hours right here in my chair, thinking. And all my thoughts upon this problem came to but one end. Minnie must be married. At once."

David looked startled. "I admit it's an excellent idea, but I doubt if even Mary with all her matchmaking schemes would ever tackle that one."

Mr. Dilling waved a deprecating hand and drew slowly upon his pipe.

"It's like this. Minnie has known one great romantic love. She is an unusual woman of deep feeling. At her age she will never love again and she will never marry anyone in the usual sense even if there were a candidate, which is extremely unlikely. I have made sure of these facts. What is needed for her then is a marriage in name only so that she and her child may live on here with some degree of honorable convention." Mr. Dilling stopped and smoked on thoughtfully.

David felt his hair slowly rising on his head. His sudden intuition must be insane, he told himself, and yet a heavy sense of foreboding slowly crept upon him.

"Go on," he said with difficulty. "Have you thought of a husband for your plan?"

"I have," Mr. Dilling said calmly. "Myself."

David leaped from his chair.

"Dilling," he cried, "you can't do such a thing. It's not . . . it's not . . . *decent.*"

"What's indecent about it?" Mr. Dilling asked coldly. "I have an honorable name even if I haven't added particularly to its luster. If I choose to bestow it upon a woman and a child who need it for their protection, whose damned business is it?"

"But," David stammered, "it's so . . . so irregular. You must know how queer the thing will look, what the town will . . ."

"What the town will say! I knew that would come. You've lived so long amidst this miserable pipsqueaking gossip that it's caught you too. What will the people say? So that's what you think of first, instead of Minnie and her child? Let us not offend the town, let us keep talk down no matter what lives are sacrificed."

"Dilling, stop! You're unfair. It's only that your proposal shocked the breath out of me. Give me time to collect myself. You've had a whole night to get used to this idea and I've had five minutes."

"Five minutes is enough," Mr. Dilling said acidly.

"What I really meant was whether in the eyes of the community this that you propose would help Minnie's cause or hinder it. I've got to think about it, can't you see?"

"I can't see. You have actually nothing to do with it. I'm

not asking you for advice. I'm merely telling you of my intention and I thought the news would come to you as a very great relief. I see I was mistaken."

"But I'm thinking of my part in it, too. How can I perform a marriage ceremony that I know is a travesty and a sham? How can I do that?"

Mr. Dilling rose and for the first time in their long friendship he looked upon David with anger.

"You don't have to. We have a Squire in this town. I'd rather have a plain civil service anyway, come to think of it. We expect to be married tomorrow afternoon at four. And if you'll be kind enough to leave now, I'll take some much needed rest."

"Dilling, you must let me talk this out with you. I'll do anything I can, but. . . ."

"You need do nothing but go. Good day, sir."

David walked out blindly and all but fell down the stairs because of a blackness that seemed to envelop him. The shock of Mr. Dilling's news was coupled with an inordinate wound in his heart. That Dilling, his close and steadfast friend, should turn against him was devastating.

He made his way up the street holding his umbrella as low as he could before his face. He crossed automatically to the post office. No one was in except Mr. Shotwell, the postmaster. He took a letter out of the Lyall box, scrutinized the envelope with care and then, with a shade of reluctance, handed it over. Even David, in spite of his preoccupation, found himself staring at it with interest. It was a large square envelope of a quality he did not often encounter. It was addressed in a firm backhand to Miss Lucy Lyall and the postmark was Pittsburgh.

"Guess that one's all for today, R-reverend. Very light mail this morning. Wait a m-minute."

He came out from behind the letter boxes and stood close

to David. He was a very tall man, angular and stooped, with eyes that seemed to swim like small blue seas behind his glasses. His nose extended thinly a shade too long, but his mouth contradicted the rest of his face by being generous. His slight stammer gave to all he said an effect of eagerness, of words falling over each other.

"P-place has been full last night and this m-morning till now. One t-topic. *You* know. W-what do you th-think of it?"

David shook his head.

"I'm g-goin' on sixty but this is the b-biggest shock I've ever known the t-town to get. H-how's it goin' to effect church affairs? Ben's an Elder and Minnie has another year to go in her office unless she r-resigns. She'll have to, won't she? Course Ben ain't to blame, you might say, but still it's in his f-family. What do you think, R-reverend?"

David moistened his lips. "I believe we'll just have to trust God and await developments."

Mr. Shotwell's blue eyes brightened. You th-think there's going to be some?"

"There might be," David answered.

"Any chance of g-gettin' the surveyor back to m-marry her?"

"I doubt it."

"The whole business just ain't credible yet it's h-happened. That's the way with a lot of things I've n-noticed. Can't b-be, and yet they are. Well, it's a queer world, b-but the best we've got at p-present."

"That's right," said David, and went out again into the rain, wondering uncomfortably if he had done well to let even the small hint drop. For Wes Shotwell had caught it at once.

He dropped the square envelope into his coat pocket and splashed up the street feeling that the tears of heaven were falling in his own heart. He was deeply hurt, he was angry, he was appalled. That Dilling should consider such an expedient was to him actually shocking. He could not adjust to it. Yet he knew his friend well enough to know that his mind was made up. Through the long hours of the previous night he had weighed all the evidence and come to his decision. Apparently too, a fact David had up until now overlooked, he had told Minnie and she had agreed to the preposterous plan. She must have, or Dilling would not have spoken with such a note of certainty.

He had come to the oddly shaped frame house where Squire Hendrick lived. It was in a sense the showplace of Ladykirk. Even Mrs. Crombie's big brick could not compete in interest. The Squire's father had been a carpenter and with his own hands had built the home for his bride. Outwardly, people said, he had seemed unimaginative even to dullness, but some young dream of love and beauty had risen within him as he had worked. There were bowed windows, there was a carved cornice along the eaves with a rose design cut out with patient care. There was a front porch with slender pillars and one on the side with fancy trellises, still strong in spite of the years. The Squire loved the house and at some sacrifice always kept it neatly painted and in repair, even when his own suits were shiny.

David paused now, looking up at it. The small room jutting into the garden which the old man had built, it was said, as a sewing room for his bride, was now the office with a separate brick walk leading to it. The door bore the legend, JAMES K. HENDRICK, JUSTICE OF THE PEACE. Here the community came to get *law:* a frightened girl from back in the country to swear to a fact and demand redress; a farmer to testify that a neighbor's dog was killing his sheep; a woman in fury over a *spite fence,* or perhaps a heavy-faced man fresh from a talk with Dr. Faraday, wanting to make his will. The Squire met them all with homely wit and common sense flavored with optimism.

"Go ahead, Dan. Don't get scared about making your will.

Won't make you die a day sooner. Fact is, it always seems to me to kind of lengthen out the span."

"Now just calm down, Myra. Nobody ever builds a spite fence when the spite's all on the one side."

"All right, sissy, stop crying and tell me whether you want money or marriage and we'll see what we can do for you. When you're young, lives can usually be mended somehow, eh?"

So it went year after year. The Squire never made much money for his fees were small, but they were sufficient for him and his sister, Miss Het, who lived with him.

David looked for another moment at the sign and then slowly started up the brick walk. The Squire was in, leaning back in his old swivel chair, hands behind his head, staring at the ceiling above his littered desk, and chewing meditatively on his quid of tobacco. An amazingly large spittoon of maroon porcelain stood near which gave out a resounding *ping* from time to time as compliment to the Squire's projectile accuracy. David stood in the doorway and cleared his throat. The Squire swung around lazily and then rose at once out of deference to his guest.

"Come in, come in, Mr. Lyall. Have a seat. Glad to see you. I can't seem to settle to anything this morning. This business of Minnie Masters has hit me right in the liver. I've seen plenty of silly young ones in trouble, but Minnie!"

He lowered his voice.

"I've always thought she was one of the finest women in the town. Never far away when anybody was in trouble, always faithful in the church, best voice in the choir, and the way she's taken care of those boys! Waited on them hand and foot. Well, what do you make of it, anyway?"

"I don't." said David. "Nobody can. It's a mystery and will always remain so. But there's a new development which I feel I must talk over with you. Can you take it straight?"

The Squire's keen gray eyes narrowed under their grizzled brows.

"I've taken a good many things in my time," he observed dryly.

"Well, here it is. Horace Dilling is planning to go through a marriage with Minnie so that she and her child may have a name."

The Squire plunged forward on his chair, his thick shoes striking hard on the bare floor.

"The devil he is!"

David nodded. "My heart's pretty heavy over it for we all but quarreled. The thing seems to me . . . well, I respect Dilling so deeply. His inherent dignity has been one of the things I've admired in him. To throw himself to the lions this way so that he and his motives will be the butt of every jest in the livery stable and the barbershop . . . well, it's repulsive to me somehow. It *hurts*. You know everybody is always ready to criticize him anyway. But after this . . ."

David put his head in his hands.

"Now, now," said the Squire, "don't take it too hard. Let's kinda look round the edges of the thing a little. First place, Dilling must know all you've said as well as you do. He's nobody's fool. And in spite of all that, he's willing to go ahead with it. I don't believe he's cantankerous enough to just *want* to stir up the town, though by golly it will all right. I think he's really trying to help Minnie."

"Oh, so do I," said David.

"Well, then," said the Squire reasonably, "give him credit for it. Maybe other folks will too. Tell you what." He tilted back again in his favorite position and studied the ceiling. "Dilling's lived here a long time and he's never got to be part of Ladykirk. No sir, he's just sat on the side, as it were, and looked on, sort of amused, and superior like. That's one reason people never took to him too much. Now if he goes ahead and marries Minnie, he'll be part of the town all right. First time. Might make a big difference."

David slowly raised his head.

"You're a wise man," he said, "I never thought of that. I was too close to Dilling to get any perspective on the thing. Here he was all set to do something really big and unselfish and I threw cold water all over it. No wonder he was angry. And as you say, the town, after the first jolt, may actually think the better of him for it. You could put in a good word here and there and so could I."

"It'll make a stir all right at first, but things have a way here of shaking down."

"I know," said David, "into the old pattern. It's amazing."

"Not a bad idea, either," said the Squire. "And I'll tell you how it's done. Folks talk a thing over together so much that it gets to be kind of familiar to them, then they can just go along as usual. They'll do the same with this, but oh, Moses, it'll take a while!"

David rose. "Thanks, Squire, you've been a big help. I'm going right back to Dilling and apologize. By the way, when I told him I would have qualms about performing the ceremony he said he'd get you to do it. If that's the way he wants it, you know it's all right with me."

The Squire shook his head violently.

"Not me," he said. "Not for this one. I'm good enough for the fly-by-nighters, but if this goes through you've got to do the job. It'll make it look a little more regular . . . if anything could help," he added.

When David reached the hotel again he found Mr. Dilling at the door in top coat and overshoes, trying shakily to raise his umbrella. At sight of David his face twitched and he turned at once signing for him to follow. David helped him up the stairs and into his room.

"I was going to you," the old man began, and his voice broke.

"I came as fast as I could," David said, his own unsteady. "Dilling, I see it all now so differently. It's a fine thing you're going to do. An unselfish, noble thing. Count on me to stand back of you, and try to forgive me!"

"I'm the one to be forgiven. I was exhausted and overwrought . . . you must know that I'd never have spoken so, otherwise. David, if I lost your friendship . . ."

"Nonsense," David said. "You couldn't lose it if you kicked me downstairs. Which I probably deserved this morning. Now, tell me the plans and I'll work to them."

Mr. Dilling was very grave.

"Minnie accepted my offer. We both decided it was best to have the ceremony as soon as possible. I shall simply go over, be married, and return at once. That will emphasize to all that there will be no change whatever in our manner of living. One request only, I have made of her. That is that she will bring the baby over frequently to see me."

Mr. Dilling's eyes filled.

"You are so accustomed to it that you may not understand that it will mean something to me to have a child bearing my name. She is to be called *Victoria* after my mother."

"Dilling!" David began, and then could go no further.

When he reached the manse again, lunch was long overdue and Mary was concerned.

"You look strange, Davy. Is anything wrong? Anything new, I mean?"

"No," he said slowly, "no, I think on the whole today is a better day than yesterday, don't you think so, Lucy?"

She flashed him a bright smile. "Oh, today is wonderful! The only trouble is I made an omelet for lunch and it's fallen. Do hurry now, Father, before it gets any flatter."

"We had very good success with our sewing," Mary told them at the table. "Jennie and I each had some old material and we bought some new. Becky told me last night the boys will pay for it. We have enough little garments finished already to last a few days. Jennie has promised to go down with me this afternoon and take them to Minnie. I . . . I suppose you weren't in to see her?"

"No, I was talking to Mr. Dilling. Oh, by the way . . ." he felt in his coat pocket, "I have a missive here for you, Lucy. A circular, doubtless, or an advertisement."

He held the rich, square envelope as though studying it.

"Pittsburgh," he remarked absently. "The postmark is a little blurred but it definitely is . . ."

"Father! *Please!*"

He handed it to her, smiling. "He didn't lose much time."

Lucy caught the letter in both hands, devouring the inscription with her eyes. Then, excusing herself hastily, she left the table and flew upstairs to her room.

"Davy, it is pleasant, isn't it, about Ninian? I believe I'm as excited as Lucy. Now tell me what really happened this morning."

"It's most inconvenient having a wife who reads one's face like a book. But I flatter myself I've got a piece of news for you now that even you couldn't guess if you tried all day. It's beyond all surmise or conjecture. It's stranger even than yesterday's event. It will rock the town to its foundations. It will . . ."

"Davy, for goodness sake, tell me. It . . . it must be about Minnie and . . . and Mr. Dilling for you were with him! *David*," she almost screamed the words, "he's not . . . he couldn't be going to . . ."

"Marry Minnie tomorrow afternoon at four and I did get it out before you did! You're completely uncanny as a mind reader and I don't know how you do it! But there it is. Now, what do you say?"

Mary leaned back weakly in her chair and said nothing for

a long moment. Then, as often happened, she gave utterance to what seemed an oblique statement but one which nevertheless carried deep significance.

"I've never been good enough to Mr. Dilling," she said, "but from now on I will try to be very, very kind to him."

Then she rose and walked to the window, wiping her eyes. David followed and they stood close, watching the rain as it fell upon the beehives and the garden.

"I could have gone to see him sometimes," Mary went on, "I could have gone and invited him to dinner myself instead of sending word by you. Maybe that's why he never came. All these years I should have been kinder to him."

There was no need to ask further how she felt about the plan.

The next day was beautifully fair, the heavens having forgotten their "great and little showers" as Jeremy Taylor would put it. David jogged along the country roads toward the Wesleys' for the ten o'clock funeral in company with Josiah Hunt who was driving him out since Jeremy needed the pastoral horse and buggy for his own work. Mary was coming with Jennie McLean in her buggy. David pondered as he watched the rolling fields just what he should say to Josiah. Would it be wise to prepare him a little for the news of the afternoon? For wherever the men's groups gathered at post office, smithy, barbershop or livery stable, there Josiah seemed to be.

David finally spoke. "You've known Mr. Dilling a long time, haven't you?"

Josiah glanced sideways in surprise and then flicked the horse lightly with the whip.

"'Bout as well as anybody's knowed him outside of you. Never felt I got past the front door with him somehow. Always seems stuck-up to me. 'Course there was once . . ."

"Yes?" David prompted.

"Well, I never told this to a soul, for it didn't seem right somehow to laugh about it. Fact is, I never felt less like laughin' in my life than when I saw him do it."

"Do what, Josiah?"

"Well, as I say I never mentioned it. Happened above two years ago. He got the habit of takin' a little walk late at night. Always sits up late, readin', you know. Well, one night round about twelve I was comin' up the street an' nobody else round an' I see the old gentleman comin' out of the hotel with his overcoat an' his checked cap on — it was Aprile an' chilly, but clear, with the stars all poppin'. Well, I followed him up Main Street an' out the turn of Paxton Road to the pasture field. Just thought the old fellah might keel over an' nobody know it till morning. Besides, I was nosy enough to want to see what he was up to."

"Yes?"

"Well, he stopped there an' leaned on the fence an' looked up at the stars. Thought he'd never get done lookin'. An' then he straightened an' took off his cap, still lookin' up, an' held it again his chest like folks do when the flag passes or somethin'. Gave me goose pimples, some way, to watch him. I hid behind Hendrick's stable till he finally put it back on his head an' turned round. I trailed him till he was safe inside the hotel, then I went home. An' I've never told it till now."

David did not reply. He was remembering Dilling's favorite lines about the stars which he had often heard him repeat.

"At the commandment of the Holy One they will stand in their order and never faint in their watches."

But even he had never known the depth of his friend's soul.

"Josiah," he said at last, "will you promise to think of that scene often in the next few days, and say a good word for Mr. Dilling as you have opportunity?"

"Sure," Josiah agreed. "Think the old chap's goin' to kick the bucket?"

"I sincerely hope not," David replied, and then they rode on in silence.

It was a full day. But the funeral of old Mrs. Wesley, since she had died replete with years and at the end in peace, did not have in it the strain of vicarious suffering which many did for David and for Mary also. The real tension was in connection with the other strange service at four. The Masters boys had been apprised of Mr. Dilling's intention the afternoon before, and had received it variously. Ben had at first said with violence that they would have no atheists mixed up with their family and any disgrace was better than that and how would it look for a member of the Session to have Mr. Dilling for a brother-in-law? Robbie had been singularly quiet for him, as though weighing the two evils before committing himself. Jacob, still bemused with his delight in the baby, had agreed at once and then, startled at himself, had retracted and waited for the decision of the others.

In the end, with all the facts before them, Ben and Robbie, outwardly stiff of mien and inwardly bruised of spirit, had given their consent. Jacob, creaking eagerly up the stairs once again to Minnie's room, had called back to them over his shoulder.

"It'll make it better for *her* . . . the little one, mind you."

Squire Hendrick had taken care of the license; David had made a few mental revisions in the marriage service; Mary had taken a pink silk shawl of her grandmother's out of its lavender in the big hall chest and conveyed it to Becky Bates whose place of importance in the whole affair well-nigh threatened to overcome her.

"After all, Becky," Mary had said in the quiet of the kitchen, as woman to woman, "Minnie is going to be married, no matter how queer the circumstances, and I just thought this shawl thrown around her shoulders over her nightdress would make it seem, well, a little more . . ."

"Just you trust me, Mrs. Lyall. I'm going to braid her hair up around her head and set a bowl of pink roses on the stand. It'll be no harm and poor soul, she'll need all the bolsterin' up she can get. My, what lovely silk this is! I'll put it back in its paper as soon as everyone gets gone so no harm befalls it. Would you think I ought to wear my good black or just my dark calico? I'm nervous as a cat. And what the town's going to say, clean beats me. Do you think any hint of it's got out yet?"

"I don't believe so for it's all happening so suddenly. How does Minnie seem?"

"Just looks away off into nothing and never speaks. She always was quiet anyway, but now she's like a graven image. Just when she has the child in her arms, her face lights up. I talk away as best I can, but she's hard hit, Minnie is. That you have to say for her. Do you think my dark calico is good enough for the . . . the ceremony, with my white lawn apron?"

At a quarter to four on this afternoon David and Mary walked down the street as unobtrusively as possible. As they reached the Masters' porch they saw Mr. Dilling in his best black suit crossing toward them, leaning heavily upon his cane. David hurried to meet him though Dilling had stated expressly that he wished to come over alone. Becky greeted them at the front door with an air of lugubrious excitement, and they all climbed the stairs in silence and entered Minnie's room. The three brothers were lined up with funereal faces before the mantel. Minnie leaned against the big white pillow shams, her coronet of braids showing dark gold against them. The pink shawl and the roses near her gave her sculptured face faint color; the large eyes beneath the delicate wing eyebrows and heavy lashes were cast down. She did not raise them until Mr. Dilling and David had taken their places one on either side of the bed, then she looked up, beseeching and fearful at the man she was about to marry. He smiled down at her.

"It's all right, Minnie. Don't be disturbed. Go ahead, David."

David cleared his throat and proceeded. When it came time for the ring, Mr. Dilling drew from his vest pocket not only one circlet but two. He slipped the first, a plain worn gold band, upon Minnie's finger. Then in the eyes of them all he put above it a great solitaire diamond that flashed in the light. Becky's muttered "Well, I never!" penetrated to the four corners of the room. Mary, like David, knew at once that the rings must have belonged to the first Victoria Dilling.

David's closing prayer was brief and tender; then came the final sentence that hung strangely, incongruously upon the air.

"I now pronounce you man and wife."

As the words died away there was a dead hush in which the witnesses seemed to freeze in their places. David, himself, was completely unprepared for the awkwardness of this moment. Mary, usually ready of speech, stood mute also. Then it was that Minnie performed the unexpected act of beauty and of grace. She reached up her arms and drew the old man's face down to hers and kissed him on the lips.

"Thank you, Mr. Dilling," she said brokenly. "Thank you."

For a moment his wrinkled cheek rested against her rounded one, then he drew himself up, reached unsteadily for his cane and, with his head high, crossed the room without a word and went out. David started to follow him, for he had swayed a little in the doorway, but another was quicker than he. It was Jacob who got there first, who helped the old man down the stairs. Those in the room could see the two crossing the street together. At the door of the hotel, Jacob held out his hand hesitantly and the other grasped it. Then to the amazement of all, they saw Jacob go inside with Mr. Dilling.

Chapter Five

JUNE PASSED and there was no word from Moreswell. As those who have long been one flesh may grow also to be one mind, so David and Mary read each other's thoughts and kept silent. One thing that made it easier to forget the tenuous hope, the suspense, the final fact of disappointment, was the pressing burden of Ladykirk's problems. Outwardly the town went on as usual. The roses bloomed and faded; the bees swarmed; the summer dust became thicker along Main Street, necessitating the sweeping of porches and sidewalks twice a day; Jim Croft at the livery stable bought a new pair of gray carriage horses; Mr. Wilson, the schoolteacher, bet Shotwell in the post office that he would have both new peas and potatoes, the latter as big as a hen's egg, by the Fourth; and another group of engineers and surveyors from the Keystone Coal Company arrived at the Stone Hotel to begin work in earnest upon the farm fields behind the town.

Through it all ran the even succession of the weeks, each crowned with the calm Sabbath sunshine which died away in song in the three churches at early dusk. But all this was outwardly. Far below there was a break in the steady pulse beat of the village. The discernment, the penetration with which

115

David had surprised himself on that night when he had walked and pondered alone after watching the two lighted windows, would by now, he felt, have had a solid frame work of fact to support them if it had not been for the wedding. The effect of that episode upon the town had been volcanic. Not even the birth of the child had caused such shocked reaction. This, of course, might have been anticipated. What was completely un-expected to David was the direction public opinion had taken, after the event.

Slowly, steadily, beginning at the post office, spreading to the livery stable, the store steps and the blacksmith shop, there had been a growing wave of approval toward Mr. Dilling among the men. David heard this on all sides. The male jury agreed that Mr. Dilling was the only man in town who could have given Minnie the help she needed; and, to their amazement, he had had the spunk to up and do it at once. They had never suspected he had that much gumption and get-up in him, and they viewed him with a new and surprised respect. Apparently the vulgarities David had feared in their discussion with regard to his friend were largely absent. Jacob's report of his call upon Mr. Dilling was in a measure responsible for this.

"He asked me to go up to his room, mind you, an' he wasn't stuck-up or anything. He was as kind an' gentleman-like as Mr. Lyall himself. He says all he ever wants of Minnie is for her to bring the baby over often to see him. He got me to help him into bed, he was that shaky. 'I'm an old man, Jacob,' he says, 'an' I don't suppose I've much time ahead of me, but I'm glad I lived long enough to do this for your sister,' he says. An' when I was leavin' he shook my hand an' says, 'You're a good man, Jacob.' That's exactly what he says to me. It teched me, somehow."

Jacob, whose simple soul was devoid of embarrassment, circu-lated freely amongst all the groups and told them his story. He was still full of shy delight over the miracle of a child in his house and of pride over his eminence in being now brother-in-law and friend to a man of consequence. So, like the moving tide, male opinion of Ladykirk turned toward the strange bridegroom.

It was the women's attitude which was disturbing. Before the very day of the wedding was over, a new feeling of censure had arisen on their part against Minnie. From kitchen to sidewalk, from back yard to front porch the criticism had grown more sharp. It was as though they were all suffering from that inhibited state of mind in which sympathy for a wrongdoer is suddenly arrested by the lessening of the need for it. If there had been no wedding, native kindness and affection would have welled up stronger, week by week, for in Minnie's case at first there had been room for overwhelming pity along with the blame; so very quickly, however, following upon her humiliation had come the fact that she had been made an honorably wedded woman!

Moreover, while up until now the town had viewed Mr. Dilling with something much less than affection, it had recognized him as a man of culture, a onetime citizen of the great outside world of sophistication to which Ladykirk was a stranger; and also, though no one had ever been able to come by the exact facts (a circumstance the town resented), a man of sufficient means to live for twenty years upon his income. This was the person whose name Minnie now bore. In addition to all this, as Mary kept constantly pointing out to David, there was the matter of the diamond, the size of which beggared the few others in the town. To Mrs. Crombie, who up until now had been the possessor of the largest in the community, this was unforgivable.

"She says it's simply not *respectable*," Mary reported to her husband one night, "for Minnie to wear that ring after what she did. Mrs. Crombie thinks she's just getting off too easily from the whole thing. And while none of the other women have come right out and said that to me, I have a sort of feeling that's what they all think. I'm worried about it, David."

They often lay awake these nights, talking it over. One alarming fact to both of them was that no one would call Minnie by her new name. She and her husband were still in the spoken word, *Minnie Masters and Mr. Dilling.* This was partly due to habit, of course, but not entirely so for Ladykirk, as a rule, dearly loved a marriage and savored the change of a name sweetly upon the tongue. No, there was a deeper reason.

"You know," Mary added, "I have a feeling that no one will *ever* call her 'Mrs. Dilling,' and what are we to do about the Missionary programs? They have to be made out in time to be printed before the July tea. That gives us only two more weeks. I will have to call the committee meeting soon, and *what* are we to decide, Davy? The whole responsibility seems to be on us."

David knew it; while the problem of church discipline (a business he thoroughly hated) would be ultimately involved in Minnie's case, the decision as to what her status in the town was now to be would, by curious coincidence, be settled in the innocent-seeming programs of which Mary spoke. It would be settled by the women themselves.

The next afternoon David went into the garden and sat down beside the beehives to think the thing over again. In all his ministry there had never been a problem like to this, though there had been difficult ones enough. He had tried during the years to soften the stern Calvinistic system of discipline in effect before he came. This consisted in having a wrongdoer visited first by a member of the *Session,* then brought before that body to acknowledge his fault and state his repentance, and last, in having his name and sin read publicly before the congregation. This latter David had avoided whenever possible. Moreover, when he had discovered the enmities existing in the village, some of them generations old, caused by certain visits of none too tactful Session members upon those reputedly overtaken in a fault, he had suggested that he, himself, pay the distasteful calls. At least, then, he could be sure that mercy tempered justice. He had prepared also a brief, charitably worded statement, which the Session somewhat reluctantly had finally approved, which he read from the pulpit after the various cases of "disciplinary action." All this would have to be gone through with later with Minnie, but he had determinedly postponed it. Now, before the Session had exerted its prerogative, judgment upon Minnie was to be pronounced in another way.

David listened to the droning bees, pondered upon the well-regulated sex activities in the hive as compared with those of humans, and then began thinking deeply about the position of the Missionary Society. It was, to all the women who belonged to it, the most important organization in their lives, outside the church itself. Upon it they poured out the unexpended interest of their hearts. They met once a month to read careful "papers" on China or Africa or Ceylon; to sing, "From Greenland's Icy Mountains," or "Work for the Night is Coming"; and to offer low-voiced, hesitant prayers for the extension of the Kingdom. More than this, they labored with indefatigable zeal for the cause for which they prayed. They had Silver Teas, they had Bake Sales, they had Church Suppers. David's mouth suddenly twitched as he recalled Mr. Dilling's comment that "the heathen would have indigestion if they ever knew how many chocolate cakes had gone into their salvation."

But the fact remained that to the women of the Ladykirk Presbyterian Church, the Missionary Society was both religiously and socially important in their lives, and therefore in the town. It meant something even to take part in a program or to serve upon a committee, but to be *An Officer* was an honor to be coveted. Many a quiet housewife, David knew, would cherish through the years a hope never consummated, for this pinnacle could not be reached by all. Minnie, however, had reached it. The feeling among the women at the time of her election had been that if anyone deserved recognition, Minnie did, for none had worked harder or more faithfully. No one was more capable or efficient. Now, what was to be done about it?

It had been Mary's idea a few years ago to make out the programs in advance and have the Newburt twins print them on the hand press which they used for announcements of Auction Sales or Beware of the Dog and No Trespassing signs. The little folders had been a tremendous source of pride and satisfaction from the first and when Mary had discovered how much it meant to most of the women to see their names in print, she had added a full list of membership on the back beneath the names of the officers. Now, David realized, these leaflets were about to take on the judicial quality of court circulars. If Minnie's name remained upon them, she would be enfolded again publicly in the normal life of the town; if it was omitted . . .

There was a sudden call from the back porch and David looked up to see Josiah Hunt there, bearing a large box.

"Good day, Reverend," he shouted. "This ain't for you though it feels like it might be books. It's for Lucy."

By the time David got there, Lucy had appeared.

"It's for you," Josiah repeated, indicating Lucy with one free thumb. "Where'll I put it?"

"For me?" Lucy cried. "Oh, Mr. Hunt, set it up here on the table. Whatever could it be for me?"

"Heavy all right. Want me to open it up fur you?"

"No, no thank you very much. I think I'd like to open it myself. You see, I never got a box before."

She flew for the shears, and David, seeing Josiah had no intention of leaving until he saw the contents, asked him to sit down. Mary and Faith hurried out, and Jeremy, who had been painting the buggy top in the stable, came up the path at sound of the excitement. In view of them all Lucy cut the heavy string and struggled with the wrappings. When she reached the lid, she lifted it gently, disclosing a card lying upon the white paper beneath. The color rushed to her cheeks as she read the message aloud.

For summer journeys under the pine tree.

Lucy paused, looking at the others, then spoke in a breathless, ecstatic voice.

"It couldn't be . . . oh, it couldn't be *stereopticon views!*"

"Well, open up the paper," Jeremy said practically, "and you might find out."

"I can't," Lucy said. "My hands feel shaky. You do it, Jeremy."

He pushed the inner wrappings aside. Beneath, closely packed, were rows upon rows of heavy oblong cardboards. He drew one out and then another and another.

"*The Gardens of Versailles; The Matterhorn; Paris in Spring; Anne Hathaway's Cottage.* Why, there must be fifty here," he said excitedly.

"Nearer a hundred, I'd say," David amended.

In the midst of the exclaiming Lucy sank down at the table and laying her head upon her arms, wept unrestrainedly. Josiah was noticeably upset until Mary explained the phenomenon.

"She always does that when she's especially happy over gifts. She'll be all right in a minute."

Like April sunshine Lucy soon raised a shining face.

"It's so wonderful I can't believe it! I *never* was so surprised!"

David, meanwhile, had removed the packing from one end of the box and brought to light an elegant new holder (its sides lined with pale velvet), which was found to have twice the magnifying properties of their own old one. They all tried it, including Josiah who had to have a little help adjusting *The Hall of Mirrors* to his vision. He peered for a long moment without speaking.

"I'll be blowed!" he said reverently at last. "I've heard plenty times of these contraptions but I ain't never seen into one before. You'd think you was right there in the pictures till you look down an' see your legs standin' where you left them. Could I try another one?"

He gazed for a long time at *Niagara Falls by Moonlight* and then reluctantly surrendered the holder.

"It's most amazin'. Who'd you say sent the outfit to you, Lucy?"

"Ninian Ross, a . . . a friend of mine," Lucy stammered.

"Box come from Pittsburgh I noticed. Wes Shotwell says there's somebody from there doin' a lot of letter-writin' to you, Lucy. Wes says he's a monkey's uncle if he can see what anybody can find to write about *twice a week!*" Josiah guffawed heartily. "Same feller, I spose, sent the box, eh?"

"Why . . . why, yes."

"Well, Faith, you look out, now. Don't you let this little sister of yours step off ahead of you. You'd have to wear the green stockin's then. Well, got to be movin' along. Good day, Mrs. Lyall. Good day, Reverend." He raised his hand to the young folks and started off.

The Lyalls all sat down on the porch to feast upon the pictured scenes, using their old holder and the new one time about. It was delightful, this sudden surprise and relief from tension. Mary and David exchanged pleased glances; and Jeremy teased Lucy as they sat on the step together snatching views from each other.

"I somehow surmised the box came from Ninian even before you read the card," Jeremy said slyly. "I don't know how I came to think of it! When's he coming back? Whew! Look at this one of the Swiss Alps! It's a beaut! When's he coming, Lucy?"

Lucy, her curls tumbled from their ribbon, her whole face flushed with happiness, turned toward her parents.

"I meant to tell you . . . to ask you today, anyway. Ninian would like to come out over the Fourth if it's all right with you. He says it will be just a month since he was here last, and you said a month, Father. And he says he's getting on well with his job and so he asked if he might come."

Lucy paused for breath and then rushed on.

"And I thought it would be nice to have him then for there will be the U.P. Festival the night of the Fourth, and that would be something exciting to do. Could I write him that it's all right, Father?"

"Why, I think so, don't you, Mary?"

Mary pretended to ponder, though a little flush of pleasure had crept into her cheeks also.

"Yes, I think that would be very nice. And he might like to stay here at the house. He could share Jeremy's room. Tell him, Lucy, that I invited him. Dear me, that's this coming week end! We'll have to start getting things in order to-morrow."

"What's this about the green stockings?" Jeremy asked, suddenly looking up.

"Oh, nothing," Mary said hastily, "just Josiah's funny way of talking. Let me see the *Swiss Alps*, Jeremy."

"No, but really, what did he mean? Do you know, Faith? He was talking about you."

Faith had been sitting quietly beside her father, her silence having passed unnoticed in the general confusion of voices.

"Yes," said Faith, "I know what he meant."

"It's just an old back-country saying," Mary broke in. "Just nonsense about . . . about when a younger sister marries before an older one . . ."

"The older one has to wear green stockings to the wedding," Faith finished calmly, "in token, I presume, of her humiliation."

Jeremy laughed, but a small uneasiness hovered in the air.

"Let us have no silly talk about weddings," Mary said with an anxious glance toward Lucy. "Mercy! It will be years before any of you have to plan for that!"

"You think so?" Jeremy asked, studying the toe of his shoe intently.

"Certainly. You're all really just children yet. In our opinion at least."

"How old were you and Father when you got married?"

"Oh," Mary said, "that's different. That has nothing whatever to do with it, has it, David?"

After the laughter, David reached for the holder. "Here, let me see those *Swiss Alps,* and if it isn't presumptuous, could one mention supper? Travel does create an appetite."

The coming of Ninian, who was to arrive Saturday morning on the early train, sent through the manse a warm, eager thrill. Mary and the girls cleaned the house thoroughly, draping curtains once more to conceal the mended parts, polishing the old furniture and cooking what could be prepared beforehand. By Friday afternoon everything was in readiness. To David's masculine eye the rooms looked quite festive. Wandering into the big parlor in search of a book, therefore, he was dismayed to find Lucy upon her knees in front of the sofa, darning a frayed spot in the carpet, with a tear running down each cheek.

"Lucy, child! What's the matter?"

Lucy stretched her cramped legs and wiped her eyes.

"It's this carpet. It's *so* faded and worn. I never thought much about it before, but now I feel a little ashamed. When Ninian's people are so rich, you know."

David walked over to the big reading table and leaned against it. Lucy's speech had stabbed him in the heart. The old Brussels carpet with the spreading roses had come with the other furnishings from Mary's grandmother — the old lady who had cut Mary off without a penny because she had insisted upon marrying an impecunious young country preacher, Presbyterian at that! The carpet had held together miraculously through the years, but it was worn to the woof in many spots. It had been laid, at spring cleanings, in every possible new direction. There was nothing more to be done, except place the furniture at strategic points to cover the thinnest areas. And, considering the size of the room, when could they ever afford a new one? With Jeremy's college coming on and Faith's music all the time . . . The old carpet was a concrete evidence of his life's failure. Ah, Moreswell!

He sighed, and absently picked up a book from the table. Lucy had gone back to her darning and apparently did not expect a reply to her little outburst. As he leafed through the pages, a smile touched his lips. Lucy, more than either of the other children, shared his taste in poetry, and this volume had been a mutual favorite since her small-girl days. There were pages faintly yellowed with much reading and tiny corners turned down with familiar love.

David still leafed it, a warmth easing the soreness from his heart. He had brought his children some good gifts and he would not belittle them.

"Do you know," he said slowly, "that there are people in the world, rare, choice souls, who would feel this room was better furnished with a copy of William Blake's poems on the table than with a new carpet on the floor."

Lucy looked up, her eyes wide.

"Really, truly, Father?"

"Really, truly, my dear. But I'll give you even better comfort than that. When a young man comes to see a girl he . . . likes, he doesn't even know whether there is any carpet on the floor at all, or not. This I can assure you, for," he smiled, "I was a young man once myself."

It was planned that Jeremy would meet the train which arrived at nine in the morning, then after late breakfast on the porch, Lucy and Ninian could take a picnic lunch and drive through the rural scenes, since, as Mary tactfully pointed out, it was Lucy Ninian was really coming to see and not the whole family. In the evening there would be dinner instead of supper and after that the *Festival*. Jeremy of course would be taking Peggy McDonald to that event, and since she lived in the country the evening meal would be served early to allow him time to go for her. John Harvey had called Faith up the week before to invite her to go with him, and she had accepted, so everything seemed happily arranged, unless, Mary thought, it was this latter part of the plan. Busy and content with the smaller and larger joys of the moment, she still had a passing qualm of pain as she thought of her elder daughter. Faith with the deep, still gray eyes, the richly endowed mind and the gift of music which flowed in increasing perfection from her finger tips. Faith with the sweet, calm manner, the shy and sudden smile. There was beauty here, different from, but as great as Lucy's impulsive charm. And so far no young man had seemed to desire it except John Harvey. Mary had a feeling that Faith was even now weighing this problem of John. As a matter of fact he had much to offer a Ladykirk girl. He had a rich farm which would soon be his to take over, for the old folks were moving to town in the fall. There was the large substantial brick house which any woman of taste could make into a pleasant home. (Sometimes on a fleeting trial wave of imagination she saw Faith entertaining the Missionary Society there at a summer *Tea* in the years to come!) John had a strong body and a friendly countenance. But he had only a country school education and his grip on the

English language was hopelessly insecure. His interests and Faith's were as far apart as the poles. Oh, Mary thought, as she baked a cake to be set in the coolness of the cellar against the needs of the morrow, if *only* they had heard favorably from Moreswell! The big county seat town would have been the perfect place for Faith to meet young men of her own kind. There was nothing to do as things stood but to go on hoping and trusting in a gentle Providence and Faith's own heart.

The morning of the Fourth could not have been more fair. David, strolling through the garden as he awaited the late breakfast, indulged in what he smilingly called to himself "reading his office." The familiar words of certain old prayers he loved rose up effortlessly to his mind and became the background of his consciousness.

O God, the King eternal who dividest the day from the darkness, drive far off from us all wrong desires, incline our hearts to keep Thy law, and guide our feet into the way of peace, that having done Thy will with cheerfulness while it was day, we may when the night cometh rejoice to give Thee thanks.

He paused to look intently upon the bees. The new hive was prospering and its busy hum was music to his ears. He could not imagine a garden without bees. They added an indefinable accent of beauty to the scene.

O Heavenly Father, who hast filled the world with beauty, open we beseech Thee, our eyes to behold Thy gracious hand in all Thy works, that rejoicing in Thy whole creation, we may learn to serve Thee with gladness.

He was eager to see Ninian again. He hoped that he might be guided to say the right thing to the boy. He had felt an immediate kinship, somehow, with him. If he was as fine as he seemed and really cared for Lucy, then . . . *We beseech Thee to sanctify all our thoughts and endeavors, that we may neither begin an action without a pure intention, nor continue it without Thy blessing; and grant that . . .*

"David," a voice called mutedly from the kitchen window, "David, they're here!"

It seemed a new Ninian whom Jeremy ushered in to greet them all. Thinner, perhaps, but erect, alert, eager and shining with happiness.

"Mrs. Lyall, you are *so* kind to have me here! I can't thank you. How do you do, sir. It's wonderful to see you again. Miss Faith, how are you?"

Then as he came to Lucy, in her best gingham dress and a new pink ribbon around her curls, his assurance seemed to leave him. Lucy impulsively held out both hands and he took them in his own, saying nothing at all. But at the look in his eyes, Mary spoke up quickly.

"Jeremy will show you to your room, now, and then we'll all have breakfast together. I'm sure you had such an early one that you can eat another."

"Oh, just can't I?" he said, laughing and reaching for his bag. "I'll wash up a little and be right down."

They ate on the porch even though the paper fly brush had to be wielded above the honey plate. If the quieter Ninian of the first meeting had been attractive, the present one seemed irresistible. Mary, watching, reading the faces, knew what each of her family was feeling. David approved, Jeremy admired, Lucy loved and Faith . . . She was trying to laugh with the rest, to be gay and friendly and (Mary knew instinctively) free from jealousy of her sister. Even Mary herself felt vicariously the sophisticated charm of the guest. But oh, it was as his eyes dwelt upon Lucy that her heart moved out to him.

"It's perfect!" Ninian was saying as he was told the plan for the day. "Absolutely perfect. I'll go down to the livery stable and see if I can scare up a rig."

"You can use ours," David said.

"Thank you, sir, but you may need yours."

"Do you know how to drive a horse?" Lucy asked curiously. "Being from the city," she added.

Ninian smiled at her. "Oh yes. We've always had horses. I mean . . . yes, I can manage one all right." He looked embarrassed at his small slip.

"Do you ride?" Jeremy inquired.

"Oh, a little. The big thing now is the auto. Have you seen one yet?"

"A man in Moreswell has one," Jeremy said. "He drove through here one Sunday afternoon and everybody lined up along Main Street to see it. For me, I'd rather stick to the horse. It's more responsive when you stroke its nose."

"There's farmer blood in Jeremy," David said teasingly. "It's from away back but every once in a while it crops up."

"Who knows? Maybe it will win out. Can't you see me following the plow? Look at those muscles!"

"Nothing to those of a steel puddler," Ninian insisted, and the meal ended in laughter.

When Ninian drove up later in the hired rig Lucy gave a cry of delight, for at a glance they all saw it was the choice one of the livery stable. The buggy was phaeton style, wide and low, with a curved step and a lamp on either side of the dashboard. The horse was a handsome bay and the whole effect one of dashing elegance. Ninian jumped out, grasping the reins expertly, and handed Lucy to her seat, while Jeremy placed the picnic hamper in the back of the buggy, and the others stood at the gate to watch them start.

"Put your hat on, dear, and don't get tanned," Mary adjured, seeing Lucy's headgear in its usual place — hanging from its cord upon her shoulders. "And don't be too late coming back, for we're having dinner at five-thirty."

"Houston's Hollow is about the prettiest place around, I think," David recommended.

Ninian spread the striped linen duster carefully over Lucy's knees, gathered up the reins more tightly and with a last flourish of good-byes, they were off.

Lucy sat very prim and quiet, her hands folded upon the duster, as they drove out of town and up the first long hill. Ninian seemed content to remain silent also, stealing frequent glances at his companion. At last as the country fields enfolded them, he turned around, to see her turning also toward him.

"I can't believe we're really together again," he said.

"Neither can I. I thought today would *never* come," Lucy said with artless candor.

Ninian smiled tenderly.

"I don't think there is another girl like you in the whole world."

"Am I so odd, then?"

"You are perfect," he said. "The only trouble is . . . "

"Yes?" Lucy prompted anxiously.

"That I can't stop thinking about you. All the time I'm at work I see you. The way you looked when you rushed out to intercept me, with a little spot of paint on your nose, and the way you looked at the edge of the porch in the moonlight and then in the choir and of course at the gate. . . . "

"You must tell me all about your work," Lucy said hastily.

So as they drove on unhurrying between the early harvest fields, they talked of superficial things and laughed often, chiefly with delight at their nearness, content to know that later in the cool shadows of the wood they could speak of all that lay closest to their hearts.

When they reached Houston's Hollow, Ninian secured the horse to the stake and rider fence with the tie rope, removed the bridle and produced the feed bag the livery stable had provided.

"We'll let the nag picnic first," he said, "so our consciences will be clear for our own."

When they turned into the flecked shade of the trees with their sunny upper branches, Lucy had to point out the May apples to him, which he had never seen before, and break one from under its leafy umbrella that he might sniff the delicate fragrance. A few rockets were still in bloom and here and there a bunch of fiery pinks. Ninian plucked one of these from its stem and tucked it, very slowly, in her hair.

They found the smooth rock which Lucy had explained was perfect for a table, and there near the little stream, they deposited their cushions, opened the hamper and feasted upon they knew not what, for whenever their hands accidentally touched, it was sweet white fire.

When they had finished, they made themselves comfortable, leaning against a big oak, and began to fill in all that the letters could not say.

"My whole life is changed since I met you," Ninian said earnestly. "Before, as I told your father, I didn't care much about anything. Now, I'm full of plans and can't wait to carry them out. Next year in college I'll study like blazes and after I graduate in June, I'll go to work . . ."

He paused, looking off toward the stream and then shyly up at Lucy.

"You won't think I've gone sentimental about myself — no, you're the one person who won't. You see, I've suddenly begun to wish I could do some good in the world."

"But of course," Lucy agreed without surprise, "Of course you will."

"I hardly know what it could be. I thought I'd talk it over from time to time with your father. What's Jeremy going to do after college?"

"Oh, be a minister, of course. That's been planned since before he was born, I guess. Father and Mother both think he'll be a fine one."

"How does Jeremy feel about it?"

"He never says too much for he's very modest."

Ninian was thoughtful. "I don't suppose I could ever be a minister. I would never be worthy of that calling."

"Oh, you *would!*" Lucy exclaimed. "You are so kind and wonderful and good!"

"Not good, Lucy. You don't know me."

"But I do. I believe I know you better than anyone else in the world."

"Maybe you do, after all."

It was intimate ground, this gentle probing of each other's hearts.

"Did you really understand what I wrote you last week?"

"I . . . I think so."

"It seems too soon, perhaps, and yet I have to tell you. I love you, Lucy. Tell me truly how you feel."

He had slipped his arm about her and she leaned toward him, her curls touching his shoulder.

"It's so very strange that I should know, all at once. But I do. Ever since the night we watched the fireflies. I do love you, Ninian. I couldn't be more sure."

His arm tightened. "I don't want to frighten you again," he said, a smile in his voice, "but I want so terribly to kiss you."

Her words came, very low.

"I don't believe I'm so easily frightened as . . . as I was."

And then their lips met again in the green shade beneath the golden boughs.

A little later, she had to thank him for the stereopticon views and tell him of her delight.

"It's the most beautiful present I've ever had in my whole life. I feel so cultured now, so *traveled*, as though I've been every-where. Do you know the scene I love best? I can't explain how

I feel when I look at it. It gives me little shivers like Omar. It's *Paris in the Spring!*"

"I'll take you there next summer on our wedding trip!" he said.

Lucy drew away in amazement.

"Wedding trip! *Next summer!* Why . . . why, what do you mean?"

"We love each other, don't we? Then we'll naturally want to be married as soon as possible. I thought after I graduate next spring we could . . . "

"But Ninian, I never thought of getting *married*. I do love you and I would like to be with you all the time. But I don't know whether I want to be *married* for quite a while. I'm pretty young, don't you think?"

His eyes were misty as he kissed her hair.

"Yes, darling, I understand. We will be informally engaged right now and not worry about the future." He smiled with tender assurance. "You'll soon get used to the thought of marriage. Just you wait and see."

When they were starting back, at last, Lucy rested her arms on the fence as Ninian untied the horse.

"Do you know," she said, "we've done everything backward according to the books."

Ninian paused, surprised.

"How is that?"

"Well, we've only met twice and yet we're almost . . . I mean, we're practically . . . "

"Engaged!" Ninian finished jubilantly.

"That's what I mean. We've gone so fast. We should just be taking an interest in each other now and then for a year, perhaps, get better acquainted and finally fall in love. You see we've started at the end, haven't we?"

"So, see how much time we've saved! Who cares for the old books? The authors just have to string out the story to hold the reader's interest. We know better, don't we?"

"And you don't think we have to believe Shakespeare? Not, well, not like the Bible, for instance?"

Ninian threw back his head and laughed heartily.

"I've never worried much about it, certainly. Why? What does Shakespeare say?"

"That 'the course of true love never did run smooth.' "

"Oh, that! Nonsense! The old boy just picked himself the wrong father-in-law, probably. Now, you see I'm wiser."

"Of course," Lucy said thoughtfully, "I've never met mine."

A tension appeared in Ninian's lips. His whole face set suddenly as he fixed it upon hers.

"No one, nothing, will ever touch our love," he said.

Meanwhile back in the manse Mary, answering the phone, returned to the others in a small excitement.

"It was Aunt Betsy Wade! She's invited us to tea, David, at three-thirty. It will hurry us a little but I couldn't refuse. Can you manage dinner, Faith, if we go?"

"Of course. And put on your blue voile, Mother, and your best bonnet! You know she'll have her ceremonial robes on. *Tea*, no less! Oh, that will be nice for you. Don't worry about dinner. I'll see to it."

It was not a long distance but to save time they decided to drive. Mary, looking eager and pretty in her best summer clothes, nodded to the townspeople who sat on their front porches under the flags and bunting, and waved to Mr. Dilling at the hotel. The big iron gates of the courtyard were wide open as though there had been considerable coming and going during the day.

"I'm so delighted to be going out to tea," Mary remarked as they passed through the covered bridge and turned into the shady road that bordered the Crick. "Aunt Betsy hasn't invited us now for a little while and I was afraid she was offended at something. One never knows. And I love going to her house."

"So do I. She always tones me up," David agreed. "Like taking boneset tea in the spring. Curious the effect is the same whether I'm pleased or annoyed with her."

They discussed Aunt Betsy as they followed the curved banks laden with mountain laurel, past the small graveyard where the former Wades lay in elegant seclusion under the pines, and on to the substantial brick house itself.

Aunt Betsy was the town's one aristocrat, both by birth and personal election. Like Mary herself she had come from a dignified city background and through the years had (unlike Mary) allowed no one to forget it. The village, however, had accepted her on her own terms without rancor, for her husband was a Wade and the Wades themselves had always been a little different from the common run. Old Theophilus two generations back had been in the state legislature and Aunt Betsy's late husband, Doremus, had been a man of parts who settled early into the role of gentleman farmer, with many contacts in the county seat and even in Pittsburgh. The Wades had always had money one way or another, and Aunt Betsy was known to have some in her own right. So now at ninety, sound as a nut, shrewd, wise, dominating, Victorian in form and given to prideful black silks and lace caps, she sat in her spacious house, intensely interested in all that went on in the town and yet claiming distinction from it. More immediately she ruled her own little kingdom of two-hundred-odd acres, including Job Harner the tenant farmer, his wife Josie and her own daughter Miss Miranda, who, although sixty-five, was still girlishly docile, thin, prim and self-effacing. She was a quietly familiar figure in town with her market basket and little dog by day or her lantern and little dog by night.

"I suppose Aunt Betsy wants to change her funeral plans again," David said as they neared the house. "The last time she brought me over on what she said was an urgent matter it was to tell me she didn't want 'Asleep in Jesus' sung as everyone seemed to be having it now. She switched back to 'How Firm a Foundation.' "

Mary giggled, then composed her face as David tied the horse and they went up the fern-bordered walk and over the wide front porch. Miss Miranda met them, her colorless face all smiles, and ushered them into the front parlor where Aunt Betsy sat in state, her gold-handled cane hooked over the back of her rocker.

"I'm very glad to see you," she said graciously. "This being a special day I felt like seeing company — *congenial* company," she added, looking over her glasses.

"Thank you, Mrs. Wade," Mary replied. "We're very glad to come."

"Now," Aunt Betsy said, "tell me the news of the family first. What's this I hear about a young city man showing interest in Lucy? Are you sure he's eminently suitable and trustworthy? I'm very fond of Lucy. She has charm. You must guard it. She's too young to be having love affairs."

David glanced fleetingly at Mary. Her eyelids drooped ever so slightly. They had suffered Aunt Betsy's slight condescensions through the years.

"We don't wish anything said about it," David began. "It's just a pleasant boy-and-girl friendship."

"Certainly," said Aunt Betsy eagerly, leaning forward. "You may trust me."

"He seems a very nice and well-brought-up young man. He is the son of Robert P. Ross of Pittsburgh."

"Highty-tighty-mighty!" There was no doubt that Aunt Betsy was impressed. "How did she ever meet him?"

"He was staying at the hotel and . . . well, you know how young people get to know each other," Mary explained with airy vagueness.

"Bless my soul!" said Aunt Betsy, still visibly overcome by the young man's connections. "Well, take double care if he's rich. They're the worst."

"How have you been, Mrs. Wade?" David inquired firmly to indicate the matter of Lucy's affairs was closed.

"I'm in excellent health, thank you, though not able to get about much. I keep in touch with the town, however, and before tea is brought I wish to discuss this business of Minnie Masters."

She eyed them both keenly. "I never thought Ladykirk could surprise me again, but I must say this beats all on record. What I want to know is, what's to be done about her *office?*"

Mary's bright face fell. "We don't know, Mrs. Wade. Have you any suggestions?"

"No," said the old lady, surprisingly enough for her. "I haven't, and it's a long day for me when I can't make up my mind. Of course she ought to resign and I think she will. But I keep thinking about the time I broke my hip ten years ago. Everybody thought it was the end of me and so did I, you may recall. One afternoon in came Minnie as serene and smiling as usual with a box of silk pieces. I heard later she'd collected them from all over town. 'I thought as soon as you were up,' she said, 'you'd want to get on with your quilt, so I brought over a few patches.' Well, that put the fight right back in me. I got well, and Minnie did it, though the doctor got the credit."

"There are plenty of people in town who have known Minnie's kindnesses," Mary said gravely.

"Let them remember them, then. And you, Mr. Lyall, hold the bit on that Session of yours. How is Dilling behaving himself?" she added sharply.

David controlled his lips as best he could. Aunt Betsy's dislike for Mr. Dilling dated from their first encounter twenty years ago. She had heard of the new arrival and his attitude of superior aloofness. When she met him one day in the hotel court she attempted in a few curt sentences to put him in his place and let him know at once who the real aristocrat of the village was and would continue to be. He had listened, according to the fascinated bystanders, in silence, then had made a courtly bow and spoken in utter gravity.

"Daily, with the greatest pleasure, I feast my eyes, Mrs. Wade, upon your beautiful Bottom. I am happy now to meet the owner face to face."

The wicked *bon mot* had swept the town with ribald laughter and had become one of the legendary jokes of the community. Needless to say Aunt Betsy had never forgiven him.

"He is as usual," David said now. "This has brought him a great new interest."

"Well," Aunt Betsy admitted grudgingly, "I'll warrant it's the first useful thing he's ever done in his life, but I'm glad he had the spunk to do this. Now I have another very unpleasant subject that must be brought up."

David and Mary stiffened to hear.

"It's about my sheep. You know I have the best breed in these parts. I've been at some pains to get fine ewes. And during this last week *three* of them *have disappeared!*"

"Oh, I'm sorry," David said.

"Sorry!" snapped Aunt Betsy. "I guess you would be if you'd suffered the loss. There's no doubt about it. Dave Washing took them! Stole them!"

"Oh, Mrs. Wade, I can hardly think that."

"You can't, eh? Well, I can. He's nothing but a thorn in the flesh to me. He's been badgering me and baiting me all these years. He's an *enemy* and I don't care who knows it. This is the last straw. I intend to prosecute and I think the church should bring the matter under its discipline."

"But, Mrs. Wade, have you any evidence? Could not dogs have destroyed them? Could they have wandered into the Bottom land and fallen in the Crick?"

"My fields are well fenced, Mr. Lyall, and there have been no dogs. It's Dave Washing and no other. Why the Lord had to set him on the farm adjoining mine is something I can't get reconciled to even in my prayers. But you'll hear more of this before I'm through, mark you."

Miss Miranda appeared with the large tea tray which she placed before her mother. Immediately the atmosphere cleared. Following her unbroken rule that no unpleasant conversation should take place during the partaking of food, Aunt Betsy's face lightened as she set about pouring from the big silver teapot. A gracious elegance now pervaded the room. Mary and David, relaxing in it, ate the paper-thin slices of homemade bread spread richly with the butter of the farm; and savored the squares of gingerbread, the recipe for which would die with the last Wade. They ate of the latter recklessly, knowing this was the surest way to Aunt Betsy's favor.

Mary felt deliciously content with the moment. She was conscious now of the thick Brussels carpet under her feet, the gold mirror above the mantel, the oil paintings on the walls, some of them Aunt Betsy's own work; the shine of the old mahogany, and the cool smoothness of the long horsehair sofa upon which she sat. The talk was easy and bright now: the weather; the Festival that evening; the little dog at Miss Miranda's feet; the nomination ten days before of McKinley and Roosevelt in Philadelphia. . . .

When they rose to go, expressing their thanks, Aunt Betsy made a statement.

"I have come recently to a rather important decision. Doctor

Faraday's talked me into it. I have never favored innovations, but health and comfort must, I suppose, be considered. I am having a bathroom put in the house."

Mary's hands flew together in an unconscious gesture of wistful delight.

"Oh, Mrs. Wade, I'm so glad for you. A bathroom is the greatest material comfort of which I could dream in this world!"

The old lady peered at her, keenly.

"It is, eh? Well, I've done without one very well till this age of me. I hope now I'll have a few more years to enjoy it."

As they drove back toward the town, Mary drew a long sigh.

"A bathroom!" she said. And then added quickly, "What do you think about her sheep?"

David laughed. "I think Dave Washing probably has them all right and is holding them at his convenience just to keep her on tenterhooks. Sort of revenge for the time Aunt Betsy had his bull penned up for a month. They're always in trouble over something, but I hope she won't make too much fuss over this for there is a good deal of talk of Dave for the new Trustee to fill the vacant place and he would make a good one. We'll have to have a special congregational meeting this fall, I think, for the election."

At the manse after dinner there was the ceremony of taking down the big flag, then nimble running up and down stairs, the flurry of pressing a forgotten sash, a good deal of calling back and forth from room to room and lighthearted laughter filling all the house.

David, already dressed for the evening, sat on the back porch, smiling to himself. Lucy had caught him in the upper hall when no one else was near and standing on tiptoe whispered in his ear.

"You were right, Father, he didn't!"

"Didn't what?" he had asked, bewildered.

"He didn't even look at the carpet."

"I'm not surprised," he had answered, turning his head quickly that she might not be made vain by his look.

He was thinking now of the pleasure of this quiet moment in which he could sit here communing with his own soul while the early evening drew its gradual, dusky veil, and the background of young voices lent its peculiar joy. This was one of those brief respites from care which seemed an antepast of heaven itself. There was, he decided, something deeply and intensely *moral* about happiness! The bright clean upleap of the heart represented man at his best. He searched his mind for proof of this. When the soul was least clogged with sin and selfishness, it should be most happy, should it not? Ergo, the happiest soul should then be nearest God. Was Jeremy Taylor right that the ideal religion was one that should "lead us to a huge felicity through pleasant ways"? A far cry, indeed, from Calvinism, but David frequently did not see eye to eye with Calvin any more than old Jeremy had.

Of course there was the problem of sorrow and the sufferings of the flesh. How were they to be fitted in with the moral concept of happiness? David walked to the edge of the porch, looking off at the shadowy hills using the words from Mary's girlhood prayer book: *Lighten our darkness we beseech Thee and of Thy great mercy defend us from all perils and dangers this night*. . . .

He turned at a step behind him and saw Jeremy looking very handsome in his gray pepper-and-salt suit and wing collar. They eyed each other with affection.

"Well, Peggy's a very pretty girl, Jeremy."

"I most dutifully agree with you, sir," he answered, grinning broadly and then went whistling down the path to the barn.

David's mind dwelt with rich satisfaction upon his son. He

had the best mind of the three children; he had initiative and a vigorous determination which must have come from Mary's side of the house; he would do brilliantly at college; he would go far in the ministry. The success, David thought, that he himself had missed, or failed of attaining, would be Jeremy's. He had an unspoken dream each time he looked at Magdalen Tower above the mantel that one day Jeremy might actually study among the dreaming spires! After all, there were scholarships . . . Perhaps it was deeper fruition to achieve through one's children than through one's self. A mounting continuity of experience.

As to the girl, she was a nice young thing for a first, boyish friendship. Her family was an old one in the rural community, having held their big farm through three generations. Jeremy had worked there during the summer for several years before he took up bookselling, and of course he and Peggy knew each other well. When he went away to college and found himself in a wider social life, however, he would meet someone more suited to his career. Well, in any case, there was nothing to worry about tonight, so let the sweet airs blow!

In the parlor at the moment, Mary was speaking to Ninian in some embarrassment.

"I do hope you won't be expecting too much of this Festival, since we've all been doing a good deal of talking about it. You see, in a little town like this our pleasures are very simple and we try to make the most of them. But it may all seem very rustic and *tame* to you!"

Ninian smiled a bit roguishly. "You needn't worry, Mrs. Lyall. I'm sure to enjoy it. Besides, I didn't come out just for the Festival, you know."

David and Mary set off before the young folks, since they wished to show their interest in the affair for as long a time as possible. They discussed the children as they walked along the quieter back street.

"I invited Peggy to stay overnight, since tomorrow is Sunday and she can go home after church with her parents. Jeremy seemed quite pleased with the idea. After all, the McDonalds were very kind to him when he used to be working on the farm. I wonder how fond he is of Peggy?" she added.

"Oh, it's nothing serious, I'm sure. Jeremy won't settle for years. He can't. It's Ninian who has decided what he wants and means to have it, if I'm any judge."

"I know. It's beautiful to watch him and Lucy together. Only I can't somehow believe we've reached the place where the children are having love affairs. I enjoy it, but it makes me feel queer — a little oldish."

David pressed her arm. "Don't you wish we were eighteen and twenty-one again? Don't you wish we could go back and live the years all over?" he asked eagerly.

She was silent for so long that a cold hand gripped his heart.

"No," she said simply at last.

His hurt was sharp beyond measure.

"I couldn't bear to go through losing little David again," she added.

He felt stunned. It was nearly fifteen years since their time of sorrow. After his first anguish, and the ensuing months of loneliness, the child had gradually become to him only a tender memory and his own spirit had accepted the loss without bitterness.

"You still feel it so?" he asked very low. "After all the years?"

"Yes," she answered. "I never got over it. I never became truly reconciled."

They walked on quietly. How like life, David thought, that as he passed from the serenity of his recent musings on the porch to the gaiety of the Festival, he should unexpectedly find his heart touched with sadness by the way? What could he now say to Mary, his own wife, to comfort her? Especially when he had never known through the years that her grief thus per-

sisted unassuaged? He was mute. Mary, who lay against his
breast each night and made the house of their habitation bright
by day, Mary, whose every thought he had believed open to
him, had secret places in her heart of which he had no knowledge.

There swept through his mind the faces of other women in
the town who had lost little children through the years. He had
never known until this moment what poignancy of pain might
lie behind their still eyes as they looked up at him in the pulpit
or met him on the street. From now on he would be aware —
oh, terribly aware of their need.

It was Mary who broke the silence in her usual voice, as they
neared the church lawn.

"What a perfect evening! And what a crowd!"

Old and young, dressed in their best and evincing a pleased
expectancy, were coming in all directions. Buggies were flying
up and down the street and already it was evident that the long
rows of sheds behind the three churches, which ordinarily
housed the horses during divine service, were now filling up. For
this annual festival of the U.P.'s was an event. The Presbyterians
might excel in their chicken and waffle suppers in the winter,
but no organization could touch the U.P.'s as far as festivals
were concerned. For one reason, their church was relatively
new — the other two having stood for well on to a hundred
years on their present sites — so there was no graveyard upon
the property; this meant a more extensive lawn, untouched by
lugubrious suggestion, upon which to hold the fête. Since the
weather entered so largely into the preparations, the building
and decorating of the tables was always left to the day itself. So
now from early morning there had been rattle of boards and
pounding of nails; shouting from the tops of stepladders as men
strung wires, hung Chinese lanterns and draped bunting; laughter and bustle from the women as they spread white cloths,

arranged bouquets, planned where the ice-cream freezers would stand, and then hulled strawberries and made gallons of lemonade in the shade of the big maples.

By late afternoon the farm folk of the congregation began to arrive. The women, bringing cakes of every variety, placed them on the reserve table arranged for the purpose and then set to work with their town sisters, putting last touches to the decorations, shining lamp chimneys and planning who would wait on table, who would wash dishes and who would cut cake and serve the strawberries. The men always "dished" the ice cream with the professional cone-shaped scoops lent for the occasion by Billy Kinkaid who made the confection according to his secret formula.

Everyone, those who were running the affair and those who would attend it, rejoiced in the fine weather, for if it had rained the Festival would have been held in the basement of the church, thus losing most of its romantic quality. As it was now, all was perfect: a warm evening with a delicate breeze blowing, a few late roses for the young girls' hair; a few last sporadic firecrackers to add stimulus and, as though nature intended to show special favor this year to the U.P.'s, a full moon!

David and Mary made their way now toward a corner of the lawn where chairs were always placed for the ministers and their wives. They were welcomed by Mr. and Mrs. Combs as hosts and sat down to survey the scene and greet those who came up to pay their respects.

"We ought to make out well financially tonight," Mrs. Combs said with satisfaction. "We certainly need the money to help out with the new pulpit chairs. We've set our hearts on red plush if we can reach it."

"Oh, I hope you can," Mary said generously, thinking meanwhile that the Presbyterian ones were growing rather shabby.

On the other side Mr. Combs was asking David in a low tone

whether the church had taken any action in connection with Minnie Masters.

"A difficult matter!" he was repeating. "A very *delicate* matter, that. I'm glad I'm not in your shoes."

"I don't like being in my own," David agreed.

The crowd was still increasing. All the tables were now filled; the women waiters, bustling, happy and important, exchanged pleasantries with those who were eating, while the men cracked jokes over the big ice-cream freezers. More and more young couples, many of them from far back in the country, stood about, with one large circle of young men under the catalpa tree laughing with each other as they shrewdly eyed the passing girls. Gene Holly, who presided over the bunting-draped ticket table, was kept busy making change from his square box and passing out the pasteboard slips, printed by the Newburt twins on their hand press: *Ice cream, 10 cts. Strawberries, 10 cts. Cake, 5 cts. Lemonade, 5 cts.* From the oil lamps on the tables a soft, pale glow touched the scene to which in a short time the rising moon would add its light.

Mary was scanning the newcomers when she caught sight of her own young people: Jeremy and Peggy first, then Faith with John Harvey, who looked quite nicely groomed and handsome tonight; last Lucy, with a red rose in her hair, laughing up at Ninian. As they approached the ticket stand, there was the rattle of a buckboard driven rapidly by, a sudden wave of laughter from one of the tables, the snap of firecrackers from the roadside where some small boys were bent upon frightening the horses, and shouting from a group of half-grown lads who were chasing each other on the edge of the crowd. At least, Mary thought, it was not a *dull* scene.

David leaned over to her.

"When is *my* girl ready for refreshments?" he asked.

His look made her feel young and happy. "Right this minute. And remember, I want everything. It's so nice to feel for once that extravagance is a duty. We'd better not sit anywhere near the children, though. They might think we were watching them."

"Which of course you wouldn't dream of doing!" he chuckled.

They lingered at the table, for they found places with Dr. and Mrs. Faraday so the talk was congenial. It was seldom enough that the doctor had time for a social event and David, who had sat up with him through many a long night as they watched a waning life, found it extraordinarily pleasant to visit with him under serene auspices. Mrs. Faraday was confiding on the quiet to Mary how she had arranged matters.

"I did some dreadful things to get him here," she said, "but I was determined for once he'd have a bit of fun like everybody else. Besides a woman enjoys going out with her husband *once* in a while! So when Molly Dowds came up to the office while he was dressing, I just told her to come back next week. I knew it was nothing special. She's just expecting again — her ninth — and she always comes to see the doctor about a month before her time. The worst was after we'd left the house. I went back to get my fan and the telephone was ringing!" She lowered her voice for the black confession. "*I didn't answer it!*"

"Well," Mary comforted her, "if it was anything serious you'll still hear of it."

Mrs. Faraday sighed. "That we will. Soon enough. He's on the go day and night. Thirty years it's been. But I guess he wouldn't be happy any other way." She looked left and right and leaned closer.

"Have you decided anything about Minnie yet? Has she sent in her resignation?"

Mary shook her head. "Today being a holiday I tried to put the whole problem out of my mind. I've felt the better of it, too."

"What about the Programs?"

"I'll have to call a meeting the last of next week. We can't wait longer."

"How does Mr. Lyall feel?"

"I don't think he's made up his mind. He's as troubled as we are."

"I went over today to see her and took a cherry pie."

"How did she seem?"

"Very thin and white and she has nothing to say. She had the diamond on and I never saw such a ring! I really . . . think it would be better if she didn't wear it. For a while, anyway."

"I know what you mean, but I imagine she's doing it to please Mr. Dilling."

"Yes, it could be. Well . . . we'd better talk of other things. Somebody across the table is all ears."

By leaning forward a little, Mary could glimpse the young folks who seemed to be enjoying themselves immensely. It was evident that Ninian was ordering a new round of delicacies for them all. She could see the interested faces turned in his direction and a glow of motherly importance shot through her heart.

They had been back in their chairs for some time where the Faradays joined them, and were just considering going home, when a commotion started near the ticket stand. David stood up to see more clearly and then gave a muttered exclamation.

"Good heavens!" he said, "it's Ben Losting on the rampage. He's really drunk this time. He's got his gun! I guess I'd better go and see what I can do," he added.

For the signs of panic were growing. People on the outskirts were scurrying for cover, and those near the central figure of the scene were pressing back on all sides. A group of young boys, their faces pale but avid with interest in the drama, crowded around the ticket stand, almost overturning it. Gene Holly had left his place and was trying, from a reasonably safe angle, to expostulate with the drunken man who, standing a long, lanky six-feet-three in his dirty shirt and pants, was pointing his gun around at random. His small eyes were bloodshot and perspiration and tobacco juice streaked his grizzled, unshaved face.

"There'll be none of these here fancy festivals on the Judgment Day," Ben was shouting. As usual his words came with surprising clearness. "The Methodists are the only ones goin' to heaven! I'm here to shoot down the U.P.'s *an'* the Presbyterians *an'* the Covenanters. They're all a bunch of stuck-up, lyin' hypocrites, tha's what they are. Why are people always pickin' on me? Because I'm a *Methodist!* The Lord's commanded me to get rid of all the rest of you scum, an' I'm gonna do it!"

David had come quite near by this time.

"Hello, Ben," he said calmly.

Ben gave one of the drunken yells for which he was famous.

"Get out, Reverend. Get away from here! You ain't goin' to get around me this time. No sir, I mean business. Get away!"

"Wouldn't you like some ice cream, Ben?" David continued placatingly.

Ben yelled again. "Ice cream? Hell!" he said. "All you chicken-livered men here can have is ice cream an' lemonade! Not a damned one of you can take a good slug o' whiskey." A sly look came suddenly over his face. "Or mebbe I could name a few," he added with a leer. "Mebbe I could name some that would surprise you!"

David broke hastily in.

"Listen, Ben, the Methodists are as much against drinking as we are. If there was a Methodist church here you'd have to go to the mourners' bench right now, you know you would."

There was the sound of a titter somewhere, and Ben reared his head.

"Who's that laughin' at me?" he yelled. "I'll stop him with a bullet, I will!"

"Nobody's laughing at you," David went on steadily. "But you know, Ben, there *might* be some Methodists right here in this crowd. There are a lot of strangers with us tonight. Better let me have that gun, for you might accidently shoot one of them and you wouldn't want to do that."

Ben's jaw dropped. His head wagged in slow agreement.

"By Gawd, Reverend, you're right. I wouldn't want to shoot a Methodist. Wouldn't matter about a U.P. or a Presbyterian, but I sure would go to hell if I'd shoot a Methodist."

An audible wave of relief swept the crowd as David took the gun and caught Ben firmly by the arm.

"That's right. Now you and I'll get away from here out of danger."

Ben staggered, as his lean hulk towered over David, but he managed to get turned around and allow himself to be steered toward the sidewalk. Roy Parsons, the constable, the sight of whom was anathema to Ben, grabbed the gun from David's outstretched hand and then followed them at a discreet distance.

All at once the voices and laughter were loosed and the Festival took on a new vibrancy; but only for a few minutes, for there arose another cry, this time from Gene Holly.

"We've been robbed!" he shouted. "There's a ten-dollar bill gone from the box. Somebody's . . . stole . . . a . . . ten . . . dollar . . . bill!"

Every face was aghast. Ten dollars was a great deal of money. It would represent a third or a fourth of all the evening's receipts. Besides, the ugly fact of *theft* smeared the face of the night.

"It must have been one of these boys!" Gene was still beside himself with excitement. "They were back of the stand here, when I was out front with Ben Losting. Help me line 'em up, somebody. They've got to be searched."

By the time several men had joined Gene, there had been a swift melting away of several of the boys into the shadows behind them. A few stood their ground, were searched and pronounced innocent. Gene was still half hysterical over the loss, since the money had been his responsibility.

"Where's Jim Cuppy? He was right here the closet of any! I mind that. An' he took to his heels fast enough. It must have been Jim Cuppy. Run after him, somebody. Catch him! *Stop . . . thief!*"

There was a faint sound of demurrence from a few of those who stood near, but, even to the fairest-minded, this sounded probable. The Cuppys lived in one of the log cabins in "Clatty Row," just outside the town. Old Jake was a notoriously shiftless and untrustworthy character. While Milly, his wife, a thin little scrap of a woman who did washings and house-cleanings, tried her best to bring up her large brood honestly, the heavy shadow of the father always seemed to be over them all. Yes, of all the boys in town Jim Cuppy would be the likeliest to take the money, so went opinion from lip to lip.

Mary, shaken from the Ben Losting episode, felt a sinking of the heart as she thought of Jim's shy, homely young face. She knew David believed in the boy and was working hard to get him to join the church at the next Communion. This matter would disturb him greatly. Gene could still be heard explaining how it all came about.

"I'd just checked over the bills not five minutes before. There was only the one ten-dollar one. That strange young fellah with Lucy Lyall give it to me to pay for his tickets."

At the words there was a general turning of heads in the direction of Lucy and Ninian, both of whom blushed furiously under the gaze.

When a new rush toward the tables from the latecomers began, and waves of animated conversation swept the scene, Ninian and Lucy with Jeremy and Peggy came to Mary to escort her home since they all knew David might be delayed until Ben was safely placed in the lockup behind the post office.

As a matter of fact he arrived at the manse shortly after they did, half annoyed and half amused by the whole encounter.

"You did a marvelous job, sir," Ninian said admiringly, "and a very courageous one too, if I may say so."

David laughed. "Maybe I wouldn't have been so brave if I'd known the gun was loaded! Ben always puts on quite a show when he's drunk and I supposed this was just bluff, but Ray Parsons found the thing was full of shot. So I don't know what the outcome will be. Ben's locked up for the night. He'll yell his head off and then be sober and docile enough tomorrow."

"Don't ever tell me again that Ladykirk Festivals are tame affairs, Mrs. Lyall," Ninian exclaimed. "I haven't seen so much excitement in a long time, ending in threatened murders and theft!"

"Theft?" David asked quickly. "What was that?"

When they told him, he got up again, his face very grave. "That's bad," he said. "I've got to get to that boy at once. I'll drive, Jeremy, if you'll hitch up. Oh, it was cruel to name him before the whole crowd when they had no evidence whatever. This may ruin him."

He drove once more down the street, now half quiet and darkened, half tremulously alive with the footsteps and voices of those coming home late from the Festival. He crossed the bridge and proceeded toward Clatty Row. Here all was dark. He found a post at which to tie the horse and then went toward the Cuppy ramshackle house on foot. As he neared it, he thought he saw a movement by the back porch. He followed, speaking in a low voice as he went.

"It's Mr. Lyall, Jim. I want to talk to you. I'm alone."

Slowly from the shadows the boy emerged.

"Are you all right?" David asked.

Jim's voice was husky. "I've heard about it! I never took the money, only nobody'll believe me."

"I do," David said. "That's what I came over to tell you."

There was a long silence. And then, "I'm diggin' out in the morning," came from the boy.

"Don't, Jim! Above all things don't do that. Can't you see that if you run away now it will look as though you really *had* taken the money. Stay right here. Go about your affairs as usual. Hold your head up. I'll be behind you. Give me your promise you won't go off."

There was another long silence as though the boy was thinking it over.

"Well, all right," he said grudgingly.

"Word of honor?" David persisted.

The phraseology was evidently strange to Jim.

"What's that?" he asked.

"A promise no gentleman ever goes back on."

David moved nearer and held out his hand. "Shake on it," he said.

Jim slowly put his skinny hand in the larger one.

"Now get to bed, and don't worry about it. The truth always comes out sooner or later. You have plenty of things to keep your mind busy in the meantime." He lowered his voice. "Try your hand drawing Ben Losting with his gun. Or me, leading him off! That ought to make a good one. Good night, Jim. I'll see you soon."

There was a faint reply, and David unhitched his horse and started back. He was tired, and still extremely concerned about the crime. What young burdened soul was feeling the weight of guilt now in the stillness of the night? For like Gene he felt it must have been one of the boys who had perpetrated the theft. Knowing the town as he did, he felt that this might be harder to live down than even Minnie's flagrant breach of morality. And the loss to the U.P.'s. He had caught a fleeting sight of the women waiters, pausing, their happy faces fallen in dismay as they heard the news. He decided to see Gene if he could before he went home.

Meanwhile at the manse they had been talking it all over. Faith had returned, her cheeks flushed and her voice pitched a note higher than usual. She sat on the step, leaning back slightly against Mary's knee. The garden was white and fragrant in the moonlight and when all was said of the events of the evening which could be said, the two young couples took to strolling between the flower beds, losing themselves alternately behind the fruit trees at the end of the garden.

Faith spoke suddenly, looking up.

"Mother!"

"Yes, dear."

But Faith was silent. Mary touched her daughter's hair gently. "What is it?" she prompted.

"Oh, n . . . nothing. I believe I'll go on upstairs. Will you say good night to the others for me?"

"I think I hear the buggy in the drive. Your father's back."

"I guess I'll still go on up. I'm a little . . . I think I'm tired, that's all."

She kissed her mother and slipped away. Had John spoken tonight? Mary thought. The whole problem of John Harvey with his big house and rich farm when viewed academically and from a distance was one thing. It was quite another when it came close. No, *no*, Mary's heart kept repeating. This was not for Faith. This *must not be!* And yet, if she should choose it, of what avail were a mother's pangs?

David had driven up to the stable by this time and in a few

moments they all came up the path. He told them of his interview with Jim and later with Gene Holly, saying he hoped he had made some impression on each in a different way.

"But it's still bad," he said to Mary as they climbed the stairs. "Of all the happenings in the town this is the first real *theft* I can remember. It must have been one of that group of boys, but which one? I hate the whole wretched thought."

"Why are you so sure about Jim?" Mary asked later, after they had heard the girls come up.

"It's hard to explain but I am. The boy's a gentleman though heaven knows how he came by it. Gene is still breathing out threatenings and slaughter, but I think he'll cool down. The loss of ten dollars is serious, though, to the Festival funds. Gene thinks maybe he ought to make it up himself, but I advised against that. He has enough to do to make ends meet as it is. It's the boy I'm most concerned about . . ." He stopped suddenly. "What's that?" he asked.

There were sounds from the garden below as of tentative harmonizing, then full upon the night air the two virile young voices rose, so ardently, so tenderly in serenade.

> *Soft o'er the fountain*
> *Lingering falls the southern moon.*

"It's Sabbath morning," David protested. "They mustn't keep that up! What will people think?"

Mary had run to the window and was kneeling there in her white gown, watching and listening.

"Oh, don't stop them, Davy. It's so sweet and romantic. When the girls are old women they'll still remember this!"

> *Drink to me only with thine eyes*
> *And I will pledge with mine.*

"It will be over all too soon," she murmured wistfully.

Good night, ladies, sweet dreams, ladies.

There was the sound of the kitchen door being locked, quick feet taking the stairs two at a time, a burst of boyish laughter, some small, self-conscious voices from the girls' rooms, and then at last all was still and the old manse slept beneath the moon.

Chapter Six

~~~~~~

DAVID set forth Monday afternoon for his weekly rendezvous with Mr. Dilling. The street drowsed in the hot sun; the cicadas sang with sensuous delight in the thick maples; and the Stone Hotel felt cool by contrast. He found Mr. Blackburn at his high desk, writing in his diary a record of the weather and town events which he kept daily. There was nothing personal in the account so it was consulted by many people who wished to verify a date or confirm a memory. It had even been introduced once as evidence in County Court to show that a defendant had lied about the weather on a given day!

Mr. Blackburn looked up now gravely over his beard.

"I hear that gun was loaded last night?"

"It was. I never dreamed it at the time."

Mr. Blackburn scratched his nose thoughtfully with the tip of his quill. He disliked steel points and always made his pens himself from turkey tail feathers.

"I've decided to enter no name in connection with the theft, such as 'suspicion seems to rest upon, etc.,' for nothing is proved. I'm pretty careful to put down only facts."

"Good," said David heartily. "I'm glad you feel that way."

"No light on the subject yet?"

"None. I'm *sure,* though . . . "

"Stick to facts," said Mr. Blackburn.

David smiled and went on up the stairs.

Mr. Dilling had an odd twinkle in his eye as David entered the room.

"So, you were quite the hero last night, I gather!"

"Nonsense," said David, embarrassed. "Ben's wife always sends for me to come out when he's on a spree — you know she and the children come to our church — so Ben's used to me, that's all. I thought the gun business was just bluff. Well, how are you?"

"I'm remarkably well. There's nothing like a new interest in life to limber up the arteries. Little Victoria" — His voice trembled with feeling and then suddenly became gruff. "We'll change the subject. I don't want to become a blithering, sentimental old idiot. I've got the board all set up. How are the general affairs of the church militant?" There was always a hint of mockery in his tone as he asked this question.

David made no move toward the chess-men.

"Oh," he said, "there are plenty of problems. Last night's, alone, are rather pressing. We've got to do something about Ben for he may really become dangerous. Then there's the Cuppy boy. It's a strange case. You know what the family as a whole is, but this boy is different. Heaven knows what bygone inheritance has come out in him, but he's got a gift."

Mr. Dilling removed his pipe. "So?"

"He can draw. I began watching him over a year ago ever since the day I hired him to help me dump some rubbish over the creek bank. It was spring and suddenly he looked across to the Bottom land with the sun shining on the new wheat and something passed over his face. It's hard to describe. A sort of *light.* I knew then that he was sensitive to beauty. Later I caught him at a drawing."

"And you really think he has talent?"

"I'm sure of it. His figures make me think of that line from Fra Lippo Lippi. You know the one: 'Paint the soul; never mind the arms and legs.' He hasn't the technique of the arms and legs, but he catches something like the soul every time. It's uncanny. I've been keeping his secret and biding my time. I haven't even told Mary. I think if people found out about the drawings he would destroy them and never touch a pencil again. He's like that, shy as a fawn. That's why this theft suspicion may wreck him. I've got to save him if I can!"

"Um . . . h'm." Mr. Dilling sounded noncommittal but he added, "Keep me posted about the boy, will you?"

"Then," David went on, "my Session doesn't see eye-to-eye with me about one or two matters" — (he couldn't tell his friend that one of them was the disciplinary action concerning Minnie!) — "the plans for union services for Sunday evenings in August, which I'd set my heart on, have all fallen through because the Covenanters won't join in, and last of all, Aunt Betsy Wade insists that Dave Washing has stolen three of her best sheep and she means to prosecute!"

Mr. Dilling snorted loudly at this and then after a moment said quietly, "So you're discouraged, David?"

"A little. There's something deeper, of course. Dilling, will you tell me something? Do you recall the two strange men who stopped here, and came to church the first Sunday in June?"

"Yes," Mr. Dilling said, uneasily.

"Were they a visiting committee from Moreswell? Tell me the truth."

"I . . . I believe so."

David drew a long breath. "I thought as much. Well, as you know, nothing came of it. Dilling, I'm haunted by the fact that my sermons are deteriorating. Or at least not improving. Maybe

I've never been forceful and vigorous enough. I'm too quiet. I'm never invited to be guest minister at revival services anywhere. I think I'm about the only man in Presbytery who isn't and it hurts a little. You see, I can't do the hell-fire business at all. What's wrong with me? Don't I *feel* my religion strongly enough? Haven't I any power at all as a preacher?"

Mr. Dilling did not look at David. Instead he smoked on, with his eyes on the window. Then he observed dryly, "I have always been of the opinion that the sins which are damned too eloquently in the pulpit may rouse more interest than repulsion in the minds of the listeners. People are a human lot, you know."

David smiled wanly.

"But more than this. Most of a congregation do not hear the *words* of the preacher. They hear the man behind the sermon. So, pull yourself together, David. You just go on living your life, and don't feel you have to eat fire and brimstone. And," his tone was sharp to conceal the deep sympathy of his heart, "forget about Moreswell! You might have found it completely uncongenial anyway. You don't know. And now let's get on with the chess."

In the midst of the game, Mr. Dilling remarked casually. "I suppose if you *had* known the gun was loaded you would have gone after Ben just the same."

"I suppose so," David said. *"Check!"*

When he left the hotel at last, with the score 3–2 in favor of Mr. Dilling, he crossed the street and walked up to the General Store to pick up a few articles for Mary. Old Colonel Harrison, portly and genial, came out from his little wicket office to wait on David himself. His coat was always of excellent material, albeit spotted from many good dinners, and his tie a flowing black silk, always askew. He wore his eyeglasses low upon his prominent nose so they never concealed his keen gray eyes. He was known to be the most prosperous man in town, shrewd in business foresight and close at a bargain, yet generous in hidden ways to the poor and to children. He always carried peppermints in his baggy pockets and had the habit, as he walked up Main Street where the houses all bordered the sidewalk, of laying a few of these confections on the window sills where children resided. He disliked being thanked, so the youngsters watched from within when he passed, then rushed out to collect their booty and, unconsciously, bless his large, retreating form.

"Well, well, Mr. Lyall, what can I do for you today? Bad business about last night, eh? I hear Ben's still locked up. Going to have him before the Squire tomorrow. And what's this about the Cuppy boy? Like father, like son, eh?"

"No," David said almost violently. "He's nothing like his father. He's a good boy. I'd stake my honor on that. Try to keep his name out of it if you can, Colonel!" He hesitated. "Someday I may tell you more about him. Meanwhile I want a few groceries."

"Right! Right!" He led the way past the dry goods to the back of the store, jostling hardware in the aisle as he went. "New cheese in today. Excellent! Excellent!" He removed the round wooden cover, sliced a bit from the open segment and proffered it to David on the point of the knife. He waited anxiously for the verdict.

"Delicious," said David, "I'll have a pound."

"Good." He weighed it with care, removing a tiny morsel above the amount specified. "I hear the new mining town is to be called *Kirk*ville. Nice little tribute to Ladykirk, I take it. They're starting on the tipple and the company houses this week. Change, change! We'll have to be prepared for it. 'Change and decay in all around I see'! The village will never be the same after the works open. But it may all blow us a little good on the side. There will be employment for all that want it. I hear the Masters boys all started there this morning." He lowered his voice. "Minnie's never been in the store since . . . She used to be in every day. Jacob does the marketing now. Ah, well, I suppose time will cover up the tracks. That be all, Reverend?"

David paid his bill and was starting to the door. No one else was in at the moment but Hen Harper who was opening boxes at the rear of the long storeroom. The Colonel hurried after David.

"What are we going to do about Minnie? With Ben on the Session we'll be hard put to it even to discuss it in regular meeting. How long are you going to postpone action? I'm for a certain amount of leniency myself — 'There's a wideness in God's mercy like the wideness of the sea' — but you know Oliver Coates! He's been at me every week. Thinks we should make an example of Minnie to teach the young people a lesson. How do you feel about it, Reverend?"

David's face fell into worried lines. "I don't want to do anything hastily. I want to allow time for . . ."

"For the dust to settle?"

"Yes. I hope guidance will come to us."

"Well, well, it's all right with me. I suppose no action *has* to be taken up until next Communion. November fifth, isn't it? Um. Have you sounded out the rest of the Session?"

David nodded. "A little. As it stands now, I think you and Cyrus Olden and Lute McLean and I are for clemency. The others feel very strongly against it."

"Just my impression. Well, well! We'll all have to do our duty to the best of our ability. 'Where duty calls, or danger, be never wanting there.'"

David's smile was irrepressible.

"That's right, Colonel. Good day to you."

His smile continued as he passed up the street. The Colonel loved to sing. With his stout legs somewhat apart he always stood up in the pew on Sundays or at Prayer Meetings, book held high, and boomed out the words of the hymns in a raucous and unsteady bass. In between he quoted them with constant fluency in every conversation.

David greeted Wes Shotwell at the post office and asked for the key of the lockup which was kept there for convenience. He hadn't tried to see Ben earlier, for after his vocal hours of the night he usually slept most of the day.

"Not a c-cheep out of him s-so far," Wes reported. "I t-took him h-his dinner but he was s-still snoring it off. You c-can look in on him now, though, an' s-see how he is."

The heavy door groaned as David opened it and revealed Ben, grizzled, haggard and mournful, sitting on the wooden bench, staring into space. His depression after each downfall was as profound as his spree had been violent. He did not speak at first as David greeted him.

"Have you just wakened up, Ben?"

He nodded.

"Do you remember what you did last night?"

He shook his head.

"You had your gun and threatened to shoot into the crowd at the Festival."

Ben leaped from the bench.

"My gun! What happened to it? Who's got it? Is it safe?"

"You ought to be more concerned to know whether you did any harm with it."

"What harm would I do? It wasn't loaded. Who's got my gun?"

"Roy Parsons. And it *was* loaded, Ben."

His mouth dropped open. "Couldn't be. I never have a shot in it outside huntin' season. One of my boys must ha' been tamperin' with it. I'll fix him for this. I'll have nobody touchin' my gun. Listen, Reverend."

His tone was melancholy in the extreme.

"I'm repentin' for my sin in dust an' ashes. I'm throwin' myself once again on the mercy of the Lord. It was that danged Eyetalian that lives out our way that done the damage. He made some wine there that would stir up the hair on a hog's back. I was sort of hankerin' for company an' I went over to see him. I can't mind much after that. Reverend, I'm prostrate before the throne o' Grace. But I've got to get out of here an' get my gun."

He started for the door but David blocked him.

"I'm sorry, Ben. You can't leave here tonight. You're to appear before the Squire tomorrow morning."

"What's bitin' *him?* I always stay here till I'm sobered up an' go on home. What's the Squire after me for?"

"It's the gun, Ben. You were dangerous last night."

"My Gawd," Ben said heavily. "An' I was plannin' to pick potato bugs as soon as the Fourth was over. Now it'll be another day gone."

David's mouth twitched in spite of him.

"They'll bring you some supper," he said. "Make the best of it here now till morning. And try to realize that you might have *killed* someone last night. What you did was a very, very grave offense."

"Me kill anybody? Now, Reverend, you're jokin'. You know I'd never do the likes of that. But about my . . . my *failin'*, I'm low in my mind. If we just had a Methodist church here an' I could get to the mourner's bench, I'd be all right. That's the only way you can repent. You wouldn't know about that, bein' a Presbyterian."

David opened the door. It was a signal for real panic to fall upon Ben's face.

"Just see if my gun's safe, will you, Reverend? I don't trust Roy Parsons. He might monkey with it. Could you, mebbe, take it home with you, just till I can get it?"

"I'll try," said David, and then turned the key again in the rusty lock.

He stopped at Roy Parsons', explained the situation, collected the gun, made sure it was empty, then, feeling rather like a fool, proceeded up the street with it.

As he came around the path to the back porch, Mary jumped at sight of him.

> "Ben Battle was a soldier bold,
> And used to war's alarms,"

he quoted mischievously, and then went through his story.

"I have apparently received the accolade from Ben, since I'm trusted with his gun. Poor old cuss. I could cheerfully wring his neck every time he gets drunk and then when he sobers up, I'm sorry for him. I think it's a sort of Rip Van Winkle situation with him and Sally. She's sorely tried, I know, but she's a shrew just the same. Where will I set this thing?"

"You're sure it won't go off?"

"Do you suppose I'd carry it otherwise? I'm no Nimrod."

"In the pantry behind the door, then. When does he get it back?"

"Tomorrow. I'll take it along to the Squire's. Ben's to have a hearing and I fancy the Squire will scare the hide off him and send him home. A fine is no use and county jail is a little heavy. He may remand him to the lockup, of course. Poor Ben! He wants to hurry home to pick potato bugs. Mary, if I have time, I believe I'll read a bit before supper to settle my mind."

To *elevate* it, rather, he thought as he went toward the study. To raise it for the moment above Ben and his gun and his potato bugs. Were these and all the other trivia of daily life whittling down his soul until there would be nothing of expansiveness left in it? Was his whole life to be a slave to puny and trifling objectives while the great world of accomplishment lay forever beyond him? He took down an anthology from the shelves and found a well worn page. He fixed his eyes upon the words although he knew them by heart.

> *Give me my scallop-shell of quiet,*
> *My staff of faith to walk upon,*
> *My scrip of joy, immortal diet,*
> *My bottle of salvation,*
> *My gown of glory, hope's true gage,*
> *And thus I'll take my pilgrimage.*

He read the poem through, lost in its tender beauty, and then sat brooding until Mary called for supper. The voices of the children sounded in their normal gaiety from the back of the house. He rose, shaking off his depression. Dilling was right. The thing to do was just to go on living the best one could. And the pilgrimage itself was good (even though the gown of glory did get a bit tattered at times); he had never doubted that! It was his own soul that he questioned.

As he went toward the porch, passing the pantry door behind which stood the gun, an odd thought struck him, falling into a new metaphor. Even if one never hit the mark there was always that little soaring tangent to the line of flight; that trajectory lift before the ultimate miss. Surely God took note.

The hearing was set for ten o'clock. David considered talking the whole matter over with Squire Hendrick beforehand, but decided against it; so promptly on the hour, and gingerly carrying the gun, he walked up the sidewalk to the office. The others were already there: Gene Holly, chief plaintiff for the Festival, Roy Parsons, the constable, and now, David himself.

The Squire spat accurately in the big maroon spittoon and, after greeting David, began.

"Ben, we have some pretty grave charges against you. You might state them for us, Gene."

"Well, last night at the Festival, Ben, he suddenly appeared with a loaded gun . . ."

"That gun's never loaded from one huntin' season till another. It must 'a been that danged Bill o' mine was huntin' ground hogs. I'll fix him when I get home! I'll learn him to touch my gun! I'll . . ."

"Go ahead, Gene," said the Squire.

"Well, he aimed it at the crowd and said he was goin' to shoot everybody there that wasn't a Methodist!"

Ben looked up with sudden interest. "I said that? Me?"

"You sure did. You said it wouldn't matter how many Presbyterians and U.P.'s and Covenanters got killed. That Methodists were all that mattered."

Ben began giggling in a pleased and foolish manner.

"My Gawd, Squire, that was pretty good, huh? That shows you what gettin' drunk will do for a man. Gives him spunk. Puts backbone in him. Makes him smart. How did the folks take it? I'd like to seen Mr. Combs' face, I would!"

He giggled again.

The Squire rapped sharply on the desk.

"Give us the evidence about the gun, Roy."

"Well, I just thought like the Reverend that it was empty an' all, but I decided I'd better make sure, so I found it was loaded."

He rose with exaggerated importance and laid two cartridges down on the desk. The Squire examined them.

"So the facts are, Ben, that while drunk you threatened a crowd of people with a loaded gun. If the maggot had bit you to pull the trigger there would be plenty of tragedy in Ladykirk today. Do you understand that?"

Ben's mouth suddenly dropped as though he began to feel things were taking a slightly serious turn.

"Pshaw, I wouldn't shoot nobody, Squire. My Gawd, you surely know that."

The Squire leaned back and studied the ceiling.

"I thought about this case a long time last night, Ben. Keeping you in the lockup or sending you to county jail, even, is no good. You might do the same thing over as soon as you got out. There's just one way I can protect the community; that is, to take your gun away from you."

For one frozen moment Ben sat with eyes on the Squire, apparently trying to take in what had just been said. Then with a terrible cry he sprang for his gun which stood in the corner. He reached it before Roy Parsons and Gene, and held it in a death grip while they struggled with him. His thin, reedy arms were no match for two adversaries. In a few minutes Roy had the weapon and Ben was shoved into a chair.

"My gun!" he said hoarsely. "Squire, I'll go to jail, I'll do anything if you don't take my gun away. You couldn't do that. It's my proppity. It's all I've got. Squire, I'll do anything if you leave me my gun."

David watched the Squire. He knew him to be a wise man and a just. He was never devoid of sympathy, but when he had carefully determined upon his judgment he was implacable.

"I'm sorry, Ben, but that is my ruling. It's the best I can do in everybody's interest. You can get along home now, and see that you try to stay sober and keep the peace. Case dismissed."

Ben did not yell or fight further. It would have been easier for those present if he had. Instead he slumped lower in the chair, his face wearing a mortal anguish which David had never seen surpassed in all his years' dealings with grief. The grizzled visage finally disappeared beneath his arms on the Squire's desk and the thin back and the dirty coat rose and fell as thick sobs shook it.

David felt his own heart turn over in his breast. He rose quickly and laid a hand on Ben's heaving shoulders.

"Squire, I have a request to make. May I have the gun in my keeping? Ben knows that I'll take care of it. I promise never to return it to him without your order, but I'll keep it safe."

The Squire nodded. "No objection to that, Mr. Lyall, if you want the bother. I give the gun into your custody. Now then, Ben, get up and go along home. You ought to be plenty thankful you're in no worse trouble than you are. So, *case dismissed.*"

David helped Ben to his feet, for all strength seemed to have gone out of the wretched defendant. Supporting him with one arm, David held the gun in the other. He decided to drive him out home since Jeremy was not using the horse that day. On the way he tried to reason kindly with his companion, but all to no avail. Ben sat slumped in the buggy like a poor bag of bones, heaving now and then convulsively.

"It's all I've got," he kept muttering. "When Sally gets mad I could allays take out my gun an' clean it. It did me good just to handle it. An' when I had it all shined up, I'd feel better. I'd feel kinda happy an' peaceable. I'd think about huntin' season. That kep' me goin'. That's all I've had to live for mostly. Huntin' season. Now I might as well be dead as lose my gun. I'd *ruther* be dead," he added.

When they came to the Losting shack, Sally was out to greet them. She wore a split sack for an apron and her face was dirty.

"Well, Reverend, I'm obliged to you for bringin' him back, though it ain't much difference all the good he is. What about them potato bugs you was goin' to pick?" she added fiercely to Ben.

Ben made no reply. He shuffled toward the house without a backward glance.

"You see what I've got to put up with, Reverend," Sally said plaintively.

David leaned out of the buggy. "He's had a big disappointment, Sally. Try to be a little kind to him."

Then he drove away, thinking as he often did, what super-human wisdom was needed before justice could be done to the weak and erring sons of men and daughters of Eve. In this case, though, his deepest sympathy was with Ben. *Poor old cuss,* he kept murmuring to himself. *Poor old wretch.*

After he had driven perhaps a mile he was struck by a sudden thought. He reined the horse to a stop, considering it. His whole desire was to drive on home as quickly as possible, but the thought won out. He turned the buggy with difficulty on the narrow road, and went back. At the Lostings' there was the sound of noise and strife: Sally's strident scolding and Ben's intermittent yells. He had difficulty in making himself heard, but Sally finally appeared at the door.

"Tell Ben to come out. I want to speak to him."

Ben staggered as he approached the buggy. His eyes were wild with grief and rage.

"Ben," David said quietly, "I just remembered something. That gun ought to be cleaned and oiled regularly. I can't do it. Could you come in to the manse every once in a while and attend to it?"

Ben looked dazed for a moment, then a weak tear oozed from each eye. He couldn't speak but he grabbed his benefactor's hand with his own dirty, bony one and wrung it hard.

"My Gawd," he said, "you're a good one!"

David rattled back over the dusty country road, an old rhyme of his boyhood going over and over in his head:

> *Do the duty nearest, though it's dull the whiles;*
> *Helping when you meet them, lame dogs over stiles.*

They seem to be my stock in trade, he thought ruefully — lame dogs.

When he got home, Mary ran down the garden path to meet him, her face flushed with excitement.

"David," she said when she came close, "you've got a caller in the study. It's Billy McNaughton and he acts so queer and so nervous, I couldn't help wondering if maybe . . . "

David laughed as she linked her arm in his.

"Come, come, don't imagine *that!* I thought even you had given up at last."

"Well, he seems quite jittery and he wouldn't budge till you came!"

David grinned. Mary's choicest efforts in matchmaking had been spent upon Billy McNaughton and Miss Mattie Adair who, in village vernacular, had "gone together" for twenty years. They lived now side by side, each alone in a large house. Billy escorted her to and from church and all other public meetings, sat on her porch in summer evenings and by her fire in winter, spaded her garden which joined his, in spring, picked the apples from her small orchard in the fall, but came no nearer marriage than when as a young man he had first begun to pay her attention. The town was certain that the delay was no fault of Mattie's. Opinion had finally crystallized in the judgment that Billy was a canny, slow-moving Scot, set now in his bachelorhood and afraid to alter his way of life; a few declared that owing to his extreme shyness he simply couldn't muster courage to pop the question. In any case, Miss Mattie had grown a bit pinched of feature and saddened of eye as the years advanced and not all Mary's well-laid little schemes in her behalf had brought about the consummation.

"He probably came to see if we want to order any potatoes for winter," David said, for Billy owned a farm on the edge of town from which he drew his livelihood.

He went through the hall and into the study. Billy was pacing restlessly back and forth between the windows, his face flushed and his whole attitude disturbed.

"Will you shut the door, Mr. Lyall?" were his first words. "This is *seerious* and very secret."

David closed the door and asked his guest to sit down. Billy complied, resting his heavy frame on the edge of a chair as he twirled his straw hat nervously between his knees.

"Can I help you, Mr. McNaughton?" David asked kindly.

Billy heaved deeply. "I'm in trouble and sore perplexed, Mr. Lyall. I know you'll give me honest advice, so I've come to you. It's about Mattie and me. We're in a very nasty poseetion. It may be all over town now, the dear knows."

"What has happened?" David prompted with quick curiosity.

Billy hitched his chair nearer and lowered his voice.

"Well, you see it's about . . . I mean it's really account of these here newfangled *drawers*. Umbrella drawers, they call them," he added almost in a whisper.

David set his teeth together so that his face might remain decently grave.

"I dunno what got into Mattie, but she went and bought two pair of these here things and she thought they needed bleachin' so she rinsed them out yesterday and just laid them over the line in the back yard and not being regular washday and all, she forgot about them and they were there all night."

Billy swallowed hard and continued. "And somehow I hadn't snibbed the stable door right — I don't know how it ever happened — but my cow got out and got into Mattie's yard through the break in the hedge and she trampled around and then must have walked under the clothesline and one pair of these . . . umbrella drawers caught on her horns and she walked off with them."

David's risibles threatened to overcome him, but the sight of Billy's distraught countenance held them in check.

"So she got into the alley where Mrs. Foster found her early this morning and she'd been in Harrison's store when Mattie bought the drawers so she brought them up to her and then told me where the cow was, and now Mattie's beside herself, for Nellie Foster's tongue's loose at both ends and Mattie says she'll be the laughingstock of the town. I've never seen her mad before in my life, but she says now she's been *compromised!*"

Billy had poured this out in a swift stream of words, and now looked spent with emotion and effort.

David gritted his teeth hard together again and tried to think fast.

"I agree with you, Mr. McNaughton, that it is a very delicate situation."

"You think so?" Billy asked anxiously.

David nodded, then took the plunge.

"May I be personal and ask if you are not fond of Miss Mattie?"

"Aye. I am that."

"*Very* fond?"

Billy hesitated cautiously but finally came through.

"You could say that."

"Then," said David, "I feel you have just one course. Ask Miss Mattie at once to marry you."

"Ah . . ." breathed Billy. "If I just knew how to go about it."

"It will be very simple after this. Go down now and say, 'Mattie, let's get married right away.' Then you could go to Moreswell this afternoon for your license and be married up here at the manse tonight. Don't hesitate, don't delay. You want to forestall the gossip."

"Aye. You'll be right, I guess. I should have done it long ago, but I always got scared like."

David rose. "There's no time to waste. Hurry as fast as you

can. And as soon as Miss Mattie has agreed, let me know."

Billy stood up too. "I spose you . . . couldn't come down along . . . just to the door mebbe?"

"Certainly," David agreed with instant alacrity. "I'll be glad to. Just to the door," he added.

When they reached Miss Mattie's neat white house, Billy hung back.

"It's a great step," he said. "It's *seerious*. My legs are like water."

"Nonsense," said David heartily. "It's the best thing you ever did. Go right in and get it over with and you'll feel fine. Hurry."

Miss Mattie opened the door, her eyes red and swollen. She looked wildly from one man to the other as Billy stepped inside.

David waited in the shadow of the honeysuckle vine so that no passer-by could see him, but it was no more than five minutes before the door opened and Billy beckoned him within. Mattie was laughing and crying together, but her face was radiant. Billy had suddenly become beaming and confident.

"Once I up and did it," he said to David in a stage whisper, "it was easy as skinnin' a mole. Aye, I've been a slow one."

"I'm very happy over this, Miss Mattie," David said tactfully. "Mr. McNaughton was very hopeful you would say *yes*, so he wanted me to come and see about arrangements at once. I suggest he drive into Moreswell now and get the license and then you can be married at the manse this evening. Mary will love to make a little wedding for you."

"*This evening*," Mattie said, with something like horror. "Oh, I couldn't possibly be ready by then. I need . . . I would want to . . ." Her voice suddenly trailed off as she eyed her prospective bridegroom. A change came over her face, a shadow of uneasiness, followed by determination.

"Of course I can be ready. After all, I've my new dress I got when I was a delegate to Presbyterial last spring and I've never worn it here. And it will be lovely to be married at the manse and would you think eight o'clock would suit?"

"Perfectly," said David. "Now I'll be getting home to tell Mrs. Lyall."

When he reached home with the news, the family gave themselves up to complete and uproarious mirth. Mary, verging first upon hysteria, quickly regained composure and began to plan for the evening.

"Poor little Mattie!" she said tenderly, "after waiting twenty years for her wedding to have to rush it through in a day's time! She was right to take no chances, though, once Billy was in the notion. And David, you were wonderful! I simply couldn't be more pleased over anything than this. Now let's see what we can do to make it a real occasion."

It was decided to invite a few guests: Mattie's next-door neighbors, the Oldens; her closest friend, Mrs. Shotwell, and Wes; the doctor and his wife who were privileged extras in any gathering; and the McLeans, who were cousins of Billy's.

"That," Mary said, "will make a nice little company, and no offense given to anyone."

During the long years in the manse the family had become conditioned to surprises and to sudden and unusual demands upon them; so, now through the hot summer afternoon they all sprang into action, working furiously, yet in a mood of pleasurable excitement withal, to prepare for Miss Mattie's nuptials. Faith cleaned the rooms; Lucy polished the big silver service and arranged the table; Mary baked her famous Neapolitan cake with the six layers; Jeremy made ice cream in the McLeans' big freezer while David lent a hand wherever he was needed. Every once in a while a new explosion of laughter rang through the house.

The old manse always showed its best by lamplight and that night it had never looked better. The parlor bloomed with flowers, for the girls had stripped the garden. There was even a bouquet for Miss Mattie, tied with a white satin bow which Mary salvaged from her own bridal trunk.

Lucy, surveying the fragrant whiteness of the wedding setting, drew close to her mother.

"I don't believe I want to wait *too* long to be married, after all," she said in a low voice. "It's strange how quickly you get used to the idea, isn't it?"

A wild and tender pang shot through Mary's heart. Since his first declaration to David, Ninian had said nothing more to them of his intentions. There was still a danger that Lucy might ultimately be hurt. She tried to thrust the thought from her as she spoke.

"You're too young to be thinking of marriage yet a while, dear. But the room does look lovely, doesn't it? Now we must hurry through supper and then dress."

By the time the guests arrived, Miss Mattie and Billy were safely concealed in the study. Suddenly as the big hall clock chimed eight, Faith crossed to the piano and struck up the wedding march; Jeremy opened the doors with a flourish; David in his frock coat led the way and the bride in her gray surah silk and white bouquet entered on the arm of the erstwhile reluctant groom who now, in his best black suit and a high collar which threatened to choke him, bore himself with an air of almost insufferable pride.

The solemn words were spoken and the long-delaying lovers were at last one. When Billy in the eyes of all had kissed his wife, the pent-up excitement of the guests broke loose! Never, they all said later, had there been such a gay wedding! The laughter, the congratulations and good wishes, the underlying thrills of amazement and satisfaction in all present, the refreshments set out in unaccustomed splendor, the possessive joy upon the face of Billy; the quiet ecstasy in Mattie's eyes.

When all was over at last the Lyalls discussed again each detail as they washed the dishes and set the rooms to rights.

"It was as perfect an incident as we've ever known, I think," said David, "not forgetting this." He handed Mary a five-dollar note.

Her eyes grew large. "Now I *know* Billy loves her," she said. Later as they prepared for bed she gave the money back to David.

"Just add this to the fund for . . . you know what."

"You're supposed to be surprised about that!"

"Oh, I am, I mean I will be, only I just like thinking about it ahead of time."

They were hardly settled when they both started up, listening. Loud and blatant upon the night air came the sound of music.

"The band!" David exclaimed. "They're serenading the bride and groom! It didn't take the town long to get wind of it! Trust Ladykirk!"

The martial music had scarcely died away when an earsplitting cacophony of tin pans and cowbells rent the street from end to end.

"This makes it all complete," Mary sighed with satisfaction. "Now Mattie will have everything."

"Yes," David chuckled, "I rather think she will."

It was long before the din died away and the night quiet was broken only by sporadic shouts from the more youthful serenaders.

Mary, having lain thoughtful for some time, spoke in a tender voice.

"She wore them tonight for her wedding. I thought she would."

"Wore what?" David asked drowsily.

"Why, the umbrella drawers! The ones that were on the cow's horns. The ones that brought the whole thing about. Mattie told me in confidence that she was going to lay them away in tissue paper after tonight and keep them always."

David's body heaved with mirth.

"I don't think that's so funny," Mary continued. "I know I'd do the same."

"What about the cow? Is it to be a keepsake too?" He was still amused.

"I'm sure she'll never let Billy sell it," Mary replied quite seriously. "If I were Mattie, I'd never part with it. Never!"

David gave her a convulsive little hug. "You constantly amaze me," he said. "But I love you. Now go to sleep."

In the following days life moved at a serious level. David settled at once after breakfast each morning to his work in the study to make up for the lost Tuesday. He was determined to improve his sermons; to find out if possible wherein they were lacking. He read over again each time he sat down to write, the words of the old Jeremy which he kept always before him:

Religion our employment, service to others our recreation, and patience our rest.

Of his employment he felt sure. But was his part in the episodes of Ben Losting's gun and Miss Mattie's umbrella drawers, for instance, representative of his service to mankind? And therefore his recreation? Perhaps. At least he could try harder than ever to cultivate patience.

When his work upon his sermons and Wednesday night talk was completed for the day, he read voraciously in the brief time left. Running like a question underneath all the lines, however, was the urgent problem of Minnie and the women's committee meeting on Saturday night. The programs must be in the New-burt boys' hands by Monday, if they were to be ready for the July tea. It was impossible, he and Mary had reluctantly agreed, to continue Minnie as secretary considering all that had tran-spired. On the other hand, to print the programs, flatly omitting her name, without warning after all the joy she had had in her high office, seemed a cruel thing. If she would only resign, Mary kept lamenting, but how to suggest it? By Friday Mary had come to a decision. She called Minnie on the phone, her knees unsteady beneath her. Minnie's voice came, very quiet, very low.

"This is Mrs. Lyall, Minnie. How are you?"

"I'm well, thank you."

"We're having the executive meeting here tomorrow evening to make out the programs . . . "

"I know."

"And . . . and I was wondering whether you would feel able now to continue . . . whether you would be too busy to keep your . . . "

"I wrote you, Mrs. Lyall. You ought to have the letter in the morning."

"Oh, thank you . . . I mean . . . I appreciate your remember-ing the meeting. I'm . . . I'm so sorry, Minnie," she floundered. "How is little Victoria?"

"She is well, thank you."

"And not another word out of her," Mary reported to David. "And her voice sounded so *drowned*, if you know what I mean."

David went early to the post office on Saturday and brought the letter. It was brief.

Dear Mrs. Lyall:

I wish to resign my position as recording secretary of the Woman's Missionary Society and also I request that my name be stricken from the list of members.

It was signed simply *Minnie*.

Mary wept over this missive. "It's that word *stricken* that makes my heart ache. It tells so much. I suppose we should do as she asks. It would certainly be the easiest way out and cause less talk. I almost wish I'd never thought of having all the members' names on the back of the programs. If they weren't all there in bold print for everyone to pore over, she could remain a member and there would be no publicity about it. What ought we to do, David? You must help me."

He sat up late that night, pondering, praying, reading his Bible here and there for guidance. His wandering fingers happened at last upon what he had always considered one of the most unusual sections of Holy Writ — the short letter of Saint Jude. He read it through again, savoring its magnificent English, until under his eyes appeared a sentence in connection with wrongdoers which he could not remember having noticed before. It seemed now to be printed in light.

And of some have compassion, making a difference.

David drew a long breath. "That's it," he muttered. "That's what I've been feeling for." He copied it in a careful hand upon a slip of paper. "I'll leave it here," he said to himself, "for Mary and her Committee to use in their deliberations. It says more than I can."

The next morning Mary had an unexpected phone call from Gertie Hawks at the lower end of town. She seemed extremely agitated.

"Mrs. Lyall, I know this isn't regular, and I'm not on the Executive, but we all know about the meeting tonight and what's to be discussed and, Mrs. Lyall, I asked to be included. I mean I want to come. I've got something to say to the women. Sort of . . . evidence."

Her voice broke in its eagerness. Mary was baffled.

"I don't know what to say, Mrs. Hawks, for there isn't anyone but the Executive supposed to be present. I don't know how the other ladies would feel about it."

"But it's important, Mrs. Lyall, and I'm the only one knows it." It was plain she was deeply moved.

"Well," Mary said slowly, "I'll tell you what we could do. You come up after the others are all here and wait in the parlor until I come out and call you. Just walk in the front door," she added. She felt disturbed over this new development, for Gertie had not said whether the new "evidence" was for or against Minnie.

The Committee arrived promptly at seven-thirty, settled themselves in the study and commenced at once upon the business of the programs. It was a laborious one: who might be at once fitted and willing to lead Devotionals (for Mrs. Crombie was bitterly opposed to anything but extemporaneous prayers); who should this year have original papers; who should merely read reports from Mission periodicals; who, of the few possibly gifted, should render special music, and above all, upon what countries should they expend their thought, money, prayers and interest this year.

At last the work was completed and the study clock stood at ten. The names were all written down in Jennie McLean's neat hand, including those of the hostesses for the next year's January and July teas. Mary's eyes had been studying the faces as the evening passed. Good women, all of them, capable, intelligent, kind (with the possible exception of Mrs. Crombie), all with the marks of the years' sorrows and cares upon them. And yet, in the main, comfortable, serene-looking women as though having lost springtime early, their autumn was lingering long. This, Mary often thought, was one of the characteristics of village life.

Mrs. Faraday, the doctor's wife, as President, now cleared her throat nervously and started to speak.

"We have, as you all know, a very important and difficult matter to discuss this evening. The officers all have one more year to serve. We must decide what to do in the case of Minnie Masters. I believe Mrs. Lyall has a communication to read."

Mary read the resignation and a great breath of relief rose from the group.

"Well, I think that settles it nicely," Mrs. Shotwell said. "I thought she wasn't going to resign or say a word and we'd just have to take action without it. I move you, Madam President, that we accept Minnie's resignation as secretary and that she be dropped from membership just as she asks and that will just clear up the whole thing."

"I think we should vote on the two points separately," Mary said anxiously.

"Do you so move?"

"I do."

The first motion was put and carried and Minnie's office was no more.

"Now as to her membership," said Mrs. Faraday, "we will throw the matter open for discussion."

The voices rose at once, anxious, determined or sympathetic.

"I don't see why we have to discuss it at all," Mrs. Harrison said. "All we have to do is follow Minnie's own request. For my part, I feel her name *shouldn't* be on the list for everyone to see, including the young people. What will they think of us? They all see her now, walking over to the hotel with her diamond on, safely married and all and the effect on them isn't good."

"I don't believe they'll think as much about it as if the word goes round she's been dropped from membership," Jennie McLean put in. "Young folks don't pay as much attention to older folks' doings as we think. Not till they're forced to."

"They say Mr. Dilling has bought her a handsome new carriage for the baby. One of these with fringe all round the top. None of us ever had the like for *our* children, I'll tell you," Mrs. Hays said.

"I think we should cut clean," Mrs. Crombie said sharply. "I think we should hold our standards high. There are the other churches to consider. What will *they* think? Their women all know what we're discussing tonight, and they'll be all ears to hear the verdict. And it's sure to get abroad even through the Presbyterial. News like this travels fast. I think our society would have much better standing if it was known we'd dropped Minnie from membership. And it *will* be known, mark you."

"Of course," Mary said, "she's losing her office."

"It's not enough," said Mrs. Shotwell. "I'm fond of Minnie. I'll be a neighbor to her as usual. I took her a pan of rolls only yesterday and I'm knitting booties for the baby. But the Missionary Society is different. We can't work to convert the heathen and then just condone a thing like this in our very midst. I think she should be dropped just as she's asked for."

"Question! Question!" called Mrs. Crombie, who prided herself upon her parliamentary knowledge.

"Just a minute," Mary said, rising. "There is something, I mean someone we must hear first. Gertie Hawks called me today and asked if she could present some new . . . facts before you. She's waiting in the parlor. I'll let her come in and as soon as she's told us what she has to say, she can go right out."

There were looks of surprise and intense curiosity on all faces as Mary left the room. In a few minutes Gertie entered, embarrassed. She would never be an Officer but she could make ambrosial coffee for a hundred people at a church supper and her chocolate layer cake was without peer. She folded and unfolded her handkerchief now with hands that shook a little. Her high bosom rose and fell above her tight stays and her face was damp with perspiration.

"I feel sort of funny now I'm here," she began, "but I was so touched somehow I had to come, especially seeing that a good many thinks Minnie is getting off easy and everything's all right with her now." She swallowed hard.

"It was just yesterday afternoon about four and I'd made apple turnovers and I said I'd take some over to Minnie for her and the boys' supper so I went in the side gate and I saw a satchel on the front porch but I didn't think much about it only whether it might belong to Mr. Dilling maybe, so I went along the path to the back door and just as I got to the hydrangea bush I stopped dead and I ought to have turned right away but somehow I couldn't. I felt froze to the spot."

There was not even the sound of breathing in the room. The curtains bellied gently in the light breeze, and a soft cricket song came out of the night.

"It was the surveyor. Whether he come for the coal works or whether mebbe he'd come back just to see Minnie, I don't know. I wondered if mebbe he was free now, even. But there he was, standing by the back steps and Minnie facing him with the baby carriage between them and she as white as ever she'll be in her coffin. And she was saying, 'You must go at once and never enter this town again as long as you live,' she said. 'Mr. Dilling come to me in my hour of need,' she said, 'and I'm his wife.' And then they didn't say anything, just looked at each other and my heart I thought would stop at the sight of them. I never — someway — I never knew before that a man and woman could feel like that. It was awful to watch and still I couldn't move. 'There is no hope for us then,' he said at last and she just said it back to him, 'There is no hope for us . . . and go as fast as you can for I can't bear it,' she said.

"And then I got out somehow and I leaned up against the side of Harrison's store till I righted myself, sort of, and then I went on home. But if anybody says Minnie's getting off too easy, I wish they'd seen what I seen. That's all, Mrs. Lyall."

When she had left the room, there was silence. Mary went to the desk and took up the slip of paper.

"This is something David found when he was reading the Bible last night. He said to pass it on to you and I thought I'd leave it till the very last before we voted."

She read it slowly, distinctly.

"*And of some have compassion, making a difference.* Saint Jude, verse 22."

Into the hush that followed came the voice of Jennie McLean.

"I move you, Madam President, that in our list of members on the programs we include the name of *Mrs. Horace P. Dilling.*"

Chapter Seven

~~~~~~

T HROUGH August and early September a rich seasonal peace pervaded the town. It was the time of year when apples and peaches reddened and pears turned to gold on the fruit trees, when tomatoes grew scarlet in the gardens and cucumbers waxed fat among their leaves. Rich odors lay upon the still, warm air, for in every kitchen busy women, filled with satisfaction in the year's bounty and their own skill in availing themselves of it, boiled and stirred, seasoned and tested until their cellar shelves were filled with the fruits of their labors and rows of ruby and amber jellies sunned themselves upon the window sills.

Mary was one of those who sensed deeply these weeks of plenty. It was as though in the midst of her physical activities her very soul found rest and refreshment in the perfection of their results. The tangled anxieties of life smoothed out and were temporarily forgotten in a replete contentment. No doubts, no questions, no fears engaged themselves with the rows of shining jars and glasses filled with their sweet store.

In addition to this, there was an undercurrent of excited anticipation in her days. The twenty-fifth of September would be her birthday and the time of the long, long desired kitchen cabinet! She pictured again its glossy whiteness, and its incredible convenience; and, thinking of her good fortune, she sang as she worked. There was cause for happiness in other respects also. Lucy, moving in a radiant cloud of love, was working earnestly at her lessons with her father; Faith seemed more than ever absorbed in her music and Jeremy had begun his last year of teaching in the little country school three miles away. Next fall there would be money enough for college!

Besides, Minnie's case had been wisely disposed of, as far as the Missionary Society was concerned. The appearance of her new name upon the programs had apparently turned the tide. *Mrs. Dilling* was heard now occasionally on the lips of the town, and Minnie herself, as though recognizing a visible token of sympathy and forgiveness, was appearing again on normal errands to the store or the post office. Yes, they had done wisely and well. If David could only get his Session to act as charitably! So, the warm days with their pungent odors and background chorus of cicadas moved into autumn.

David savored, too, though in lesser measure, the satisfaction of the earth's yield of kindly fruits. He was laboring earnestly over his sermons and studying every available minute. The idea of *happiness* as a moral concept kept recurring to him. He had discovered in a special translation of Ecclesiastes a verse upon which he intended to preach.

For he [man] should remember that . . . God approves of joy.

Here was to him and perhaps to others a new idea. He pondered upon it. There was a dynamic force in happiness; it was positive; it was constructive. It seemed, indeed, to be implicit in the universe even as was suffering and sacrifice, and perhaps to a greater degree. (He made hasty notes upon this thought: *a.* More beneficence and fruition in nature than destruction. *b.* More natural beauty of color, light and sound than ugliness. *c.* Songs of birds, playfulness of animals, prevalence of laughter in mankind.) It was conceivable, then, that the delicate cultivation of a happy spirit and the full exercise of joy whenever possible might actually constitute a conformity to the laws of God. Might be a libation of human praise poured out to the Creator.

He smiled suddenly. This line of thinking, and sermonizing, would never bring him an invitation to preach at a revival! So be it, he answered his heart. He must travel his own road. Take, now, the prevalence of *laughter*. He had never really thought of that phenomenon before, though he recalled now that Dilling had once spoken of man as "*the risible animal*," adding, "Can't you make any cosmic deduction from that, David?"

He considered now this strangest and commonest of man's reactions to life. There was in it a link somehow with the spirit, for only man laughed in the face of the universe. Was it pure mirth or bravado or courage or did it arise from an unconscious conviction that "all would yet be well"? Perhaps the evidence of man's ultimate indestructibility lay not in his prayers alone, then, but in his laughter. There was something here to follow up. Meanwhile he could hear Mary's voice from the kitchen rising gaily in song as though to point up his thinking. He put aside his books and stretched his arms above his head, relaxing comfortably.

"I hope I'm not merely trying to justify my own general contentment," he said half aloud. But no, there was something much bigger, much deeper in the whole idea than that.

One evening when Mary was out, he held a conference with the children in the study. They were all deliciously thrilled over the birthday plans. Through Jennie McLean, who now possessed one, they had found the exact price of kitchen cabinets. Jennie's in golden oak had been thirty-five dollars, the one in white, which Mary wanted, would be thirty-nine-fifty. David went to a corner of the bookshelves, removed three volumes of an Encyclopedia and drew forth a small brown crock. He poured the contents on the desk and they all crowded close to count it. As it was all in silver except Billy McNaughton's five-dollar bill, it took some time. They piled the "cart-wheels" in one place, the half-dollars in another and so on down to the nickels. They counted carefully aloud. Thirty-eight dollars and seventy-five cents! Close enough, they all agreed, with glee! The precious plan was assured. There remained now only the pleasure of arranging the last details. Jeremy suggested that he borrow the McLeans' spring wagon, drive to Moreswell on the twenty-fifth and bring the treasure home because it would be so much more fun to have it arrive on the birthday itself. David and the girls would drive in about a week previous to that, to select it, pay for it and have it held until then.

"I've never felt perfectly safe about it before," Lucy exclaimed, "but now it's as good as here. Let's plan the dinner."

"We'll ask someone to invite her for the afternoon and then we can have the table all set and the cabinet in its place when she comes home. Do you think she's counting on it, Father?" asked Faith.

"Yes," David said hesitantly, "I know at least she's *hoping* for it with all her heart. But it will be exciting enough at the end to overbalance that. She told me she liked thinking about it before hand, but she didn't want anybody to mention it outright for she wanted to *feel* surprised when she saw it. So we'll just proceed as though she knew nothing."

The air of the manse during the next weeks was surcharged with the happiness of which David was writing in his sermon. All sorts of little jokes at their mother's expense were perpetrated by the children; sly remarks about the general inconvenience of the kitchen were made with straight faces; foot touched foot and knee nudged knee under cover of the dining room table when anyone went dangerously close to giving name to the secret; Mary, seeing through it all as they intended she should, returned just the right answers, maintaining withal an expression of baffled innocence delightful to behold.

It was during breakfast on Friday morning, the seventeenth, that David returned from answering the telephone with an uneasy look on his face.

"Who was that?" Mary inquired.

"It was Doctor Digbee from Rushville. He says that a Reverend Miller, a missionary from Africa, is going through the Presbytery, trying to speak in all the churches in a very limited time."

David paused at sight of Lucy's stricken eyes.

"He's speaking in the church there Sabbath morning and he would like to address our evening service here. It won't give much time for spreading the word but of course I can announce it at morning service and hope for a good turnout. Someone will drive him over Sabbath afternoon and I guess we'll have to have him for supper and over night. Will that be all right?"

"Oh, yes," Mary said calmly. "We'll just have our dinner in the evening. Africa? We haven't had anyone from there for a long time. I hope he has lantern slides. When they have pictures we always get a bigger offering. . . ."

A startled look passed over her face and she suddenly excused herself from the table.

The children met later up in Faith's room.

"Well, this cooks it!" Jeremy said fiercely. "You know what will happen."

"We can't let it," Faith said, her normally gentle lips grim. "We've just got to talk to Father and tell him he doesn't *dare* use our savings."

"He won't," Jeremy said. "He'll just use his own. He's put about fifteen dollars into it. Besides, we can't dictate to Father about anything connected with . . . well, *religion*."

Lucy was in tears. "Oh, it can't be true. It's too cruel! Just when we thought we were safe. Why did God have to *let* a missionary come here just now!"

"There's one chance," Jeremy said slowly. "If he should be anything like the last one . . ."

A groan went up from the girls. For the last representative of a mission field to visit them, while oratorically persuasive in the pulpit, had not appealed to the manse family in private. He was big, bumptious and wordy and under the impression evidently that the world owed him both money and service. Jeremy had lugged his heavy baggage, they had all taken turns carrying prodigious amounts of hot water up to his room, Mary had cooked and then cooked still more to please his demanding appetite, and he had left without a word of thanks for the hospitality, only exhorting them sternly to remember his particular field with their prayers and *especially* their gifts. The children had dubbed him *Bombasty* ("because it rhymes with nasty," Jeremy said) and while their parents maintained a polite silence it was felt that they approved the term and had not contributed overmuch to his particular cause.

"Yes," Faith said, "if this one coming is anything like him we might be safe yet. But it's only one chance in a hundred."

"We could hide the crock and just be innocent about it, till next week when he's gone," suggested Lucy eagerly.

"Wouldn't solve the problem. If Father and Mother feel they ought to give, they'll do it whether it's this Sunday or next week. No," Jeremy sighed, "we're in a jam all right and I don't see what we can do but wait and keep quiet and hope for the best."

"It seems queer," said Lucy plaintively, "to pray that the missionary won't be any good, but oh, I *will*, whether it's wicked or not."

"I hope, Jeremy, that when you're a preacher you won't be always running up against these dreadful problems," Faith said soberly.

"Don't worry, I won't," her brother replied with surprising conviction.

The missionary arrived at four on Sunday afternoon. At sight of him the hearts of the children sank in their breasts. He was slight and sallow and gentle, with one shabby bag and a suit that needed pressing. His eyes were tired and kind behind their glasses and his smile was disarming.

"We're goners," Jeremy whispered to the girls in the kitchen, "as far as his personality goes. You can see he's a nice sort of chap. But he doesn't look to me as if he could preach worth a cent. If his *appeal* doesn't come off, then maybe still . . ."

David himself, as he chatted with his guest in the study and watched him as he sat at the table, listening more than he spoke, feared honestly for the success of the evening's service. The man was colorless, and quite evidently shy by nature. The congregation he felt sure would be disappointed, and Dr. Faraday, who was never too enthusiastic about Foreign Missions, would probably bring up again in Session meeting the question of whether the privileges of the pulpit should be granted to *everyone* who came along.

On the way to church, Mr. Miller spoke humbly of himself.

"I fear I'm not much of an orator," he said. "When I think of the need, and that I am the one to speak for it, I could wish for tongues of fire."

"I guess we all feel that way, even about an ordinary sermon," David returned as comfortingly as he could.

He seated his guest courteously in the center and largest pulpit chair, which had the immediate effect of making him look smaller and more insignificant than ever, and then turned to scan the congregation. It was of barely average size, since he had not even been able to promise *slides* as an inducement. There would be slim chance of a goodly offering. Many of those who could always be counted upon to contribute to visiting missionaries were not present. Aunt Betsy's daughter, Miss Miranda, *was* there, he noted, and there might possibly be a silver dollar from her. He sighed. He suffered for the embarrassment and disappointment of the man beside him. He had his fears, too, concerning a back seat filled with boys and young men. It was always hard enough to hold their attention. . . .

He rose to announce the opening hymn, "Sun of My Soul, Thou Saviour Dear." There followed the Scripture, the Prayer, and the next hymn, out of deference to the missionary, "Watchman, Tell us of the Night."

The offering, David then explained, would be taken *after* the sermon, since the Reverend James Miller of Uronga, Africa, was with them this evening to present his message. They welcomed Mr. Miller to their midst and (putting more earnestness than usual into his voice) he begged the congregation to give him their most prayerful attention. He then stepped back and Mr. Miller moved forward to the side of the pulpit and, very quietly, began to speak. There was an instinctive straining on the part of the congregation to catch the first words, and then as he continued, that deep and breathless silence which means that listeners have forgotten themselves and their surroundings. Even David, keyed nervously at first for the speaker's failure, found himself transported far away. For Mr. Miller was telling his story with the simplicity which enhances stark drama.

He had gone out to Africa to preach the gospel, he said, and was still preaching it; but he had almost at once become aware that this was not, in itself, enough. He paused to hope apologetically that this would not to any sound heretical. He had found soon that these people among whom he was working needed healing of body as well as of soul. He could not ignore this need. He had tried in his blundering way, and with the few remedies he had taken for himself, to help them. He was in a remote colony of savages. There was no other white man. He had had many very narrow escapes from death. He told, casually, of a few. Then had come the day when the Chieftain's son lay desperately ill from an infected wound. Mr. Miller had begged the frantic father to let him try what he could do. The Chieftain agreed under the conditions that the missionary's life be forfeit if the young man died. "Of course I had to take that chance," the little man said simply. But the Chief's son got well.

From that time on, he had been doing what he could to heal their diseases. He had sent back home for books, for simple medications, for any advice transferrable by letter. He had, for example, become fairly skillful in dressing wounds. "There are so many of these. Terrible ones! The constant fighting, you know." He described it. David, glancing at the boys in the back seat, realized that he need not have been concerned about their attentiveness.

At the end, the missionary leaned toward his listeners.

"My dream," he said, and his tired, sallow face shone as though in a vision of light, "my dream is that someday I may have a real doctor out there and a little hospital to which all the tribes around can come. Meanwhile on this hasty trip, for I promised my people I would not stay long away from them, I am trying to raise funds to buy dressings and simple medicines and equipment to take back with me. If . . . if any of you feel like contributing . . . "

He broke off, hesitant.

"I sing a little," he went on. "I use my voice constantly in my work. I sing to the sick. I will close now with the hymn that they call in Uronga, the 'Healing Song.' "

With the same simplicity and complete unselfconsciousness which had marked his utterance, he now lifted his head and looking off, far away and beyond his listeners, began, in a clear and melodious baritone, to sing:

> *"At even e'er the sun was set,*
> *The sick, O Lord, around Thee lay."*

The familiar words fell like a benediction. David felt his throat tighten as he listened:

Once more 'tis eventide and we,
Oppressed with various ills draw near . . .

He could see the faces of the congregation, raised, rapt. Many of the women were openly weeping, the men sat with the fixed features which revealed their emotion. Dr. Faraday, who had never been greatly interested in Foreign Missions, was wiping his eyes. The singer's voice became softer:

Thy touch has still its ancient power,
No word of Thine can fruitless fall;
Here in this quiet evening hour,
Lord, in Thy mercy, heal us all.

He turned, once again a little shy man, and sat down in the great chair which swallowed him up.

David went forward to the pulpit and found he had no words. At last he said, "The Elders will now wait upon you for your offering. As your hearts have been moved this night, so give."

When the service was over, Dr. Faraday was the first to reach the speaker. It was to invite Mr. Miller down to his office for a talk. David waited to receive the collection from the men who had taken it up. They poured it out of the reed baskets upon the marble table below the pulpit. It did not take long to count. It consisted of eight dollars and twenty-five cents.

"More than I thought it would be," Oliver Coates said. "Smallish congregation. Now, if he had had lantern slides, we'd have got more out."

"No, not bad," Colonel Harrison remarked. "If he gets that much every place . . . and of course he'll get more at morning services . . . it will count up. Good cause, though personally I would have liked to hear more of the gospel message. Very touching, though, very."

David put the money in a heavy envelope and met Mary at the door. They walked slowly up the back street.

"David," she said at last, "you know what we have to do."

"Yes," he said huskily.

"You felt it, too?"

"Yes."

"In all the years, even with the famous missionaries we've had here, I've never been so moved as by this man . . . this little, selfless brave man. . . . We have to, Davy. You agree?"

"It's your disappointment," David burst out. "I can't bear it. You've waited so long. You want it so. Duty is so hard sometimes. How can we be sure we ought to make this sacrifice?"

"I'm sure," said Mary quietly. "And what is the cabinet compared to this need?"

He stopped and kissed her in the darkness under the maples. A cool leaf fluttered down on their upturned faces.

"Besides," she whispered, "we'll just start saving for it again."

When they reached the manse they found the children already in the study, sitting quietly, as prisoners awaiting their sentence. Mary's head was high and her lips firm.

"I want to talk to you," she said. "You must all have felt what your father and I did this evening. We must do something for Mr. Miller's work. I know, my dears, what you've been planning for me for the birthday, but it doesn't matter. We'll get the cabinet later. I would like to give the five dollars that Mr. McNaughton gave for the wedding fee. That's my very own, and your father will give ten of the savings and I thought maybe you would like to give another five from the three of you."

Mary's face was all aglow with her eagerness. "That would be a really *great* gift and we'll all be glad once we've done it. Truly, I'd *rather* do this than have the cabinet now! Where is

the money, David? We ought to have it ready when Mr. Miller
comes. Do you want to help, children?"

They agreed slowly, soberly, seeing no other course open
to them. The girls' eyes were mournful and Jeremy's smoldering as David took the little crock from its hiding place. But
Mary was actually gay. She laughed over the place of conceal-
ment, and at her stupidity in not having discovered it. "You
can see that I don't dust too carefully," she joked. She laid the
money herself in a little pasteboard box and placed it beside the
collection in its brown envelope.

"There!" she said, "that will save many lives. What a wonderful feeling when we think of it!"

The rest of the evening and the next morning were pitched
upon a high note as far as she was concerned. The missionary
was moved to tears by their offering, and before he left for the
early train he brought to Mary from his shabby bag a little gift:
a small elephant carved from ebony.

"It is such a trifle compared to all you've done for me," he
said, at sight of her pleasure. "This stay with your family has
been the brightest spot in all my furlough. I shall remember
your home when I get lonely and discouraged. I can't thank
you enough for your kindness and your great help."

Mary felt lifted as upon wings as she waved him off from the
front door. Later she placed the little elephant here and then
there, experimenting to see where it showed to the best advan-
tage. She turned to her household duties buoyed up with a vast
feeling of virtue and self-sacrifice. During the twelve o'clock
dinner she talked constantly of the missionary and of the joy
of helping him in his wonderful work. Afterward the girls left
to do some errands and David went to Mr. Dilling's for his
holiday game of chess. The bright morning had darkened, a
cold rain began to fall from the ashy sky and the wind scattered
the first gusts of stricken leaves. Mary sat down suddenly in

the kitchen, when the afternoon had worn on, realizing that she was very, very tired. All the glad certainty over her sacrifice suddenly departed from her. She saw now only the old inconvenient kitchen and the place where the beautiful new cabinet was to have stood. So soon, only a few days away, she would have had it. And even as the full weight of that disappointment fell upon her, all the griefs of her life seemed to gather and press down upon her heart; the death of her child, the long sickness of hope deferred in connection with David's call to a larger church; the constant privations and rasping little economies of the years. She thought again with an aching sense of loss of all the weary steps the cabinet would have saved her. Then she got up slowly and dragged herself up to her bedroom where the sad rain was beating against the windows. She threw herself upon the bed and began to sob. The reaction from the emotion of the last twenty-four hours was swift and heavy. There was no necessity for quietness or self-control, for she was alone in the house; so she suffered the heavy audible sobs to tear and wrench her.

But she was not alone. Jeremy, coming in the back door and seeing no one below, had started up to his own room. His footsteps on the carpeted stairs made no sound. Just outside his mother's door he stopped dead. He heard the sobs; and between them he heard a muffled, moaning voice.

"I hate the heathen . . . I *hate* the heathen . . . I want . . . my . . . cabinet"

Jeremy's young face blanched and stiffened while his steady-going heart seemed to falter in his breast. In all the years of his life he could not remember seeing his mother even weep unrestrainedly and now . . . these racking sobs! He was terrified. He made a movement as though to go to her, then he stopped. If only his father were here or even the girls, they might know what to do. But he felt clumsy and ignorant and afraid somehow of hurting her more. So instead of opening her door he turned and tiptoed down the hall to his own room, entered, ran the bolt — the pride and badge of his male privacy — in its socket, then sat down, shaken and unsteady, to think.

After all Mother's outward calmness, even brightness over the gift, this was what really lay deep within her. He felt sickened with a new and mature knowledge. Mother's serene and happy demeanor had been for them all like the sure sun in the heavens. But what dark and hidden stress had perhaps often lain behind her laughter? While they, the children, never knew, never even suspected.

Then there was that bitter, and incredible cry against the heathen which still rang in his ears! It appalled him. He or Faith or Lucy might conceivably have said such a thing — but *Mother!* Of course it was probably only a temporary emotion, but even so, she felt it strongly enough to speak it aloud with that dreadful vehemence.

As he kept thinking of it, however, a sudden feeling of personal relief swept over him. The occasional rebellions in his own breast would never again seem such dark and evil things since even Mother knew the mutiny of the spirit!

He sat, hunched over, on the bed, his elbows on his knees, his knuckles pressing his cheeks. From what he had inadvertently discovered, one fact stood out above all others. *The cabinet must be bought.* And he was the one to pay for it. This was inescapable. To tell his father what he had learned would be to worry him inordinately, for he would likely be hard put to it to make up the deficit just now. He, Jeremy, had the money if he used it; and use it he would, even though it went against the inexorable family rule that next in sacredness to the gifts to the Lord was the money for education. This creed had always been considered almost as binding as the theological one. No matter what had to be done without, the money for the enrichment of the children's minds was holy and untouchable. It had been so with the expense for Faith's music, for Lucy's seminary, and now, he knew, most important of all in his parents' eyes, the fund for his college. A sharp pang shot through Jeremy's heart and was gone. He straightened and tensed his muscles. He would soon be twenty-one; he would be a man; his decision must be his own. In any case, he would take the extra money from his savings to buy the cabinet.

The details followed quickly in his mind. He would not breathe a word of it to the others. It would be the great surprise. On the morning of the birthday, which luckily fell on Saturday, he would borrow the McLeans' spring wagon and their horse, too, if he could, for it was heavier than Prince for a long haul. He would enjoin them to secrecy and then go to Moreswell and bring home the treasure. He would time his trip so that he would arrive home just before supper. What a flourish he'd make as he drove in! What wild excitement would follow! Whoopee and Hurrah! But silence, Jeremy. Guard your tongue and your movements well!

He slipped downstairs and stole softly out of the house, making a noisy re-entrance a half-hour later. He watched his mother during supper, but aside from the fact that she was a little quieter than usual he saw no change in her behavior. He pondered this deeply.

The next week went fast, for everyone was unusually busy. Failing the cabinet the girls began feverishly to embroider a collar-and-cuff set between them and to importune their father about the birthday *poem*. Since David had a little knack at versifying, his rhymes for the various natal days had become traditional. They were read at the end of the supper.

"And I was wondering," Lucy said to him one evening in confidence, "if maybe this year you couldn't make Mother's poem a little longer and more . . . well, more *poetic*, sort of, instead of just funny. To make up a little for not having the big present. What do you think?"

"I think that's a good idea," David said, smiling into Lucy's anxious face.

"And don't you think we should have bought ice cream? Because she does so like chocolate."

"I certainly do."

"I'm afraid I'm still *unreconciled*," admitted Lucy, "but maybe someday we'll feel it was all for the best. I wonder, though, if I'll ever be as good as Mother when I grow up. One thing that will help out on the birthday will be Ninian's present. He's sending something. He told me. I think it's gloves, for he hinted about sizes."

"That's very nice of him. Still fond of him, Lucy?"

She colored until her face was pure rose. "Oh, Father, I couldn't *tell* you how much! I can't imagine, though, how he ever fell in love with me, can you?"

"I think I could if I made the effort," David said. "What's the latest word from college?"

"He's working terribly hard. He says he's determined to get top marks so that I . . . we . . . will be proud of him."

"Good boy."

"And you'll make the poem very nice? Sort of a little like Shelley, maybe, or well, not as sad as the ending in Omar, but . . . you know, just a little bit like it?"

"An extremely modest request," David grinned, "to a writer of doggerel. But I think I know what you mean. Instead of trying to be funny, perhaps I can strike a little more tender note for this one."

"That's it! I knew you'd understand. Because she gave up the cabinet, you know."

When Jeremy went to inquire about the loan of the horse and wagon, Mr. McLean seemed embarrassed but had to tell him that it had been already bespoken for Saturday. This was a setback, but he finally secured the promise of Josiah Hunt's extra horse and larger wagon which he kept for hire. Of course, this would mean additional expense, but there seemed no help for it. He had to take Josiah into his confidence, for he needed a place to leave Prince and the buggy since the family must assume he was off on an extra day's bookselling, a habit he had been following all fall since his school had begun. It seemed like heavy deception, but it would all be cleared up by afternoon.

Saturday was a perfect autumnal day: the sky gentian blue, the first changing color showing in the maples, the air warm and rich with odors of the earth's repleteness. Everyone was bright at breakfast, making silly jokes about birthdays and guessing what words David could find to rhyme with fifty-two, in his poem. No one, of course, spoke of the cabinet, and Mary seemed the gayest of them all. To Jeremy's relief his movements later went unquestioned. The girls and his mother were busy in the house, his father had gone out, so he drove off, all unsuspected, left the rig in Josiah's stable and then, feeling strange and full of subterfuge, rattled off in the wagon, down the hill, over the bridge and on out the Moreswell road.

He had ample time for thought as he drove along. He wondered seriously if he had done well to keep his plans to himself. While young, he was keenly perceptive and he had the sudden feeling that the knowledge he had acquired that day outside his mother's door should have been shared with his father. Well, it was too late now, and the main thing after all was to get the cabinet. He smiled to himself as he recalled how closely he had been to getting caught when he removed the remainder of the money from the little crock. He had just finished putting it in his pocket the night before when Lucy came into the study. He had quickly grabbed one of the Encyclopedias, muttering "Archimedes . . . Archimedes. . . ."

"You're always looking up such funny people," Lucy had remarked innocently and, securing the book she had been hunting, left the room.

He watched the passing fields and far rising ridges now with a heart both warm and fearful. The matter in hand was really a very large one for him to handle alone. He hoped all would be well. He felt much more like a boy at this moment than the man he had thought himself as he dressed that morning. The wagon jolted and jounced over the rutty road and Jeremy pushed back his cap, put a foot on the side board and whistled, trying to feel jaunty and secure.

When he reached Moreswell he tied the horse to a hitching post on lower Main Street as close as he could get to the big hardware store where he expected to make his purchase. He felt his inner pocket to make sure the money was safe, and then, with a quick-beating heart entered the store and started toward the far end where he could see the tops of the cabinets rearing their heads above the clutter of gadgets and implements in the middle distance.

As he came nearer he discerned a worn black felt hat appearing and disappearing in the semi-gloom of the long storeroom. It was moving about amongst the cabinets and it could belong to but one person! They met, face to face, each too amazed for a moment to speak.

Then, "Jeremy!" David cried. "Where did you come from?"

"Father! How did you get here?"

They waved the salesman momentarily aside and got together in a dark corner.

"You see," David explained, "as it came nearer the day, I couldn't stand it, so I just went to Colonel Harrison and made a clean breast of the whole thing and drew an advance on my salary. We'll make out someway, and I thought I'd surprise everybody. . . ."

"And I heard her crying the day the missionary left. She was so terribly disappointed and I decided to take some of my savings and the rest of what was in the crock and of course make it a complete surprise. . . ."

Then all at once, as though they were the same age, they clapped each other on the shoulder and laughed and were greatly jubilant!

When they finally set about making their selection, they were almost lofty in their demeanor. They took their time, both conscious of the unaccustomed and delightful experience of having a large sum of money in their pockets; they savored to the full their mastery of the situation as the salesman, sensing the hidden wealth, grew obsequious and deferential. They examined the cabinets from all sides, judicially praising or condemning the workmanship; they explored the inner recesses critically; they pronounced upon the quality of the enamel finish, knowing nothing whatever about it. Finally, when they could prolong this sweet time of power no longer, they made their choice, David paid the bill, and then while the hardware men were encasing their prize and stowing it away in the wagon (Jeremy's, David insisted, because it was larger, but really because his heart was bursting with tender pride in his son) the two of them had a bit of lunch at a small restaurant and afterward started triumphantly for home, David leading in the McLeans' light spring wagon, Jeremy following.

They had agreed to try to reach the house at five o'clock, just before supper, so when they found they were making better time than they had expected, they drew up at a quiet watering trough under the trees and there, side by side, discussed it all again while the horses drank and rested and the sun moved nearer the west.

It was a few minutes past five when they rattled along the drive at home. David had left his equipage at the McLeans' as he passed, so he now sat beside Jeremy on the high seat of Josiah's big wagon, and together they called and shouted as they came opposite the back porch, for they could contain themselves no longer.

The girls came out first, looked, wild and incredulous, and then Mary came, and both Jeremy and David threw their hats in the air at once. She saw, she knew, and ran to the wagon side, her face white and then scarlet with the shock and joy of it.

"David, Jeremy, why, how *could* you do it! Oh, David! Oh, Jeremy!"

There never had been, of course, such a birthday celebration in the history of the manse. There was the uncrating, the unwrapping, the final setting up of the cabinet against the kitchen wall as they all crowded about.

"Easy now. Take care, Jeremy."

"I've got her, Father. Lower your side."

"A little more to the window, David, could you? Not so far . . . there . . . there . . . that's just right!"

It stood then, white, shining and completely real in the very spot of the dreams. Mary had to show them all, then, each shelf, each drawer; had to demonstrate how now as she baked and brewed she need take no extra step! She caressed the smooth sides, she cried out over new and unsuspected conveniences within it: a flour sifter fastened in its place, a cunning rack for spices, a holder for the rolling pin!

It was late when they seated themselves at last in the dining room for the supper Faith had prepared and the cake which Lucy had baked all herself and which now stood, garlanded with ivy, in the center of the table. There was much talk and laughter. The other gifts were displayed again: the collar-and-cuff set from the girls, the elegant kid gloves from Ninian, a crocheted doily from Jennie McLean. Most of all, David and Jeremy had to tell over and over just how they felt when they met in the hardware store in Moreswell!

It was growing dusk by the time the bought ice cream had been eaten and Jeremy lighted the hanging lamp above the table so that David could see to read the poem. There was the usual flutter of anticipation as he rose now, put on his glasses, drew a sheet of paper from his inside pocket, leaned nearer to the light and while everyone listened eagerly, began to read.

"To Mother, at Fifty-two."

Lucy, drawing little satisfied breaths betimes, found her wish fulfilled. It was not a funny poem at all, but it was nice. It was long, too, describing the whole day. The last stanza just suited, for you could hear the crickets now right outside the window.

> *"Soft the minstrels of the garden*
> *Twang their harp strings in the dark,*
> *While the stars in heaven are shining*
> *With a faintly glowing spark;*
> *Sinks the quiet house to slumber*
> *After gala day and night;*
> *Sleep, to dream her 'Happy Birthdays';*
> *Mother's fifty-two tonight!"*

There was great applause and everyone pronounced it the best he had ever done.

"It does sound just a little like Shelly's 'Serenade,' honestly, Father," Lucy maintained stoutly. And Mary thanked him with her eyes.

It was before they went up to bed when they had all gone out to the kitchen to look once again upon the cabinet that Mary made her confession. In spite of the gaiety of the evening a little shadow had fallen upon her face during the last hours. Now she stood up bravely among them (on the very spot, indeed, where she had stood that first day when the mouse ran across the floor) and raised her hand for silence.

"There's something I must tell you," she said, "it's so on my conscience and I couldn't go to sleep after this wonderful day, having you think I'm better than I am. You see I truly wanted to give the money to the missionary. I felt it was our duty and just at first I was glad. And then Monday afternoon it rained and I was so tired and all at once I wished we *hadn't* given it and I . . . I didn't feel kindly toward the poor heathen, and my thoughts were *very* wicked. But I want you to know . . . " she was looking at David but he couldn't see her face distinctly just then . . . "that now since I'm *so* happy and rich and blessed by your kindness, I'll try hard to be better and to . . . *grow in grace.*"

Chapter Eight

IT WAS TOWARD the end of October before David felt he had his sermon upon happiness ready to preach. True, about the usual number of tired farmers drowsed through his hard-thought-out and carefully prepared discourse; there was also that more disturbing element in the congregation — those who eyed him blankly, their thoughts though waking, still quite evidently far away; but here and there he could feel a response, an even startled interest.

As a rule there were no comments upon a sermon, but this time there were two. Martha Olden, Cyrus the Miller's bright-eyed wife whose laughter was so frequent and so hearty as to be proverbial in the town ("There's Martha laughing again! Just listen to her!"), shook hands at the door and said shyly, "I liked what you preached about today." Mr. Wilson, the school-teacher, was more articulate. He wrung David's hand and looked him in the eye. "That's the best sermon I ever heard," he said. "My father was a Scot who thought it was a sin to whistle on the Sabbath and I guess I've been a little tarred with the same stick. I needed that. Thank you."

So, David felt, if he had touched opposite poles of life philosophy in his members, justifying the one, converting the other, his labor had not been in vain. There was still another sermon

208

that would have to be preached, however. How was the problem of sorrow to be fitted into this fine new moral concept of his? Ah, there was the rub, indeed. And yet he held tightly to his theory that *every* life involved a certain amount of happiness in excess of pain. Ergo . . . Well, he would let this thought simmer for a while, before attempting to do anything with it. The practical problems of his flock claimed him right now.

The Congregational meeting was to be held Saturday of the following week for the purpose of electing a new trustee. It was David's plan that the Session would convene just after the meeting and receive those who wished to state their repentance for wrongdoing and be reinstated before Communion the last Sunday in November. To this end he had visited each member of the Session to discuss again the problem of Minnie. He had now won over all except Oliver Coates who held out for a public reading of her name and offense. This, David told him courteously but firmly, he would not do. Aside from Oliver there were several others who at least felt she should be severely dealt with in the Session meeting itself. David feared for this and yet hoped that in the embarrassment of seeing Minnie before them, they would all abstain from heavy-handed judgment. He had seen this happen before.

On Tuesday the Squire called him in to tell him that Aunt Betsy Wade had been to his office to get him to swear out a warrant against Dave Washing for stealing three ewes.

"She's rarin' to go after him," the Squire reported, "and I don't like the business. Dave's as straight as a string. He wouldn't steal a hair, but he does like a practical joke. If he has her sheep penned up, as I assume he has, it's because she goaded him into it. But I've got to have a hearing. Set it for Friday. You know that woman! Durn me if I can see how Doremus ever stood her. And yet . . . "

He grinned shamefacedly.

"I know," David agreed. "The town will lose a great deal of its savor when Aunt Betsy leaves it. I'd like to be behind the door at the hearing."

"You can be in front of it. I'll call you for a character witness for Dave."

David shook his head. "I couldn't possibly do that. You can get plenty of others. I'm upset that this should come up just now before the Congregational meeting. It's rather nasty having the whole town mulling over it when Dave's a candidate. I wouldn't put it past Aunt Betsy to have waited for that very reason. I know she's been planning to bring action since early July."

"She has? Well then, that's about it, the old schemer. I'll do my best for Dave, but of course nothing will keep the talk down. He'd make a good Trustee too. By the way, any clue ever turn up about the Festival money?"

"Not that I ever heard of," said David, turning more serious still. "I've kept in close touch with Jim Cuppy and he hasn't run off as he threatened, but the suspicion has done something unfortunate to him. I'm still pondering what more I can do to help him. Did you know that the ten dollars was made up to the U.P.'s?" he added hesitantly.

"Oh, yes, that leaked out, all right. Gene Holly couldn't keep it. All you need to spread a thing in this town is to say it's a secret. Pretty generous of that young man, I call it."

"Ninian's a fine boy," David said, a hint of pride in his tone. "He felt that since it was his bill that had been taken he would like to contribute another to the cause. I didn't know anything about it until Gene showed me his letter and I've never mentioned it before outside the family since Ninian meant it to be confidential."

"Son of R. P. Ross, eh? Well, if he and Lucy make a match she'll certainly be sitting down in a butter keg, as the saying goes."

David tried to be casual. "Oh, they're just boy and girl yet. He enjoys coming out to visit in the country."

"Tut! Tut!" said the Squire. "I saw them together. A girl can hide her feelings, but a man's eyes give him away every time. That young fellah's in love if I ever saw one. Can't blame him. Lucy's a sweet little morsel. Well, as I say, if the thing goes through, it will set the whole town up. Millionaire's son from city comes out to Ladykirk for a bride. Pretty good headlines for the county paper, eh?"

As David walked down the street his heart beat a little faster than usual at the thought of the Squire's parting remark. It *was* the most incredible coincidence that Ninian and Lucy should ever have met at all, and then had loved at first sight! He and Mary had tried to hold their own fancy in check as they watched the young people together. And yet, who could be passive before the light in their eyes? Who could deny the low, changing tenderness of their voices as they spoke, or the throbs and little beatings of their hearts. It was love. Love at its sweetest and best. And, though this fact was rarely mentioned even between him and Mary in private, it yet was authentic and undeniable: Lucy would have in addition to love itself, wealth and a social position beyond their wildest dreams for any of their children. One thing only rose occasionally as a question to their minds. That was the attitude of Ninian's parents. There had been no word from them. Of course there would probably not be until the engagement was official and the ring given and received.

He stopped suddenly in front of Billy Kinkaid's ice-cream store. It might be well to check now on his particular state of grace. Billy was the town's periodic drunkard. He was a bachelor, living alone in rooms behind the store. He was neat, witty, kindly, and possessed of a secret formula for the making of ice cream so delicious that young skylarking couples from all the nearby towns made his "parlor" the objective of their summer drives. His sprees, unlike those of Ben Losting, were quiet, almost decorous in nature, for when intoxicated he became filled with a vast dignity and a politeness that was quite overpowering. The town, being a violently temperance one, had difficulty in fitting Billy into the role of the Scarlet Son of Satan which his vice demanded. The ladies of the W.C.T.U. discussed the matter in their meetings, as they fingered their bows of white ribbons nervously. The greatest difficulty was, they felt, in regard to the children! These, gathered early into the ranks of the Loyal Temperance Legion, met once a month to hear of the evils of Demon Alcohol, to recite the *Pledge*, and to sing: "We'll turn our glasses upside down," and other songs in praise of Aqua Pura. It was disconcerting then to know that these young Crusaders eagerly awaited Billy's lapses and when one of these occurred, crowded into the store where he, with a broad grin and impeccable manners, opened his big freezers and dispensed spoonfuls of ice cream, gratis.

Yes, Billy was a problem in a local-option temperance town where every woman felt that strong drink was hell's own beverage, where the young girls in recitations at church sociables declaimed earnestly that "lips that touch liquor shall never touch mine!" and where the great majority of the male populace, whatever their inhibited desires, conformed outwardly to these doctrines. For Billy, when intoxicated, to grow more polite, more generous, more skillful in his work (for everyone conceded that the ice cream he made when "under the influence" was even better than that made when sober, probably because he was more reckless then with the cream) upset all the rules. Moreover, he added to his other good qualities that of penitence. After each spree he came solemnly to meet the Session, confess his fault, promise new endeavor and be reinstated in his church standing. When the Elders evinced some impatience over the regularity of these episodes, David merely reminded them that on the highest authority they must continue until "seventy times seven." This, he felt, should cover Billy for life.

He decided now to look in upon him and mention the coming Session meeting, for he had recognized by the flavor of the dessert at Mary's birthday dinner that Billy must have been very drunk indeed when he made it.

He opened the door into the small store which showed the two huge freezers standing against the wall and the long counter in front where men and boys sat when they dropped in casually for a dish of ice cream. Beyond, through an open door at the side, was the "parlor" filled with small marble-topped tables at which couples or ladies alone sat to partake of refreshments.

Billy came out from his quarters at the back wearing his long white apron.

"Hello, Billy," David began, "how are things going with you?"

Billy shook his head mournfully. "I'm afraid, Reverend, I've had another *attack*."

It was characteristic of Billy that he never used any of the words usually connected with intoxication. He always had an *attack* or an *unfortunate happening* or a *little difficulty*.

"Could you not try my plan," David pleaded earnestly, "of coming to me when you feel this urge coming on you? Maybe together we could get the best of it."

Billy shook his head while his blue eyes twinkled shrewdly.

"It's like this, Reverend. When the desire ain't on me I don't need help. When it is on me I dont *want* any. See? Like the old fellah that never mended his roof. Said on a wet day he couldn't do it and on a dry day it was as good as anybody's."

David looked back into Billy's honest, humor-lined face. He had long ago decided that it was hopeless to try to change him, and yet, as his pastor, he felt a weight upon his conscience in connection with this erring member of his flock.

He lowered his voice and leaned nearer.

"Are you faithful with *all* the means of grace, Billy? Your prayers and reading the scriptures? This will strengthen you against your time of need."

"Well . . ." Billy admitted, "I mebbe do get a little lax about that. After a long night in the store here, I kinda roll into bed the quick way. But when I'm having a *little difficulty*, I seem to take to prayin' like a duck to water. The words just come, flowin' as fast as Colonel Harrison's himself. I even get to quotin' hymns. Just like him. It's a funny thing how it takes me that way, ain't it, Reverend?"

David drew a long despairing sigh. "Well, try hard to keep up your devotions *between* 'difficulties,' Billy, and do you wish to meet with the Session, then, a week from Saturday?"

"I'll be there," said Billy. "I'd never let myself miss a Communion. Would you like to taste something different? Instead of chocolate this week I made banana. Just a minute."

He bustled back to the big freezers, opened one with care, drew out a liberal spoonful and extended it to David. He accepted it, and the two men eyed each other seriously as he slowly sampled it.

"Wonderful!" David said at last. "About the best I ever tasted. Will you be making it regularly?"

"Just once in so often," Billy said. "Don't do to overwork a new flavor. Not in Ladykirk anyway. As I always say, this is a vanilla and chocolate town. I know them all so well here I can pretty near guess when a person comes in the door which kind they want. Well, I've tried to do right by them. Good ice cream. Good measure. A little free for the kids and the sick. 'Bout all I can do in this world, I guess."

David impulsively reached out his hand.

"You're a good man, Billy," he said, "in spite of everything," and then left precipitately, embarrassed and ashamed of the end of the interview. He felt that he was never severe enough with

Billy. That was not the way to save his soul alive. Or was it? He never could be sure.

He walked on down the street, greeting familiar faces by the way, overcame the temptation to go into the hotel and visit with Mr. Dilling, passed the Masters' house, postponing the embarrassing call he must make there until he returned, and finally arrived at the old mill which stood by the creek. He strolled in the winding road, filled with a pleasant anticipation. Cyrus Olden, the miller and husband to the laughing Martha who had approved his Sunday sermon, was perhaps the best-liked man in the community. Tall, heavily built, red-haired and ruddy, with a fine dust of flour always powdering his working coat, he performed his daily task with a sort of joyous abandon. His father and grandfather had been millers before him. As he often said he had grown up in the old mill and loved every beam and timber in it. Moreover, as he confessed with a freedom somewhat alien to the reserved Scotch-Irish populace, he felt he was "called" to this work. "I take the golden wheat," he would say, "and make it fit for bread." There was a faintly poetic and philosophic streak in his make-up which he was not ashamed to show. He was interested in politics, too, and when the farmers stood about in the mill he always set them discussing the affairs of the nation instead of the gossip of the town. The mill, as a social center then, had a distinct *tone* quite different from the livery stable, for example.

David loved an errand here and walked in now, pleasantly bemused as always by the hum of the machinery and the sweet grainy smell. He found Cyrus tossing heavy sacks about on the upper mill floor and leaned against the wall for a chat.

"When I give up preaching, Cyrus, I think I'll get you to take me into partnership," he said smiling at the big man before him.

Cyrus smiled back warmly. "Don't talk about giving up preaching, Mr. Lyall, not after that sermon last Sunday. I never heard one like it. We had plenty talk about it here yesterday."

"You did?" David asked, surprised and pleased.

"That we did. There were some that said the text, *that God approves of joy*, didn't seem like Scripture, but I said, Scripture or not it sounded good to me. You know how Martha's always laughing. Well, one day Mrs. Crombie came in and Martha was off over something, and Mrs. Crombie says, 'I'd be afraid to do that,' she says. 'You might bring a judgment down on yourself.' I declare if she'd been a man I'm afraid I'd have given her the sharp edge of my tongue. I wonder what she thinks now after the sermon. That ought to set her down a peg."

He came over to David, and leaned with graceful ease against a pile of grain sacks. "I've done a lot of thinking someway about life. It's a puzzle all right. But you know I've always felt like you said, that people ought to enjoy it all they can. If folks are happy every least little chance they get, it may be like money, saved up when trouble comes. Like a little house all warm inside when the winter snows hit the roof, eh? Could be, couldn't it?"

David nodded. "I wish I'd consulted with you, Cyrus, before I wrote my sermon. I believe I'd have made a better job of it. But I'm glad you liked it, you and Martha. I just dropped in to speak again about the Session meeting. I'm counting on you more than anyone else to help Minnie out a little when she comes, and hold the other men in check."

"I won't fail you. I'm not much for judging."

"Thanks, Cyrus. I suppose you've heard about Dave Washing and Aunt Betsy."

Cyrus laughed. "It's funny but it could be serious too. I've been putting in a word for Dave here and there as I could. I don't think there will be any other important candidates unless this business upsets things. You never can tell how people are going to jump in an election, but I'll still be working on it."

David started up the street again, bracing himself for his interview with Minnie. A certain innate shyness, a delicacy of nature, had prevented him from ever mentioning her irregularity to her in the months intervening. He knew the time must arrive for that but had put it off as long as possible. In addition to his own natural hesitancy, he had now to consider that Mr. Dilling was involved, with his pride and his lack of sympathy with the church and its rules. *Tread delicately,* he whispered to himself now, as with a quick-beating heart he ascended the Masters' porch and rang the bell.

Minnie came at last, evidently from the garden, her cheeks flushed and her lovely hair loosed a little and soft about her face. She smiled slightly, but her eyes were grave as she ushered him into the parlor. They exchanged the usual greetings, David inquired in detail about little Victoria, and then he knew the time had come.

"Miss Minnie," he began, changing in quick embarrassment to *Mrs. Dilling,* "as your pastor and friend, I feel I should speak to you about meeting with the Session and discussing with them your . . . your . . ." In spite of all his prepared sentences, he floundered now under her calm, sad eyes. "Your problem," he ended. "They will convene next week after the Saturday service, and I felt of course you would wish to come then and give your . . . that is, say what you cared to say. I assure you that I will make it as easy for you as I can."

He looked at her, and under his gaze the sadness in her eyes turned to anguish. Her face was white.

"I can't," she said very low. "I've wanted to tell you before, but it was so hard. You see I could confess about my shame, but if they would ask me if I was sorry I did what I did . . ." She shook her head despairingly. "I'm afraid I couldn't say yes. Love is so strange, and now since I have my baby . . ." Her voice sank to a whisper. "I can't seem to repent as I should. That's why I haven't been able to pray ever since. I couldn't say this to anyone but you, but I have to explain. It haunts me all the time, night and day. I'm so confused and so wretched. And then there's something else."

Dave waited.

"It's my husband. It's Mr. Dilling. He has forbidden me *ever* to meet the Session whether I could answer everything they asked me or not. He says it would be . . . be *indecent* for me to do such a thing. That it would disgrace him and me both. That's the way he feels, and how — after what he's done for me — could I go against him?"

Minnie tried for self-control, but the tears suddenly ran down her cheeks. There was a look of mortal pain in her eyes. David's own heart felt wrenched as he watched her for, fortunately or unfortunately, he understood his old friend's attitude. For Minnie Masters, an unmarried woman, and one of Ladykirk's own, to have confessed her sin before the Session and received reinstatement would have been in conformity with all village experience. For Horace P. Dilling's *wife* to unbare the intimacies of her heart before a group of men was another matter entirely. David saw it all, but his mind felt blocked by the revelation.

"I think I understand your position, Minnie," he said slowly, "but I must have time to consider what we can do about it. Try not to worry too much, and above all, do not feel that you cannot *pray*. Remember we are all creatures of the earth. We do not know which sins in God's sight are the greater, and which the less. So say your prayers and do your duty now day by day as you see it. Later on we'll talk this over again and I feel sure we'll find a way out."

Then a tremendous embarrassment befell him. As he rose to go and held out his hand, Minnie, the reticent, Minnie the dignified, the aloof, raised it impulsively and for a second rested her lips upon it.

When David was out on the street again he felt hot and cold. In all his life, he had received no comparable demonstration of affection from anyone outside his own family. Certainly *no one* had ever before kissed his hand! He buried the honored member now in his coat pocket as though the light of day must not play upon the secret it bore, while a deep flush slowly dyed his face. This that had happened to him was something he could not tell even to Mary, but in the dead of the night when his heart was heavy with temporary discouragements he would take out the memory and regard it as one might take pleasure in a hidden treasure. Perhaps after all his doubts as to how he should handle Minnie's case he had blunderingly said or done something to help her. If so, he humbly thanked God. A faint, and, he felt, rather unecclesiastical, chuckle escaped him as he neared home, when he thought of his unremitting efforts to bring the Session into line to be ready next week to receive Minnie who, he had never once doubted, would present herself. Now, Minnie was not coming. At least not then. He must keep on working, but with an entirely different objective from now on.

On Friday morning two hours before the hearing for Dave Washing, Aunt Betsy Wade called the Squire on the phone. Her voice was cold with fury.

"I have to report to you," she announced, "that my farmer found my three missing ewes shut up in the barn this morning! If that isn't evidence enough that Dave Washing has had them, I don't know what is. He keeps my sheep for nearly four months and returns them just in time to save his skin. I want to know now whether you feel it's best to have the hearing this morning as planned, or whether it would be better just to send the constable out to arrest him without delay."

"We can't do that, Mrs. Wade. You've no proof. Did anyone see him take them?"

"No, but . . ."

"Did anyone see him bring them back?"

"No, but I tell you . . ."

"Well, then. We can't arrest him. And there's no sense in

going on this morning with the hearing. You've got your sheep. They've had four months free boarding somewhere. Now, my advice to you is to let the whole matter rest."

"I will never let it rest, Squire Hendrick. Never! I have been humiliated. I've been persecuted, outraged by this man. I've been . . ."

"Mrs. Wade, was there not a little matter of Dave Washing's bull spending a time in your barn last year?"

"That," replied Aunt Betsy with dignity, "was an entirely different matter. That bull broke into my field. What I did was in self-defense. And I want you to know, Squire, that if you will not do your duty by me in prosecuting my charges, I shall take the matter of retribution into my own hands. There will be a way," she ended darkly.

"She's got something up her sleeve," the Squire said anxiously to David as he reported the interview later, "but gosh only knows what. She's a deep one. At any rate things are cleared up now before the election. Of course there are a few folks I hear that have been making a good deal of this sheep business. I'll spread the word now that Aunt Betsy's ewes are safe in the fold and we'll see what that'll do."

There fell then upon the countryside that strangest, most soul-satisfying time of all the year — Indian summer. There was in the November air a pause, a hush as though hidden wings were beating back the winds of winter; as though a benison, a bounty of sunny blue skies, of warm haze on the hills and smoky red sunsets, was being bestowed by the lingering year. The last leaves fell lightly, not in saddened gusts, and a mellow undertide of peace, past all describing, settled upon the town.

David felt he had never so loved the old manse as in these days. Everything in the far garden suggested past fruition; the summer flowers were gone, but white and gold chrysanthemums lifted cool spicy blooms along the fence, and the peculiar rich sweetness from the last ripe grapes filled the air. Mary had pressed much of the fruit and had rows of bottles of the unfermented juice upon the cellar shelves. In the cold winter nights they would drink it from Grandmother's delicate wineglasses which in the manse had held no stronger beverage.

"*Tremit absens,*" David murmured one day, recalling the old Latin poem, as he paused by the arbor.

> "*Trembles the absent vine and swells the grape*
> *In thy clear crystal. . . .*"

The absent, yet all-pervading vine; the sacred, the hallowed vine, chosen to be the immortal symbol. Its summer life would rise and tremble in the winter's glass, even as did the sacramental wine within the soul. He touched the great gnarled stalks with reverent fingers.

His mind was curiously active during these weeks. He did much reading and felt that his sermons were going better. Sometimes of an evening he would leave the lighted room where the family sat about the first grate fire, put on an old topcoat and step out on the back porch to study the sky, engage in his private devotions and think in the cool freshness of the air. The words of old Jeremy often rose caressingly.

God sends him a little star to stand over his dwelling, and then again covers it with a cloud.

A great love for all struggling, erring, eager, happy, sorrowing humanity possessed him. Blessed, he thought to himself, were all the innumerable dwellings of the sons of men, each with its little star above it and sheltered by its cloud. And nearer, closer, the houses of Ladykirk seemed to draw together in the darkness.

As he stood here one night he had, irrelevantly enough, a

sudden idea connected with Ben Losting and his gun. Odd that it should come in the midst of deeper musings. It was now hunting season and the sight of Ben's ravaged face had haunted him. The gun, Ben's one joy, stood in the hall closet. David had appealed to Squire Hendrick to ask if it could not be returned to Ben just for these few weeks, but the Squire was firm. What assurance had they that it would be safe to do so?

Now, out of the nowhere of the night, David had a plan. The next morning he went to the hotel and spoke to Mr. Blackburn at his desk.

"Your diaries cover a good many years, don't they?"

"About thirty, I'd say."

"Could I run through the November entries of perhaps the last ten?"

"Of course," Mr. Blackburn agreed. "Could I help you?"

"I want to see if Ben Losting has ever been drunk in hunting season."

"Don't think so," Mr. Blackburn said, "but we'll look. If he was, I'll have it down."

Together they went over the neatly written entries of the weather, the births, deaths and town happenings of the years. Only once did Ben Losting figure in the record. This noted that he boasted of having shot a rabbit at fifty yards.

David thanked Mr. Blackburn and went on up to Mr. Dilling's room for a brief chat. The old man was a trifle edgy and David suspected the reason. Minnie had doubtless told her husband of his call. He tried to divert his old friend now by telling him his plan for Ben to have his gun temporarily.

"You give yourself a lot of unnecessary trouble," Mr. Dilling said testily. "You wear yourself to tatters over all sorts of trifles. Why don't you save your strength for more important work?"

"Oh, I don't know," David replied uncomfortably, for the

criticism was in line with his own thinking. "I just feel sorry for the poor cuss. I suppose it is foolish."

Mr. Dilling's face instantly softened.

"Well, according to Mr. R. Browning, 'All service ranks the same with God.' Maybe your halo will come by way of Ben Losting, after all. Who am I to criticize you? I've been wanting to talk to you, though, David, about other matters."

"I suspected so."

"Through the years we've discussed many things including religion but I've always purposely kept from telling you exactly how I feel toward it, for fear of hurting you. Now, for certain reasons, I have to make my own position clear."

"Very well," said David, "go ahead."

"It's hard to say this to you, but I've been driven to it. I respect truth above all. I strive for honesty of mind. Therefore I can't accept the whole framework of your theology. The creed is shot through with statements as outmoded as that the earth is flat. Yet the church demands our blind belief in them. It will not admit what any man can find out if he reads, that much of all this that has become sacrosanct by usage really came down from older primitive faiths."

He looked down at his nervous hands.

"So, since I am completely out of sympathy with organized religion in general, the idea of any group of church members playing God and sitting in judgment upon another human being, especially someone I love . . . Well, it is unspeakably repugnant to me and I will have no part in it."

David's face had fallen and Mr. Dilling looked at him anxiously.

"I've hurt you!" he said. "I was afraid of this."

"No," David said slowly, "you haven't. You've hinted at all this before even if you never came right out with it. I've done some reading and thinking for myself, too. But here is where you make your mistake. Suppose I always dressed in an out-worn suit?"

He paused, smiling whimsically. "Not such a far-fetched metaphor at that. The point is, would that affect the real *me?* Might you not even disregard what you didn't like in my outward trappings for sake of something deeper and more important underneath?"

He stopped, distressed.

"I know that may seem to you like begging the question. I can't find the right words to answer you, Dilling. I guess real religion is like love, it cometh not by argumentation. You simply find it . . . or, more likely, it finds you."

He rose and held out his hand. "But don't worry about Minnie. I promise you nothing will ever be done which will give you embarrassment or pain."

Dilling grasped his hand but made no answer.

The Saturday of the Congregational meeting was golden-warm. Up and down the streets and from one country-line telephone to another had buzzed the discussion of the election, for church offices were important in the community. While nominations were given from the floor, it was always pretty well arranged from lip to lip beforehand just what these were to be. The more influential and substantial element in the congregation had been agreed upon Dave Washing for the new Trustee. While there would be small factions here and there who might suggest other names, yet the controlling majority were settled upon Dave. That is, until the matter of Aunt Betsy's ewes had arisen. Now, though most of his adherents laughed the matter off, there was a feeling amongst them that a summons to the Squire's, even though canceled, left a small cloud upon Dave's reputation. Had he, for example, meant to *keep* the sheep, or was he holding them merely as a joke in retaliation for the bull episode of last year? These were questions that were asked in every gathering place that week. At the livery stable Dave was completely exonerated; in the blacksmith shop and at the post office, the verdict was not unanimous. And in church elections, as the men went, so went the women. So the matter hung in the balance.

The meeting was unusually large. The "basement," as the first floor of the church was uneuphoniously called, was packed to the doors. This in itself presaged no good, David thought as he walked forward to take his place at the low pulpit as the Presiding Officer of the Day. This meant that there was going to be close voting with faction ranged against faction.

Just as the hands of the round clock on the side wall pointed to the hour of three, a small stir arose about the door. This was followed by a hush. Through this abnormal silence, Aunt Betsy Wade — who had not been inside the church for over five years — Aunt Betsy, in a black plumed bonnet tied under her chin and her black embroidered silk shawl draped majestically about her shoulders, advanced slowly up the aisle. Her right hand grasped her cane upon which she leaned with dignity; her left held a wide-opened lace fan against her breast. There was not a sound, a breath during her long progress to the front row of seats. Here, with the help of Miss Miranda who had followed her like a negligible shadow, she finally arranged herself, adjusted her cane, applied her fan, and nodded to David, as implying that proceedings might now begin.

David, his heart pumping too fast, rose and offered the opening prayer. The Clerk of Session then read the minutes of the last Congregational meeting, and after a spattering of delayed comment upon diverse matters, the real business of the day began. David gave a brief summation concerning the duty and dignity of a church officer, and then asked for nominations for the vacant position of Trustee. At once Colonel Harrison rose ponderously and named David Washing in a good round voice. Quickly following came the heads of the three small factions entering their men in the race. David quailed inwardly at the mention of these. They were not men upon whose judgment he would care to lean. And yet any one of them might easily so divide the vote under the circumstances that the main candidate would be defeated.

At this point Aunt Betsy, making the same regal business of rising as she had of sitting down, got to her feet, leaned both hands upon her cane and faced the congregation.

"Mr. Moderator," she said over her shoulder to David.

"Mrs. Wade," he responded, quaking inwardly.

"I wish to make an observation upon the nomination of David Washing for the office of Trustee of the Ladykirk Presbyterian Church," she said with great distinctness. "I would call it to your attention that no one is better qualified by experience to look after the *lost sheep of the house of Israel* than he!"

She sat down in a hush like that which had attended her entrance. Then like a low rising wind there passed over the congregation a stir, a movement, a flutter of small controlled sounds, not laughter exactly, but certainly not those pertaining to the ordinary decorum of the occasion. Aunt Betsy turned, startled, fixing keen, baleful eyes upon the people behind her. It was evident to all that she had intended her remarks to make a different and more sinister impression.

"I move the nominations be closed!"

"I second the motion!"

It was put and carried. In record time the tellers with suspiciously unsettled faces passed the ballot slips, waited for the usual delays while pencils were exchanged, and finally collected the papers in their hats and retired to the corner at the side of the pulpit to count them. In a very few minutes the report was ready. David Washing was the new Trustee.

At the announcement and without waiting for the concluding prayer, Aunt Betsy rose, and with head high and lips grim, made her way down the aisle and out to her carriage.

When actual adjournment came, the room was in a hubbub. Many crowded around Dave Washing to shake his hand. It was apparent that Aunt Betsy's remark had swung the balance uproariously in his favor. Squire Hendrick and Colonel Harrison were seen in a rear corner chuckling until they were forced to wipe their eyes. Indeed, everyone moved out on a wave of high good feeling in which even the defeated factions joined.

In the small room at one side of the hall where the Session convened, the usual gravity befitting them was utterly lacking.

"The *lost sheep* of the house of Israel!"

They quoted and requoted it to each other, with many slappings of knees and shoulders. When Billy Kinkaid appeared to make his confession there was nothing added to David's own brief questions and the atmosphere of the room was almost one of bonhomie.

If only Minnie *could* have come today it would have been so easy, David thought on his way home. They were all in such an expansive mood.

That night Ladykirk was swept from end to end by laughter. Not since Mr. Dilling's wicked remark about Aunt Betsy's *Bottom* had there been such general mirth. The only trouble about it all, David and Mary agreed, was Aunt Betsy's humiliation. She had come in a full state of arrogant assurance to deliver a clever and crushing blow to her adversary. Instead she had been hoisted by her own petard. She had sent Dave straight to victory and made herself a town laughingstock at the same time.

"She'll be crushed," David said. "It's no use saying she deserved it. Of course she did. But she's old and proud and Dave *did* annoy her, and I'm sorry for her. I'll try to think up some way to salve her wounds."

And Indian Summer continued. David presented the evidence

of Mr. Blackburn's Diary to Squire Hendrick and received permission to return Ben Losting's gun to him for the duration of the hunting season. The abject delight and gratitude of the latter warmed David's heart curiously. After all it was something to bring such happiness to any human soul, wasn't it? He must try to make Dilling see this.

He thought much of his old friend in these days as he worked among his bees. There was — had always been — a hardness, a bitter cynicism in his thinking; an almost fanatical fear of deceiving himself. He was not an atheist. He would take off his hat to the Infinite, but it was with a distant respect. There was no warmth, no love, no holy hope within it. And he was growing very old.

One day David stopped his work suddenly and went to the study. He took down a book, found a marked paragraph and copied it carefully.

Late, late have I loved Thee . . . Thou didst call and very loud and didst break through my deafness. Thou didst shine and my darkness was scattered. Thou didst touch me, and I burned for Thy peace.

"I'm not sure how he'll take this," David muttered, "but I'll leave it on his table anyway next time I'm down."

One afternoon as he was putting winter feeding in the hives (the honey crop had been smaller than usual that summer) Mary called him from the house. Her voice was anxious when he went in.

"There's something wrong," she said. "I could tell by the way *Central* rang. Over and over quickly, you know."

David went to the hall and picked up the receiver. His words were few, but as he hung up, he swayed ever so slightly and sank down on the chair nearby.

"What, David? Oh, what is it?"

"It's quite dreadful, Mary. Sit down and brace yourself. It's

Cyrus Olden. He fell backwards out of the upper mill door."

"Not . . . dead?"

David nodded, and leaned forward upon the hall table.

"I must go as quickly as I can pull myself together, but this has hit me hard."

She came close and put her arms about him.

"I'll make you a cup of tea at once. You must have something before you go. You're so white!"

"No, I must get to them as fast as I can. I'll be all right."

He put his head in his hands for a moment, then rose, kissed her and was gone. Mary watching him from the front door, leaned weakly against the lintel.

"Poor Martha! Oh, poor Martha! I wonder if she'll ever laugh again."

And Ladykirk mourned. From one end of it to the other a pall hung upon the town, while the very houses seemed to draw together in the tragedy. Men talked low in their gathering places; women with tears in their eyes baked and cooked their best to carry to the Olden family, or sponged and pressed a black veil or skirt that Martha might be able to wear at the funeral. Kind hands took over the routine work of the stricken household; strong men stood at the door, offering their help in broken tones. The town mourned for a friend and brother, whose cheerful voice was silenced even as the steady hum of the mill was still.

David, his own heart sore beyond telling, walked the streets, thinking of all this. He could not know in that tender year of grace, nineteen hundred, that there would come a time when the quiet dead would be hurried from their homes as though they bore a plague upon them, and left to lie alone in strange places until they quitted all human habitations forever! He only knew that now once again the village drank of the same cup, and that the gentleness of grief lay upon them all as old and young made their way to the upper room where Cyrus Olden lay close and near to those who loved him, to look upon his face and bow again before the mystery.

It was the largest funeral Ladykirk had ever seen. From far back in the hills unknown farmers who had at some time brought their grain to the mill and lingered long to talk with Cyrus came now to do him honor. The women crowded the big, spreading white house, and the men filled the yard, standing bareheaded, their hats against their breasts. When the time came David took his place in the front doorway where he could be heard by those within and without. The mild pleasant air lay sweetly upon the town where all sounds were stilled for this hour. There were no wheels upon the street, no trafficking about the stores; the blacksmith's anvil was silent. Only David's voice rose in words of consolation and prayer.

And at the end, as at every funeral service in Ladykirk, the whole company sang together the Twenty-Third Psalm in the old metrical version which they had all known by heart from childhood. David himself raised the tune and for the first line his clear tenor rang alone.

The Lord's my shepherd; I'll not want;

Gradually the women joined him. It was not until the second verse that the deep voices of the men, hesitant at first, began to sing. Then, steadily increasing in volume, the rich harmony rolled along the quiet street.

E'en though I walk through death's dark vale,
Yet will I fear no ill;

Mr. Dilling, sitting up in his hotel room beside the open window, his head supported upon a thin hand, listened and heard the diapason of faith as it reached its climax.

Goodness and mercy all my life
Will surely follow me;
And in God's house for evermore
My dwelling place shall be.

He leaned back in his chair with a long, quivering sigh.

"They have something, these people," he spoke to himself. "I'm not sure just what it is, but they have something I do not have."

Chapter Nine

NINIAN'S VISIT at Thanksgiving was planned with the gentle decorum of the times. First he wrote Lucy that he would like very much to come out to Ladykirk that last November week-end, as *early* as might be agreeable to her, he being free from Wednesday afternoon until Monday. He would stay at the Stone Hotel. The receipt of this letter was at once the subject of a family conclave. Did he mean he could be with them on Thanksgiving Day itself? It sounded like it. It was finally decided to invite him to the manse for the long week-end, beginning Wednesday evening, if he cared to come, and Mary sent a little note in Lucy's letter to this effect. The reply was practically instantaneous. Ninian was grateful, delighted, wildly excited and accepted with pleasure.

This turn of events sent a more than customary thrill into anticipation of the national holiday.

"Mother," Lucy said one morning, "do we *have* to have Miss Tilly this year for Thanksgiving dinner?"

Faith and Mary stopped their work and looked at each other.

"I do think," Faith said in her even voice, "that some other family might take her for once. Isn't she a distant cousin of the Fosters? Couldn't you ask them, Mother, if they would invite her?"

232

Mary considered. "I know how you feel, but we've always thought that on this day we should share with someone who has less than we do. Mill Tilly is the only person in the congregation who is not only very poor but absolutely alone. I don't know how your father would feel about not having her."

"Oh," Lucy lamented, "if we could just rest up from our consciences once in a while, how *comfortable* it would be! I would like everything to be perfect when Ninian comes, and you know how it will be if Miss Tilly's here. First of all when she gets too close to the fire . . . " Lucy held her nose delicately. "Then she always spills gravy over the tablecloth and dips her bread in her coffee . . . "

She dropped dejectedly into a chair and Mary looked worried.

"Maybe you children should have a chance to decide this year about the matter," she said slowly. "At least we can discuss it with your father tonight. He's still sad over Mr. Olden's death and he has plenty of problems on his mind, but I know he'll consider this carefully. You can talk it over with Jeremy when he comes home."

That evening after dinner, they all repaired to the study where David sat judicially in his big desk chair. Jeremy presented the case.

"We feel it's high time we had one Thanksgiving *sans* Tilly," he began. "We've had her every year as long as I can remember and frankly we feel . . . Faith and Lucy and I . . . as if we deserved a little respite."

"You know," Lucy put in, "that Mother's planning to use Grandmother's damask tablecloth and all the best china and silver and we would like a really *elegant* meal for once with no one upsetting her coffee or not using her napkin or . . . "

"There are nice people we could invite who are lonely too. The Wilsons have no relatives," Faith suggested.

"When it comes to that," Jeremy said somewhat shyly, "what about the MacDonalds? There are just three of them and they haven't an aunt or a cousin or anybody. Peggy always says holidays don't seem right when you have a small family." Then quite unaccountably he blushed to his ears.

"Oh, the MacDonalds would be perfect, Father! Wouldn't they, Mother? And Ninian knows Peggy and likes her so much!" Lucy was enthusiastic.

"And say," Jeremy put in excitedly, "if we asked them I'll bet they'd send in a turkey! You know they did one year anyhow."

"Jeremy!" his father reproved mildly.

"Well, that was just a thought. Not my chief reason," he defended.

"A *turkey!*" Lucy cried. "I never dreamed beyond roasting chickens! Oh, do let's have them."

David and Mary looked at each other, weighing the matter.

"I could ask Mrs. Foster to invite Miss Tilly," she said.

David stroked his cheeks.

"She's come here for so many years, I feel she's our responsibility," he said slowly. "And yet I understand how you children feel. It's hard for me to make the decision."

"Listen, Father," Jeremy said suddenly, "why can't we draw slips from a hat and leave it to fate. Then we've got a chance to get rid of Tilly. . . ."

"*Miss* Tilly, Jeremy."

"All right, only I never think of her that way. And yet she's got a chance to win too. Why, I say, wasn't that a Scriptural custom — drawing lots?"

David smiled. "It was practiced, I believe, quite extensively among the early Christians."

"Well, there you are! Let's get a hat and I'll write the slips. There are five of us to insure a majority so we can all draw. We'll put three *MacDonalds* in and three *Tillys*, Miss," he added, "What do you say, girls? Gee, it's going to be exciting!"

"But we're taking a chance not only on the guests but the *turkey*," Lucy said anxiously.

"Oh, well, some of the other farmers just *might* send in a turkey anyway. What do you say, Faith?"

"I think this way is right. I don't want Miss Tilly, but maybe we ought to give her a chance."

"I think so, too," Mary echoed.

"I don't believe I'm as good as the rest of the family," Lucy admitted mournfully, "but let's go ahead and get it over with. I've got goose pimples already."

David collected some bits of paper and wrote the names while Jeremy got his father's hat from the hall, then as master of ceremonies he put the slips in it and shook them vigorously.

"Come on now," he shouted, lost in the game, "Mother first."

Mary drew, and smiled widely as she read her slip. "The *MacDonalds*."

Wild clapping from the children.

Lucy begged to draw next because she was so nervous. She reached her hand in, shut her eyes, then opened them and read in a hollow voice, "*Miss Tilly*."

"Don't despair," cried Jeremy, "we have three more tries. Come on, Faith."

Faith drew the MacDonalds to prolonged applause; but David's slip was Miss Tilly, so the outcome hung in the balance. Lucy was close to tears. "I think this is worse than just deciding and sticking by it," she said. "The suspense is so awful."

Jeremy now raised his right hand in a melodramatic gesture, while his left fumbled in the hat which David held for him. He raised his eyes.

> "*Dear Heavenly Powers, think me not silly,*
> *But grant that I may not draw Tilly.*"

"Miss," he added as an afterthought amid the general laughter. He drew, opened the slip slowly, read it and sank down on a chair. *"The MacDonalds,"* he breathed.

"Well, I guess that settles it," said David. "You'll speak to Mrs. Foster soon, won't you?" he asked Mary.

"Oh, at once," she said. "And I'm sure she'll agree."

Jeremy was right. Early the morning before Thanksgiving Mr. MacDonald brought a turkey to the back door of the manse. A noble bird of incredible weight. It was evident his family were much gratified over their invitation. Other gifts from the farm members of the congregation had been arriving all week: pumpkins; a print of butter; spare ribs; a crock of freshly made sausage, a bushel of apples and (to the children's mind the best of all) a sack of black walnuts! It was customary during all the year for the country folk to stop their sleds or wagons or buggies at the manse gate and with an air of pleased importance to come up the walk with their humble but highly useful offerings. It had been so in Ladykirk time out of mind, but it was quietly spoken that the Lyalls were more fortunate than other manse families before them in this regard because they took none of the kindness for granted. Mary's exclamations of spontaneous pleasure, David's honest-voiced appreciation, sent many a farmer away with a warm spot in his heart.

Now, on this particular Wednesday, the house hummed with activity and happy anticipation. Only Mary thought betimes of Miss Tilly, living in her one room, her ancient black cashmere, greening with the years, hung behind the door along with her knitted hood, both absorbing freely the odors of her unvaried cooking; her white hair up in crimping pins against her great day's outing; her woolen shawl refolded so the moth holes would not show. Mary hoped there had been no slip in the plan for the Fosters to take her. Mrs. Foster had agreed to it, but without enthusiasm.

Ninian arrived late that evening, alighting with his bag from a hired conveyance at the manse gate and literally running up the walk. Lucy, watching from the window, met him at the door and stood for a long moment close in his arms before the family in general were aware he had come. Mary, in the upper hall, could not help but see that first kiss and then the dark cheek pressed to the fair one.

Soon he was swept into the welcome of the family. He was in great spirits! His marks, he confided to David, had turned out rather well so far. To Mary he told his gratitude at being in the manse instead of at the hotel. "You mustn't ever feel you have to have me if it's inconvenient," he said earnestly, "but being here with you all is really like being in a different world! From what I'm used to," he added.

He had to be shown the turkey, which he praised inordinately; he gloated over the golden pumpkin pies, he helped Lucy arrange fruit on the tall glass cake stand for tomorrow's centerpiece; he suddenly remembered the boxes of sweets he had brought for Mary and for Faith and rushed to get them, he helped Jeremy bring up more coal for the grate.

"I've never been here before when the fire was going," he said, watching the lumps of soft coal flame and glow. "It's beautiful! Oh, I say, can we have a *sing* tonight?"

The family with delicate tact retired early, leaving the young lovers to sit on the sofa beside the fire. There was so very much to say, which was surprising, considering the frequent letters. Then Ninian, his cheeks flushed, drew a small box from his pocket and placed it in Lucy's hand.

"This is just a little in-between gift," he said. "I thought if you were willing, I'd bring the ring at Christmas."

Lucy opened the box slowly. Within on its snowy bed, lay a little heart-shaped gold locket on a chain, with a shining stone gleaming in its center. She looked at it incredulously.

"Do you like it?" he asked eagerly.

"*Like it?*" she repeated, and then as usual in extreme delight, dissolved in tears. But Ninian, understanding apparently, wiped them away and bade her open the locket.

"I feel a bit of a fool, putting in what I did, but I somehow thought you'd like it," he said.

She pressed the tiny spring and Ninian's own face looked back at her!

"I brought my camera along and I'm going to snap you to-morrow so I can put you in the back of my watch and look at you whenever I want," he added.

How fast the hours flew! Little by little their voices dropped lower. Lucy, raising her beautiful, innocent eyes to his, confided that somehow she did not feel startled at the thought of marriage any more. Not since it was Ninian she would be with forever and ever. And he told her he couldn't wait longer than next year to have her for his very own. How could he, loving her as he did?

The great hall clock struck midnight and they knew they must soon go up. Ninian blew out the lamp and they sat in the fire's glow, watching the shadows dance upon the walls.

"I'm a little worried over something," he confessed. "I'm not sure whether I should tell you or not."

"Of course you should," Lucy encouraged fervently.

"Well, it would be a comfort to talk it over. You see . . . there's a girl . . ."

At her startled look he swept her closer to him.

"Darling, what a blundering idiot I am to start that way. This is a girl I don't even *like*, but I've known her all my life and my parents have always sort of had her laid out for me. She's the daughter of old friends of theirs. And she — well, it sounds caddish of me to say so even to you, but she's always cooking up things and scheming around — oh, I can't quite explain, but . . ."

"She likes you," Lucy finished.

"I guess so. It's all a horrible mix-up as far as I'm concerned, for Mother gets ideas and she's a very hard person to convince if she's really set on something. That's one reason I'll be glad when our engagement is announced. Gladder still, when we're married."

Lucy was puzzled. "But if she knows that you l . . . love *me?*" she queried.

Ninian was embarrassed. "I've tried to explain, but she and Dad feel I'm young and don't know my own mind . . . you know all that argument. They've always refused to take me seriously except in matters of their own choosing. Your father believed me right away when I told him I loved you. I'll never forget that all my life long!"

"Did your parents mind your coming here this week-end instead of going home?" Lucy asked astutely.

"Well, yes, they did rather," he admitted. "That's what I really started to explain. You see Mother had planned a big do-dad for this Saturday afternoon, in honor of this girl. Trina. She's just come out."

"From where?" Lucy asked innocently.

"In society. You know. A débutante. I hadn't heard that this thing was arranged for till I wrote Mother I was coming out here for the holidays. Then there's been the very dev — mischief to pay ever since. But why should I give my plans up? Why should she blame me for going ahead and making my own? I'm sure she always has. Last year she and Dad were away on a cruise at Thanksgiving. Did they consider me? I've had more lonesome holidays in my life than I could ever count!" His young voice was bitter.

Lucy had to take time to draw his head down to hers. "But never again," she whispered. "You'll never be lonely again." Then she questioned him about the party.

"Oh, it will be one of those big shindigs. I'm sick of them.

Orchestra behind palms, white crash on all the carpets, food and drink galore, fancy flowers, a hundred people or so milling around, receiving line grinning and shaking hands till they're limp — *you* know."

Lucy didn't know but she tried to picture it. "*A hundred people*," she echoed, "in your house! It must be beautiful."

Ninian looked around the shabby manse parlor. The friendly voices so lately raised in song and laughter seemed to fill it now, to furnish it. He looked down at Lucy. "Not so beautiful as this one," he said quietly. "Not nearly so."

They talked it all over carefully. On the one hand Lucy felt honestly that he should not disappoint his mother. On the other, Ninian maintained that his parents must learn he was in earnest in his love and expectation of an early marriage and that his being at this reception for Trina would only give them something more to go on in their wholly unwarranted plans for him.

They decided at last to do nothing and to forbear worrying about the situation. They were now safely together. Why allow any past problems or future possibilities to mar that happiness? What was youth for if not to enjoy the present and be confident that on the morrow all would be well? They banked the fire, and softly climbed the stairs.

In the upper hall Lucy paused, touching the locket which he had fastened about her neck.

"I just wondered," she whispered, "the stone — it shines so — I just wondered . . . what it was?"

"It's a diamond." He smiled.

Lucy flung her arms about him. "I didn't like to ask and yet I had to know. A diamond! Oh, Ninian, I know I won't sleep a wink tonight!"

But they did, at last, the two tender young hearts, with only a wall between them.

Thanksgiving Day was dull and gray outside with clouds of

snowflakes scurrying through the air and a wind in the chimney. Just the weather for feasting and roaring fires within. Ninian had been apprized of the narrow escape they had all had in connection with Miss Tilly and rejoiced with the others over the coming of the MacDonalds.

"Peggy's a most awfully nice girl, Jeremy," he remarked while the young men were tying their neckties with particular care up in their rooms. And Jeremy in an oddly muffled voice had answered, "You just bet she is!"

There was great bustle on the part of all to get the house in order, the turkey in the oven and the long table laid before the eleven o'clock Union church service. It was Faith who worked closely with her mother, thought of everything and added the last touches to the preparations.

"What would I do without you, dear?" Mary said in the final rush. "Especially now since Lucy's head is in the clouds. Isn't the locket charming? A little too valuable a gift, I fear, but what can we say?"

"Oh, just let her enjoy it," Faith answered in a low voice.

Looking up, Mary caught the wistfulness on her elder daughter's face.

"Do you know, Faith," she said impulsively, "I've never seen you look as pretty as you do this minute!"

"Why, Mother!" the girl said, flushing with surprise and pleasure, "thank you. How . . . how nice of you to say such a thing!"

That, Mary thought to herself, will give her a little something to hug to her heart today when she is rather shut out of the happiness around her. And why, indeed, shouldn't parents pay compliments to their children She had been thinking a good deal about Faith and John Harvey, recently, for Faith had been increasingly quiet and brooding. Were matters coming to a head between them? He was taking her to the entertainment that night as he did to everything that went on. In the eyes of the town it was a settled thing. A *match!* But it wasn't right for Faith. Poor child! Every night Mary prayed longer than usual that *The Call*, the long awaited call to a larger town, might somehow come so that Faith, dear Faith with her gifts and gentle graces, might have her chance.

Mary slipped into a back seat in church in order to leave instantly when the service was over. The responsibility of the enormous turkey and the MacDonalds to dinner weighed upon her. Lucy, profiting by the fact that it was a Union choir, sat with Ninian (very close) in the pastoral pew, for all to see and report upon later. Jeremy, waiting for them outside, entered with the MacDonalds and sat next to Peggy for the first time, thus providing more fireside conversation for the town that day. Mary saw it all and John Harvey too, who sat far back with his eyes fixed upon Faith in the choir. Her own heart felt suddenly overborne. *Deep as first love and wild with all regret. . . .* The words rose in her mind, drowning out the opening hymn. God grant it be not so with any of them, she prayed. I mean the *regret* part, she added hastily, giving as she frequently did a parenthetical explanation to the Deity.

One person she tried hard not to see was Miss Tilly. Her conscience was not entirely at ease about her, though she felt the children's wishes had deserved consideration. If Mrs. Foster had been as good as her word, then all would be well.

When the benediction was pronounced, Mary waited to speak to no one but hurried home by the shortest route. The turkey, she found, was browning beautifully, and she began hurriedly to attend to the rest of the dinner, giving a glance to the elegantly set table which today would remain unmarred by accidents. It really *was* a great relief.

Soon there was quick stamping of feet at the front door, for the ground was already lightly covered with snow, and the voices of the family and the MacDonalds as they all entered. The parlor grate was set to blazing its best and there was much easy laughter and running to and fro with offers of help on everybody's part, while the rich fragrance of the coming dinner filled the house.

It was perhaps a half-hour later that Lucy, glancing out the front window, gave a sharp scream.

"*Look*," she cried, and could say no more.

All the young folks rushed to see. There coming slowly up the walk, protected from the snowflakes by a large, rusty umbrella, was a thin figure clad in an ancient knitted hood, and a gray woolen shawl. It was, it *was* Miss Tilly!

"No!" Jeremy all but yelled, "It can't be!"

"I was afraid all the time the Fosters wouldn't ask her," Faith's voice was tragic.

It was Ninian who saved the day. "I think," he said, fairly choking with laughter, "that this is the funniest thing that ever happened!"

So it came to pass that Miss Tilly was received amid wild spasms of mirth which she accepted without surprise as her due welcome, while her bonnet and shawl were being removed and she was ushered to a seat by the fire.

"The Fosters invited me," she remarked casually to Mrs. MacDonald in her high, cackling voice, "but I just said no, I always et Thanksgiving dinner at the preacher's. I thought you'd forgot me today, though," she added to David, "when you didn't wait for me. "

"No, Miss Tilly," Jeremy broke in dramatically, "we certainly didn't forget about you. Indeed you've been in our minds constantly for a week. Hasn't she, girls?"

They could not reply, but fled to tell their mother the news, a train of outrageous giggles following them. David, seized with a convenient fit of coughing (for which Miss Tilly offered him a hoarhound lozenge from her all too unsanitary pocket!), managed to get general conversation going finally and distract his guests from the children's levity.

When Mary in the kitchen had regained her own self-control she insisted she was glad it had all ended as it had and hurried to set a place for the latest guest beside her own where she could watch over her. Indeed, far from casting a gloom over the party, Miss Tilly's unexpected presence gave grounds for unwanted hilarity all during dinner.

"About the casting of lots, Father," Jeremy said as they were finishing their pie, "do you approve of the custom?" His countenance was wickedly serious.

"Well," David began, seeing Mr. MacDonald look up with interest, "it was used by the early church, so perhaps we should not entirely discredit it, but personally I feel it is not a very dependable . . ."

He was interrupted by gales of laughter.

When the older folks had retired to the parlor, the gaiety continued in the kitchen amidst the clearing up and rattle of dishes. They all made rhymes to celebrate the main event of the day, but gave the palm finally to Jeremy for his succinct summing up of the situation in one couplet.

Willy-nilly
We get Tilly!

Ninian and Lucy lingered after the others had left, while she told him all the story of the cabinet, displaying its charms as she spoke. He listened with an odd expression on his face and then walked to the window and stood staring out at the snowy garden. When he turned he still did not speak, only looked at the cabinet and then at her, before he put his arms about her.

Faith was playing to them all in the parlor when the telephone in the hall rang. The call, Jeremy reported with some surprise, was for Ninian, who did not close the door after him when he went out to answer it. His words, therefore, came disjointedly through the music, with long pauses between them.

"Yes . . . yes. . . . Oh, hello . . . I'm very sorry, but I can't Trina. . . . Yes, I realize that, but I've already explained. . . . I don't feel you have any right to say that. . . . I'm sorry but you see . . . Well, it might have, but as it is . . . Yes, of course. . . . Well, all right, good-bye."

His face was flushed and his manner embarrassed when he re-entered the room. He was quieter than usual the rest of the afternoon and only brightened as they prepared to go out that evening to hear "The Swiss Bell Ringers" perform in Harrison's Hall, above the store. Peggy was staying overnight, and when John Harvey called for Faith the three young couples set out together lightheartedly. Even Faith was suddenly bright and laughing as John towered above her, holding her coat.

David and Mary did not go. Instead, they put more coal on the fire and sat down to talk the day over.

"You know," Mary said later, "I believe it was a girl who called Ninian up this afternoon."

"*A girl?*" David echoed in astonishment.

"Yes, I heard him say *Tina* or *Trina* or something like that. It must mean that he's had a rather close involvement with her when she would find out where he was, from his family, I suppose, and call him up. It disturbs me, somehow, coming when everything seemed so beautiful between him and Lucy."

"I confess that's something of a shock to me, too," David said slowly, "but after all he must know dozens of girls and I fancy he's quite sought after for more reasons than one."

"This girl was definitely begging him to do something. It seemed to me he was very positive at first in his refusal and then weakened a tiny bit at the last. Of course I'm not sure, hearing only the one side."

"He may have told Lucy all about it. I trust that boy, absolutely."

"Oh, yes," Mary agreed, brightening. "It's silly to imagine things."

The next morning Ninian proposed that they all drive up to see the new coal works and to that end he went down to the livery stable and returned with *a carriage*. Mary declined the trip, but the young people filled the fine equipage in high feather and David followed in his own buggy, for he had not been up to Kirkville recently. They viewed together the changes wrought on the erstwhile peaceful hillside. The great, gaunt tipple now reared its head, with the outlines of the washer beside it; the Company store and offices were under way; and streets of uniform small house skeletons rose bleakly from the mud and the snow. Along the level not far from the tipple appeared the sketchy outlines of the future coke ovens.

"They've had an army of men working here," David said, surprised, "but I didn't know they'd gotten this far. The works will be starting up by spring at this rate."

"It doesn't take long," Ninian said, eyeing it all keenly. "There's something about the coal business that fascinates me. I guess because I used to play around a mine when I was a kid. I was allowed to go out to visit the Superintendent's son at Haverty, since Father had an interest in the mines there. I think he has some sort of hookup with this one here," he added casually.

"He has?" Lucy asked in awe.

"Well, you have to have coke to make steel," Ninian smiled at her, "so the steel men usually keep a finger on a coal mine or two if they can. I wonder what sort of ovens they're building."

He scrambled up to the first rough foundations and peered at them interestedly.

"You can't tell much yet, but I'm sure they're beehive design." He looked across the small valley to where the manse showed, a mere white spot amongst its trees. "You'll get a great view of these at night when they start going," he said. "My word, what a sight they are when you're too far away to see anything but the flames. Dante's Inferno wasn't in it with coke ovens!"

"I'm thinking more just now about the human element," David said slowly, "I don't know why I've been so naïve, but I never pictured a town the size this is going to be! Why, it will have as many people in it as Ladykirk!"

"Enlarge your parish, sir?" Ninian laughed. "I can tell you they'll be a mixed lot. They always are. More interested in the beer wagons than in religion, I'm afraid, most of them."

David was thoughtful as he drove back, pondering the light words.

When they returned, Mary told Ninian he had had another phone call and the operator had left a number with which he was to make connection as soon as he got back. He glanced at the slip of paper she handed him and then looked at Lucy.

"It's Mother," he said in a low voice, "I told you she never gave up. I guess I'm beaten."

He put in the call and the family went at once out of hearing. When he rejoined them, his dark eyes were smoldering.

"I'm afraid I'll have to leave tonight," he said, looking at Mary. "I'm so terribly disappointed, when you asked me for the whole week-end, but Mother had something planned for tomorrow afternoon and it's going to make trouble, I guess, if I'm not there."

"We're sorry, too," Mary said hastily, "but you mustn't disappoint your mother."

"You understand?" Ninian said anxiously, his eyes searching hers.

"Of course. Your parents will want a part of your visit. That's only natural." She tried to convince herself with the words, but a small fear once more assailed her heart.

In the afternoon Ninian and Lucy set out on foot to call upon Aunt Betsy Wade. After hearing the Lost Sheep episode, Ninian insisted he must meet the old lady; but the family all knew also that the long walk through the covered bridge and along the winding creek to the Wade farm was the most romantic and secluded about town.

Ninian and Lucy did not hurry. As soon as they had left the village behind, he drew her arm close to his and held her small mittened hand in his own gloved one. He was angry, even bitter, and Lucy tried to cheer him as best she could.

"You couldn't come back tomorrow night after the party?" she asked hopefully.

He looked troubled. "No, I'm afraid when everything's over it would be much too late. But it isn't long until Christmas. I'd come out in between but I've been working like a dog every week-end, and I want to keep it up if I can."

They spoke of the ring as they paused beside the little Wade graveyard, hearsed with its pines. There was nothing somber in the spot to them. To their warm-blooded youth the evidences of mortality were dim and unreal, and their love stretched ahead endlessly. They kissed long and gravely, feeling nothing in the quiet place but enchanted ground since they could be alone there with their bliss.

"I've been saving up for the ring. I'm sending to Tiffany's for it. Don't let me forget to measure your finger when we get back," he said at last. "And we can be married next summer, can't we? You could always come home whenever you wished, and I'd take such care of you! Oh, darling. I'll be *so* good to you!"

"I know," Lucy whispered. "I must try to be ready, though. I'm studying, too, as hard as I can. Father says I'll have covered about three years of college by spring. And then I should know a little more about cooking, shouldn't I?"

Ninian smiled. "Don't worry too much about that. I'll take a chance. Our time now is so short — do we have to go to Aunt Betsy's after all?"

"I think we should. Mother's probably called up to tell her we're on our way, and Father thinks our visit may cheer her up. She's been feeling quite low since the Lost Sheep meeting. We'll stay only a minute."

But they stayed an hour, without knowing it, for Aunt Betsy in their presence rose to her old sprightly best, and Ninian put forth every effort to charm her. With great success. The famous Wade gingerbread melted magically from the plate and Miss Miranda, with pleased twitterings, kept replenishing it. The last unconscious stroke of genius on Ninian's part was an unfeigned admiration of Aunt Betsy's paintings to which Lucy called his attention.

"I'm no artist myself," he said, "but my father goes in for collecting pictures a bit, so I've gotten interested. These are good, Mrs. Wade. I think they're most terribly good. Weren't you told so, when you did them?"

Aunt Betsy's face softened.

"Oh, yes, my teacher said I had talent, but in those days young ladies didn't have *careers*. All they were interested in was falling in love and getting married. And as I observe things, they haven't changed much, eh, Lucy?"

They left, flushed and happy over the old lady's approval, calling back their promises to come again, and very slowly made their way back along the quiet road.

The family again left them alone for a little while in the parlor that evening while Ninian awaited the rig which was to drive him to the main-line train, six miles away.

"You're sure you understand about tomorrow," he kept asking with concern. "You don't feel . . . I mean, you don't *doubt* me?"

Lucy raised worshipful eyes.

"Why Ninian, even if you . . . if you *killed* me, I'd never doubt you!"

They didn't hear the arrival of Josiah Hunt with the rig.

There had to be a voice to call, before they came forth from their dear and private world.

When he had gone, Lucy, suddenly looking tired, went on up to her own room; Jeremy left to take Peggy home; and David had a Trustees' meeting. Mary relaxed by the parlor fire, watching Faith as she moved about, straightening the room, glad of a chance to discuss with her elder daughter some of the problems connected with Lucy which lay upon her heart. As it befell, however, it was of Faith herself that they talked.

She sat down on the hassock before the grate and began to take the hair pins from her hair.

"I don't think anyone will be in tonight," she said. "I'll run if there is a ring at the doorbell."

Her hair fell, blonde and silken, around her shoulders, making her face young and appealing in its frame.

"We're so seldom alone," she began. "I've been wanting to talk to you. I'm so unhappy and worried."

"Is it about John?" her mother asked.

"Yes. He wants to get married. He asked me first this summer — that night of the Festival — but I put him off. I told him I must have time to think it over. Now he's pressing me. And this is one thing that disturbs me if nothing else did. He wants a wife. I'm his first choice but if I refuse, I know he'll try at once to find someone else. His father and mother are moving to town like the MacDonalds before too long, and he'll be alone. It's like that."

She clasped her knees and looked into the fire.

"I don't know what to do. You see, I *want* to get married and have a home and . . . children. It doesn't sound maidenly to say it, but *you* understand."

"Of course, dear."

"And I'll be twenty-five my next birthday and then if we go

on living here, and I don't marry John, I'll just get older and older and keep on giving music lessons . . . John *is* nice and kind and would be good to me and the big house would be ours and I'd be sort of *important,* in a way, in the community. . . ."

"I understand, dear."

"That's the one part. And sometimes when I just sit quietly beside him, he's so big and strong, I think it's enough and I'll say *yes.* But when we try to talk by ourselves . . ." she broke off and wiped the tears away, "then I know I don't love him at all. We haven't anything in common. He never reads a book. He doesn't like music except a few popular songs. He's a little tiny bit *coarse* sometimes. He doesn't mean to be. He just doesn't feel about things as I do. I know I shouldn't marry him, only . . ."

She moved suddenly over to Mary and knelt before her, her stricken young eyes raised to her mother's.

"Only . . . isn't it *sad* that he can't be right for me the way Ninian is for Lucy?"

She sank upon the floor and dropped her head on Mary's knee while sobs shook her.

"I try not to be jealous of her. I'm glad she's so happy, but it's hard to watch her with Ninian and know that John and I couldn't ever be like that."

Mary stroked the soft hanging hair.

"I know," she kept repeating, "I understand it all, but I'm afraid to advise you. I think your own heart must tell you the answer."

At last Faith raised her head. The fairness of her young face smote Mary afresh.

"I can't marry him," she said with a sort of despairing finality. "Deep down I've always known that. I've just been playing with the idea because I want so much to love and be loved. But I could never be happy with him, and that would be dreadful for both of us. I'll tell him soon . . . I'll tell him next time he comes. . . ."

She buried her face again. "But I'm afraid it will be my only chance, *ever!*"

Then Mary found words.

"Nonsense," she said with brave assurance. "You musn't even think of such a thing! Most girls have several offers of marriage before they really decide. You're young and who knows what may happen? We may not always live here. I'm always expecting your father to get a call somewhere to a big town. He's so clever and good and such a student. You know he had honors from college and the Seminary both! And his book and everything. Besides, by another winter you might go into the city to study and stay there so you could . . . could meet people and . . ."

Her voice trailed off, but soon grew strong again.

"So don't ever for a minute think you are just tied to Ladykirk. You must believe that something wonderful is just around the corner for you and it will come! And I'm glad you are not going to marry John."

"You are, truly? I was afraid . . ."

Faith's gray eyes were wide.

"Truly. The big house and all the rest are not enough without love."

"Faith drew a long breath. "I'm glad you think I'm doing right. I feel better since I've talked it all out with you. I believe I'll go up now, and thank you, Mother, so much!"

Mary knelt for a long, long time by her bed that night.

On Monday when the city paper came she took it to her own room and shut the door. She turned to the Society page, which she usually glanced at casually if at all, and scanned it now with care. What she sought was not difficult to see. At the top was the picture of a proud-looking, handsome young girl with an extravagant pompadour and low-cut evening dress. *Débutante Honored*, ran the heading. Below was her name, Miss Katrina Van Doren. At the side in a long column was the write-up of a reception of one hundred fifty guests given on Saturday afternoon by Mr. and Mrs. R. P. Ross at their home, "Craigie Hill," for Miss Van Doren. Receiving with Mrs. Ross and the débutante had been Mr. Ross and their son, Ninian, home from college for the holidays. After full description of the decorations and gowns and a partial list of names, there was this brief statement: "Following the reception the younger guests all went on to the Thanksgiving Cotillion at the Hotel Hamilton."

Mary put down the paper and sat for a long time looking straight ahead. She did not see the familiar furniture, however. She saw the reception; she saw the receiving line with Ninian and the débutante standing so near each other, bowing and smiling; she saw into his mother's heart and knew that she intended this girl for her son.

Her cheeks burned with a painful flame as she pictured on the one hand, Ninian in the old manse, having dinner with the MacDonalds *and Miss Tilly*, drying dishes in the kitchen or walking along the rutty creek road to Aunt Betsy's; then saw him in a day's time, as the heir of R. P. Ross, at home in "Craigie Hill" which could house a hundred and fifty guests, and later, dancing the Cotillion at the Hamilton. With the débutante!

The bright dream they had all shared faded and died. The contrast between it and reality was too great. They should have known better from the first, she and David. They should have warned Lucy, guarded her, prepared her for what might come. Compared to this new problem, that of Faith now seemed almost negligible. For while Faith with her normal serenity and deep inner resources would overcome her temporary unhappiness, Lucy's heart was made to soar as a lark to heaven or fall in dying anguish to the earth.

"I never knew life *could* be so hard," Mary moaned as she put the paper where Lucy would not see it. Ah, Lucy, the creature, as David always said, "of spirit, fire and dew." Must the bright fire be quenched? Must the fresh morning dew turn to gall?

She and David talked that night well into the morning. He read the paper and his face grew fixed and still. He too saw the background of the Ross family as he had never even imagined it before. Like Mary he read between the lines and knew that Ninian and the girl Trina had been destined by their parents for each other.

"And of course the Rosses will be able to exert great pressure," he said slowly.

"And Ninian is young. He seems detetrmined and sure of himself, but you see in this case he yielded — he went back."

"He called Lucy on the telephone yesterday," David reminded, clutching at the straw.

"Yes. I only hope he didn't give material for gossip to any listeners. He's not used to a party line. What I heard Lucy say was discreet. Bewitchingly so, I thought. Oh, David, if things go wrong for her I don't know how I can endure it. It's so much harder to bear your children's pain than your own," she ended piteously.

"We may be quite mistaken. I'm not going to doubt Ninian until I have to. I'm sure he loves Lucy and he may stick to her through thick and thin. It's possible he was caught in this Saturday's affair and couldn't extricate himself. I see the dark threats in the whole picture, naturally, but let's try to see a little hope, too." David endeavored to sound convincing.

Mary shook her head sadly. "I'll try," she said, "but I can't help wondering if we've all been living in a fairy tale." A heaviness, in which all the disappointments of her life settled upon her as they had the afternoon she had rebelled against the gift to the missionary, made her voice weak. "I'm afraid it was all too beautiful to be real," she added.

They agreed to say nothing of their fears to Lucy for the time being, so in the following days she was the only gay and care-free person in the house. Faith had told John her decision and now his fine bay mare was seen no longer tied to the manse hitching post; as the normal round of village social events came along, Faith went unattended, or stayed at home. She looked wistful and a little wan, but there was always the refuge of her music to which she applied herself with greater fervor than ever. Jeremy too, seemed in these days unlike himself, but his more serious mien passed for the most part unnoticed in the face of greater anxieties.

For David, there was a new and heavy burden. Oliver Coates had called him into the tinning shop one day as he passed by and with a great air of secrecy tinged with a sort of complacent horror, told him the news of the night before. Mr. Wilson, the schoolmaster, had come home from Greenville the worse for liquor. *Mr. Wilson*, the teacher of the youth, the exemplary citizen, the pillar of community respectability! It was un-thinkable, but Oliver said it was true, and David, knowing the exactness with which Ladykirk men had knowledge of each other, believed it.

"I was down at the livery stable last night," Oliver went on with grave relish. "A bunch of us were sittin' there round the stove when there was a noise at the big door and when Sim opened it there was Mr. Wilson in a hired rig. How he ever got out from Moreswell with his life is beyond me, for he pretty near took the side off the door just drivin' in. He'd been to some kind of a college dinner or something. Left early yester-day morning so's to get there."

Oliver lowered his voice. "He was so drunk we had to fairly pull him out of the buggy. Then Bill Weller and I helped him up home. When Mrs. Wilson opened the door an' saw him, I thought she was goin' to faint. She taught school for him today herself, an' give out he was sick."

David leaned against the counter, feeling as though his own legs would not support him.

"He was talkin' a blue streak when we were helpin' him home. You know how dignified he always is, an' quiet. Well, he wasn't last night. He was singin' some crazy song an' he'd stop an' say, 'Once in my life I cut loose an' damme but it feels good,' he'd say. Then he'd start singin' again. Well, what do you think of that, Mr. Lyall?"

David's voice was heavy. "I'll go to see him, of course," he said. "Meanwhile, I think it shouldn't be talked about."

"*Talked about!*" Oliver cried. "How are you goin' to stop that? There were eight of us down in the livery stable an' saw him come in, an' Wes Shotwell an' at least three women saw us takin' him home! Dear knows how many more heard the singin' an looked out. You know this town!"

"Yes," David echoed sadly, "but I hope the judgment won't be too harsh."

Oliver came close to his pastor. His face was stern.

"You know what I think, Mr. Lyall? I think there's been entirely too much softness an' clemency lately toward those who commit flagrant sins. I think the church has to put a stop to this an' take a firm stand. Look at Minnie Masters! Look at the theft on the Fourth of July. Was anything ever done about that? Just dropped. Look at Ben Losting for that matter. I hear you got the Squire to give him back his gun."

"Only for hunting season," David interjected.

"Well, that's just mollycoddling him. Look at Billy Kinkaid. Still in the church, an' getting drunk whenever he feels like it. Now, it's Mr. Wilson. I say, it's time we had some *discipline*. I'm not satisfied, Mr. Lyall, the way things are goin' in our church an' community. I might as well tell you out plain. I suppose you'll wait upon Mr. Wilson *soon*."

"Yes," said David uneasily. "Yes, of course. Soon."

"Well, get a little iron in your blood before you go. Get a little starch in your backbone. This is a sight worse than Billy Kinkaid's sprees. This is serious to the youth of the town. I think the School Board should take action too. But you let him have it good an' hard, Reverend. He deserves it."

David felt sickened as he left. There was within him along with the shock a great sympathy for Mr. Wilson. Like himself, he had always surmised that the schoolmaster had unfulfilled ambitions. He was not a strong man. Dr. Faraday sounded his chest frequently to make sure. So he had stayed on, as the years passed, in Ladykirk. He had kept up on all the humanities however, and had prepared many boys for college who could not have afforded secondary schooling beforehand. He had helped with Jeremy. Sometimes he had conferred over a bit of classical Latin with David; sometimes they had tossed theories of education back and forth between them. He was one man in the congregation whose eyes David searched for Sunday after Sunday as he preached. He remembered suddenly Mr. Wilson's remark about his sermon on God's approving of joy. Could that have had anything to do with the present downfall and disgrace? Oh, surely not. Yet any relaxing from stiff, accustomed standards was perhaps, after all, dangerous. What a checkered thing was life!

He waited for a week before he left one night with the oil lantern to guide him, and darkness to cover him, for the Wilson home. It was a small, neat brick house that stood back from the street. David, hating himself and his errand, crossed the side porch on leaden feet and knocked upon the door. He had spent most of the afternoon preparing the line of thought his remarks would take. There would have to be first some words of censure (at least serious recognition of the offense) then pastoral counsel and last encouragement in grace, with prayer.

Mr. Wilson opened the door, started, paled, and then unsmilingly invited him in and drew a chair to the grate. Mrs. Wilson, after an embarrassed greeting in which her eyes entreated him, fled precipitously, stumbling over a stool as she did so, to another room. It was all too evident that they sensed the reason for his call.

David sat back in the chair and cleared his throat.

"There's a feel of snow in the air tonight," he remarked.

"I noticed that," said Mr. Wilson.

"I see by the Hagerstown Almanac that we're to have a great deal of it later in the winter."

"You follow the Almanac too?" Mr. Wilson inquired.

They discussed the signs of the zodiac then and their possible effect upon gardening, roof-shingling, weaning calves, etc., for at least fifteen minutes. Then as the subject dropped of itself, David cleared his throat again and thought of his prepared introduction.

He looked up and met Mr. Wilson's stricken eyes. "How are your bees doing?" he suddenly found himself asking.

They talked then of winter feeding, drone traps, wax combs, swarming and the glass box. It was a fruitful topic, for Mr. Wilson was one of the few other men in town who kept bees. When no more could be said, a hard little silence fell. David tried again but the planned words stuck in his throat. "W . . . What are you reading now?" he asked desperately.

It was good to feel the ground of Scott and Thackeray safely beneath their feet. They spoke of their favorites. They challenged each other fiercely on points of style. They tossed in a bit of Dickens for good measure. They laughed together once, forgetting. When David looked at the clock at last, he jumped up in great relief.

"Dear me, it's ten o'clock," he said. "I must go at once. I'm sorry I've stayed so late."

He made a quick movement toward his overcoat.

Mr. Wilson helped him on with it and handed him his hat. His lips were not quite steady.

"I'll meet the Session," he said very low, "whenever you say."

David wrung his hand. His own voice was husky. "I'll let you know," he said, "and don't worry."

At first on the way home he chided himself sharply again for his own weakness, but having done so, he looked up at the stars and slowly began to feel at peace. God himself, knowing all, must pity more than He judged. *Thou art a man and not God; thou art flesh, not an angel.* The words from old Thomas à Kempis had often encouraged him. Surely they applied now to Mr. Wilson.

The time just preceding Christmas was usually the happiest of all the year in the manse. There was very little money to spend on gifts, but there was no lack of gay preparation and of ingenious little surprises. There were young voices singing from morning till night out of sheer exuberance of spirits. . . .

> *Sleighbells sweet go jingle, jingle, jingle,*
> *Frosty ears go tingle, tingle, tingle;*
> *Fires burn bright and hearts beat light*
> *And winter brings us Christmas!*

Then in the evenings there were meetings of all sorts to prepare for the big Sunday School entertainment on Christmas Eve, and before the family went to bed, carols around the piano. It had always been a beautiful time.

But this year as the weeks passed, it was different. Faith was evidently trying with difficulty to keep a front of proud indifference, for John was already beginning to "go with" Seena Harris, daughter of the new miller. Seena was buxom, rosy and self-assured, and was taking a leading place among the older young people of the town. She had a strong soprano voice, which no one but Faith knew was consistently off key, so she was hailed as a great addition to the choir. Faith, therefore, was thrown constantly with her and found her faint patronage hard to bear. For in the eyes of the town in general — and of Seena in particular — it looked as though John had suddenly dropped his attentions to Faith in order to center them upon the new girl.

"I almost wish sometimes I could wear a placard saying that I could have had John if I'd wanted him," Faith said to her mother one day, a little bitterly, for her.

"Never mind, dear. I'm sure Mrs. McLean suspects the real state of affairs and if only a few people do — well, you know how things spread in Ladykirk. Besides, it is only your heart that matters, not your pride, and you don't regret your decision, do you?"

"No," Faith sighed. "I know now more than ever that it was just the attention I liked. I do miss that, though," she added honestly, "but it wouldn't have been fair to keep him dangling any longer. He'll probably marry Seena!" Her voice was flat.

In addition to this, Jeremy, the fount of all high spirits, capers and quips, grew more serious and moody with traces of irritability at times, all out of keeping with his character; while Lucy suddenly stopped singing, "Fires burn bright and hearts beat light," and took to spending long hours in her own room. She had nothing now to say about Ninian. Some months before, she had begged to take over the morning trip to the post office, explaining that she loved getting the first *feel* of The Letters, and David had willingly given in to her request although he had always enjoyed the excuse of the mail for his morning walk. Now, she returned from these daily pilgrimages silent and noncommittal.

So, all in all, the old joyous pre-Christmas atmosphere was lacking and although Mary tried desperately to recreate it, she failed. The fears that she and David had both felt in regard to Ninian multiplied and filled her mind waking and sleeping. She watched Lucy with love-anxious eyes. The child was nervous and pale. She jumped at the slightest noise and the tears sprang when there was no reason for them.

"Is anything troubling you, dear?" Mary finally asked her one day, superfluously enough.

But Lucy only shook her head and went upstairs.

Because she thought she knew the cause of it all, Mary could not bring herself to frame the question, "How is Ninian?" No, she must wait even though her own heart seemed like to break with the fear and suspense.

David, unhappily aware of the clouds that hung over his household, tried to rise above them as he went his normally busy way, and comfort Mary on the side with a stout insistence that all young love had its waxings and wanings, and the reason they, as parents, were so particularly burdened now was because they had three affairs of the heart to consider at once. As to Jeremy's erratic behavior, it might mean that he and Peggy were growing apart a little, and while she was a very nice girl this, if it were true, might be a blessing in disguise, considering the years of study ahead of Jeremy. David reassured Mary on all points, even as he enjoined himself to hope against hope that the tender hearts in their keeping might be spared pain.

One snowy afternoon as he passed Squire Hendrick's home he met Dan Holding, the horse trader, starting back to the office. Dan was a big, handsome man, now past forty, with a thick brown mustache, heavy curly hair and a pair of quick, dark, roving eyes. It was the look in these eyes which made Ladykirk mothers at some time or other issue veiled warnings to their young daughters, and which made even chaste wives and spinsters flush a little and feel an inward trembling as he passed them by on the street, for at every woman, unless she were really old or devoid of all comeliness, Dan looked with his dark, questioning, insolent stare.

Mr. Dilling, who up until the time of Minnie's fate always took a light, even humorous view of the community immoralities, had long ago dubbed him "The Parish Bull." David had never shared the jest. As nearly as he came to loathing a human being, he felt dislike and abhorrence for Dan Holding. For the trader, as he journeyed about the country, buying and selling horses, left tragedy behind.

Then two stricken parents, usually from far back in the hills, would bring a weeping, frightened young girl to the Squire's office to swear to a fact and demand redress. The procedure from then on was to David iniquitously simple. Dan, at the Squire's summons, would swagger one day back to the little office, grin behind his soft, thick mustache, leave the price of a good horse on the Squire's desk and drive off again, considering the matter closed.

Now, David found himself face to face with this man whom Squire Hendrick had evidently called again to come and render account.

"Afternoon, Reverend," Dan drawled, smiling his arrogant, inscrutable smile. "Good winter weather we're havin', eh?"

David felt his blood hot within him.

"Mr. Holding," he said, "have you no conscience, no decency, no *mercy* in you, that you bring trouble and pain to so many hearts? That you persist in your evil ways?" Then he fought down his disgust for the man and spoke quietly. "Mr. Holding, won't you seek the help of God and try to lead a better life? Won't you start coming to church as a beginning? You and your wife?"

Dan looked at him, amused, assured. "Reverend," he said, "my business is horse-tradin'. I've watched that old nag you drive and I've itched to sell you a new one. But I say to myself, No, I won't interfere with the Reverend, till he asks for it. Your business is religion. Now suppose you just wait till I ask for it before you try to sell me any. Fair enough?"

He opened the gate and was halfway up the walk in a moment. David went on, seething within himself. Was the man impenetrable? Was there no way to reach him? He had driven out to the Holding farm times without number through the years to see if by any means he could win Dan to a better way of life. He had always been hampered in anything like a frank discussion of the situation by the presence of Annie, Dan's wife, a woman of faded prettiness and an amazingly sweet smile. It was clear that she worshiped her big, swaggering, handsome husband. It was also clear that she was unaware of the irregularities of his life. Their house was on a lonely wooded road, they had no children, there were no near neighbors. Annie was a shy, quiet creature of the hills; she drove to town once a week with her butter and eggs, chatted a little perhaps with those she met in the store and drove home again to her remote farm. How would she ever know of Dan's misbehavior, David often thought. Who would there be to tell her? So she spoke Dan's name still with a little smile of wonder, as though she marveled that he had chosen her for his own. But, although she looked wistful when David invited her, she never came to church either. Probably because Dan wouldn't allow it.

When David had finished his errands, he saw Dan again, hitching his sleigh in front of Harrison's store. He went up to him through the snow.

"Mr. Holding," he said. "I will stick to the bargain you proposed to me just now, if you will make me one promise."

Dan's black eyes viewed him, considering.

"Well, let's hear it," he said.

"Promise me that if you ever do need me, if I can ever help you in any way, you'll come to me."

Dan's big head was thrown up in amusement and relief.

"Why, that's easy. I guess that promise won't ever give me any trouble. An' how about you doin' the same? If you ever need a new horse, you come to me for it. Fair enough, ain't it?"

David was taken aback. He would certainly not choose to have business dealings with Dan. His reputation was nearly as questionable upon matters of horseflesh as upon morals. But David knew he was fairly caught. Also he felt Prince was good for many years to come.

"I promise you," he said slowly,

Dan grinned widely, saluted with his big, fur-mittened hand and went into the store.

But the news of his latest summons to the Squire's soon spread. It was the thing, David later realized, which precipitated the specially called meeting of the Session. It was Oliver Coates who approached him with the request. The members of the Session, he said, had been doing some private talking on a certain matter and would like to discuss it with him if he would specify a night for the meeting. He called the men at once for the following Saturday night.

When he told Mary she caught her hands at her breast as she did when pleasant excitement overtook her.

"David," she breathed, "do you think they *could* be thinking about putting a bathroom in the manse? You know since Doctor Faraday's and the Wilsons', and Mrs. Crombie's, and now Aunt Betsy's . . . Oh, David do you think it *could* be?"

"I doubt it, dear. Don't get your hopes up. It's probably something about the church. The problem of Minnie again, maybe."

"But to ask for a special meeting! It must be something unusual."

As a matter of fact, the thought of the bathroom had crossed David's mind also, though he would not confess it. He knew Dr. Faraday had mentioned the matter to several Session members, stating that he felt one should be installed now in the manse, but David had heard no more about it. The Christmas season would be an appropriate time, however, for the Session to announce such a magnificent gift. And after all, during his long time of service he had had few raises in salary. And these, small ones. There had been no major improvement in the manse except the furnace eight years ago. He tried to keep his imagination in check, but a certain extra warmth crept into his voice as he greeted the men Saturday night, and ushered them into the study. He spoke cheerfully of the heavy snow, of the coming Christmas services and then, deferring to Oliver Coates, he asked that the matter upon their minds should be presented.

Oliver coughed and Colonel Harrison cleared his throat with embarrassment. There was indeed a rather general recrossing of legs and shifting of facial expression. Suddenly David realized that they did not look like a group of men who had come upon a pleasant errand.

"Well, Mr. Lyall," Oliver began, his thin lips twitching slightly, "we hope you'll accept this criticism in the spirit in which it's given, for you know we all have nothing but the good of our church at heart. But," here he coughed again, "the plain truth is, as I told you, we're not satisfied about the way things are being handled. What I mean is, it looks to us like there's a low state of religion in Ladykirk and nothing's being done about it. We've had too many things happen round here this year, and the church never takin' a firm stand. In the old days there was *discipline*, an' what have we now? Just sermons about God approvin' of happiness an' everybody gettin' into heaven by laughin' or some such thing. That's not what builds people up in their most holy faith, Mr. Lyall."

Oliver had grown more and more heated so that the last sentence fairly burst from him. The other men looked desperately uncomfortable and David was white as death.

"We'll hear now from some of the rest of the members," Oliver said.

There was a silence, then Colonel Harrison leaned forward, his capacious vest wrinkling, and looked over the top of his glasses.

"Now, Mr. Lyall, we don't want to seem critical of you. We all know how faithfully you've served this congregation and this town. The only thing in our minds is that there maybe should be a *little* more firmness, a little more vigor in our efforts. 'Onward, Christian soldiers, marching as to war.' The church militant, you know."

"I feel," said Wes Shotwell, "that mebbe you could put a little more fire in your preachin'. Have some sermons on *predestination* an' *the elect* an' *original sin* an' that. Some good hard theology would mebbe rouse people up some."

"Of course," Lute McLean put in thoughtfully, "as I've told you men before I feel we've all just got a little wrought up over recent happenings and we're forgetting that most folks are living their regular Christian lives as usual. For my part I'm not one to criticize as fine a man as Reverend Lyall on anything, but I said I'd go along with you in the Revival idea."

Oliver then stated the plan they wished to present. "We just thought if we had a good Revival, say early in January just after Week of Prayer, it might stir people up in the church an' shake up the whole town mebbe. You know at Revivals people come from far an' near. We thought we could get the Revivalist to concentrate on special sinners like Ben Losting an' Billy Kinkaid an' *Dan Holding,* for instance. Did you know, Reverend, Dan's been up to his dirty tricks again?"

"I did. I spoke to him on Tuesday when he was in town."

"He told me in the store he'd just made a bargain with you," the Colonel put in. "Said it was a good one. I must say I felt a trifle curious."

"The bargain was," David said slowly, "that if he ever needed me he would come to me and if I ever needed a new horse, I would buy it from him."

The men looked faintly shocked.

"Do we understand then that you are to make no more effort to reform him, to *save his soul?*" the Colonel asked.

David colored furiously, in spite of himself. "I have tried steadily through the years to reach Dan Holding. My visits only seemed to irritate him. I spoke to him again the other day on the matter of reforming his habits and coming to church and he practically told me I was to stop bothering him. Later, not wanting to shut off contact with him, I got him to promise to come to me if I could ever help him. And he added the horse-deal part."

"Well, well," the Colonel said, "well, well, we must trust Mr. Lyall to handle things in his own way. I hear Dan's victim this time is one of the Emlinger girls out on Bill Dowling's tenant farm. Too bad, too bad. Only seventeen, I hear. Dan always gets off light. No judgment can reach him, I guess."

"The judgments of the Lord are true and righteous altogether," David quoted quietly. "We might perhaps leave it with Him."

"Well, meanwhile," Oliver renewed the attack, "what I think is a *Revivalist* might do something where a minister everybody knows so well, I mean everybody's used to, couldn't. Here, as I told Mr. Lyall not long ago, is Minnie Masters — an' Mr. Dilling too, for that matter — never darkenin' a church door, an atheist, almost, an' Billy Kinkaid, an' Ben Losting an' Dan Holding an' the Cuppy boy — I know you won't let that be said, Mr. Lyall, but if the screws had been put on him, I'll bet we'd had that theft solved by this time. An' last of all — Mr. Wilson! Is it any wonder some of us feels we need a stirrin' up of religion in this town?" Oliver's face was glistening again with his earnestness. "I suppose you've been to see Mr. Wilson, Reverend?"

"Yes," said David. "He will come to meet the Session whenever we wish."

"You lit into him, good an' strong?"

David looked at his questioner.

"I spoke, I believe, as the Lord gave me utterance," he said.

"Good."

"And," David went on, "I will begin at once to make arrangements for the Revival. You know my feelings in regard to them. I feel they depend entirely on overstimulated emotions which do not as a rule produce permanent results. But there are exceptions. I will accede now to your wishes and throw myself completely into the plans. I wish to add one thing. I have my own ideals as to the function of a minister of the Gospel. I have tried earnestly to follow these. If at any time you do not . . . do not feel my service here is . . . adequate . . . if you feel it is unsuccessful, I . . ."

An outcry answered him. Lute McLean was angry. "I told you," he said, "that after all he's done for the whole community it was a sin and a shame to bring this thing up the way it was done."

"Now, now," came the Colonel's pacific voice, "you surely know, Mr. Lyall, the standing you have with all of us. What we've said is only a mere suggestion for you to think over in the interest of the church's good. 'I love Thy Kingdom, Lord, the house of Thine abode.' Nothing personal against you. Never!"

They all shook hands warmly and a little shamefacedly. "All we mean is for the Session and the minister to take a firmer stand against all these things that have gone on here."

"You mebbe just have too kind a heart, Reverend, that's all. No offense meant."

"We aren't really *criticizing*, Reverend, you know that. We certainly appreciate all you do for us."

Lute's voice was the last. "It was Oliver Coates stirred up all this hornet's nest and for the love of the Lord, forget it — all but the Revival . . . We've had them before and I suppose we can live through another."

When they were all gone, David sat down before the fire, his hands clenched together. So his professional tragedy was not that he had received no call to a larger church; it was rather that he was proving too small even for Ladykirk. For in spite of their protestations there *had* been criticism. Perhaps it was even abroad in the town. His very soul cringed at this thought. He had felt so secure here. Perhaps even a little condescendingly secure. And now . . .

The door opened softly; Mary entered and came slowly over to him. She touched his shoulder.

"It wasn't . . . the bathroom?"

He shook his head.

"It doesn't seem to matter too much just now. Oh, David, I'm afraid our worst fears are true about Ninian. Lucy broke down utterly an hour ago and told me she hasn't heard a word from him *for two weeks!*"

Chapter Ten

CHRISTMAS was over and the New Year almost upon them and still there was no word from Ninian. With aching hearts and a tenderness greater than they had ever known, David and Mary tried to reason with Lucy. They pointed out to her with gentle honesty that Ninian's station in life was infinitely diverse from her own. "Not above yours," David always put in firmly. "We do not recognize the values that would imply. But *different*. Oh, very, very different."

They forced her to remember the pressure exerted upon him to make him return at Thanksgiving for the reception *and ball*. Mary even brought out the paper with that last utterly damning sentence: *Afterward, the younger guests all went on to the Cotillion at the Hamilton Hotel.* She felt as though she were handling a surgeon's knife as she did so, but drastic measures were necessary. Lucy read it, turned very white and handed the paper back to her mother.

"I'm sure he still loves me," was her only comment.

She begged piteously to be allowed to telephone the Ross home in the city. This was the only point upon which David and Mary forced upon her their parental will. She *must* not do that. She could continue her letters if she wished, but their advice was against this, also. If Ninian still felt for her as she insisted he did, then he would assuredly get in touch with her. If — and here the sight of Lucy's eyes upon them always made the words stick in their throats — if he should have changed in his intentions under great stress of family influence, then she must accept the fact, try to put him out of her thoughts and remember only the pleasant part of their friendship, etc., etc. After all, it had covered only a few months and they were both very young, and as time passed she would find other interests and forget. . . .

Oh, the empty worn-out words that parents' tongues have framed from time out of mind as they try to cry down young love and bury its warmth under the cold snow of reason! So David and Mary felt as they watched Lucy's still face turned upon them in sad disillusionment, not for her own heart but for theirs that they could doubt.

David had to thrust aside the heaviness of family burdens as he gave himself up to his work. He had been, according to popular opinion, very fortunate in securing Mr. Homer Turbenroth to conduct revival services during the last week of January. Mr. Turbenroth's efforts, so the folders regarding his work stated, had been signally blessed. In Moreswell, crowds had thronged to hear him and the number of converts had been beyond all expectation. In Statetown, Rushville and Waverly the churches could scarcely contain the people. There were testimonials from pastors and laymen and converts alike; he was described by one as a "fisher of men who came up with a full net every time." David's eyebrows quirked slightly over this summary as he studied the photograph of Mr. Turbenroth which occupied considerable space in the folder. It showed a man of large physique and heavy waving hair who was looking forcefully into the camera, chin extended.

David had consulted with Dr. Digbee of Rushville as to the

Revivalist's qualifications. Dr. Digbee reported that the latter's meetings there had packed the church and it was felt that a number of souls had been saved. David, therefore, proceeded to engage him, the Session agreeing with unusual alacrity to pay the fifty dollars *and expenses* which constituted his fee. It was arranged among them that he would be lodged at the home of Mrs. Crombie who enjoyed displaying her large house and elegantly furnished guest rooms. She offered to give him his breakfasts also and for the other meals he would be the guest of the minister and the church officers. So, they reasoned, there would be no expense except the fifty dollars, which, while high, would be an investment, so Oliver Coates said, in ransomed souls.

On a gray Monday, David sat at his desk preparing *The Annual Narrative of the State of Religion of the Presbyterian Church of Ladykirk*. This document, sent out each year at this time by Presbytery to be filled in and returned thither, somehow made David's heart heavier than it already was because of one item upon it. For the most part the answers to the questions were simple enough.

Has your church been supplied with preaching during the year? Yes. Is the attendance good? Yes, except in bad weather. Are the children and youth generally present at the Lord's Day public services? Yes. Is the condition of the Sunday School good? Yes. Is the Shorter Cathechism regularly taught? Yes.

Then came the question which had disturbed David each time he had made the report during all his twenty-odd years in Ladykirk.

Has there been any *unusual* interest in religion in the congregation?

David leaned back in his chair now, thinking. He was seeing the faces of his people as he looked down upon them, Sunday after Sunday. There was old Mr. Collins, long an Elder, now resigned because of the infirmities of age. Whenever he was able to be at Wednesday night Prayer Meeting, David always called upon him to pray. Mr. Collins was a Scot and the accent of his boyhood still clung softly to his speech. He prayed with his white head raised, his closed eyes seeing an inner vision of grace. He always ended with the same words. "And now, Lord, what wait we for? Our hope and our trust is in Thee."

David saw Miss Margaret Trask. He saw her strong, noble, lined face raised to his in holy expectation, Sunday after Sunday. She had, according to Mary, worn the same black bonnet for more than ten years. When her brother in the city sent her five dollars for a new one, and whatever else her woman's soul might crave, she had put the bill in the collection basket at Missionary Meeting. When Mary's intuition had penetrated the secret, she had remonstrated with the giver. "Why, my dear," Miss Margaret had answered gently, "I don't in the least need a new bonnet and they do need the money so *Out There*." He thought now of Miss Margaret.

He thought of dozens of others, good, kindly people, doing their humble duty day by day, as they saw it, sometimes against great odds. There was nothing dramatic, nothing spectacular about it. Just the patient perseverance of the saints. He read the question once more. Has there been any unusual interest in religion in the congregation? Then he wrote again, honestly, as each year: Nothing unusual.

The annual Week of Prayer passed uneventfully with no guest preachers at the services since the Revival would follow so soon. David, working upon his daily talks, sometimes far into the night, put forth an earnest effort at first to inject into them a note of theological threat. He was not pleased with the results (though Oliver Coates complimented him once with a "That's more like it, Reverend!") and always announced a closing hymn like *There's a Wideness in God's Mercy*, or *Softly and Tenderly Jesus is Calling*, to counteract the effect. Before the week was out he was preaching in his own style and from the heart.

The heaviest snow of the winter fell in the second week of January. It shut the little town securely in between its white hills. The blue smoke curled in clouds from every chimney, grate fires blazed high while great drifts lined the streets. The chime of sleigh bells and the heavier clang from the big farm sleds with their accompanying creak and rumble could be heard every hour of the day. There was, David noted, a subtle undercurrent of pleased anticipation abroad in connection with the coming Revival. It made the women feel almost gay to realize that in this month there would be not only Reading Circle for the elect who belonged to that group, an *Elocutionist*, presented as the third number of the Lecture Course in Harrison's Hall, but also seven meetings to which all the girls could wear their new hoods, hats or fascinators as the case might be and the good mothers in Israel their best bonnets and capes. There would be for seven nights Some Place To Go, where not only familiar but strange faces could be seen and where at the outer church door, rows of young men would wait to see the young ladies home. There would be emotional excitement, too, in the songs, and in the exhorting of the Revivalist. There would be the quivering, constant wonder as to which human brands might be snatched from the burning. Even the men around the postoffice stove or in the livery stable and blacksmith shop talked constantly of the Revival.

David, with his unfailing insight, knew all this and understood. In the manse itself Faith was feverishly trying to finish crocheting a red fascinator, which with a large bow on the top and its ends open and lying gracefully about her shoulders, would be a copy of the one Seena Harris was already wearing, and would be very noticeable indeed in the choir during the meetings. So were the little vanities of the flesh linked with the larger affairs of the spirit.

David himself was not exempt from this warring of the members. While he strove earnestly to make preparations for the Revival, he wrestled in prayer daily over his own weaknesses. For he *had* felt keenly the criticism directed at his sermons and his general pastoral work even though he knew it had stemmed from one Elder in particular. His pride was deeply wounded and for the first time in the years he wondered as he walked the familiar streets if the steady flow of village conversation was centered in any censorious manner upon him. He struggled against dark thoughts which crossed his consciousness with an unholy stain: the hope that the Revival would be a failure; the fear that Homer Turgenroth would convert those for whom he, David, had worked and striven for years, and thereby receive for it all the glory. Against these unworthy but extremely human reactions, David wrestled in an agony of remorse. "I am man and not God," he pleaded. "I am flesh, not an angel." Then he set himself earnestly to devise new ways to insure the success of the Revival.

One of these was the music. At his instigation the choir was now practicing three nights a week to prepare special selections. Another idea he had which the Session approved with interest was that of having *ushers* at the meetings. This would be a distinct innovation and would lend a certain air of dignity to the occasions. There would be many strangers present, and the basement would in all likelihood be crowded, so ushers would be useful as well as impressive. David's suggestion was to have the older teen-age boys act in this capacity, thus insuring their presence and also that of their whole group. He named Oliver Coates, Junior, as Captain, not, as he told himself sternly, as a stroke of diplomacy, but because young Oliver was the most serious and conscientious lad about town. David had always, indeed, felt an instinctive pity for the boy, who, apparently overborne by his father's strictness, seemed to have little normal life or spirit of his own.

When young Oliver was first approached on the matter of

heading the band of ushers he refused with something like actual fright. He was a tall, thin boy, with pasty cheeks and large, wistful eyes behind spectacles. David did not urge him, sensing the real embarrassment beneath his words, but later Oliver Senior told him quite definitely that his son would serve. He appeared, then, with the others at the practice sessions David held with them after school in the church. Another group of young people met in the study night after night to address the printed notices of the Revival, done by the Newburt twins, which were then mailed far and wide to all members of the Community, not forgetting Ben Losting and Dan Holding!

As he lay down to sleep one night David told Mary wearily that he felt he had done all he could at that point for the meetings and had decided to relax for a day or two and forget the arduous time yet to come.

And it was the next morning that Lucy was gone!

In the rush of getting Jeremy off to his school, Mary had done no more than call the girls to breakfast. Faith had appeared as the rest were finishing; then Jeremy, a little belated, had forgotten his lunch and returned in a whirl to get it; Mary had had a lengthy telephone call about the coming program for Reading Circle, David had settled in the study for an hour's reading, Faith had gone on to her practicing and so it was nearly nine, and the little branch train long since gone its whistling, lurching way through the woods when it was discovered that Lucy was not in her room. The note pinned to her pillow was a model of brevity:

Don't be angry for I have to go and please
don't come after me.

It had seemed strange to Lucy during those last days that the burning decision in her heart did not show through her flesh and tell them all of her intent. For when the fourth week of

Ninian's silence began, she knew she could wait no longer. Something had happened, but not what her parents thought. Never, even in the strange, sleepless hours of darkness, did Lucy doubt her lover. To her it was quite simply incredible that he would change; or that he would leave the wild, despairing questioning of her letters unanswered, if he were able to hold a pen. *Something had happened to Ninian.* She had waited long enough now, too long. She must go to him and find out for herself.

It was her first great subterfuge. She was distressed to deceive but determined upon the necessity. So, she abstracted the small black valise which David used when he went to Presbytery, from his closet, bringing it to her own. In it she laid the few articles of underwear she deemed necessary. She asked Mary to sponge and press her garnet cashmere, ostensibly to be ready for the Revival meetings. She added to the valise a ruffled white apron, her best, in case she *would* need it; she had borrowed two dollars from Jeremy, vaguely mentioning a *surprise*, and thus equipped, slipped down the stairs this morning when she saw from the landing that the others were at the breakfast table and, almost suffocated by the beating of her heart, hurried out and along the snowy street. She caught a ride over the bridge with Josiah Hunt, and managed to purchase her ticket and get on the icy steps of the train in a steamy cloud just as it was leaving. She sat, hunched very low, in a rear seat, hoping no one would take special notice of her. As it happened, no one did.

The train was sickeningly hot after the frosty air outside and Lucy's head felt very heavy. She tried not to think of the manse as she finally reached Moreswell, and managed by means of constant interrogation to get on the city train. There, surrounded by wholly unknown companions, she felt both better and worse than she had before. She was safe from prying comment, but she was in a strange world, going she knew not where.

She sat up very straight now, and tried to look like an experienced traveler. She wore with her black coat and small felt hat her precious Christmas gift which her mother had made for her. Mary, torn by her child's distress, had taken from its careful storage Grandmother's seal-skin coat, which she herself had worn until the bare spots became too prominent and then laid away, intending to have a cape made sometime when she could afford it. But the present need to brighten Christmas had been too great. So, with skillful fingers she had fashioned for Lucy, from part of it, a small muff, lined with bright red silk from Harrison's counter. It added a touch of elegance now to her otherwise simple costume, and the feel of the soft fur was comforting. She stroked the muff and tried to decide what to do when she reached the city. Written carefully on a paper in her pocketbook was the address of the Ross home. This she must find if she had to walk the streets all day to do so.

She got off the train somewhat shakily, carrying the small valise, and followed the crowd into the great station where she felt completely lost and alone. She began to realize, too, that she had had no breakfast. A glimpse of a large restaurant to one side of the main waiting room sent through her a gnawing ache, but she looked the other way resolutely, uncertain as to how her funds would hold out.

"They'll surely give me something to eat when I get there," she murmured to herself.

She inquired of many people in the passing crowd how to reach the address on the paper slip, but all, though kindly, told her they were strangers too. One man at last looked with concern into her anxious young eyes, and taking her by the arm, piloted her to the street where he signaled a policeman. The officer was full of knowledge. She would take the streetcar there — he would put her on it himself — and ride to the end of that line. Then she would get another trolley, and it would take her to the avenue she wanted, whereupon she would walk until she found the right number.

"You're goin' out where the big bugs live, sissy, so it's goin' to take you a little while to get there."

He was right. The route seemed endless, as she carefully followed her directions. Little by little the ordinary dwellings melted away, the streets became wider, spreading white lawns appeared with glimpses of stone mansions showing behind trees. When she left the second trolley and began the final search she found that the spacious lawns had become wooded estates. She was very tired but she trudged on, changing hands frequently so that one could warm itself in the muff while the other carried the valise. She watched now with an ever increasing tension for the numbers on the entrances. She was beginning to feel very cold and a little lightheaded when she came at last to two great stone lions on either side of a driveway. Below them on matching blocks of stone were carved the words *Craigie Hill.* Lucy leaned for a minute against the nearest lion to breathe her relief and muster her courage, and then began the last long walk to the house.

If she had not been so frightened and so utterly weary she would have paused to feast her eyes upon the magnificence of the snowy grounds and the palatial structure itself. As it was she ascended the wide stone steps, reached the front door and rang the bell, with scarcely a glance about her. It seemed a long time before the door opened. A tall, serious old man in a black suit stood there and looked down a long nose at her and her little black satchel.

"If you're selling something, Miss, you should go around the side drive to the servants' entrance," he said.

Lucy's chilled and anxious face suddenly broke into a smile.

"You really thought I was selling something — *books*, maybe?" she asked.

"I assumed so, Miss."

"Well, I'm not," she assured him with a small laugh, "but it's so very funny that you should think so. Are you Mr. Ross?"

"No, Miss," the nose growing longer, "I am the butler. Mr. Ross is not in."

"Ninian . . ." Lucy said, her voice unsteady now, "is Ninian at home?"

A change came over the old man's face. "You know Mr. Ninian?" he asked.

"Oh, very, *very* well, but I've been so anxious lately, I . . . I had to come. Is he . . . ?"

He opened the door wider and took the satchel from her.

"Won't you step in, Miss? You must be chilled through, this cold day. Just come on down to our sitting room and the wife will give you a cup of tea."

She followed him blindly through the great hall and finally downstairs to a cozy room where she sank, quite forlorn, in a chair he set for her. Her lips trembled so she could barely frame the question, but she must.

"Ninian," she said, "is . . . is he all right?"

"He's been ill, Miss, very ill these weeks back. It's typhoid. Something awful it's been."

"Is he . . . better?"

"Aye, a little, maybe, the last few days, but it's been touch and go, I'll tell you."

Lucy suddenly leaned her head back while the color left her face and the room roared and grew dark.

"Quick, Maggie, the child's in a faint." The words came dimly. "Bring some tea. . . . Watch her now. I'll get a bit brandy to put in it."

Lucy felt someone loosening the coat collar, chafing her hands, putting a cup to her lips. She sipped obediently and slowly began to feel warm again. The room righted itself and she saw a short, plump woman with gray hair and a kind face moving about her.

"There now," she was saying, "you'll just be starved with

the cold likely. Sup up the rest of your tea and you'll feel better. Could you eat a bit scone, think you?"

"I had no breakfast," Lucy said feebly.

"Oo-aye, that's it, then. Saunders, she's had nothing to eat! Fancy! Fetch her a tray. There's scones still in the oven, and oatmeal in the pan. Just give it a warm and hurry up about it."

But before she ate Lucy had to ask again. "Is he really better? Is he going to get well?" Her heart stopped as she waited.

It was the man Saunders who answered as he brought the tray.

"There's a bit more life in him the last day or so, the doctor says. But the danger's not clear past yet. . . ."

The woman spoke up strongly, giving him a sharp look. "Of course he's better! Didn't one of the nurses say yesterday that in her opeenion he'd turned the corner? *Sair*-tenly he'll do well from now on. Make a good breakfast, Miss, and you'll feel stronger. Then we'll see . . ."

She looked questioningly at her husband and then went out to the kitchen with him leaving Lucy to finish the scones and marmalade alone. She was still half stunned by the extremity of the news, with only the small hope lightening it. Ninian sick unto death and she never knowing! Only her heart had warned her truly. What if she had not listened to it, even now?

When Saunders and Maggie, his wife, returned, they seemed embarrassed and hesitant.

"Would you be the little lady Mr. Ninian's been out to see at Ladykirk?" Saunders asked.

"Yes," she said eagerly. "I'm Lucy Lyall. Has he told you of me?"

"Well, he sort of mentioned it once, secret-like, to Maggie and me. We don't know how to put it to you, Miss, but it may be a little surprise to Mr. and Mrs. Ross that you've come. You see they're both pretty busy and just now with Mr. Ninian so sick and all . . ."

Lucy was naïve but not obtuse.

"I understand," she said with dignity. "I knew before I came how they might feel, but I had to find out about Ninian. And oh, I'm *so* glad I came, no matter whether they think it's odd of me or not. Could you take me to him now? You think I can see him, don't you?"

The old couple looked at each other again.

"It's them domned nurses — excuse me, Miss — but they're bossy from the word go. I think maybe your best plan is to . . ."

"Speak to Mr. Ross, himself. He'll be here shortly for his lunch. Mrs. Ross has hers in her boodwar so she won't be down. We want to help you, Miss, and if you . . . if things get . . . I mean if you want anything you can always slip down here and Saunders and me will . . ."

"That we will, Miss, and don't fash yourself now, more than you can help. Maybe she'd like a bit wash-up, Maggie?"

When Lucy had made herself fresh and recombed her hair she ascended the stairs again with Saunders and was left to wait alone in what he called the "back library," for the arrival of Mr. Ross. It was a room she would at any other time have enjoyed, with the walls filled with books — rather unused looking, Lucy thought — a handsomely carved desk and table and large leather fireside chairs in one of which she tried to fit her slender form. Saunders turned up the gas in the fireplace and withdrew while oppression fell upon Lucy. She held her hands tightly together and prayed incoherent little prayers that Ninian might soon be better, that she might see him, that Mr. Ross would not be too stern with her, that she might say the right thing when he came. . . .

When he did come, she was startled, for there had been no sound of footsteps on the thick carpet. She was leaning forward, her head on her hands, when she heard a quick voice.

"Miss Lyall?"

She started up, seeing a heavy-set man with gray burnsides and mustache looking at her with a rather distant and expressionless stare.

"Yes," she said, her voice shaking from fright. "I know it seems strange for me to come. . . . Father and Mother wouldn't even allow me to telephone because they felt it would look undignified . . . but I *had* to find out, Mr. Ross. I knew something had happened to Ninian when he didn't write and I couldn't stand it any longer."

"Sit down, Miss Lyall," the big man said in his clipped voice. "I have, of course, heard your name from my son, but we did not deem it necessary to inform you of his illness." He sat opposite her, looking off above her head as though considering. "Certainly not to send for you," he added, not exactly unkindly, but distantly.

Lucy leaned toward him. "It doesn't matter about me," she said, "but is he really better? Is he out of danger now?"

He looked at her then, very keenly indeed, for Lucy's eyes were brimming and her whole tender young face full of tragic intensity.

"We are not sure," he said more slowly. "We have at least strong hope now. He has been very, very ill."

"But has he not *asked* for me?" Lucy said piteously.

"Not to my knowledge. He has been delirious much of the time. Most of what he said was unintelligible and wild. About his studies chiefly and a dove. That seemed to be an obsession. The doctor says often in these cases some unusual object . . ."

"But that was *me*," Lucy cried out. "Oh, it's so terrible that I didn't come sooner, or you didn't send for me. That's what he calls me in his letters or when we're alone. I've never even told Mother and Father. It's been a secret between us. It's from the Lucy poem, you know."

"I'm afraid I don't understand."

Lucy's face had the luminous quality now which often fell upon it.

"You see, Father loves poetry so, and he named me out of Wordsworth. And when Ninian knew, he wanted to see all the Lucy poems so we read them together one day last summer out in the woods and when we came to that one — don't you remember? —

She dwelt among the untrodden ways
Beside the springs of Dove.

He said, 'that's what I'll always call you to myself — Dove.' He . . . he said it suited me. Please don't tell this to anyone else, for it's something just between Ninian and me, but oh, Mr. Ross, couldn't you take me up to see him right away? We've wasted too much time as it is."

She had sprung to her feet and he slowly rose to his. He was regarding her with a strange look, amazed but certainly not cold or distant any longer.

"Perhaps you are right," he said gravely. "Just follow me."

They went up wide, curving stairs, soft to the foot, along halls that seemed endless and stopped at last before a door.

"You must be prepared for a shock," he whispered. "Ninian is quite emaciated, and he may not recognize you."

He pushed the door open a little way and an elderly nurse appeared at once. She looked askance at Lucy and was starting to speak when Mr. Ross beckoned her aside with a gesture of authority.

When Lucy saw the face on the pillow, she suddenly felt very sick, for it was wasted to the bones and the closed eyelids seemed to cover sunken pits. She set her lips tightly and took a long breath, then advanced to the bed. All at once the sickness eased and she thought only of the fact that the long separation and uncertainty were over.

"Ninian," she spoke softly, "Ninian, I've come to see you."

His eyes opened. He looked at her without expression as though too often before he had dreamed and wakened to find no substance.

She reached out and took his thin fingers in her own, while he watched her still with no light of recognition — rather, a sad startled distrust of his own senses. She went on speaking.

"I couldn't endure it any longer, not knowing what had happened to you. So I came this morning to find out. You know me, don't you?"

She leaned over and whispered in his ear, and then smiled at him. Suddenly his poor lips moved. A light came into his eyes.

"It's really *you?*" he said weakly.

"Really and truly. Would you like me to sit beside you for a little?"

"Yes. Oh, please stay." And he smiled at her with sudden content. "Don't leave me."

It was that painful, twisted smile, the first in all the weeks, which made the nurse look keenly at her patient and caused Mr. Ross to blow his nose, mutedly, at the foot of the bed.

Lucy sat down, still holding the thin hand in her own.

"I think," she said over her shoulder with sweet assurance, "he'll get well quite fast, now."

Mr. Ross motioned the nurse to his side and spoke in low tones.

"I will have Saunders bring some lunch up for Miss Lyall to the sitting room. If she wishes, I think she should stay with the boy this afternoon."

The nurse's face was firm.

"I do not feel that is wise, Mr. Ross. It may only excite him and put too much tax on his strength just now. I cannot be responsible for the results of having a stranger in the room."

Lucy, glancing up in fright, saw an expression on Mr. Ross's face which she felt she would not care to have turned upon her.

"I will take the responsibility, Miss Davis. You will see, please, that Miss Lyall is treated with every consideration. When does the doctor come next?"

"This afternoon at three."

"I will be downstairs to speak to him at that time."

He gave a slight signal of the hand to Lucy and left. The door was closed and the nurse sat down at the desk. Ninian lay watching his love.

"Talk to me," he whispered.

So she talked gently (trying to forget the presence of Miss Davis) about all the manse family; of her trip in and how she would have missed the train if Josiah Hunt had not picked her up near the bridge; she told how Jeremy had upset in a snow-drift one morning as he drove to school in the sleigh. Ninian smiled again at that, and then lay with his eyes closed, clinging to her hand, sometimes speaking her name and listening until she said, "I'm here."

He had fallen asleep by the time Saunders brought her lunch up to Ninian's sitting room. He waited there until she came in.

"I thought I'd tell you, Miss, your father telephoned and I took the great liberty of talking to him myself, you and Mr. Ross being up here at the time. I told him of Mr. Ninian's illness and that you had arrived here safely and we would see you were well looked after and you would probably call him yourself, later on."

"Oh, thank you, Mr. Saunders!"

"Just *Saunders*, if you please, Miss, and my wife is *Maggie*.

If at any time you want anything, you have just to press any of the bells that says B above it. You'll find them all over the house. Like this," he added, pointing to the small row of buttons beside the door. "Now is there anything more I can do for you, Miss?"

Lucy came close to him. "There is something I would like to ask, if I may. Where is Mrs. Ross? Is she not at home?"

Saunders paused before he replied. "Aye, she's at home, Miss, but she spends a deal of time in her own private soote of rooms. She's been worn out some over Mr. Ninian, so she has most of her meals to herself up there."

"Oughtn't I to go to see her or something?" Lucy asked anxiously. "It seems strange for me to be here and not even to have met her yet."

Saunders slowly shook his gray head.

"If I was you I wouldn't fash myself over it just now. She knows you're here and when she's ready she'll greet you. Just mind me and Maggie will do anything for you. We're that fond of Mr. Ninian, and we're glad you came, Miss."

When she returned to the sickroom she found two nurses there, the older woman and a very pretty young one with a huge golden pompadour. Lucy had an instant feeling that the latter disapproved of her presence more even than Miss Davis had done. They glanced her way and went on conferring in low tones. Then Miss Davis left, and the young one took rather ostentatious charge. When she bent over Ninian she smiled extravagantly, supporting him in her arms, her head very close to his as she gave him his medicine.

"Where's Lucy?" he asked.

"Here I am," she spoke quickly while the smile upon the golden one faded at once. She sat again close to the bed, until the doctor came at three. She liked him on sight, for he reminded her of Dr. Faraday at home.

"So," he said, extending his hand to Lucy, "there are medicines that are not put up in bottles, eh? Sometimes they work wonders, too. Now, let's have a look at our patient. Maybe you will be good enough to wait in the sitting room until I have finished here and then I'll come and talk to you."

When he came, his face was more serious than it had been at Ninian's bedside.

"He's been a very sick young man," he said, "and we're not entirely out of the woods yet, but we're coming that way. The great problem now is care and nourishment, and we have three good nurses on the case. He must be kept quiet and yet peaceful and happy. He must be coaxed to eat what is prescribed. I think perhaps you can help us. He's been a very violent and distraught patient until his strength gave out. Even since that he's been too restless. I have a sort of idea" — he paused smiling — "that he is going to be more relaxed from now on. You can stay for some time, I hope?"

"If Mr. and Mrs. Ross will have me. I . . . I think Ninian would like me to."

"I am not surprised," the doctor smiled, "and from my conversation with Mr. Ross just now I think he is very willing to try this new cure. So I'll expect to find you here."

Lucy looked up anxiously. "The nurses seem to feel I'm rather in the way, or something."

He patted her shoulder. "Don't mind that, my dear. Just keep Ninian happy. Nurses never think family or sweethearts belong in a sickroom. But we doctors know professional care isn't everything, no matter how good it is. So, you just do your part and let them do theirs. Among us we ought to get results, eh?"

He went back to Ninian's room and she heard him talking to the golden-pompadoured nurse in firm tones. Then they both appeared at the door.

"Miss Lyall, this is Miss Cosgrove. I've suggested she let you try to give our young gentleman his broth. Good day now, to you both."

By five-thirty, Lucy was very, very tired, if triumphant. Ninian had had a long nap, had taken all his broth, and had told her in his weak voice that he felt better! When she rose at a summons from the hall, she explained to him that she was staying in the house and would see him later on after he had another sleep. He understood and was, apparently, content.

She found Saunders waiting outside the door with her valise in his hand.

"I'll show you to your room, Miss, and Mr. Ross says to tell you dinner is at seven and he will be pleased to have you join him. Mrs. Ross will not be down."

He led the way up and down thick-carpeted halls, their walls lined with heavy oil paintings.

"I'm afraid I'll not find my way," Lucy said anxiously. "It's such a *very* large house."

"Here we are, Miss. It's the wee guest soote we're putting you in, for it's more cozy, like. Just make yourself at home now and would you be wanting Jennie, the upstairs girl, to help you unpack?" He glanced at the small and very light bag in his hand. "Or maybe you'd just rather settle yourself, belike?"

"I think so, Saunders. Oh, what a lovely place!"

He lighted the gas fire and the lights on the wall. The elegant little room glowed with rose and gold. He opened the inner door to show the bedroom beyond and another to reveal the immaculate white wonder of a bathroom. A private one!

"Just for me?" Lucy gasped. "I can't believe it! You see at home we don't have one *at all*. It's Mother's great dream, but we really never expect it to come true. Oh, if she could only see this!"

"In small towns," Saunders said hastily, "everything's different like. I'll show you how to work the faucets."

When she was alone, Lucy looked her fill at the luxury about her, and then almost without volition of her own, dropped upon the bed and fell instantly to sleep. The knocking on the door at last had to be very loud to wake her.

"It's seven, Miss, and Mr. Ross sent me to fetch you to dinner," Saunders was repeating.

It was a very nervous Lucy who followed him downstairs, after her hasty toilette. Mr. Ross met her in the lower hall and escorted her to the dining room, where he seated her beside him; and Lucy, seeing the great table glittering with silver and candles, could, at first, not speak at all.

Little by little, however, she regained composure and made a few timid remarks. Mr. Ross asked about Ninian, seemed pleased with the reports he had heard, and volunteered a few general comments of his own. It was on the whole, though, a silent meal and Lucy would fain have taken refuge in conversation with Saunders as he waited upon them. Her only attempt in this direction, however, was abortive as Saunders' face froze to such an alarming degree that she realized she had made a mistake.

When dessert was finished, Mr. Ross rose. "Will you come into the library, Miss Lyall?" he said. "I should like to talk to you."

It was hard to bear the fright she felt all alone, and the ghastly burden of being disapproved of. But there was a gentle dauntlessness about her, as she went with him. She had done no wrong; perhaps she had even done Ninian good already; she would fight for her love if that must be.

Saunders brought coffee in small cups, turned up the gas in the fireplace, rearranged the lights to Mr. Ross's satisfaction and withdrew the comfort of his presence. Mr. Ross lighted a long stogie, asking her perfunctorily as he did so if she minded tobacco smoke, and then settling back in his chair, studied her. Lucy, with a completely untaught wisdom, forestalled what she felt was coming by speaking first.

"I know," she said, "just how you must feel about me, and about my coming here without being invited. I am very much embarrassed, but I've explained to you why I had to do it. Besides that, though, I know you and Mrs. Ross may think I'm all wrong for Ninian."

The man in the chair looked startled. But Lucy went on before he could speak.

"When I didn't hear from him for so long Father and Mother tried to explain to me what could have happened. They said you probably wanted him to fall in love with a girl you knew and that maybe you had persuaded him to give me up. Father said his station in life was so different from mine. *Not above mine*," Lucy's lovely young face took on something of David's own dignity as she repeated this, "but very different. And I want you to know I understand that."

Mr. Ross had removed his stogie and was looking at her fixedly.

"When your parents pointed out these facts to you, do you mean to say you did not doubt Ninian's . . . ah . . . attachment for you?"

Lucy smiled at the absurdity of the question.

"Why, how could I? We love each other, Mr. Ross. It's forever, you know, when you love the way we do."

The man's eyes dropped before the beautiful light in hers. He sat quiet for a few moments as though considering.

"Suppose," he said, "that you start at the beginning and tell me all about it. How you and Ninian met . . ."

"Oh," Lucy's laugh rang deliciously through the room. "You don't know about that?"

"No, I know very little about any of it, indeed. Tell me in your own way. Of that, and your family and your life in general. About what you do when Ninian visits you. All that."

Lucy was suddenly at ease and smiling. "I'd love to," she said. "I'll tell you everything."

And she did. Beginning with the day she had been painting the black rocker under the pine tree and had rushed out to intercept the imagined bookseller. She told him just as they came to her mind, many things: the Festival and how Ninian and Jeremy had serenaded them that night when it was all over; how brave Father had been with Ben Losting and the theft of the ten dollars which Ninian had ultimately made up "because it was such a *dreadful* loss"; the picnics in the woods; the *sings* on the back porch or around the piano; Thanksgiving Day and Miss Tilly and how Ninian's laughing as he saw her coming up the walk had made them all forget their disappointment and see the funny side of it. She interpolated innocently as she went along much revealing information: how worried she had been over the parlor carpet, for example, before Ninian's first real visit and how Father had comforted her.

"And now," she told her listener happily, "I never think of things like that at all because . . . it's strange when he has been used to all this," she gestured at the luxury about her, "but he says our house is *beautiful!*"

The man watching her did not reply, but his eyes, to Lucy, looked suddenly very tired and sad.

She went on then, as brightly as she could, searching for something that might cheer him. She told of their call on Aunt Betsy and the story of the sheep and he smiled, at least, over that. She described the family, each one — Faith and Jeremy and Father and his work. When she was speaking of Mother she told of her little muff and how it had been the only bright spot for her in the whole dark Christmas.

"It's the loveliest thing I've ever had," she told him, "except this, of course."

She went over to him quickly and showed him the locket, opening it to reveal the picture. Mr. Ross touched it, nodded, but did not speak.

"Mother and Father thought it was maybe too valuable for me to accept. You see — you won't think me rude, will you? — the one thing that has kept me from being *perfectly* happy with Ninian is the thought that he's . . . that you're . . . I mean, the money. It *is* a sort of barrier. When I first knew about it I wished so much he had been really selling books, like Jeremy. There would have been no problems then." She sighed.

"I can't think of anything else to say. Oh, yes, there is something. I'll tell you about it because Ninian says it's the nicest story he ever heard in all his life."

She told him, then, the whole episode of the kitchen cabinet.

When she had finished finally, quoting the last lines (which she had particularly liked and remembered) of Father's birthday poem, she, too, sat silent, waiting. Mr. Ross, whose stogie had long since been laid aside, rose and walked over to the fireplace. He pulled out his handkerchief and Lucy thought with some dismay that he was wiping his eyes. This she could not understand, for she felt that on the whole her narrative had been very cheerful. After what seemed a long time he turned, came close to her and laid his hand gently on the top of her brown curls.

"My child," he said, "you have transported me to a world of which, sadly enough, I know little. Would that I did! But if some day you and Ninian . . . " He stopped while Lucy ceased to breathe. "There will be a great deal to talk over later on, and I'm sure you will both be patient, and do nothing in haste."

"But you mean you really don't mind his being in love with me, then? You don't want anyone else for him?"

He looked into her bright, eager eyes.

"You have beauty, Lucy, but you have something much more important. You have strength of character — that was shown by your coming here — and you have a loving, gentle heart. What more could I ask for my son?"

Lucy rose then and caught his hands in her own.

"I'll make him so happy and . . ." still seeing the sadness in his eyes, "I'll try to make you happy too."

Then, she didn't know how it happened, whether she reached up or he reached down, but they kissed, she and Ninian's father!

"You'd better run along to your room now, and get some rest," he said quickly. "You've had a long day."

He walked with her to the stairway and stood there, watching as she climbed them. At the landing she paused for a bright wave of her hand. She did not know it but Mr. Ross watched until the last fleck of the garnet cashmere was out of sight. Then, slowly, he walked through the great, empty downstairs, looking into first this room and then that. At last he went back to the library and sitting down, began to think over, as a traveler might recall enchanting foreign scenes, all that Lucy had told him.

Meanwhile she had slipped into Ninian's room, and after a grudging permission from the nurse, had gone close to the bed. He was awake, as though waiting. A long, peaceful sigh escaped him.

"I didn't dream you?" he said, smiling.

She leaned over him.

"I'm as real as real and *so* happy. I've had a talk with your father and oh, Ninian, I think he likes me!"

"As if he could help it!" But she could see the sudden pleasure in his eyes.

"And now I'm going to bed. I have the little guest-room suite and it's like a storybook. You must try to get a good sleep and I'll be in to see you the first thing after breakfast and stay all day if you wish. How do you feel tonight?"

"Oh, better. I love you!"

Their voices were very low. Lucy smoothed his hair with a tender hand.

"Good night, Ninian."

"Good night, Dove."

Once back in her *wee soote*, Lucy gave herself over to warm delight. The dark fears of the morning only accented the present rapturous relief. There was only one marring trifle, which increasingly made itself felt. She looked for the row of little buttons and found them next the outer door. It was most bold of her, but her happiness gave her courage. She pressed B with a quick-beating heart, and waited. It seemed but a minute until there was a discreet tap. She opened the door to see Saunders beaming upon her. It was surprising how much shorter his nose looked as he smiled.

"Yes, Miss. What can I do for you?"

Lucy looked both ways carefully and then told him in a whisper.

"I'm so sorry to trouble you but you see at lunch I was very nervous and at dinner I was just a little afraid of Mr. Ross, I think — I never will be again — but I didn't eat much and now, Saunders, I'm *so* hungry!"

If possible his smile widened. "Exactly, Miss. I'll have a nice little supper up to you in a minute. Maggie'll be pleased to see to it. We just mentioned not five minutes past that you'd eaten like a bird all day. Right, Miss. I won't be long."

"Thank you so much, and Saunders, my name is Lucy."

"Miss Lucy, then, thank you, Miss."

As she sat in her pink challis wrapper in the chintz chair by the gas fire, consuming to the last crumb the bountiful supper which Saunders had brought, she began slowly to review all the days since those first dreadful ones when no letter had come from Ninian. And the nights! Never until then had she dreamed that a heart could truly ache. Yet during all those weeks she had been moving steadily toward this hour of content! She thought of the family back in the manse, who were doubtless at this moment thinking of her. She would call them on the telephone tomorrow. Suddenly she remembered some lines which Father had once marked for her in her own copy of Blake's Poems. They occurred in her favorite one which she had known by heart from childhood, yet this quatrain she had never understood until now. She said the words aloud once and then again savoring them with her new knowledge.

> *Joy and woe are woven fine,*
> *A clothing for the soul divine;*
> *Under every grief and pine*
> *Runs a joy with silken twine.*

At last she fell asleep, her young limbs folded in the biggest and softest bed she had ever known.

It was not until the fifth day of her stay that she met Mrs. Ross. She had heard her voice several times in the hall speaking to one of the maids, and she knew from Ninian that she had been in to see him when she herself had been downstairs for her meals, but that was all. The strangeness of it distressed her, and the more so because Ninian did not seem inclined to discuss it, being completely satisfied with her presence. She started violently, therefore, when Miss Cosgrove came into the sickroom one afternoon and said, "Mrs. Ross would like for you to come to her boudoir, Miss Lyall. I'll show you the way."

Lucy looked wildly for help at Ninian, who was at the moment half asleep, then rose and followed the nurse, her heart

jumping in her throat. She was wearing the white ruffled pina-
fore apron she had brought with her, because Ninian had taken a
great fancy to it, so it was in this garb that she presented herself
before the great lady, who from her high-backed satin sofa
surveyed her guest with an astonishment she could not conceal.
Whatever she had expected to see it was clear that the reality
was very different from her mental picture.

"Sit down, Miss Lyall," she said, pointing to a chair opposite.
"I have been quite unnerved by my son's illness and so have
been keeping rather strictly to my own rooms."

She stopped, as though somewhat baffled. Lucy of course
could not know that in the white apron she looked a bare
thirteen.

"I had expected to see a much older girl," Mrs. Ross added
involuntarily, still studying her guest with amazement.

"I'm nearly nineteen," Lucy said as pleasantly as she could
for fright. She glanced down suddenly and smiled.

"It's my apron! Ninian likes it so I wear it when I'm with
him." She quickly removed it. "Now, you see, I look more my
age. I suppose," she went on earnestly, "that Mr. Ross has explained why I came as I did and how embarrassed I am. . . . I've
been wanting so much to see you."

"Indeed?"

"Yes, I couldn't be perfectly comfortable until I knew you
didn't think too badly of me for coming. Mr. Ross has been *so*
kind to me!"

"Oh, he has!" There was no escaping the bitterness in the
voice. It was Lucy's turn to look amazed.

"Yes," she said simply, "has he not told you?"

Mrs. Ross ignored the question. "Miss Lyall," she said, "I am
a woman of some experience in the world and I think I understand perfectly the situation between you and my son. You, a

country girl, with a background quite different from his own, have caught his fancy temporarily because you are a type he has not known before. And you, on your part, are dazzled naturally by a sophisticated young man from the city. I do not wish to seem unkind, but sometimes the truth is best even when it hurts."

Lucy watched her, curiously and without speaking as she went on.

"It so happens that Ninian is in the somewhat rare and fortunate position of being able to offer everything to the girl he ultimately marries, and therefore can choose. . . . I mean he can . . . *choose*. He is handsome, I think I may say without undue pride, he has charm, a good mind, a pleasant disposition and in addition, wealth. His father has large interests *as you doubtless know*, and I, myself, have independent means. If he marries *suitably* he will inherit accordingly. If he does not . . . "

Lucy's face wore an expression disturbing to Mrs. Ross. There was on it no pallor of shock, and no trace of resentment.

"You can surely see, then," she went on, "why we wish this little passing fancy of yours and Ninian's to terminate for the good of you both. It was impulsive and unconventional of you to come here uninvited, to say the least. It showed you were not versed in social decorum even if you did not have any ulterior motives. You see I'm trying to give you the benefit of the doubt. But my advice is for you to return to your home as soon as possible, and center your affections upon some young man of your own social level while Ninian will lead the life his own position demands. In fact I may say this is what I *expect* you to do." Her voice was stern.

She stopped again for breath, finding their positions uncomfortably reversed. Lucy's eyes watched her with a calm, almost pitying expression while she herself felt less than at ease.

"You look like an intelligent girl and I'm sure you understand.

Ninian is our only son and naturally we have plans for him. We want the best for him. If you really care for him you will want this for him, too. But whether you do or not, *this is what I intend!*" She rose to end the interview.

Lucy rose, too, folding the white apron over her arm. She stood for a moment, looking upon the hard, handsome features of the woman before her. Although in the last few minutes she had traversed a realm of emotions to which she was a stranger, she had suddenly divined during the conversation the situation which existed between Mr. and Mrs. Ross.

She stood silent, wondering what she could say, knowing her own love to be beyond the reach of this woman whose dark eyes burned into hers as though by their intensity to threaten and disarm her.

At last she found words.

"I'm so sorry to disappoint you, Mrs. Ross, or make you unhappy, but you said yourself that Ninian was in a position to choose, and, well, you see he has already chosen — *me.*"

It was such a simple little speech, and yet so utterly final.

Lucy went out and walked slowly through the long hall. She felt shaken and completely humiliated. She entered her beautiful little *soote* to think it over. She knew that in a sense she was afraid of Mrs. Ross. That proud head with its fashionably dressed hair; the unsmiling mouth and unfriendly eyes; the flowing elegance of her peignoir that curled in soft circles around her feet as she sat on the satin sofa like a queen giving audience — everything about her made Lucy feel awkward and timid and ordinary, even without the hostility of her words and manner. If it were not for Ninian, Lucy decided, she would pack her valise and leave the house instantly. But it was for Ninian she had come, so she must do nothing to harm him.

She began to tremble, a queer sensation in itself. She spread her palms to the gas blaze and set her teeth firmly together to keep them from chattering. She realized that most of all she craved human companionship, so when she was sufficiently controlled she got up and made her way down the stairs and down again until she had reached the big, warm kitchen where Saunders and Maggie were having one of their endless cups of tea at the heavy oak table. At sight of her they both rose and hurried to her.

"You're white as a ghost, Miss, and shivering! Sit down now, and Saunders, fetch a cup. It's not . . . it's not Mr. Ninian?"

"No," Lucy managed. "He's much better. I . . . I think I would like some tea, though."

Saunders and Maggie gave each other a long look above her head.

"That's right. Nothing fettles you like a nice, hot cup of tea, and Maggie, cut a slice of your fresh cake. I'd have taken it up to you, Miss, if you'd have rung."

"I just thought I'd like to come down for a few minutes, if you don't mind," Lucy said, unsteadily.

"You're maybe a bit overlong in the sickroom. It often takes people that way," said Maggie, bustling solicitously about her, "but you'd just be surprised now how Miss Davis and Miss Cosgrove and the night one are all mentioning you, Saunders says. A nice young lady they say and no trouble at all."

"They are more friendly now," Lucy put in weakly.

"And here's Jennie, the chambermaid, can't be doing enough for you, and as to the doctor . . . "

"What was it he said to you, Saunders, only yesterday, mind?"

"He said, 'She's done more for that boy in five days, than medicine could in five weeks!' Meaning you, Miss."

So they talked on, comforting her while the name in all their minds was never spoken. And as Lucy ate and listened the trembling slowly went out of her limbs and something of the humiliation also left her. She thanked them at last and went back to Ninian, escorted by Saunders all the way.

"And if ever you're feeling a bit lonely, like, Miss Lucy, just come down again and Maggie and me will be very pleased to have you."

The evenings had been growing each more pleasant. Lucy chatted away at ease now during dinner, and after, before she went upstairs, Mr. Ross talked to her of many things. It seemed as though through her he was coming to know his own son for the first time. And always as she left him to go upstairs, he stooped and kissed her.

Tonight she prepared for dinner eagerly, for they would have good news to talk over together. There had been a very satisfactory report from the doctor that afternoon. Ninian was more than out of danger; he was showing definite improvement. He had laughed that day; he had eaten everything given him and asked for more; he was beginning to show a better color; his voice was stronger. Lucy, with fresh white edging in her collar and her brightest hair bow smartly tied, ran down to dinner, determined not to think of the earlier unpleasantness, certainly not to speak of it, except to ask advice about the length of her stay. She drew the heavy portières apart and entered the room in a small flurry of haste. Then she stopped dead. Mrs. Ross, in a trailing black gown, stood by the fireplace, one arm gracefully resting on the mantelpiece.

Mr. Ross rose at once. "Oh, come in, Lucy. I believe you and Mrs. Ross have already met."

"We have," Mrs. Ross answered with a frigid smile which managed to encompass critically the whole small figure before her from hair bow to buttoned shoes.

Saunders announced dinner which proved a sorry affair, indeed. Mrs. Ross, ignoring Lucy completely, addressed herself to her husband, who replied chiefly in monosyllables. When the meal was ended, she rose and said, "I have some matters I wish to discuss with you, Robert, in the library, if Miss Lyall will excuse us."

There was a curt finality in her tone which sent the blood flushing through Lucy's cheeks. As she was leaving the dining room, Mr. Ross caught her arm and detained her after his wife had passed on.

"May I stop in at your sitting room later this evening and chat a while?" he asked in a low voice.

"Oh, I wish you would. I always leave Ninian at nine-thirty," she said.

So they talked it all over then, with Mr. Ross choosing his words with particular care. He spoke with considered respect of Mrs. Ross, but he managed to convey to Lucy at once how she felt toward their guest and how he, himself, did. The warmth of his own attitude seemed to soften and cover the other, so that Lucy was more than ever conscious of the nearness of her relation to him when he had finished.

"Mrs. Ross is planning to leave for Atlantic City in about ten days. We expect Ninian to be quite convalescent by then. She will be gone for a month probably and during that time you must come back and stay as long as you please. I'll count upon that and I'm very sure Ninian will and I'll write to your parents, myself."

He looked at her then almost beseechingly.

"I hope," he said, "that you understand."

"Oh, I do," Lucy assured him. "I'm afraid I can't leave before the afternoon train tomorrow since I must explain first to Ninian that I'm going. But I'll go home then and come back, if you really want me, later on. Ninian will be content, I think, for we'll be in touch. I'll write him every day." She drew a long sigh. "The main thing is that he's safe now."

He leaned over and took her hand in his. His voice was husky.

"I haven't words," he said, "but thank you, my dear, for *everything!*"

When they had each voiced their affection all over again and he had said good night and closed the door behind him, he reopened it quickly, and stood there for a moment with something of Ninian's own twinkle in his eyes.

"Do you know what you've done to me — among other things? Set me *to reading Wordsworth!*"

The next morning Lucy told Ninian gently of her plan to leave that day. He was at first rather wild, then depressed but finally acquiescent. She had been here practically a week, she reminded him, when she had come merely to *inquire* about him, thinking to go back home that same night or, if it was necessary, to stay a day or two at the most. So she must go now, but she would return. She really, she added earnestly, should be home for the *Revival!* At which, to her surprise, he laughed outright.

"You surely don't think *you* need converting?"

"Well, I hope not," she replied seriously, "but I do sing in the choir, you know, and besides if I were not at the meetings, everyone would wonder . . ."

"And talk about it?"

"Of course."

Then she laughed too, and for a long, happy hour they discussed Ladykirk and what great things they would give it to talk about some day.

She had a late lunch in Ninian's room and then came a little time all alone with him, by benefit of Miss Davis. There was a small babel of good-byes in the hall from the nurses and Jennie, during which the door to Mrs. Ross's rooms remained significantly closed; there was the almost tender parting with Saunders and Maggie, and she was ready to leave.

The hour must have been inconvenient for him, but Mr. Ross was there in the front hall ready to ride with her to the station, to buy her ticket and see her safely on the train. He uncovered his head in courtly fashion as they parted and stood in the bleak air, still with his hat off, as he waved to her passing window.

Jeremy met her that night at Ladykirk station with Prince and the sleigh. They talked fast all the way home, mostly of what had transpired during her absence. The story of the strange week in the great Ross mansion she would save to tell later when they were all together. Lucy knew as they passed swiftly over the snowy track to the chiming of the sleigh bells — past the lights of the Stone Hotel and Harrison's store and the post office and all the familiar houses — she knew how much she had lived in the few days since the morning she had hurried along this very street clutching the small valise. She knew suddenly too, and with great surprise, that she had been brave to do what she had done. But most of all she knew that now she was very weary and very homesick!

She stumbled in her eagerness as she climbed the manse steps, and then as the door was flung open with the warmth and light behind it, she ran over the threshold and all but fell into the arms outstretched to receive her.

Chapter Eleven

＊＊＊＊＊＊＊＊＊＊＊＊＊＊＊＊＊＊＊＊＊＊＊＊＊＊＊＊

HOMER TURBENROTH arrived Monday morning and
David with Oliver Coates met the train as a welcoming committee. From the moment he laid eyes on the man, David was
seized with violent dislike, and in remorse for the feeling tried
to put more warmth than usual into his greeting. Mr. Turbenroth was even larger than his photograph indicated and his voice
matched his physical proportions. There was an unctuous
heartiness about it which grated upon David's ear.

"Brother Lyall, it is a pleasure, indeed, to meet you. And
Brother Coates! One of your Elders, you say? It is always a
privilege to know those engaged in the Lord's work. I hope that
my stay among you will be richly blessed to the saving of souls."

His eyes roved with a professional quickness over the station
and the travelers, coming or going, as though he were scanning
the scene already for prospective converts. David led him to
the sleigh, explaining as they went the plans for his entertainment. It was here the first hitch occurred. Mr. Turbenroth
very definitely preferred to stay at the hotel. He must, he said,
be undisturbed during the hours he spent in preparation and
prayer and this was more easily effected in public rather than
private lodgings. David, able as usual to see both sides to a

question, admitted the reasonableness of this argument, while still courteously presenting the advantages of Mrs. Crombie's hospitality. When he found this to no avail he sought Oliver Coates who was going to convey the Evangelist's not inconsiderable luggage to its destination in Josiah Hunt's hack.

Oliver was nonplussed. They had not reckoned on this additional expense. Mr. Blackburn might give them a special rate at the hotel but even so . . .

"You can't budge him?" he asked.

"I cannot," David replied somewhat shortly.

"Well," Oliver said, "I don't know what the rest of the Session will say about it but I can't see what else we can do than drop him off at the hotel. You'll see about the rates, won't you?"

"I'll do my best."

When they reached the hotel desk, David introduced Mr. Blackburn to the new guest, who all but upset the old man with his violent handshake and then signed the register with flowing strokes.

"It will be a great pleasure I'm sure, to be with you," the Evangelist said to his host. "I have heard reports of your wonderful chicken and waffle suppers as far away as Moreswell and Rushville."

David, seeing a slight bulge of flesh above Mr. Turbenroth's collar, felt another unworthy thought, which he throttled immediately.

When he had done everything he could to assure the guest's comfort and given all the immediate information necessary, he set out with a troubled spirit to placate Mrs. Crombie if this were possible. To tell the truth he felt genuinely sorry for her. She lived alone in her big house and the idea of having the Evangelist for the week had doubtless been a thrilling one to her. She was getting on in years but was still remarkably active.

David had heard from Mary of how she had cleaned the house from garret to cellar, had gone to Moreswell to buy new curtains for the spare bedchamber and had told all and sundry that she expected to serve *every breakfast* in her big, golden-oak, seldom-used dining room. For years to come she would have been able to mention in conversation: "When I entertained the Evangelist," or "Mr. Turbenroth said thus-and-so the week he stayed with me."

David had scarcely rung the bell when the door flew open and Mrs. Crombie in her lavender crocheted breakfast shawl stood before him.

"Didn't he come?" she asked anxiously.

David stepped inside and as gently as possible made her aware of the facts. He watched her face change as he spoke from anger to a dismal resignation. She looked, all at once, small and withered and old. He laid his hand kindly on her shoulder.

"I'm so sorry about this, Mrs. Crombie, after all your work and preparations! You were so generous to agree to take him in the first place and I can't tell you how I regret the change in plans."

"Well," she said, her voice for once more heavy than sharp, "if that's the way he feels, I guess there's no help for it."

He left her at last to her disappointment, telling himself that the week had not begun auspiciously.

By evening, however, something of the excitement of the general public communicated itself to David also. There was a large crowd in the basement for the first night, and the ushers, captained by the serious and conscientious young Oliver Coates, gave an almost flawless performance. Their offices lent an indefinable dignity to the occasion and David, as he watched the pleasantly self-conscious expression on the faces of the men and women, unaccustomed to this courtesy, was gratified.

When the meeting began, Mr. Turbenroth, with a copy of

Moody and Sankey's Hymns 1 to 6 in his hand, stood in front of the low pulpit platform and led the singing in a powerful tenor voice.

"Now, folks, you'll learn that at these meetings we're always going to warm up first with song. Throw out your chests now, let your souls expand, let the Holy Spirit come right into your hearts! Now then, ready, everybody SING!

> *Throw out the life-line across the dark wave!*

That's it! Come on now! Still a few folks aren't singing. EVERY-BODY!

> *Throw out the life-line; throw out the life-line,*
> *Someone is drifting away.* . . .

Now, that was good, folks, but we can do better. I want to see every man, woman and child in this room just opening up their souls to God in song! If you never sang before in your lives, SING NOW. Ready, just a chord, please, from the organ. Come on, the next verse:

> *Throw out the life-line with hand quick and strong.*"

Suddenly he stopped the singing with upraised hands.

"Now I want you to picture to yourselves a small boat on the great ocean, tossed with the waves, ready to sink. See, there's a man in it! Terrified, desperate, *lost*, ready to be sucked down to his death in the icy waters. But look, someone on shore has a rope! He flings it out! It misses! It falls short. *Throw it again! Throw out the life-line!* He throws it again. Look, the man in the boat has caught it! He's pulled to shore! *He's saved!* But oh, my friends, that picture is as nothing to the one of the sinner, lost, hopeless, *helpless*, ready to be sucked down by the waves of sin into everlasting *Hell!* Think of that, my friends. That's why I'm here this week to save some of the lost from hell fire, by *Throwing out the life-line!* Now, once more with that thought in mind — a chord again, please . . ."

By the last chorus the volume of sound was overwhelming. David listened with wonder and aching eardrums. He was permitted to read the Scripture and his quiet voice seemed to drop into a vacuum as he proceeded. Then again the singing, this time with variations. Mr. Turbenroth's face was red and perspiring with his zeal.

"Now then, the men — only the men — sing it out, now!

When the roll is called up yonder —

Now the ladies. Don't let the men beat you! Show them what you can do. Ready!

When the roll is called up yonder.

Fine! Now, all together. Put your hearts in it! SING!

When the roll is called up yonder, I'll be there!"

In the hush that followed the final outburst, the Evangelist dropped his voice to a hoarse whisper.

"But *will* you be there? You and you and *you?* Are there some souls here tonight who will not be found before the Great White Throne? Who will be instead in that place of eternal torment where . . . their . . . worm . . . dieth . . . not . . . and . their . . . fire . . . is . . . not . . . *quenched?* Search your hearts! Let us all bow now for a word of prayer."

The sermon was, to David's orderly mind, distressingly chaotic. While purporting to start from the text: *Cut it down. Why cumbereth it the ground?* it wandered through a series of anecdotes and exhortations with only occasional references to the original theme. Mr. Turbenroth, however, by his strange mesmeric powers, held the listeners in the hollow of his hand. He shouted, he whispered; he threatened, he besought; he moved them to laughter and then caught them up in terror. Something vital and powerful seemed to flow from his huge body to the people seated before him. David, studying the faces, honestly admitted this, even as his sensitive soul shrank from the words and the manner of the discourse.

At the end there came the climax for which all waited. It was the time when the Evangelist would beseech those who felt the need of conversion to give the sign. This was preceded by the singing of a hymn. But there was no bursting of throats now. The choir at first sang alone, softly, then, at the direction of Mr. Turbenroth the congregation joined in muted tones:

> *Along the River of Time we glide,*
> *Along the River, along the River;*

Then the refrain:

> *Drifting, drifting, out on the sea of eternity.*

The Evangelist had told David that sometimes there was no *response* the first night, but that he strove as hard then as at later meetings for results. He besought now, his voice rising and falling, while the choir alone kept up the dirge-like refrain.

"Keep your heads bowed. Pray, pray that the Spirit will work mightily in our midst tonight! Is there a soul here who realizes he or she needs the Cleansing Power? Who is drifting out on that eternal sea to his own damnation? Is there a soul who will come *now*, this moment, to the safety of salvation? Raise your hand. I'll see it. Pray, everyone, for the ones who are hesitating. Don't delay. Tomorrow may be too late. Death comes as a thief in the night. Now, *now*, cross over the line. It is only a step. Just raise your hand. I'll see it . . . *A hand is raised!* Thank you, brother. Hallelulia! There is joy in Heaven when a sinner repents . . . *Another hand is raised!* I see it, sister. Hallelulia! Keep praying now, while the spirit is working . . . Keep your heads bowed. . . ."

He turned to the choir. "Once again now, very softly, the whole hymn."

David, who had been asked to watch for the raised hands and note to whom they belonged in order to give Mr. Turbenroth information later, saw now that the two who had given this sign were Billy Kinkaid, and Hetty May Sykes who lived with the Burroughs out in the country and who was slightly below normal mentally.

The exhortation finally ceased, the last hymn was sung with fervor, the room gradually emptied of its congregation except for the Session, Billy, Hetty May and the Burroughs family who were attempting to persuade her to leave without further delay. David joined their group and tried to assist in calming Hetty May, who was now in a state of mild hysteria. Mr. Turbenroth, looking eager and gratified, left Billy and hurried to the girl.

"I think," David said to him in a low voice, "that Hetty May should go on home as soon as possible. She is rather emotionally unstable."

"She get fits," Mr. Burroughs put in, shortly, "when she gets too excited. Come on, now, Hetty May, an' no more nonsense."

"I told you we oughtn't to have brought her. Not to a *Revival!*" said Mrs. Burroughs.

Mr. Turbenroth tried to take charge. "This may be really the working of the Spirit," he urged. "In one place I had three different converts who had seizures. Let me talk to this young girl about her soul's salvation . . . Just step aside, please."

But Mr. Burroughs solved the problem by picking Hetty May up bodily and carrying her from the room. His family followed with scattered good nights over their shoulders and the door closed behind them. Mr. Turbenroth's blue eyes looked sultry.

"I am shocked," he said to David, "that you permitted such a proceeding. That young girl's soul may now be forever lost."

David explained briefly the situation in regard to Hetty May.

She was already a member of the church. She was a good girl, but easily moved by any excitement into hysteria or worse.

"She is slightly unbalanced," he concluded with a touch of asperity, "but I do not consider her soul in any danger. Shall we join the Session?"

The men sat in the far corner of the room, with Billy Kinkaid in their midst twirling his hat nervously in his hands. David introduced Mr. Turbenroth to each one and then let him take charge. As a matter of fact, Billy made it all quite simple.

"Yes sir," he admitted freely, "I'm a sinner in need of help. My trouble is . . . the bottle!" He raised an imaginary one to his lips. "I just get rightly back in the church till . . ." he snapped his fingers, "out I go again like that. The Reverend here, can tell you. It's discouragin'."

Mr. Turbenroth now showed his full skill in dealing with the repentant. He argued, he warned, he held out visions of hope. He had them all kneel as he offered prayer. The Session members took the position with some hesitation, their Calvinistic knees being stiff and unaccustomed to it. At the end, Billy, overcome with the flood of persuasion and petition, shook hands all around, his eyes moist and his lips a-tremble, and left the room, as he said, a *saved man*.

The Session were visibly impressed and spoke with warm respect to Mr. Turbenroth.

"It's even better than we ever expected for the first night," Oliver Coates said in awe.

"A wonderful moving of the Spirit in our midst," Colonel Harrison pronounced solemnly.

On the faces of the Session there was to David's eye a certain light of earnest excitement, not unmixed with importance. It was quite natural, he thought to himself. They would share personally with Mr. Turbenroth all the dramatic events which might occur during the week. He walked home wearily, pondering. At the manse gate he smiled wryly, then quoted Billy Kinkaid as he addressed the stars. "It's discouragin'," he said.

The meetings gained swiftly in momentum. The condition of the snow and a full moon helped, of course, for as more and more people from far out in the country heard the reports of the Revival on the party-line telephones, they jingled in big sleds or in "cutters" — wrapped cozily in buffalo robes or horse blankets — over the shining white tracks to swell the crowds which thronged the basement. It was necessary soon to secure all the undertakers' chairs and bring in the long benches from the small side rooms. A wave of electric interest swept the town. Mr. Turbenroth early distributed printed copies of an extra hymn not to be found in *Moody and Sankey*, and inaugurated a fifteen-minute song service before each meeting. The new hymn was caught up immediately:

> *Will there be any stars, any stars in my crown,*
> *When at evening the sun goeth down?*
> *When I wake with the blest in the mansions of rest,*
> *Will there be any stars in my crown?*

The tune was whistled on the street and around the post-office stove; women hummed it at their work, young people sang it around parlor organs or pianos. It became the *motif* of the Revival. Colonel Harrison was one who reveled in the song services, his unsteady bass booming out often by itself at the end in a low descending echo: *In . . . my . . . crown.* The choir too outdid itself in leadership with Seena Harris' shrill soprano rising above all the rest. But *everybody* sang, until the incredible volume of sound (which was the apparent aim of the Evangelist) took possession of the place, all but rocking the sturdy brick walls, surging and swelling until the people were bathed in it, lost in it and intoxicated by it.

Once as David listened and marveled he wondered if any of the congregation were at all conscious of the words they were singing, or indeed whether, for the purposes of the Evangelist, it mattered whether they were or not. Of course he realized that his taste in hymns was not the same as that of Mr. Turbenroth. The later was, for example, greatly addicted to that group which David always classified mentally as *the eternal vague-ities.* So he studied his people as now with complete abandon they chanted with all their vocal powers: "Beautiful Isle of Somewhere" or "In the Sweet Bye and Bye."

He saw suddenly by inward vision the missionary as he had stood in the quiet upper sanctuary that autumn night and sung "The Healing Hymn." The contrast between him and Mr. Turbenroth was shockingly great. Yet perhaps . . . Well, in any case he, David, must try to curb his thoughts, suppress his criticism and give himself wholly with all the faith he could muster to the processes of the Revival.

On Wednesday night, in the middle of the song service, Ben Losting, his wife and five progeny were ushered up the center aisle and took their places near the front. A ripple ran through the congregation. There were subdued whispers, a shifting of positions and then the voices rose louder than ever, stimulated by suspense and excitement. It was the first time Ben Losting had been inside a church since he had lived in the community; now, shaven and reasonably clean, he reared tall and gaunt from his chair and studied the Evangelist critically with his bloodshot, watery eyes.

The service proceeded with more than usual dramatic effect. Mr. Turbenroth grew each night more stern in his denunciation, more violent in his pleading, more lurid in his illustrations. At the last, when with bowed heads the people waited for those in sin to give the sign, it happened. Ben, who, as David watched him, had grown more and more restless, giving utterance to frequent groans, interspersed with Amens, suddenly lurched to his feet and cried out as though in mortal terror.

"I'm a lost man! I gotta confess my sins an' get converted or I'm on my way to hell."

Mr. Turbenroth was instantly beside him, where he had collapsed in his chair.

"There is salvation just waiting for you! Pray, everyone, pray for our erring brother. While I speak with him will the choir sing softly, *There is power, power, wonder-working power . . .*"

Ben's voice rose above the music and the low urgent tones of the Evangelist, with more groans and once almost a yell.

"It's the burden o' my sin!" he kept repeating, "I've gotta confess it. I've gotta confess it before men!"

Mr. Turbenroth finally signaled for complete silence, while he helped Ben to his feet.

"Courage, brother, courage! Make your confession now, while we all pray for you. Don't be afraid! We're all sinners and sojourners together with death and judgment awaiting us all. Pour out now what's on your conscience!"

Ben's voice began in a hoarse whisper and increased in volume with each sentence.

"I'm a sinner in the eyes of the Lord. I'm a drunkard an' I ain't a good pervider for my fam'ly. I might a been a murderer. I went to the Festible with my gun an' I was dead drunk. I might a shot into the crowd. They've took my gun away from me. I ain't no good. I'm set for hell unless I get converted."

Ben was now shaken and groaning, and no matter how familiar one was with the story, David thought, the effect was distressingly upsetting to the nerves. The Evangelist called for the congregaion to sing softly, *Throw out the life-line*, while he worked and prayed with the unhappy man. Toward the end of the singing there was a series of sounds from Ben that became words in a rising crescendo.

"Amen! Praise the Lord! I'm saved! I'm converted! I've got religion at last. Hallelulia!"

The Evangelist, flushed wtih triumph, spread his great arms wide and swung the congregation into: *Shall we gather at the river?* then with dramatic suddenness pronounced the benediction. Any further converts that night would have been anticlimactic.

But Ben's public confession of his sins established a new order of procedure. In fact it paved the way for the week's great disclosure. The following night as Mr. Turbenroth asked for a show of hands he spoke of the weight of misery which lay upon a guilty conscience. There would come relief from confession to the Session and himself and the minister, but how much more from public confession! Was there not someone there that night who would have the courage, when all heads were bowed, to tell the sin which had kept him from the path of righteousness? Maybe there were some, long Christians in name, who had fallen from grace, who needed the Wonder-Working Power?

"As you raise your hand, name the sin which so easily besets you. Confess! Confess the burden on your soul! It will help us all! Now, while we're all praying, who will be the first?"

From far in the back a young man's muffled voice said, "Drinking." David saw the hand but could not see the face. With amazing quickness others followed, naming their sins, asking for prayer. When one final blurred and seldom spoken word fell upon the air, David grew hot all over and the Evangelist brought the meeting to a close with a rousing hymn. There was plenty to talk about in Ladykirk that night, for no one knew who had made that final confession!

"It's repulsive to me," David said to Mary later, "hearing people expose their souls which are certainly more intimate than their bodies. I hate this whole business, and then I hate myself for hating it. I'm afraid I'm jealous or hypercritical. Maybe Turbenroth is doing good. Maybe even Billy Kinkaid and Ben Losting have actually been converted."

"Do you believe that?" Mary asked.

"I'm trying to," said David. Then he added honestly, "No, I don't, but I'm praying for faith."

The next afternoon, urged by the fact that he had not been to see his old friend all week and also by the need of talking over the meetings with him, David dropped in on Mr. Dilling. He found him looking unusually well, smoking a rich cigar and fingering *Horace* affectionately.

"Well," he began, "how are you making out with your Wild Bull of Bashan?"

"Meaning . . . ?" said David.

"Who else? I've been having most of my meals sent up here lately as I can't stand the strain of seeing souls saved under my eyes. All the drummers have been attacked by Mr. Turbenroth, and I rather think I'm next on the list. So far I've succeeded in avoiding him. Well, how are the meetings? You look as though you were among the damned yourself."

"I do feel rather used up," David admitted. He had just begun his account when a loud knock upon the door interrupted him. He glanced at Mr. Dilling.

"Oh, open it," he said philosophically. "If it's what I think, I might as well get it over with. But don't leave."

It was Mr. Turbenroth. He showed surprise and slight disapproval at sight of David, but covered it quickly.

"You were just leaving?" he asked hopefully.

"No," Mr. Dilling said, "he's just come. Will you have a chair, sir?"

The Evangelist sat down and cleared his throat heavily.

"Mr. Dilling," he began, "I have a great deal upon my mind

in connection with the Revival services and so must come directly to the point. I cannot stay here any longer under the same roof and not speak to you about your soul's salvation."

"Ah!" said Mr. Dilling, lifting the cigar box and offering it to his guest.

Mr. Turbenroth's nostrils contracted with apparent longing, but he shook his head.

"I have learned that you are not a professing Christian."

"Ah!" said Mr. Dilling.

"That many people here even consider you an *atheist!*"

"Ah!" said Mr. Dilling again.

The Evangelist leaned forward and spoke as to a child.

"So, let us start at the very beginning. Do you believe in God?"

"I do," said Mr. Dilling.

"Very good!" said his questioner, looking gratified.

"I had a feeling if it were put straight to you . . . Now the next thing is, have you made your peace with Him?"

"Well, I should say that God himself is the only one who could answer that."

Mr. Turbenroth looked baffled but only for a moment. "Let us approach it from a slightly different angle. Do you understand what we mean by The Plan of Salvation?"

"Oh, perfectly."

"Good! And you believe in it?"

"No," said Mr. Dilling.

The Evangelist jumped. "You understand what it means and yet do not believe it?"

"That is correct."

"*Why?*" The question exploded from him.

"Because I consider it a primitive, irrational and wholly untenable concept."

Mr. Turbenroth looked stunned. He felt himself now on unfamiliar ground, so he switched back hastily to his accustomed phraseology. He dropped his voice to an ominous tone.

"Mr. Dilling, you believe, of course, in the everlasting punishment of hell fire!"

"No," said Mr. Dilling politely.

"What?" The Evangelist sprang to his feet. "In all my life, in all my experience with sinners, I've never met a man who didn't believe in hell!"

"Really?" said Mr. Dilling with interest.

Mr. Turbenroth's full face was now almost purple. He started to speak, but his usual fluency failed him.

"How," he sputtered at last to David, "can you talk to a man about his soul's salvation when he doesn't believe in *hell fire?*"

"How, indeed?" agreed Mr. Dilling cheerfully.

The Evangelist gave him one look of near loathing and made for the door. David hastened to open it for him.

"Excuse me for not rising," Mr. Dilling said, "and a very good day to you, sir." A deep chuckle pursued the guest as the door closed.

David returned and stood looking down at the old man.

"I almost felt sorry for him," he said. "He was so stumped, so deflated. He couldn't get a handle to you. Maybe you've shattered his confidence in himself."

Then suddenly they laughed together while David felt the first release from the tension he had known all week. When he was leaving, Mr. Dilling grew serious.

"While I don't care to have Mr. Homer Turbenroth tinkering with the affairs of my soul, you know you're always welcome to try. I suppose because you never have! But I've been doing some thinking, lately, David. When I have a majority decision in my own mind, I'll tell you."

"Any time," said David, "and thanks for the visit. It's done me good."

The public testimony continued in the meetings, even though David made so bold as to argue with the Evangelist against it. When pressed by Mr. Turbenroth for the reason for his opposition, David had been driven to confess that it was his sense of dignity and privacy that was offended.

"The people are emotionally worked up into a kind of hysteria or they wouldn't do it," he urged.

"Well," said the Evangelist bluntly, "isn't that what you got me here for? Isn't that what I'm paid to do? If I didn't work 'em up, I tell you, *nothing* would happen?"

So David was forced to desist, master his distaste and wrestle in his petitions that good might come of it all. And the confessions continued. All the small sins of the category and occasionally larger ones were breathed hoarsely upon the heavy air of the basement, and the town was rent with the gossip of it.

By Saturday night the crowd broke all previous records, for a large group of men had to stand along the back walls. As the people poured in, David was conscious of a great relief that the week was over. He and Mary had decided that they couldn't have stood the strain of another. He felt he could detect signs of fatigue in others as well, certainly in the members of the Session, some of them old men, in the choir, and in the ushers, especially in young Oliver Coates. His complexion was always pasty, but for the last few nights it had been a chalky white. Once as he passed the printed hymn sheets David noticed that his hands trembled. He had taken his work too seriously, that was quite evident and David had a rush of remorse that he had not had a second corps of older men to relieve the boys.

Into this last service the Evangelist now threw all his powers. The congregation rocked with the singing; it shuddered in the hush of foretold doom; it waited at the last, breathless, electric, for the revelations of the confession period. But none came. Perhaps, David thought as he waited tensely, the souls had grown weary along with the bodies, and were resting now in their own deep, normal secrecy. Perhaps all who could bring themselves to public avowal had already done so. There must be an end to it sooner or later. Meanwhile Mr. Turbenroth urged, threatened, besought. David, scanning the bent heads, saw the face before the words came. It was a young face, chalky white, back by the door. Then into the momentary silence came a voice, broken and breathless.

"I took the ten dollars at the U.P. Festival."

It was young Oliver Coates.

Before the Evangelist could speak, David was on his feet, breaking the atmosphere of mortal shock.

"The hour is now late and we must draw this series of meetings to a close. In the name of the Session and the congregation, I wish to express to Mr. Turbenroth our appreciation of his earnest efforts this week. Our prayers and good wishes will follow him in all his work. Any who care to meet with him and the Session may do so at the close of the service. Let us stand now and sing, 'God Be With You Till We Meet Again.'"

He gave a quick signal to Faith at the organ. In a second the release of the voices came. David himself pronounced the benediction. Tenderly. The people passed quietly out. The Great Revival was over.

But not quite. The Session waited silently in their corner, with one member ashen as death. The boy waited in another corner, his dark eyes behind their glasses unseeing in their despair.

"I hope you didn't mind my suddenly taking over, Turbenroth," David said quietly. "I was to close the service anyway, you know, and I felt it had to be done promptly. This is a tragic thing that came out. For Mr. Coates, as an Elder, you know. I'll go and speak to the boy."

David made his way to where young Oliver stood and held out his hand.

"That took courage," he said, "but I'm sure, in a way, you're relieved. Don't be frightened now. Come on over and speak to the Session and clear it all up."

"My father . . ." he began.

"Yes, that's the hardest part. But you must go through it like a man."

Mr. Turbenroth, who had joined the other men, was for once lacking in his easy, professional urgency. He looked anxiously into the set faces around him. This was very different from the other nights when he had triumphantly presented the converts to the church officers. He started several times to speak but the sentences were abortive and he finally nodded to David.

"We all know Oliver," David began. "He has always been a good boy. A model boy. I have asked him to tell us just what occurred, and I have told him that we have all made mistakes, not only in our youth, but later on as well. You showed courage to confess in the meeting, Oliver. Now be brave and tell us all about it."

The boy wet his stiff lips and swallowed painfully. He was trembling.

" Well," he said in his unsteady, changing young voice. "I was there at the Festival when Ben Losting come in with his gun and Gene Holly left the stand an' run toward him. Us fellows all sort of leaned again' the stand to see better an' I looked down an' the money box was right under me, sort of. An' I've been savin' up for a bicycle." He stopped and a quivering sigh escaped him. "I've been tryin' this long time to save for a bicycle."

He repeated the words as though by that to make his listeners understand the extremity of his longing.

"I don't know yet how I come to do it. The ten-dollar bill was there an' I just slipped my hand on it an' nobody saw me. There was a lot of us run when Mr. Holly yelled about the money bein' gone. Soon as I got home, I'd have give anything to put it back, but I didn't know how. I never put it with my bicycle money. I've just kep' it. When Lucy's fellah sent the ten dollars to the U.P.'s, then it was harder'n ever to get rid of it. I've just kep' it. Here it is."

He drew the crumpled bill out of his pants pocket and held it out to David.

David's eyes swept the group. "You have all heard Oliver's story," he said quietly. "He took the bill on sudden impulse, under unusual temptation, regretted the act at once, wanted to return the money, has never spent it or even put it with his savings. He now restores it to whatever use will be decided upon. In my opinion he is completely absolved from his mistake and with God's help will, I'm sure, be scrupulously honest all the rest of his life. Have any of the Session an expression of opinion?"

Lute McLean spoke quickly.

"I agree."

Colonel Harrison followed, then one after another, including Mr. Turbenroth, the men assented. All but Oliver Coates, Senior. He still sat, his face frozen in shame and misery. He did not speak after his son had gone and the members of the Session were trying with painful awkwardness to say something of brotherly kindness. Mr. Turbenroth offered his hand and suggested further prayer, but Oliver with glassy eyes that scarcely saw his idol, got his coat and hurried out before even David could overtake him. There was a little discussion then, but the men had small heart for more words, so very soon they all went quietly out into the beauty of the still, white night. The Evangelist walked beside David in a strange silence, except for the crunch of the snow under their feet.

"That man," he said at last, "Mr. Coates, looked as though he might even *do* something to himself. I feel he needs the full support of the Wonder-Working Power tonight. I could stop and speak with him at his home."

"I'm not sure," David said hesitantly, "whether that would be best, though you're very kind. I was going down myself. He's known me for so long he might speak more freely to me. If I can just get him to talk it all out he'll feel better. Shakespeare was right. 'Give sorrow words,' you know."

"What was that again?" asked Mr. Turbenroth quickly. "I could use it perhaps in my confession periods. Just say it over, will you?"

David smiled, but complied.

> "*Give sorrow words; the grief that does not speak*
> *Whispers the o-er-fraught heart and bids it break.*

I'll write it out for you if you wish. You'll have dinner with us, then, tomorrow after church?"

"Yes, thanks." He stopped as David did outside the Coates' house.

"I'm tired," he said. "I'm *dog*-tired. If you won't be offended, I don't think I'll go to church tomorrow."

It was, David felt, the first completely natural remark he had made all week.

"Of course I won't be," he answered. "It will be poor pickings, I fear, as far as the sermon goes, for I've been concentrating so hard myself on the meetings. Take a good sleep and we'll see you at one-thirty. Then we've arranged for our son, Jeremy, to drive you to the main-line train, leaving about three. Good night. You must be tired. But congratulations on all your earnest work and the results that have come of it."

"I don't know about this last one." The Evangelist's voice had in it now no unctuousness.

"I think," David replied earnestly, "it may be the best result of all. The boy is relieved of his burden of guilt which he might have carried indefinitely. The town will forget and forgive. It does that with its own, and the parents will somehow get over it. But perhaps best of all, another young boy, who has been under suspicion, is now cleared! You see, you have accomplished something very far reaching."

"You think so? Sometimes I get to wondering whether . . . The people here seem to think an awful lot of you," he ended with apparent irrelevance.

"Oh, I've been here for a long time. In a small town we get fond of each other sooner or later."

"Well," said Mr. Turbenroth, reclothing himself in his spiritual heartiness, "I'll say good night then, Brother Lyall, and thanks for your fine cooperation. All we ask is souls for our hire. May you be guided in your work now in this distressed household."

David opened the side gate and followed the walk to the kitchen, the only room showing light. He knocked and after a slight wait the door was opened a little way by Mrs. Coates, her eyes red and the tears wet upon her cheeks.

"Come in, Mr. Lyall," she said brokenly.

He grasped her hand reassuringly and turned to her husband who sat beside the kitchen range, his face in his hands.

"Oliver," he said, using his given name for the first time. "I had to see you again before I could rest. You and Mrs. Coates must not take this thing too terribly to heart. I know the shock it is to you, but remember the boy is essentially a *good* boy. He was overcome in a grave fault, but he's made all the expiation he can. If he had *used* the money, it would be quite different. He repented almost at the moment of the act. So, you must forgive him and show him you are proud at least of his courage tonight. His real integrity has not been hurt, of that I'm certain."

There was no reply. David sat down in one of the kitchen chairs. He had learned through the many said crises of the years that even the steady, quiet flow of a human voice can help to break the spell of anguish.

"We all suffer more for our children's mistakes and troubles than for our own," he began. "That is natural and unselfish. But there is a selfish side which creeps in. We are proud of our children. We expect them somehow to justify our own existence. We want them to fulfill our own lives and conform to our ambitions for them. Now, you have probably taken great satisfaction in the fact that Oliver has always been such a model boy."

"That's maybe the trouble," Mrs. Coates put in. "We've maybe held him down too close, him being the only one we had and all. We wanted him to be so perfect. You know you've always been awful strict with him, Oliver."

"So," David went quietly on, "when our children make mistakes it is often our pride that suffers. We must watch that. Have you talked to your boy, Oliver?"

"Not a word," Mrs. Coates answered, "he won't speak to him. He won't speak to me."

David sat for a moment watching the bowed head of his Elder. Once in a while a great gusty breath like a sob shook Oliver's lean frame.

"Perhaps," he said gently, "you are thinking of the town's attitude. Surely you have lived here long enough to know what that will be. People here have kind hearts. They will think first of all of young Oliver's courage in confessing and honorably returning the money. In a very short time it will all be forgotten. Don't worry about that."

Then at last Oliver spoke through the hands that still covered his face.

"An' it was me that wanted the Revival and got the man here! It was me that brought it all on us."

David considered carefully and then said, "And it's well you did."

The only answer was a groan.

At last when he had done all he could, David rose to go.

"You must get to bed," he said, "and try to rest. We are all worn out from the week. And Oliver, I beseech you, be kind to your boy, and don't take this too hard." The words sounded stereotyped and futile against the stricken misery of the man's face.

Mrs. Coates led him to the front door and shook hands. "What you said has helped me, anyway, Mr. Lyall, and thank you for coming. He's proud, Oliver is, and this is terrible for him. I'll get over it first, I guess. I said all the time we ought to have got the bicycle. Oliver's had good work this year and we could have done without something else for the sake of the boy. Oh, well," she sighed, "it's done, now. But thanks again, Mr. Lyall."

David walked home heavily. As he passed one lighted parlor window close to the sidewalk he heard the notes of a piano and young voices singing:

> *When I wake with the blest in the mansions of rest,*
> *Will there be any stars in my crown?*

Could the Revival, he wondered — looking up at the real stars, shining golden in the frosty sky — could the Revival after all have been part of the unfathomable plan for Ladykirk? A necessary bit of a strange and infinite design? Could it be?

Whether this was so or not, he knew now that in spite of his hurt, his inner conflict, his soul's distaste and his hard-fought, miserable little jealousies, he was glad there had been the Revival. Perhaps Billy Kinkaid and Ben Losting were, as the Evangelist put it, *truly redeemed*. One could hope. As to the others who had met the Session, most of them had been the young people he had been expecting to receive into the church soon anyway. Yet, it was well, as it was. Moreover, there had been two strange young men from down toward Wassing, who had evidently come for the sleigh ride and remained to be moved by Mr. Turbenroth's appeals. These were the two who had confessed to the most glaring sins. They might indeed constitute stars for the Evangelist's crown!

But most of all, two young hearts had been freed by the meetings from the burden of guilt and suspicion: young Oliver Coates and Jim Cuppy! This alone was worth it all. His spirit rose as he thought of Jim. The boy had kept his word; he had not run away, but he had so withdrawn into himself that even he, David, could not reach him. Now there could be talk again between them of his drawing, maybe definite help somehow. He would get that boy yet! In some far-off day, it was conceivable that Ladykirk would be famous because of him.

His thoughts returned to his stricken Elder, and his heart ached for the man. The shock, the wounded pride, the utter humiliation, the sudden wall of grief between him and his son. Oh, it was hard! It was bitter! Poor Oliver, who had been so concerned that all the sinners of the community should be brought under the spell of the Evangelist! He knew Oliver had personally escorted Mr. Turbenroth to call upon Minnie (knowing David would not) and had also driven him clear out to Dan Holding's, though Dan, he gathered, had not been home at the time. It was now a perilously sad defeat to Oliver's lofty plans for the town's spiritual awakening — this that had fallen upon his own heart.

If only the inevitable *talk* of the next few days could be done away with! But this, David knew, was as impossible as trying to switch daylight and darkness. It would, though, as always, have its healing properties and at last the incident would be woven into Ladykirk's own pattern.

He had reached the gate and as always at night, paused a moment to lift his soul above the stars, then made his way slowly up the walk.

It had been Mary's thought to invite Mr. Turbenroth to dinner.

"It seems as though we should, David, don't you think, for his last meal?"

And the Evangelist had accepted with alacrity. He arrived, rested, full again of his extraordinary vitality, and ready, as he told them, for the next call of God, whenever it came.

The dinner went pleasantly enough until near the end. Then Mr. Turbenroth turned suddenly to Jeremy.

"I hear you are going to enter the ministry?" he said.

Jeremy's face turned scarlet. He hesitated. "Well," he said when the little silence had grown appreciable, "I did think of it."

"I heard it was all settled," pursued Mr. Turbenroth, "do you mean you've given it up?"

"It . . . it needs great consideration," said Jeremy painfully.

"Well, it would be too bad if you changed your mind, wouldn't it, Brother Lyall?"

He glanced at David's startled face and back again to Jeremy. "What would you think of if you don't go into the ministry?"

"F . . . farming," Jeremy brought out.

David broke in with a relieved laugh. It was evident, he felt, that Jeremy did not care to discuss his plans with the stranger.

"Oh, he's always had a green thumb. Anything he sticks in the ground will grow. Are you a gardener, Mr. Turbenroth?"

The conversation was firmly shifted, and it was not until the farewells had been said and Jeremy with the departing Evangelist had set out for the main-line train — the trip a very definite, but it was felt necessary, breach of Sabbatarian observance — that David stopped suddenly in passing through the study as though something had clutched his heart. Why had Jeremy turned crimson when that question had been put to him? Why had he hesitated and stammered and been embarrassed? He was perfectly capable of polite evasion without that. After all, why should he have evaded at all? And, as he remembered now, the boy's eyes had looked frightened and distressed.

A dozen little omens, portents of the last months, disregarded at the time, now rose in his mind to add weight to the fear that possessed him. He could not discover the truth until he had returned from the evening service when Jeremy would be home from his trip. That intervening space seemed interminable and the tension within him mounted. He could not even confide in Mary. The very voicing of his thoughts would give them substance when, he assured himself stoutly, there was none.

Mary did not go to church that evening, since she wanted to have a hot supper ready for Jeremy at the end of his long, cold drive. It was to David a hard service, since he knew that in the eyes of all it should be a sort of *follow up* of the previous week's meetings. He put into it all the strength, all the prayerful effort he possessed, to find at the end his body was wet from the strain of it. He left as soon as he could and hurried home. The girls were not back yet, but Jeremy sat with his mother in the parlor.

"Jeremy," he said at once, "I've just been wondering why you hesitated when Mr. Turbenroth asked you today about your going into the ministry."

The boy looked at his parents beseechingly. "It's hard to tell you," he said in a strange voice. "I've been trying to for months but every time I started I found I couldn't go on. I don't want to be a preacher."

"Why, Jeremy!" his father said huskily, "What do you mean?"

"I want to get married," Jeremy said. "I want to marry Peggy."

A great wave of relief passed over David. He threw a fleeting glance of assurance and understanding to Mary.

"I know how you feel! Every young man who is fond of a nice girl has sudden moments when he thinks of marriage even though it may be quite impossible at the time. When that thought seems to take precedence over all other . . . other plans. Now, in your case you have a good many years ahead of you before you finish your education. Why not explain this to Peggy, even though it seems hard right now? Then, by the time you're through college . . ."

"But that's what I have to tell you," Jeremy burst out. "I don't want to go to college. I want to marry Peggy and take over the MacDonald place next fall. You know how I've always liked the country and all those summers I worked out there, I got to thinking more and more about it. I didn't decide, though, until this last spring. Then I knew. Books have always come easily to me, but I'm not a real student like you, Father, and I don't honestly think I'm cut out for a preacher. Lots of people aren't," he added ingenuously. "I like to work out in the open. It may sound crazy to you, but I like to plow and plant things and watch them grow. I like to harvest. It's hard work but I'm strong. I like animals. I like everything about a farm. And I want to marry Peggy. Soon. I can't wait for seven years or even for four. I've . . . I've been in love with her since I was sixteen. It cuts me all up to disappoint you both, after you've saved and planned for me, but I can't do anything else. I've absolutely decided and that's . . . that's the way it is."

There was in the words and the tone a considered finality beyond argument.

"You see, Father," he went on, "you *like* the ministry. When you were young you chose the thing you wanted to do. Surely I have the right to do the same, haven't I?"

David's lips were stiff in his white face, but he managed the words.

"Yes," he said, "yes, you have. But oh, Jeremy, have you given this enough thought and *prayer?*"

The boy flushed a little. "Yes," he answered, very earnestly, "I have. For myself I am absolutely sure about everything. It's disappointing you both that nearly kills me. I know how you've counted on my going into the ministry, Father, and sacrificed for it. You know I would do it if I could, don't you?"

Then, as there was no answer, he got up abruptly, and went out. David and Mary sat in silence, listening to his feet climbing the stairs, then David, finding speech still impossible, crossed to the study and closed and locked the door behind him. He walked over to the mantel and put a foot wearily upon the fender. He looked up dully at Magdalen Tower, at the curving stone bridge and the summer sky reflected in the Isis, but his thoughts took no clear form. People near death, he mused, must feel this slow, creeping numbness of all the senses.

The door knob turned once, softly; he heard the girls come in; he heard voices raised, questioning and incredulous; then finally more footsteps on the stairs and utter quiet. It was then, as though relieved from all human nearness, that he sat down to face the bitter facts.

Jeremy, so dedicated from his cradle, would never be a minister. *Would never even go to college.* The sacrifices, the confident plans of the years had all been in vain. The Dream of Jeremy, the great preacher, who would fulfill the prophecy of his name, who would in his own person bring alive the ambitions of his father's heart — this was over. Not until now did David realize how steady, how persistent, how all pervading that Dream had been in his life; how completely he had transferred the hopes of his own youth to Jeremy for achievement. Now, he, his only son, was not even going to college, would never see the Seminary, nor win a possible scholarship to take him to study beneath the dreaming spires, would never sway congregations by the fire and fervor of his words. Oh, this was what came of the long years in Ladykirk! Was it his father's own failure that had driven Jeremy from the pulpit to the plow? Bitterness ate in upon bitterness.

The slow hours followed each other and the big hall clock chimed them as they passed.

It was two o'clock when David through his insupportable pain and disappointment suddenly saw another face as though it looked at him from the opposite chair. It was that of Oliver Coates. He heard his own voice so lately raised in words of wisdom and advice to another man whose son had disappointed him. The irony of it! The desperate, impossible emptiness of those words as he turned them upon himself!

But were they empty? He recalled them with scrupulous care. They had been true words as he spoke them. They still were. Steadily, painfully, honestly then, as a surgeon might probe, he considered the secret places of his own heart. Was it chiefly his own ambition and pride which now lay slain? Had it always been God's will and his son's best good which he had truly sought, or a vicarious fulfillment of his own desires? He did not spare himself. At last he knew, as he had often told others, that *acceptance* was the first law for the wounded spirit. From that point on, the hurt would begin to heal. He recalled his last admonition to Oliver. "Be kind to your boy and don't take this too hard."

He sat quietly as another hour passed, then he rose, blew out the lamp, unlocked the door and went slowly up the stairs. There was a light still showing under the door of Jeremy's room! He tapped softly and went in. The boy was sitting, still clothed, on the side of his bed, complete dejection in every line of his body, waiting, evidently, for his father to come. David sat down beside him, put his arm about his shoulders and smiled into the troubled young face.

"You did give us a shock tonight, but after we get used to it, we'll be happy for you." He knew them for brave words.

Jeremy's body quivered. "You don't hate me then?"

"Oh, my dear boy!"

They sat close, each feeling the power of a love he could not speak.

"It's a noble calling, that of a farmer. I've often said so,"

David remarked slowly at last. "And you needn't let your fine mind go to seed even if you don't go to college."

"That's it!" Jeremy answered eagerly. "Peggy and I have talked that over. We're going to join the Reading Circle as soon as we're married and start our own library, and, Father . . ."

"Yes, son."

"Don't think because I'm not going to be a preacher that I'm not interested in . . . well, the *church*. I thought . . . maybe I oughtn't to say this . . . but I thought some time when I'm older, I might even get to be an Elder. And right now, if there's anything I can do for you . . ."

"Thank you, Jeremy."

"And you're not too disappointed in me?"

"I could never be disappointed in you," David said gently. "I am proud of you. Someday I know you will be a man of influence here, a pillar in the church and the community. God bless you, Jeremy. Good night."

He went out, closing the door softly, and stood for a moment, gathering his forces after the effort of the conversation. Yes, the Dream was dead. Dead. Dead. But he had buried it. There was a triumph of overcoming in that. He could now hold fast to the reality. Here, so close to him, were still his children: his son with his determined young strength; his daughters sleeping safely in their quiet beds; and just down the hall, where another light was still burning, Mary with her sweet body and sweeter spirit — Mary, his beloved, awaited him.

Chapter Twelve

~~~~~~

T HE WHOLE VILLAGE settled back, weary and relaxed, after the Revival. The gossip slowly spent itself until
even conversation took on its usual, easy-running content.
There was, as David had predicted, a general attitude of kindli-
ness toward the Coates family. The town, while uncompro-
mising in its standards of conduct and its denunciation of any
breach of them, was yet quick to sense true repentance and to
enjoy indulging in that pity for another's humiliation which
brings a comfortable, if unconscious, sense of self-satisfaction
along with it. The Coates family fulfilled these conditions
perfectly. Maria Coates, always a favorite among the women,
confided freely in all her neighbors, with tears; Oliver Senior
went his way in silent and terrible humility, and the boy himself,
with his shy, beseeching eyes, made a constant, mute appeal to
the town's sympathies. In time, David was sure, it would all
come right with the Coateses, even with the stricken Elder himself.

Urged on by an almost fanatical zeal, born partly of his need
to smother the ache in his own heart, David worked now upon
his sermons each morning and caught up with the loose ends of
his pastoral work in the afternoons. He went to see Jim Cuppy

and found him now willing, even eager to talk. His thin, sensitive face was bright with his new justification. He had already felt the town's changed attitude toward him and he seemed to have grown taller under it. He spoke of his drawing and how he meant to get at it again in earnest and, greatest surprise of all, promised to join the church at the April Communion. As David left him he was struck with a sudden thought. Could Aunt Betsy Wade do something to guide the boy in his work? At least until plans could be made for his further schooling? He dashed back to Jim and begged for a little sketch.

"That one of Mr. Moss!" he said. "Could you let me borrow it, Jim? I'll keep it safe."

Jim went into the house and at last emerged with the small sheet. It showed old Henry Moss, the town paperhanger, seated upon a chair, a roll of wall paper cascading from his knee, his head tilted to the side, his one cheek slightly bulging from his tobacco quid, his ragged beard streaked with the juice, his expression mournful as always, as he operated the trimming shears with a knotted hand. The body was a bit out of proportion, but the likeness was uncanny.

"Trust me with this, will you, Jim? I won't embarrass you in any way."

He stopped to see Billy Kinkaid to offer again a helping hand if he needed it; he drove out to Ben Losting's one cold afternoon; he made his routine rounds of the sick and sorrowing; he married a young couple one night in the manse parlor; he smoothed a small rift in the choir due, he surmised, to general weariness of the flesh on the part of the members after their hard week's work; and he eagerly answered a summons from Aunt Betsy Wade which came before he had been able to get over to see her.

He found that her ostensible reason for calling him was to

change the psalm for her burial service back again from the Twenty-Seventh to the Nintieth, but really, he knew, to hear all the news of the Revival first hand, Miss Miranda not being in her opinion an inspired reporter.

"So it was the Coates boy after all! That will set old Oliver down a peg, I should think. A good man, nobody better to mend a roof, but a touch of the Pharisee in him. So this clears the Cuppy lad, eh?"

"Yes, and I want to talk to you about him. I'm very interested in that boy. He has, I believe, a great gift."

"Gift!" snorted Aunt Betsy. "The only gift in the Cuppy family is for procreation on a large scale. I hear Milly is just about to have her thirteenth, and doing washings every week as usual. It's a crime! Somebody ought to give the old man rat poison! What do you mean, *a gift?*"

"Judge for yourself," David answered, drawing the little sheet from his pocket and laying it in her hands. She looked at it, turned nearer to the light, looked again.

"Henry Moss!" she breathed. "To the very life!" And then, "You don't mean the boy did this?"

"I do. And a great many more. I've been fond of Jim for a long time and I've been over to see him often the last year trying to persuade him to come into the church. One day I caught him at a sketch. That's how I found out."

"It's incredible!" Aunt Betsy said in a voice curiously subdued, for her. There was wonder, there was respect in it. "It's amazing! The squint in the eyes, the sag of that mouth . . . he's caught it all. I can't believe it!"

"Now I've got an idea," David went on. "It occurred to me that you could give Jim some help with his art, and in return for it maybe he could be of use around here. He's a good worker. I'd like to get him away from the surroundings he's in. I believe the boy will go far, but he's in the rough now, of course. You could teach him manners along with color and perspective. Please don't feel I'm presumptuous in suggesting it."

"Do you think he'd come?" she asked humbly, her eyes still glued on the sketch.

"I think he might."

"We could use a boy," she said slowly. "Miranda isn't very spry. There's not too much I can teach him at my age . . . but I guess I still remember the elementals. I'd like to work with him." Her old eyes glistened. "I could introduce him to oils and help him start landscapes. David Lyall, you'll maybe get a star in your crown for this! I hear," she added, peering over her glasses, "that the whole town's singing that song. Miranda's at it every day. For myself, I'll stick to Isaac Watts."

"Me too," David said smiling. "I'm more than happy that you'll consider taking the boy. Shall I speak to him about it?"

"No," said Aunt Betsy in her peremptory way, "I'll send for him myself and we'll have a talk and I'll keep the sketch till he comes."

It was left so, and David went home with an elated sense of accomplishment.

Darkly in the nights, however, there settled upon him the cloud of his disappointment about Jeremy. That wound, while covered, would take long to heal. He still wondered if his own conspicuous lack of professional advancement had affected Jeremy's decision. He saw again constantly his own eager, confident youth against the background of the present, and a sadness seeped through his being. He would lie these nights, very still, beside Mary's sleeping body, as though a mortal weight had settled upon his limbs and heart together.

But in the mornings a strange thing happened. With the soft, insistent light there came an amelioration of his pain. The normal early sounds of life broke pleasantly upon him. All the residual joys of his heart rose again even as spring was now gradually rising above the cold, gray theme of winter. Once he thought of Martha Olden. She had been troubled the last time he was to see her because the town evidently thought she was laughing again too soon after her sorrow.

"Deep down inside, my heart's broken for Cyrus. I'll never get over it. But when something funny happens, I just laugh in spite of myself. Is it wrong?"

He had caught her hands in both his own. "God give you grace," he had said, "to laugh all you can."

He still believed he was somehow on the right track in thinking that the scale in every life tipped greatly or ever so slightly toward happiness. "Saint Paul's groaning and travailing creation to the contrary," he muttered, smiling, to himself.

Mary had more quickly adjusted to Jeremy's altered career. She still looked paler than usual, David thought, but she had begun to speak with cheerfulness about Peggy's fine qualities, the beauty of the MacDonald farm and the comfort of the big house. She even ventured small jokes occasionally about how she expected to be invited there later on for the big events of the farm year: harvesting, cider-making, etc. David marveled at this, but admitted that the little pleasantries helped bridge the awkward gap between the old plans and the new.

As a matter of fact Mary's mind and activities were already becoming engaged upon another matter. For years she had dreamed of the possibility of having *Presbyterial* meet at Ladykirk. This was an impressive organization made up of representatives from every Woman's Missionary Society in the Presbytery, covering roughly the entire county. To its annual convention came denominational delegates of every church from the smallest hilltop to the largest town and city.

As a rule these two-day meetings were held in the more important centers, but Mary, urged by various motives, had boldly determined to issue her invitation at the last Presbyterial. So she had arisen in the big Rushville church April a year ago, and with all the gracious assurance her quick-beating heart would permit, told the women assembled that the Ladykirk church warmly invited them to meet there the following spring. The invitation was promptly accepted.

Her first motive — Mary told herself fiercely it *was* the first — had been to secure for their church and local Society the tremendous stimulus and prestige which the Presbyterial's meeting there would give; the other motive had been a personal one. Among the delegates would be women from the biggest and finest churches in the county — wives of Elders, wives of Trustees, wives of potential Visiting Committees. They would all see David. He *was* handsome and young looking for his age. He would give the formal address of welcome at the big "open" evening meeting and he always did that sort of thing so well. But most important of all, by far, she would arrange to entertain overnight at the manse the delegates from *Moreswell* and from *Waverly*, where the pulpits were now vacant.

In a sense it seemed futile to cling further to hopes of Moreswell, yet two facts were undeniably true. The congregation there had not yet called a new minister. They had been without one for almost a year, which was a long time. And the committee *had* been interested enough in David to come out to hear him last June. Was it not possible that this interest might be reawakened? Be stimulated?

The Waverly pulpit had been vacant now for a shorter time. The church there was not too much larger than their own; the town, however, would have certain advantages over Ladykirk. But oh, *Moreswell!* The county seat! Well, who knew what might happen now? Mary never for a moment underestimated women's influential power.

The whole prospect, indeed, had yielded a certain nebulous

hope to her heart throughout the year, although because her conscience twitched in connection with such long-range plans, she had refused actually to acknowledge this balm so far ahead of time. And in her tender, innocent agonizings for David's success and the children's happiness (Faith's especially), she had tried earnestly to justify her procedure to the Almighty.

But now as February drew to a close with the great occasion only a little more than a month away, she could not only begin her preparations for it but indulge in the optimism which was involved in it. The women of the church, rested now from the emotions of the Revival, were eager and enthusiastic also. The conference would give full scope to their various abilities. A luncheon would be served at the church on both days so that those specially gifted in making coffee or chicken salad for a hundred and fifty people would be in their glory. Others, differently talented, would serve on committees of all sorts, and all who had a "spare" room would have guests in their homes overnight.

There was about the whole affair a delightful mixture of religious and social import, making it the most important event the townswomen had known in years. Even the U.P. and Covenanter sisters were interested, for they would be invited to attend the meetings and would naturally stand ready to lend anything their Presbyterian neighbors wanted to borrow when the time came, cakepans and salad crocks knowing no denominational barriers.

Within the manse, Mary worked indefatigably. The house must be cleaned throughout, every curtain washed, stretched and mended, every carpet beaten and scrubbed to revive the dim colors, cushions recovered, portières redyed, David's study renovated (he winced slightly over this item); and if it could possibly be managed, their faded and stained bedroom paper replaced with new.

It was an ambitious campaign, but like a small, dauntless general she set about it. The family, ever quick to seize upon material for jokes, soon developed a new one.

"I think," Mary would say, "that this week, we'll launder the downstairs curtains. . . . "

"Because they must be nice
For the Pres-by-ter-ial!"

The children would shout it in chorus.

One day Jeremy looked up gravely from the supper table. "I believe," he said reflectively, "that I'll crop Prince's tail. Shortened and tied up with a blue ribbon, it would look rather smart. . . . "

"For the Pres-byt-erial!" the girls chanted.

In spite of their badinage, however, the family threw themselves heartily into the preparations. The girls house-cleaned, and mended fragile lace curtains; Jeremy valiantly beat carpets each Saturday and tacked them down again in the big rooms; David, eschewing all help, dusted and rearranged the books in his study; and finally Henry Moss, the town's one and only paperhanger, who had to be handled with infinite tact because of his temperamental attitude toward his work, was, after several breaches of promise, maneuvered into the bedroom where he sat, as in Jim Cuppy's sketch, mournfully chewing his quid as he trimmed the rolls with his grimy-looking, knotted hands. His final accomplishment was always above reproach, however, and in four days' time the old room bloomed fresh with roses. Mary was beside herself with pleasure. She felt sure the Trustees would agree to pay for it, for David had always asked for so little in the way of improvements. But in any case it was worth the cost, she thought recklessly. She would put the delegates from Moreswell in this room, let the Waverly ladies have

Faith's, which now with its fresh curtains and small refurbishings looked very nice; Faith would share Lucy's, she and David take Jeremy's, and Jeremy would go to the eaves room in the garret. Oh, if they only had a bathroom, how really comfortable their guests would be!

The weeks flew. Lucy made her second visit to the Ross home and returned in a state of radiant contentment. Ninian was almost well; Mr. Ross had been increasingly kind; she was to have her ring in June on the anniversary of their first meeting, but they would not be married until fall owing to the fact that Ninian would now have so much work to make up at college; the only cloud was Mrs. Ross's opposition and this was a dark one; but they had decided to try to forget this, hoping that one day it might disappear.

Mary hugged the vicarious joy to her heart as she worked. If something *should* happen to David because of the Presbyterial (and it could, she always reassured herself stoutly), then Faith might get her chance too. And there was no doubt about Jeremy's happiness! Since his confession he had been his old debonair, high-spirited self, with occasional touches of becoming maturity as he spoke of his future responsibilities.

March passed with its bright, racing clouds, its crying wind and early golden evening star. Kites flew, the maples and lilacs budded, the snow all disappeared and the roads became hub-deep with mud.

Out in the garden along the fence, the great spring *brood* had begun in the hives. David went out one mild afternoon, lifted a box lid and peered below the sections at the miracle within. There was the Queen already engaged upon her vast processes of procreation; there were the golden-brown brood cells each housing its own mystery; there was the whole complex structure of the hive, ready to welcome its new life and to prepare for the coming summer's flow of sweetness.

He raised the corner of each box carefully to satisfy himself by the weight that there was enough honey still within to carry the bees on to flower time. All was well, he decided.

He passed up the walk and paused as he so often did by the grapevine. It would have to be pruned this spring. He must speak to Josiah Hunt about it. Josiah had the knack of this as of many other things. He thought of the old vine soon to go under the knife, to bleed, and then to burst anew into glorious leaf, into perfumed incipient fruit and finally the full purple grape! *I am the vine; ye are the branches.* He would preach soon upon that text.

Within the manse all that could be done was now done. Mary was glad, for she was very tired. David remonstrated with her frequently during the last week of March, as she constantly answered the telephone or consulted with committees.

"Don't work so hard, Mary. You look thin to me. For heaven's sake, don't wear yourself out over this business. Everything will go all right."

She only smiled. Her eyes, in spite of her weariness, were bright. He knew she was going to entertain four delegates, but she had not told him they were to be the women from Moreswell and Waverly! There might be other vacant pulpits in the Presbytery just now, but she was sure of these. And men never knew how often women pulled the strings! How often from behind the scenes they prompted the real actors!

Everything in a larger sense was now well organized, for Mrs. Faraday, their President, had done her work well. There was a committee to cover every phase of the Presbyterial from *Devotionals* down to *Hot Rolls.* The decorations were positively inspired: quantities of laurel cut from the Creek bank were massed at either side of the pulpit with blooming house plants showing between! Minnie, who had volunteered to help without being on the committee, had brought all her red geraniums, and her artistic touch in their arrangement was now evident.

One minor problem that had confronted the women was what to do with Mrs. Crombie. All through the years she had held a place of peculiar importance owing to her wealth, her big house, her own sharp-tongued assurance and, it had to be admitted, her extraordinary efficiency. Now she was not as strong as she used to be and so could not be given the chairmanship of one of the regular committees. However, she must not be slighted, for when offended she could in the most unaccountable ways create friction.

It was finally decided to make her chairman of *Hospitality*, her only duty being to sit at a table just inside the basement room and register all guests, assigning them to the homes where they would be entertained overnight and later to read this list aloud at the afternoon meeting. Mrs. Crombie was highly satisfied with this arrangement, engaged Winnie Ames, the town seamstress, at once to make her a new silk dress, prepared a large notebook with parallel columns labeled *Delegates* and *Hostesses*, and on a sheet of foolscap, wrote the long list of those who wished overnight guests. Mary had been especially eager to see Mrs. Crombie properly mollified, for ever since the episode of the Evangelist she had been very cool both to David and herself. From various sources she had heard that Mrs. Crombie blamed David for the change of plan. "If Mr. Lyall had just put his foot down and told the Evangelist plain out that he was to come to me, he'd have come and an end to it," she had told all and sundry. Well now, Mary thought, she could assign herself as many guests as she pleased and make up for her former disappointment.

She went over one morning to tell Mrs. Crombie that she herself was prepared to entertain *four*, and her preference would be the delegates from Moreswell and Waverly, if that could be conveniently arranged. She watched as this notation was entered in the notebook, pleased with her diplomatic phrasing and also that she had mentioned it in good time.

The day of the Presbyterial dawned clear and perfect. April put aside her earlier tears of the week and smiled entrancingly upon Ladykirk and all within it. Mary woke before daylight, made up "light cakes" from sponge set the night before and after breakfast was over with, gave a last careful scrutiny to the whole house. She had laid *Religious Aspects of the Greater Poets* by David Lyall in a conspicuous place on the parlor table, before she went up to bed the night before, and had privately cautioned the girls to be sure to put it back if their father removed it. Somehow, she would draw the guests' attention to it if they overlooked it. She had her little speech all prepared to give — casually of course — when they showed interest.

"My husband's the most modest man in the world *about his writing*, but I'll see if he won't autograph a copy for each of you, if you'd care to have it. Just a little souvenir of your visit!"

Then she would take four books from the sad stack in the corner of the study and *make David sign them*, no matter what he said to her afterwards. Sometimes a woman just had to go ahead, regardless!

She gave the girls now the last instructions concerning the setting of the table and the cooking of the evening dinner which had to be left to them, then after receiving their excited assurances, and commendation upon her freshly pressed surah silk and retrimmed spring hat, set off for the church where she would need to remain during the entire day.

Already there was great activity. Women were bustling about in the small rooms at the side of the hall arranging the luncheon or putting last touches to the long tables set in the basement. Already a number of guests had been registered and more were arriving constantly. Mary in her official capacity as wife of the minister and Mrs. Faraday as President of their society, greeted them cordially, introduced them to each other and directed them to Mrs. Crombie's table to register. There was a delightful stir and chatter which made Mary's cheeks flush rosy with the pleasure of it. It was a very big thing, this that she had boldly undertaken, but it was going to be a success! Anyone could feel that already in the very air.

All at once two women entered, younger and more fashionably dressed than most of the others, and bearing upon them in clothes and manner the indefinable imprint of social distinction.

"We are the delegates from Moreswell," the one said to Mary, smiling, while an evasive and delicate fragrance drifted from her person. "I am Mrs. Rollins, and this is Mrs. Darby."

"I am Mrs. Lyall, the minister's wife, and I'm delighted to meet you." Mary's heartbeats all but choked her.

"What a quaint old town Ladykirk is," Mrs. Darby said in her beautifully modulated voice.

"And so historic," Mrs. Rollins added with her charming smile. "I have to do a paper for our Reading Circle on Old Hostelries of the State and I want so much to include the Stone Hotel here."

"It *is* interesting," Mary said brightly. "Perhaps my husband could give you some facts about it. You'll have a chance, I'm sure, to talk with him later."

She didn't want to tell them outright that she was entertaining them, for that would give away the fact that she had deliberately planned it so, but she chatted on, feeling herself lifted into a different atmosphere. In her mind she could see these two in the newly papered bedroom; around the table with Grandmother's best giving it the grace to which they were accustomed; she could see them in the parlor while Faith played for them; she could see them talking to David, *looking at his book*. Surely, surely they would like her family! She grew more and more animated and knew intuitively that she was making a good impression, herself.

"We mustn't monopolize you," Mrs. Darby said, with apparent regret, "but it's lovely indeed to meet you. We'll see you again, I hope."

"Oh, of course," Mary replied gaily, "I shall look forward to it," and handed them on to Mrs. Faraday.

Through the day Mary's spirit soared as upon eagle's wings. The morning session got under way with enthusiasm; the sanctuary room above looked beautiful, decorated with the laurel which incidentally quite hid the worn pulpit chairs; the surpassing excellence of the luncheon was commented upon on all sides; the afternoon service was interesting even to the reports. An undercurrent of pleasure seemed to run subtly below the serious business of the occasion. The delegates apparently felt the warmth of their welcome, more noticeable in the village than in larger town churches, and were responding to it. Deep in her heart Mary felt that she had been led by Providence to bring this all about, and that in addition to the success of the Presbyterial the hidden prayers of her heart were going to be answered.

Toward the end of the session she and Mrs. Faraday quietly slipped out and returned to the basement to assist delegates and hostesses in finding each other when they all came downstairs. Even now Mrs. Crombie in her new silk would be standing up in front of the audience with her notebook, reading out the assignments, at each of which the women designated would rise and thus have a chance to see each other. There would still be plenty of further inquiries, however, even with this arrangement, and Mary and Mrs. Faraday would be there to answer them.

"It's going well, isn't it?" Mrs. Faraday said excitedly now as they waited. "I never knew a Presbyterial to start off like this one. It's wonderful!"

"And the luncheon!" Mary beamed. "The women at the table near me all said they had never tasted anything like it!"

"Well," Mrs. Faraday chuckled, "they'll find out what Lady-kirk can do when it tries. Oh, here they come!"

There was the sound of feet upon the wide stairs leading to the vestibule, then the basement was suddenly full again of laughter and many voices. Mary and Mrs. Faraday directed the visitors to the right and the local women to the left and answered questions as fast as they could.

"Could you point out Mrs. Wilson? We are to go with her."

"I couldn't see my delegates' faces when they stood up. If you'd just call out *Rushville* now . . ."

It was all pleasant, happy confusion. As soon as the crowd thinned a little, Mary hurried over to Mrs. Crombie's table. It would be tactful before claiming her guests to show proper deference.

"Everything's going beautifully, Mrs. Crombie, and I hope you aren't too tired. I met the Moreswell ladies this morning, but I haven't seen those from Waverly. I think they must have come late, but I'll find them now as soon as . . ."

Mrs. Crombie interrupted her, crisply.

"You aren't having the Moreswell delegates. They're going to the hotel."

"*The hotel?*" Mary breathed.

"Yes. It wasn't my doing. They just said when they registered that they'd already got rooms at the hotel and wished to stay there." She lowered her voice. "They're pretty uppish, if you ask me. But I guess now you'll know how I felt about the Evangelist. It's exactly the same thing, only this time it's in *your* lap."

Mary's face had turned white. She held the table with both hands, for she felt weak.

"Who did you assign me then in their place?" she asked.

"Waverly. That's what you asked for. There's just one came from there. That old lady sitting over in the corner."

"You mean . . . you gave me . . . just *one delegate?*"

To do Mrs. Crombie justice she now looked decidedly embarrassed. Her face flushed. "Well, you specified Moreswell and Waverly. You seemed set on those two places. There were plenty of hostesses ready to take *anybody*. I did what you asked as far as I could." She began rustling her papers nervously, trying apparently not to look at Mary's face.

"And everybody's placed now . . . *everybody?*"

"Everybody's placed, and a big job it's been, too. Well, you've got one, anyway. Lots of women have just one. And about the Moreswell pair, as I say, you'll know now, you and Mr. Lyall, how *I* felt!"

Mary turned away and to her horror saw the room rising and falling around her. Worst of all, she felt tears imminent. She got a chair and sat down, biting her lips hard, fighting the faintness back. She felt, indeed, as though she could never rise. Mrs. Faraday hurried over. "Are you sick, Mrs. Lyall? You're just overdone. You've worked so hard over this thing. Sit still and I'll see to the rest. They're pretty well gone now anyway. Are you sure you're all right?"

"Yes . . . just a little faint for the moment. Thanks so much."

She got to her feet. The room was nearly emptied now and she could see clearly the old woman in the corner. She sat there, waiting to be claimed, her faded eyes somewhat anxious behind the spectacles, her veined hands clutching a small reticule on her capacious lap. She had a round, wrinkled, gentle face and white hair drawn tightly back under a black silk bonnet which tied beneath her chin. There was about her person a soft, bulging abundance of flesh owing to a comfortable, uncorseted old age. She looked up and smiled happily as Mary approached.

"I just sat here out of the way till you'd come. I've been watching you. Course I knew who you was. I'm Mrs. Jenkins, and I never thought I'd be entertained *at the preacher's*. When the lady at the table told me I said any place would be all right, but she said no, you'd asked special for Waverly!" Her smile widened.

Mary, with a great effort, rallied her stricken forces.

"We're glad to have you, Mrs. Jenkins, and perhaps we'd better be going now. You're to be our only guest as the others I expected have arranged to stop at the hotel. I was prepared for four," she added, the words bursting from her.

Mrs. Jenkins' eyes filled with quick sympathy.

"My, that's too bad, and you all ready for them! It's a disappointment, ain't it, when you work and prepare for company and they don't come. There would have been two of us, but the other lady took an upset last night late and there wasn't time for either of the alternates to get ready. So I just said when she phoned that I'd come on by myself. Henry, that's our hired man, he drove me to the Junction and I got along fine. I do love a Presbyterial! I haven't got appointed a delegate for dear knows when till this time. I guess they think I'm not stylish enough mebbe for the big places." She chuckled gently and without resentment. "But wait till I tell them what a grand meeting it was and that I got entertained *at the preacher's!* They'll open their eyes. And so will my John. He's my son." Her whole face became suffused with unspeakable pride.

They were at the front door now. Jeremy was to be waiting with the buggy to take the luggage and drive any one of the ladies who might not care to walk. (Oh, how carefully planned the details! All but the most important!)

He was there now, as they reached the pavement. He wore his best suit and stood proudly beside the freshly polished buggy. Although Prince wore no blue ribbon on his tail, he was curried within an inch of his life and his harness had been cleaned and oiled with infinite care. Jeremy came forward, a large question in his eyes.

"This is our son Jeremy, Mrs. Jenkins. He'll drive you home. There was a slight misunderstanding, Jeremy, so we are having no other guests."

For a second he stood motionless as though trying to take in the meaning of her words; then his dark eyes caught fire.

"Mrs. Crombie, I take it," he said in a low voice.

"Partly. Now if you'll help Mrs. Jenkins into the buggy . . ."

"You get in too, Mother, and drive. I'll walk home and be there ahead of you!" He smiled at the old woman who smiled happily back.

"You're a little like my John was at your age," she said. "He's my son. All I've got."

Jeremy was as good as his word. By cutting corners and coming up through the garden he managed to reach home first and prepare them there for the tragic denouement. David was out in the drive when the buggy drew up, warmly hospitable to their guest, his eyes and touch on Mary's arm, tender beyond words.

They all rose to her need. The girls helped Mrs. Jenkins up the stairs to the big bedroom with the new roses; then they cleared away the extra places from the table and attended to the final demands of the dinner, having sent their mother up to rest. The soup, served from Great-grandmother's hand-painted china tureen, was to have set the ultimate seal of elegance upon the meal — that and the bought ice cream for dessert making *three courses*. Could Moreswell itself go farther? Mary had thought. Now, as the girls with Jeremy returned to the kitchen where everything was ready except the guests for whom it was all prepared, the very perfection of the viands smote them for, for once everything they had touched had turned out well.

"Oh, it's *cruel*," Lucy said, her voice breaking.

"I *hate* that Crombie woman!" Jeremy ground out through his teeth. "She was at the bottom of this. You can bet on that!"

"We've got to conceal our own feelings and make it as easy for Mother as we can. Oh, when I think of the way she's planned and worked. . . ." Faith's eyes brimmed over.

"The way we've all worked," Jeremy added. "And for one old woman."

"But it's a hundred times worse for Mother than for us. She really *cared*, and looked forward to it so, and this awful disappointment now on top of . . ."

"On top of what?" Jeremy asked sharply.

"Well, I mean . . ."

"You mean me. You mean she took it hard about me."

"N . . . not nearly as hard as Father," Faith stammered, embarrassed, "but you know she did feel it, I mean she was rather . . ."

"You needn't elaborate."

"Don't sound like that, Jeremy, I just . . . Oh, we mustn't argue. Won't you try to be as funny as you can at dinner? It might cheer her up."

"I never felt less like it."

"Well, none of us do, but we've got to try. And don't think of what I said. Mother's satisfied now about you. It was just a shock at first and now *this* is a shock. That's all I meant. Come on, Lucy, let's get the soup ready."

Upstairs Mary had dropped down for a moment upon Jeremy's bed and David sat beside her, to hear all the story. She had to confess now that she had *asked* for Moreswell and Waverly, if that could be arranged. She had to tell all. David's mouth, as he listened, was white and set. Between the broken words he understood Mary's secret plans. There was more then to her disappointment than the absence of expected guests, though that in itself was very great. There was the loss of a last, dimly descried hope for the future.

He sat quietly smoothing her hair, but his heart was sore and very, very angry.

At last he kissed her and rose. "It's a burning shame," he said, "but try if you can, not to feel *too* badly. I know that's easy to say. I know how you've looked forward to this." He stopped and Mary read his countenance. In some strange and unholy way it comforted her to know that he was angry for her sake.

"Mrs. Jenkins seems a nice old soul. I imagine it's a tremendous event for her. We'll have to do the best we can to make things pleasant, Mary, dear. I think I could cheerfully *throttle* Mrs. Crombie!"

At the door, he turned with a wry smile. "You needn't quote me," he said.

There was no doubt of the visit's importance to Mrs. Jenkins. She came downstairs in her black silk dress, her white hair smoothed back to a tight little knot on the top of her head, her round, wrinkled cheeks shining from fresh water and her eyes bright with pleasure, as she scanned first the parlor, then the dining room table, and the faces of all the family around it. In a slow, easy, gentle voice she chatted on throughout the meal, as she ate the viands with hearty zest.

"My, but this is a treat for me! Just wait till I write to my John and tell him I was entertained *at the preacher's.* He'll be that pleased. He's awful good to his old mother. He's always after me to leave the farm and move to town but I like the country. Henry, that's our hired man, and Lizzie, that's his wife, they take good care of me. And John comes as often as he can."

She paused to chuckle at Jeremy's antics as he helped remove the soup plates.

"My, you've got a lovely family here," she said, looking from one face to another. "My John is all we ever had and I said I was a'most like Abraham's Sarah when I had him. He's been a good son, though. He's just give me one big disappointment. He's never got married. I always keep hoping he will yet."

She looked with a pleased intentness at Faith. "Every place I go I just size up the young ladies," her artless old voice went on, "and I just tell them my John ain't to be sneezed at. He's done awful well, John has. He's a teacher. We always hoped he'd be a preacher, Father and I, but I guess a *perfessor* is next best."

"Teaching is a fine calling," David said hastily, fearing for the risibles of the young people. "Jeremy is teaching now. Just a country school, of course."

"My, that's just how my John started. Are you going to keep at it?" she asked Jeremy.

This lead at once to a discussion of farming, a subject upon which their guest was completely and intelligently versed. It lasted for the rest of the meal with frequent references to her John's opinion upon all points.

After dinner Mrs. Jenkins sat in the big parlor rocking chair, rocking happily as she looked about her, one foot (encased in an old fashioned "straight" shoe) stretched out sufficiently to keep rhythmic time to the movement. Her voice flowed on softly, continuously, until time to leave for the evening session.

It was the next morning that she discovered the "pretty" blue book upon the parlor table. She had peered at it keenly through her spectacles, read the gilt lettering on the cover and quite matter-of-factly associated the name at once with that of her host.

"Why, my, my! Did Mr. Lyall write this book himself?"

"Yes," Mary said quietly. "Would . . . would you like to have a copy?"

She was overcome. At Mary's behest David came and, shame-facedly, prepared to sign it.

"Perhaps she would like to have her name in it along with yours?" Mary suggested, adding, though the others did not know from what bitter depths, "as a little souvenir of her visit."

It was done. *For Mrs. Lucinda Jenkins with best regards from the author, David Lyall.* She read it over and over aloud in her delight. Then her face clouded a little.

"I wish a'most I'd had you put Father's name in instead of mine. He'd be that pleased if he could just know."

David added in parenthesis, *For Mrs. Nathaniel Jenkins.*

She was then completely content. "I'll show this to my John and won't he be surprised I've met an Author! He won't believe it, hardly. But he'll read this, you may be sure. Such a reader he's always been! I guess that's why he's got to be a perfessor. He'll be that pleased to see this book. My, my! I guess I'll let him have it first."

Her final good-bye was touching.

"I guess this has been about the nicest visit I ever had except the time Father and I went to Ohio on our weddin' trip. Your house is so pretty and you've all been so kind to me. I'll never forget it. Many's the time at home I'll just sit and live it over. That bedroom with the roses and everything. I'll write my John all about it tomorrow. . . . And mind now, if ever you're going through Waverly just come right on out to the farm. We'll be that pleased to see you. It's just two mile from town and you turn left at the post office . . ."

When the day was all over Mary felt strangely still and quiet. The Presbyterial had been an outstanding success. The vote of thanks to the Ladykirk women had been unprecedented in its enthusiasm.

The women of the local society themselves were exuberant, even though weary, and for days now would talk about it with satisfaction. For the second luncheon had, if possible, surpassed the first. *Everything* had gone smoothly. As Mrs. Harrison remarked, there had not been a single jarring note. None, thought Mary as she climbed the manse steps with difficulty, except the one which had jarred her own heart.

She had felt queer all through the day. Her mind had wandered during the speaking because her head ached persistently. She had had a slight cold for a week, but had ignored it in her excited activity. Now, she knew, as she entered the house, that it was worse. Almost without volition, she mounted the stairs to her own room, undressed and got into bed. Everything about her felt heavy: her head, her limbs, her spirit. She lay still, stretched out under the shadow of the fresh new roses, unseeing, uncaring.

When the family discovered her they were greatly alarmed. This was not like Mother. She should have been in the midst of them now, laughing with them over *my John,* praising the girls for the dinner last night, and Father for his speech of welcome, and Jeremy for the shined-up buggy and harness which had been a surprise for her, talking everything over together the way they always did.

But Mother lay with her eyes closed and scarcely spoke at all. David, although anxious himself, thought he understood and tried to reassure the children. It was just reaction from the weeks of work and nervous tension. The anticipation had been so keen, and then there had been . . . the disappointment. All this took its toll. She was just worn out and needed rest. They would keep her in bed tomorrow so that she could take care of the cold and in a day's time she would be all right. Lucy put a cool cloth over her eyes, Faith brought a headache powder, and David, listening to a little sharp cough, prepared a mustard plaster with his own hands.

"Now, no squirming. You probably don't need this but we'll be on the safe side. There! After our various *simples,* and a good night's sleep you'll be fresh as a daisy! You're just tired out." Then he added tenderly, "You're not grieving too much over what happened?"

She shook her head. If she spoke the tears would come.

The next morning the cold seemed worse and David went down to Dr. Faraday's office to get some medicine.

"She's had too much Presbyterial," the doctor said as he made up some powders and folded them carefully in small papers, then poured cough medicine from his huge bottle to a small one.

"My wife said she got a little faint spell the first afternoon. Well, I hear it was all a great success and a feather in the women's caps for bringing it off so well. Tell Mrs. Lyall I said she deserved a rest-up in bed. Let me know," he added, "if she isn't better in a few days."

But on Friday David called the doctor to come up. It was still, he was sure, just weariness and a severe cold, but he had felt a sharp anxiety that morning as he looked at Mary's heavy eyes and heard the cough. He must be sure. Dr. Faraday chatted a moment with the girls downstairs when he came, and spoke cheerfully with David as he climbed the stairs.

"Cold still hangs on, eh? Best to check the chest, then. She may need a little stronger cough syrup. Lots of grippe around now. We'll all be better when the warm days come."

He had reached the room. The door was open and he stopped dead upon the threshold. He was listening to the heavy breathing from the bed. Then silently and with a grave face, as though his diagnosis was already made, he went forward to examine his patient.

When he told David downstairs, his kind, work-weary eyes brooded upon his pastor, but his voice was quick.

"We've no time to lose, Mr. Lyall. This is pneumonia and it's gone deep already. We must get Mrs. Marling at once. I think she's free. This will take careful watching. Call the girls and I'll tell them what must be done meanwhile . . ."

David's face was stone-white.

"You mean it's *serious?*"

"Very. It would be foolish to pretend otherwise. Now, we'll all get to work."

He gave his instructions, crisply, concisely. David should telephone for Mrs. Marling, Ladykirk's one nurse, who was not ordinarily called except when the danger was grave. ("They've got Mrs. Marling!" one townsman would report to another in hushed tones, knowing then that a life-and-death struggle was on.) Lucy must run to Harrison's store for cotton batting, for a jacket must be made of it to cover the poor, tortured chest. Faith was set to stay closely by the bed until the nurse arrived and David must hurry down to the cellar as soon as possible and send more heat up to the sickroom, for it must be kept at the same temperature day and night since the weather had grown cold and raw again.

"I'll go to the office for some more medicine now," he said, "and be back with Mrs. Marling. I want to talk with her here. Keep your chin up, Mr. Lyall. We'll do everything humanly possible, you can be sure."

The whole house bowed under its sudden weight of terror. For the feeling which enveloped David and the children was nothing short of that. Mary had never been seriously ill in her life. Like the punctual return of daylight, so had she gone about her duties, making bright the house of their habitation. Now, the very center and soul of their lives was threatened, and a cloud of blackness settled upon the old manse and all within it.

The strange, heavy breathing grew worse as the day wore on and Mrs. Marling listened and watched and would not leave the bedside even for her meals. The doctor came back that night and stayed longer than usual. When he left he put a hand on David's shoulder.

"It's pretty bad, I'm afraid. You've been brave for a great many people through the years, Mr. Lyall. Now, you must be brave for yourself and your children."

"You mean there's . . . no . . . hope?"

"No. Not quite that. We're in a tight spot, though. Just pray as you've never done before."

But when they gathered for family worship that night as usual David found he could not finish. He got through the Twenty-Seventh Psalm, Mary's favorite, but then his voice failed him.

"We'll each pray silently," he said. And the room was still except for the soft settling of the burning coal in the grate and the sound of the girls' weeping.

There was no change on Saturday. All the town knew now of course and besieged the house with inquiries. Women with strained faces came to the back door with a loaf of bread, a baked chicken or a pie, to relieve Faith and Lucy in their unaccustomed responsibilities. When they had done all they could, the people of Ladykirk hushed their very hearts to hope and pray; to listen for news, to wait. . . . The terrible quiet of suspense fell upon the town.

On Saturday evening Mrs. Crombie came over, bringing a pan of her famous rolls. Her eyes were red and swollen.

"How is she, Mr. Lyall?"

David slowly shook his head.

Her eyes ran over and her mouth trembled.

"I feel as though I did it. She turned white when I told her about the delegates. I don't know what made me do what I did, and her so kind to everybody. I just wanted to get even, but oh, it was wicked! I don't deserve ever to be forgiven."

"It wasn't that, Mrs. Crombie," David managed to say. "The doctor told me this must have been coming on for a week."

She looked at him, waiting, but he could say no more. She put her shawl quickly over her head and turned to the door, sobbing as she left.

There was no change by Sunday morning. Mrs. Marling told David to go on to church if he felt he could get through the service. He could do nothing there and they would send for him instantly if there was any more unfavorable sign. Dr. Faraday felt the crisis would not come for another day at least.

It was the Sabbath of the April Communion. It was the Sabbath when, among others, Jim Cuppy, in his hard-earned new suit, was to join the church and (as Colonel Harris always put it in the Session minutes) "be admitted to the sealing ordinance of the Lord's Supper." David's body felt weak and the anguish in his soul made him fear for his self-control. But he must go, must try to go through with it. This was his duty, his work, and above all, he must not fail Jim. There would be no sermon, which would make the service easier. He dressed in Jeremy's room, his hands unsteady like those of an old man.

As he tried to recall it afterwards, the church hour was an utter blank except for one thing. Strange, he thought as he pondered this, how the inner spirit of a man, immersed in its misery, could withdraw to its own depths and remain oblivious to the outward motions of the body. For, he knew, he must have moved and spoken according to the ancient pattern of the Communion service; he must have seen the anxious eyes of the congregation raised to his, he must have watched his Elders as they solemnly distributed the elements; but all he remembered was the one moment when the boy had stood before him, and he had spoken the words of initiation, *James Cuppy, soldier of Christ* . . . and had seen that tender light flooding the young face.

As he walked home, avoiding interception as much as possible, a line from the prophet Ezekiel flashed through his mind with searing pain. *So I spake unto the people in the morning and at even my wife died.* So brief, so terse the statement to cover a man's broken heart. Oh, tragedy unutterable for Ezekiel, to carry on his work when the desire of his eyes was slipping from him. Was it so, even now, with himself?

The manse was very still by midafternoon. Mrs. Marling, silent and tireless, went about her ministrations. Beside her trained skill the family felt futile. David talked tenderly to the children gathered in Faith's room like lost and frightened sheep. He made himself strong for them. They must hope, they must pray, they must do their usual duties to keep themselves busy. He kissed the girls and wrung Jeremy's hand. He told them they must all be brave together and support each other. Then he went back to stand beside the bed and look upon the beloved face, now flushed and heedless, and hear again the labored breathing.

At last he turned and went down to the study to wrestle with the angel of God. How strong in prayer he had been all through the years when lives in other homes had hung in the balance! He had felt then a triumphant power within him. Sometimes it had seemed to him that he had gone into the very valley of the shadow and forcibly turned Death back by the unrelenting faith of his petitions.

But now, for Mary, for his own heart's beloved, he felt impotent, despairing as though the craving cry of his heart fell unavailing to earth, and the heavens were brass above him. He dropped his head upon the desk. *My God, my God, why hast thou forsaken me?*

He was shaken abruptly by the loud peal of the doorbell. This was strange, for all the townspeople on their anxious errands of inquiry went softly over the path to the back porch David got up, stumbled toward the hall, and opened the door. Dan Holding stood there before him and for a long moment they looked at each other in silence.

"So I've come, Reverend, like you told me," Dan said at last.

David moved aside and signaled him to enter. He felt distraught at this unbearable intrusion. Dan sat down in the study, holding his wide felt hat, and looked at the floor. He had now, David slowly noted, none of his old insolent bearing. The arrogant, flashing smile was absent. Instead his face looked haggard and his broad shoulders sagged.

"Can I do anything for you, Dan?" The usual words came automatically.

"When we made that bargain I never thought I'd need it. But now I'm in the worst trouble I ever was in. So, I've come."

"Another girl?" David asked sharply.

He shook his head. "It's Annie. It's my wife." His voice fell to a husky whisper. "She's found out about me. After all these years. It was that damned Evangelist told her. Oh," he gritted,

"I could kill him with my bare hands for what he's done to me!"

David could not speak. He watched Dan with a fascinated horror as he went on. "He came out to see me that week he was preachin' here. Oliver Coates drove him. I wasn't home, so he talked to Annie. *And he told her.* She never knew before. From then on she acted different and I couldn't understand it. Finally I got it out of her."

His head sank lower. "I don't know what to do. Unless things change I don't want to go on livin'. I can't stand it, Reverend. I can't stand it!" The cry was wrung from the man's soul.

"You . . . you *love* your wife, Dan?" David's amazement showed in his tone.

Dan looked up then. "Love her?" he said. "Why, I'd cut off my right arm for her. Why, I don't care for nothin' in this world but her. I'd die for her. I'd . . ."

He stopped at the dark question in David's eyes.

"I guess you don't believe me," he said slowly, "after the things I've done. I guess it would sound crazy to try to tell you. I ain't good at expressin' myself. I guess mebbe I *was* crazy."

"Suppose you try to tell me, Dan."

Dan sat silent, his handsome face working.

"I don't know as I can, Reverend," he said at last. "I don't think I can explain it to nobody. It's so mixed up, like. You see I never thought Annie'd have me in the first place. God, she was pretty. But she married me and then I got sort of scared and — jealous, mebbe — I don't know what it was. She was always above me, sort of. Not that she acted like that, but I knew it. She was kind of gentle in her ways and refined and she read books and all. I hadn't anything about me to brag of only that I could always get a girl. *You* know. Like putty in my hands. Always been like that."

He swallowed hard.

"So I just begun showin' my power to myself every onct in a

while. It made me feel big, smart, sort of, and I'd come home and swagger round in front of Annie, lickin' my lips over my secret, feelin' I could get *any* woman, almost, if I wanted her. Made me feel sort of strong, sort of master over Annie. Oh, *I* don't know exactly why I done it. You wouldn't understand."

"On the contrary," said David, looking steadily at the great, handsome creature before him, bowed now in his woe. "I think I do understand. It was a foolish, a wicked course of action, but I believe I know what was going on in your heart. Have you ever told Annie all this?"

"Me? Tell Annie? No."

"Then, Dan, you must do exactly as I tell you. Go home, as fast as you can. Tell Annie every word you've told me as soon as you get into the house. Remember," he repeated sternly, "every word. How much you love her, why you did what you've done. And tell her . . . " He broke off. "Can you go straight from now on as to other . . . women?"

"No woman means anything to me but Annie. The rest are no more than that." He snapped his finger. "It was just . . . like I told you."

"I believe you," David said. "And one thing more. Tell Annie that beginning next week you'll bring her to church every Sunday. I know she wants to come and this may prove to her you mean what you say."

Dan nodded humbly. "She'll listen. She don't act mad. Be easier if she did. She does . . . everything . . . I want. It's just that she don't talk or smile any longer. It's like livin' with a *dead* woman."

A sudden pallor swept David's face. Dan noticed it sharply.

"Are you sick, Reverend? Anything wrong?"

"It's *my* wife," David managed to form the words. "She's very, very ill."

"Not . . . *serious?*"

David nodded.

Dan's distress was pathetic. "And here I've been takin' up your time with my troubles! Reverend, I'd do *anything* for you. Look what you've done for me! Isn't there something I can do to help?"

"Yes," David said quietly. "You pray for my wife and I'll pray for yours. Another bargain," he added, though he was not able to smile at the words.

Suddenly Dan grasped him by the shoulders. All the power of the big, vital body seemed at the touch to be poured into David. It was as though an electric current of strength went through him.

"Don't you give up," Dan said fiercely. "Don't you dare give up. She'll get well. I know she will."

He turned swiftly, then added over his shoulder, "I'll be up tomorrow to hear how she is, and Reverend, I'll do the best I can . . . about what you just asked."

David turned back to the study and knelt down beside his old desk chair. For some reason, for some miraculous reason the floodgates were open heavenward and he poured out his soul.

That night Dr. Faraday came back at nine and did not leave. They knew then. Jennie McLean stayed too, making what feeble excuse she could.

"The girls want to be together tonight, Mr. Lyall, so I'll just sleep in Lucy's room and be here if . . . if you need me . . ."

Her tears interrupted the words.

Dr. Faraday sat close to the bed, watching, watching. Occasionally he would meet David's eyes, but he gave no sign. So often through the years they had kept vigil together, as the heavy hours of the night wore away. But never like this! Never before like this!

In that hush, that breathless darkness just before the dawn, a soft whisper of rain began to fall. The watchers saw Mary turn slightly and reach her hands across to where David would ordinarily have lain.

"Davy?" she said.

He leaned over her. "Darling, I'm here . . ."

"Are . . . the . . . sweet . . . peas . . . planted?" she asked weakly.

"We'll plant them tomorrow." He said it, though the words tore his heart out. Tomorrow?.

She sighed as if content, and fell again to sleep.

When the full chorus of birds woke the morning, Dr. Faraday leaned over and blew out the lamp. He sat then, tensely, one hand upon the slender pulse, his eyes fixed upon Mary's face, as though he counted each faint breath.

At seven he rose, took the temperature and walked to the window. David watched him peer at the mercury in his hand, bend forward sharply and peer again. Then slowly he turned. He was the most kindly of men, but he rarely smiled. He was smiling now straight across into David's heavy, anguished eyes.

"It's dropped," he said. "The fever has broken!"

David could not grasp it at once. "What does it mean?" he asked, thickly.

"It means," Dr. Faraday said in his careful courtly way, "that your wife, Mr. Lyall, is going to recover."

Oh, the beauty of those April days! Mary thought as she sat propped against her pillows, the whole house athrob with happiness, that she had never known such utter, blissful content. She realized now that she had been close to the last far, mortal gate, and had returned. What room for past concern when she was enfolded safely once more within the love of David and the children?

She watched the bright, blossoming fruit trees through the window; she heard the familiar gee-whoa, haw of the plowmen as they turned over the village gardens; she listened to the soft iterant refrain of the doves in the morning, the twilight note of the robins in the pine trees, and at night the delicate pipings of the young frogs from the springtime swamps along Paxton Road.

One Sunday evening she lay alone in the early dusk, having insisted that there was no need for anyone to remain with her during the church hour. She thought over then carefully her own part in the Presbyterial: the determined plans, the hopes, the infinite labors, the final crushing disappointment. She lay very still as she heard Ladykirk Creek running over its stones in the spring freshet, and the faint echoes of the last hymn, as they died away upon the spring air. Perhaps it had been wrong of her to take life in her hands and try to wrest it to her own purpose. Perhaps all her ardent devising had been wicked and misguided. At least it had come to naught. She sighed but without bitterness. From now on, no matter what came she would accept it. She would not struggle; she would not repine; so, she prayed, she might be forgiven.

On the last day of April, Lucy, coming in from the post office, knocked at the study door to leave a letter.

"That's all for you, Father," she said, as she hurried away to read the latest from Ninian.

David picked up the envelope somewhat absently, his mind still upon his own train of thought. It bore the mark of Bethel College, his own Alma Mater, a small denominational institution in the Middle West.

David groaned. "Money again, I suppose," he muttered. "I'm sure I sent my alumni dues."

He slit the envelope carelessly and pulled out the sheet.

My dear Mr. Lyall [*he read*]:

At our coming Commencement on June 21, Bethel College wishes to confer upon you the degree of Doctor of Divinity. Your book entitled Religious Aspects of the Greater Poets, *written some years ago, has only recently been brought to our attention by the head of our English department, Professor John Jenkins. We consider it a distinguished piece of work. The college therefore wishes to recognize one of its Alumni as scholar and man of God. We trust you may be able to be with us on this date. Sincerely yours,*

WILLIAM J. MASTERS, President.

David's glassy eyes read it over and then over again, fixing at last upon one sentence: . . . brought to our attention by the head of our English department, Professor John Jenkins. . . .

He straightened. "Good God!" he said, for the first time in his life using the name of the Deity as an expletive. *"My John!"*

Then he tore out of the study. "Mary!" he shouted as he took the stairs two at a time, even as Jeremy. "Mary!"

With the letter flying from his outstretched hand he burst into her room. But for a whole minute he found he could not speak.

Chapter Thirteen

~~~~~~

OFTEN WITH LIVES — as with weather — a long period of undimmed brightness follows a cloudy season. So, as May advanced with all its unfolding beauty, the hearts within the manse expanded with happiness. The news of the coming degree had rocked the household with surprise as nothing else had ever done. The children, inordinately proud and excited, treated their father as a rare being from another world and rolled the *Doctor* upon their tongues with infinite relish.

Mary, still weak, lay in her room, wrapped in warm delight, her heart all but bursting with her new justification. What she had done *had* been right after all! It had brought this wonderful, this incredible thing to David. If she had not planned for the Presbyterial, if she had not *asked* for Waverly, if she had not put the book on the parlor table, it would never have happened. Instead then, of trespassing against the divine will, she felt rather that she had been working along with a gentle Providence which had strangely manipulated events toward this end. She rested now in this thought, her cheeks showing their first faint color, a continual smile upon her lips.

And David? Schooled as he had been to humility and a quiet acceptance of defeated ambition, this sudden honor, the first in all the years, well-nigh overwhelmed him. Outwardly he was casual enough, teased the children about their taking it so seriously, made somewhat light of it also to those in the town who, owing to the usual mysterious news osmosis, had already heard about it and congratulated him. Only to Dilling and when alone at night with Mary did he acknowledge the depths of his pleasure. Dilling's own delight was touching in its intensity.

"Don't you dare say to me," after David's first attempt at modest disclaimer, "that it was this John Jenkins' gratitude for his mother's visit that brought it about. The very thought is unworthy of you! You have earned this degree by that book. And why in Heaven's name didn't I think of sending it out to your college long before this? David, nothing could give me more joy than this whole business." He blew his nose violently. "Now let some of your lame dogs go for awhile and settle down and write something else. You've been a perfect mule in that particular, you know. I . . . I'm terribly pleased. I can't tell you how much."

So, they talked it all over. Mr. Dilling was adamant upon one point. The *hood* was to be his gift. He would order it at once, so David could be invested with his own and have it to keep always.

The whole town seemed suddenly to David to be bathed in sparkling light. A delicious new zest for living ran through his veins. Just after the elysium of Mary's return to him from the dark valley, there had been added this too . . . this *gift*, the gladness of which accompanied him wherever he went. He woke with it in the heavenly fragrance of the May mornings; he hugged it close in the dim half-slumbers of midnight. I will be *Doctor* Lyall for the rest of my life, he would think, refusing to be ashamed of his quiet pride. Sometimes he and Mary repeated the words aloud to each other in the darkness, not quite as the children did, but rather as the seal, the first consummation of the hopes of long ago.

When Dilling called him down one day, David supposed of course it was to discuss the matter again, but he found it was quite a different one which was engaging his friend's mind. He was very serious.

"I've been doing a great deal of thinking lately," he said, "about Minnie and little Victoria."

David's throat still tightened whenever he heard the way the old man's voice dwelt upon the child's name.

"I have made my will of course, and arranged all secular details to the best of my ability. Little Victoria is now legally adopted and I have even selected her college if, when the time comes, the choice should prove agreeable to her and to her mother. But it has been increasingly borne in upon me that I have omitted something important."

He stopped as though what he was about to say was difficult.

"I have been bitterly opposed, as you know, to Minnie's meeting the Session and making any sort of . . . confession. I am yet. My very gorge rises at the thought. But the point I have overlooked is that little Victoria will be growing up in this town. To be happy in it she must conform to its way of life. And so must Minnie."

"That is true," David said.

"The church constitutes a very large part of that way of life, so I cannot debar them from that. I have talked with Minnie about this. While she accepted my first dictum without question, I find her deepest desire is to be reinstated and have the child baptized."

He sat, looking down at his thin, veined hands. He sighed.

"Her happiness and little Victoria's good are all I want in this world. So, do what you must to bring this about. I'll oppose it no longer."

David was deeply moved. "I am more relieved than I can say, and Dilling, I honor you for this decision. I'll make it all as easy as possible for Minnie. In the case of Mr. Wilson I called a special Session meeting at the manse, and I'll do it again. Then if she wishes, she can have the baby baptized the first Sunday in June. There is a regular baptism service then!"

Mr. Dilling nodded. "Ever since the day of Cyrus Olden's funeral I have been thinking this over."

"Why, you weren't there," David said in surprise.

"No, but I sat here at the window and heard those voices singing the Twenty-Third Psalm. Something melted in me that day, my pride, I suppose. Don't misunderstand me, David. My own beliefs — and disbeliefs — remain as they have always been, but I had at that moment a new insight into the character of these people around me. I realized that while in matters of the mind their experience may be limited, in matters of the soul . . . Well, at any rate, I can't take the responsibility of shutting little Victoria and Minnie, too, away from this. So that's that. Have you time for a game?"

Mr. Dilling rarely spoke as they played, but today he made one remark, showing that his concentration upon his queen was not complete.

"If Turbenroth or one of his ilk was the minister here instead of you, I don't believe even now I could agree to it."

David flushed a little. "Don't worry," he said. "Everything will be all right."

As he walked home, his heart was lifted anew. The whole problem of Minnie and her child with reference to the church had lain heavily upon him. Now it was to be resolved by Dilling's own wish. He had no fears now, as he would have had some months ago, about Oliver Coate's compliance in the matter of an extra Session meeting at the manse to receive Minnie. Nor had he any dread of certain questions Oliver might ask. Poor Oliver was very quiet now in the Session. David mused again over the results of the Evangelist's visit. Dan Holding and Annie had now been added to the strange procession of those whose lives had been affected by it. They were coming to church each Sunday, Dan with a show of his old arrogance to cover his embarrassment, Annie with her blue eyes full of an incredulous and wistful wonder. Dan and he had wrung each other's hands after their first service, the clasp speaking what their lips could not.

In Billy Kinkaid's case there had been one small lapse. A drummer had gone in to his store for a dish of ice cream late one night and offered Billy a swig of whiskey from the bottle in his overcoat pocket. Billy had accepted with alacrity and together they had finished it.

"But you see, Reverend," Billy had explained conscientiously later, "there wasn't a full quart to start with so I couldn't possibly run into any *difficulty*. You know. Just enough to taste my mouth as you might say but not enough to *repent* over. So, if it's all right with you, Reverend, I'll just count I've still got a clean slate."

In Ben Losting's case there had been a violent explosion. Ben had gone importantly to the Squire's a short time after the Revival and with complete and blustering confidence, demanded the permanent return of his gun. The Squire had refused point-blank.

"My Gawd!" Ben had yelled at the top of his lungs, "don't you know I got converted? Wasn't you at the meetin'? Don't you know I'm a sinner saved by grace?"

The Squire had spat accurately in his maroon spittoon and squinted in Ben's direction.

"Hope so," he replied with moderation, "hope so."

Ben was furious. "Why you ain't no Christian yourself! You're a damned, pigheaded, son-of-a — "

"That'll do, Ben," the Squire broke in sharply. "One more word out of you and I'll put you in the cooler. Go on home and behave yourself."

"When am I gettin' my gun, you old . . ."

"Ah! Ah! Tell you what I'll do. If you keep sober and keep

the peace till next huntin' season, I'll give you back your gun. Now get along."

Ben had gone straight up to the manse and poured out the conversation unexpurgated to David. He was frantic with rage and disappointment.

"But," David remonstrated, "you won't really need your gun again until next fall and you expect to keep sober in any case, so it's not so bad, Ben."

"It's the principul of it," Ben said. "Here I get converted an' everybody says it was the biggest one at the whole Revival an' the Squire don't pay no more attention to it than if I'd spit on the sidewalk. Well," he added heavily, "since I'm here I might as well shine 'er up."

David watched him as he caressed the gun like a lover. When he was all finished he had set it back in its place and turned to go.

"You'll be careful, Ben," David admonished, "and keep sober. You must hold hard to what you have gained."

Ben heaved a prodigious sigh. "All that there trouble I went to, lettin' myself go, groanin' an' shoutin', and rarin' round at the Revival. Thinkin' I'd get my proppity right off. Course I'll have to keep sober now till huntin' season, but I tell you, Reverend, if it wasn't for my gun, I'd say it was hardly worth it."

He had gone, deflated, on his way.

As the May evenings passed with their clouds of perfumed snows beneath the fruit trees and the sharp point of the little new moon caught in the lace of the garden elm, Mary from her upper window was the first to see it one night, a ridge of fire along the western hill behind the town. She called the others excitedly.

"The coke ovens! They're starting up at Kirkville!" Jeremy exclaimed, as they all crowded to look.

Night after night then, the wavering crimson flames rose against the sky, and the dwellers in Ladykirk acknowledged with a touch of sadness that the old era had passed and a new one had begun. More and more village men now worked at the mines, coming home grimy with coal dust; strange faces appeared in the post office; foreign tongues sounded along the quiet stretches of Main Street.

David had been steadily watching the growth of the town beneath the hill. He drove up frequently and sat in the buggy as he studied the rows of red frame houses with their shabby entourage of outbuildings. He wondered just how to go about work in what he felt was to be his enlarged field. By nature shy and a gentleman, he had a horror of professional intrusiveness. It was different, of course, with Dr. Faraday. He was being called already day and night by the people of the Patch. He needed no further introduction than the sign upon his door. He was not only welcomed, he was begged to go to them.

But with a minister it was not quite like that. The cure of souls was more subtle and not so likely to be sought after. He could of course try knocking at door after door inviting those who answered him to come to church, but acceptance would involve a very long walk for the women even if they cared to come. They shopped at the Company store and only the men came to the post office in Ladykirk.

He introduced himself to the big Scotchman who ran the Company store and he described the people of the Patch (even as Ninian had done) as a mixed lot. Some Slavs and Polaks, a few Italians, and a great many Irish, English and Scotch.

"The Welsh all seem to keep to the hard-coal fields," he said, "but there's a little of most everything else here, and that's a fact."

"I would like to serve them if I can," David said, "but while I'm getting my bearings, will you send me word if you hear of anyone who needs a minister? And I hope you'll come down to church yourself and bring your family."

"We'll be glad to," said the Scotchman, "as soon as I can pick me up a rig. We're Presbyterians, of course. I wonder," he added, "if it's struck you that half of these people anyway are Catholics?"

David showed his surprise. "It was stupid of me not to realize that! You see, Ladykirk is such a completely Protestant Community that I rather forgot. . . . Well, as it looks to me there will be plenty of work for two of us. Has any priest been here?"

"Oh, aye. One's been out. He's Father Dunn, a short, stocky chap from Moreswell. He was in here, too. Pleasant enough, though I don't hold with them, as you might say."

"How does he find the people of his own faith here, I wonder? Does he go from door to door?"

"I wouldn't know," said the Scotchman. "I've an idea he just smells them out."

David smiled. "Well, I'll have to do the same, I guess. If Father Dunn comes in again, tell him I'm anxious to meet him, will you?"

But the first call to David came unexpectedly and soon. Dr. Faraday tied his horse to the manse hitching post one late afternoon and hurried up the walk. When David came to the door, the doctor was breathing heavily.

"I'm glad I found you in," he said briefly. "I need you badly at once up at Kirkville. Can you come?"

"Of course," David said. He took his hat, called to Mary and went out.

"I think you'd better drive yourself," the doctor said, "for I may be detained longer than you'll need to stay. I'll tell you the situation, then you can follow me up. I was called on an obstetrical case last night. A young slip of an Irish girl and it was hard going. A breach birth. The child was born this morning and only lived for an hour. I did my best. Now the mother is beside herself because the baby wasn't baptized. She's running a temperature and if she starts to hemorrhage we're lost. I've kept her under sedation all day, but she's awake now and in a frenzy."

"Shouldn't you have tried for the priest? There is one who comes out, from Moreswell, I hear. . . ."

"I know. I know. I wanted to call him, but the husband is a Scot and won't have it. To be fair to the young fellow, I don't think it's only because he's a Protestant. I think he's not quite sure what the priest would say to her. It's all a tragic situation. She was so built up, of course, about having the baby so she's got her grief now, and her fears on top of that. And she's far from home, poor child! Well, if you'll get your rig, we'll go. And for heaven's sake, do your best, Mr. Lyall. We're on touchy ground here, both physically and theologically, I doubt."

David was nervous as they climbed the jerry-built steps, and entered the front room of one of the unbroken line of small red houses. He heard the crying before his eyes adjusted to the dimmer light. Then he saw the big cheap oak bed which took up most of the space. Leaning over it was a tall, white-faced young man, and against the pillows lay a girl who looked no older than Lucy. Her face was flushed and swollen from weeping, and her eyes were wild and distraught. Great shuddering sobs shook her and at each she cried out with pain. Dr. Faraday moved swiftly. He took her temperature, checked the pulse, all the while talking firmly to her.

"Now Mrs. MacDonald, you must control yourself or you may be very sick indeed. You must try to relax and stop this sobbing. I've brought someone to talk to you, Reverend Lyall."

"Oh, Kathleen," the young man said brokenly, "here's a good man come to help us. Och, listen to him, now, dearie. Sit you down, Mr. Lyall, and see if you can quieten her."

He drew a chair to the bed. David sat down and took the young woman's hands in his own. He had been praying with all his strength for wisdom, for guidance, for some word of comfort for the pitiful figure on the bed.

"I want to tell you, Mrs. MacDonald," he began in a steady voice, "how greatly I grieve for you in the loss of your baby. My wife and I lost a little child, a boy, my own namesake. That was years ago, but we never forget him and my wife grieves even yet, I know. But I want to tell you about our family."

She hardly seemed to be listening but he went on quietly.

"We have three fine children, a son and two daughters. They are the joy of our lives, and while it is hard for you to think of this now, someday I know this same joy will come to you and your husband. You will . . ."

She turned her stricken face then toward him. "But it wasn't *baptized*," she said hoarsely. "And they've taken it away . . ."

"I know," David said, "but how could that make any difference in the sight of a loving God?"

Her eyes widened, almost with horror at his words.

"You remember how the Master loved children," he went on. " 'And they brought unto him also infants that he would touch them, but when his disciples saw it, they rebuked them. But Jesus said, Suffer little children to come unto me and forbid them not, for of such is the kingdom of God.' Can't you take comfort from those words?"

But the young woman only shuddered as though she had not heard.

"I'm scared," she sobbed, "for my baby. Oh, I'm scared . . ."

Dr. Faraday came forward. His voice was almost stern. "You must control yourself, Mrs. MacDonald. If you can just listen to Reverend Lyall now and heed him."

"He's not a priest," she moaned.

"Yes," David said with dignity. "I am a priest. I am an ordained Christian minister with authority to speak peace to you."

His voice sounded strong, but within he was desperate as to how to reach this frightened young soul. He glanced at the wall beside the bed. A cheap print of the Madonna and child hung there. Suddenly a certain fact struck his mind as though it were an inspiration. He leaned near, and because she looked no older than Lucy, her name slipped from his lips.

"Kathleen," he said tenderly, "I know you must often look at the beautiful picture you have here over your bed. Did you ever think that Jesus himself was not baptized when he was a little child? Not until he was a grown man, thirty years old."

She turned her face then and looked directly at him. He could see first blank astonishment in her eyes and then gradually something else. Her sobbing stopped, and she lay quiet.

"Would you be sayin' that again, please?" she asked at length.

David repeated his words. "You probably know this but never thought before of its significance. Now I want you to hold it in your mind as you look at the picture. Say the prayers you have been taught to say. You have a duty now to get well and strong. You can't help your grief. Dear child, we know that. But you must not distress yourself with evil fears. That is wrong. Would you . . ." He hesitated, looking up at the young husband. "Should I offer prayer?" he asked.

"If you would, please, sir," he said.

David stood with the other two men, and bowed his head.

"Father of all mercies and God of all comfort, receive into thy gracious keeping the soul of the child. Comfort and sustain the parents. Restore speedily to health the young mother; give her rest of body and of mind. Give them both the oil of joy for mourning; the garment of praise for the spirit of heaviness." He raised his hands. "And may the *peace* of God which passeth all understanding be upon you and remain with you always. Amen."

He said good-bye in the room but the young man followed him out to the buggy and gripped his hand again.

"You'll come back?" he begged.

"If you want me. Are you sure it's . . . all right?"

"You helped her. I could see that. The wild look's gone. Beside, mebbe I'm needin' a bit lift up myself."

"I'll come again tomorrow," said David, "And remember I'm always ready if you need to call me. We live in the manse at the far end of Main Street — anyone can direct you. And God bless you, my boy."

He felt deeply moved. The young fellow, he was sure, was no older than Jeremy! As he reached the main road, he drew Prince to a halt and looked back over the Patch. There was work to be done here. It would be hopeless, he felt sure, to try to bring these people to Ladykirk. The church and all its offices must come to them. Perhaps they could use the old schoolhouse on the hill for a four o'clock service. If he could locate anywhere a little portable organ they could come up soon on Sunday afternoons and sing some hymns in the streets to begin with. But strongly, clearly in his mind he saw rising above the smoky red houses a tiny chapel with a white spire.

It was a week later that he — literally — ran into Father Dunn. He was walking along the main Patch street when he recalled his promise to be home by five and, after looking at his watch, wheeled suddenly around and collided with a heavily built middle-aged man who had just come out of the house behind him. It was the priest. They both smiled as they righted themselves.

"Father Dunn? I am David Lyall, the Presbyterian minister in Ladykirk. I'm terribly sorry I charged around like that. I'm really not a dangerous person." He held out his hand.

Father Dunn had a fine Irish twinkle in his eye.

"I'm sure the attack was unintentional," he said.

They walked along together, talking pleasantly enough of generalities. David had a feeling that the priest preferred to hold the conversation at this level, but he himself was eager to touch essential problems.

"We each have plenty of work here," he said at last. "I think our parishes, so to speak, are fairly evenly divided. I was called a week ago to the bedside of a young Mrs. MacDonald, one of your flock. She was in distress of mind and her life was in danger, so I did what I could. But if you should hear of it I want you to know I was not proselyting."

They had reached the end of the street.

"I have been looking forward to meeting you," David added. "As a matter of fact I've never known a Catholic priest before! And perhaps you haven't known a Presbyterian!"

Father Dunn admitted it. In spite of his evident likability there was a distinct reserve, even a trace of condescension in his manner. David acted on impulse.

"Maybe I should explain ourselves a little. The polity of the Presbyterian church actually antedates that of Rome. It is the one established by Saint Paul and . . . " he added with a twinkle of his own . . . "Saint Peter. That's not my idea, by the way. It's easily verifiable. We have an honorable history, a doctrine based solely upon the Scriptures and a dignified but very simple service. I guess that, perhaps, sums it up. As to the doctrine . . . "

He stopped and looked off across the rolling hills. "As I grow older I'm not sure just exactly how much emphasis any of us should put upon it. There," he said, bringing his eyes back to Father Dunn's questioning ones. "Perhaps that sums me up, too, without my realizing it. Well, we'll be running into each other often here. I hope we can be friends."

Father Dunn had an odd look upon his face.

"I think we'd better not ever try to discuss doctrine or church matters, but as man to man, friends it is. Only don't try to knock me over next time! I used to be quite a fighter back in Ireland."

They laughed as they parted, each still studying the other with interest and a growing liking.

As David drove home, he drew in long breaths of the spring air and felt again stronger than ever the sudden lightness of the spirit amounting to afflatus, which had overtaken him these last weeks. His eyes roved over the countryside, where the new wheat was touched by the late afternoon sun. He let the reins fall slack in his hands and sang softly to himself as he rode along:

> "*Sweet fields beyond the swelling flood,*
> *Stand dressed in living green.*"

He agreed with Aunt Betsy on the subject of hymnology. For pure poetic expression no one could surpass old *Watts*. His mind drifted to Jim Cuppy. The plan for his residence in the Wade household was working out well. A little later he would try to get money collected to send the boy to school. Mr. Dilling had volunteered to help and he knew Aunt Betsy would. Perhaps they themselves could donate a little of what they had saved for Jeremy if Mary were willing. Ah, that thought still hurt but he must bury it deep under the new joys.

As he passed up Main Street he saw that the iron gates of the hotel fence were closed and that the big yard was filled with cattle! He knew the drovers were in town. Poor Dilling! He hated these annual spring visitations, most of all when the men were buying up sheep, and he must listen from his bedroom window to the continual bleating.

"Silly beasts!" he said once, venting his wrath. "Silly, brainless, dirty, noisy beasts. I believe I would walk a mile to kick a sheep! Not hard, of course, but the gesture would relieve me."

David had laughed. "I'm ashamed of you! You haven't the poetic attitude at all. What about Blake's 'Little lamb' and Milton's 'nibbling flocks' and . . ."

"Well," Mr. Dilling replied, "I will tolerate one small lamb for the sake of the Muses, but for the grown sheep . . . Bah! Spelled with an *h*," he added.

David wondered if he should run in for a moment to cheer up his old friend, but seeing Dr. Faraday's buggy in front of the office, he decided to stop there to talk over a certain matter in private. While Mary's improvement was steady, it was very slow. She came downstairs now each day and sat on the porch or in the parlor, her "Pretty Thoughts" box on her knee and a stack of books and papers beside her, while she culled and copied selections suitable for coming obituaries. Jeremy teased her constantly.

"Such a nice, lively, convalescent pastime!" he remarked once with a grin. "Just don't get too *hilarious* over it, Mother!"

And Mary as usual explained earnestly that it didn't depress her in the least and it was so comforting to feel she had enough material on hand since one never knew when . . . Since things sometimes happened so . . .

Then, at the sudden look in Jeremy's eyes she stopped, as he bent to kiss her.

David tied Prince now, and went into the office. There was a pungent smell of medicines, since the doctor dispensed these himself along with his skill. There was a large secretary filled with medical volumes, shelves of bottles, a flat-topped desk with a large "student's" lamp, a worn leather couch and two straight chairs in addition to the doctor's own swivel one. For forty years the people of Ladykirk had come here with their ills. The shabby black bag that sat upon the couch ready to be grasped in a moment, contained along with its instruments the confidence of the countryside. This, although nobody ever dreamed that Dr. Faraday could tell many a brash young city physician more than he had learned in his courses!

The doctor rose now to greet his caller.

"Well, Mr. Lyall, nothing wrong I hope?"

"Not with me," David said as he sat down. " 'A lean dog for a long chase,' you know. I just dropped in to speak about our coming trip, I mean to my old college for . . . "

"Your degree!"

"Yes," David smiled. "It's quite a little journey. We can do it in a day of course, if that wouldn't be too hard for Mary. Just how much do you think she can stand by that time? It's only three weeks away."

Dr. Faraday looked out the window and tapped gently on his desk with a small powder spatula.

"Mr. Lyall," he said very gently, "I am sorry to be compelled to say this, but I do not feel Mrs. Lyall will be sufficiently strong by then to go at all."

David half rose from his chair. *"Not go?"* he burst out. "Oh, Doctor, that would nearly kill us both. This is a . . . to us, I mean, a big thing. Surely if we took the trip by easy stages . . . " He broke off. "Is there something about her condition that you've not told me?" His face was tense.

"Now, now, don't alarm yourself, Mr. Lyall. She's doing very well indeed. The point is, her heart is still weak. It's a muscle, you know, and can get overstrained like any other muscle. In time I am convinced it will be as good as new, but for another two months, let us say, she must rest a great deal and avoid any extra fatigue. The excitement and exertion of this trip would be unwise and might be dangerous."

"But you feel sure she'll be all right eventually?"

"I'm sure of it."

David drew a long breath. "Well," he said, "that's all that truly matters, only this other disappointment comes pretty heavy. It will really be harder on Mary, I suppose, than on me. To stay at home and miss everything . . . Oh, I don't know how I can ever tell her!"

"You won't have to. She knows already."

"What!"

"Yes," Dr. Faraday nodded. "She asked me point-blank a week ago and I told her. She had a bad moment and then she took it like a soldier. You can talk it all over now, for she's been afraid to tell *you!* It's a great pity, but after what we went through a short time ago even this doesn't seem too important."

"You're right," David said. "I'll try to forget my own selfish side of it and cheer her up. I don't need to ask you to watch her carefully?"

"I believe that's hardly necessary," said the doctor. "And I'm glad you stopped in."

They smiled with the understanding of the long years in their eyes and then David went on home.

It was in the evening after Mary had gone upstairs that he told her he knew. Mary was bright even though two small inescapable tears coursed down her cheeks.

"Next to the degree itself," David groaned, "the trip out there together and having you see it all . . . but I'm a selfish swine to talk about my own feelings. I truly care more about your disappointment. You know that."

"I know, dear. I've had a whole week to think it over and get reconciled while you've had only a few hours. But David, I've thought of the loveliest plan!"

He looked up, surprised.

"I want Faith to go! There must be some member of the family there to see you get your honor and she's the logical one really. I've been wishing all spring that we could think of something exciting for Faith to do, and this is it! You see Jeremy and Peggy are so happy and Lucy is to get her ring next week and it does leave Faith rather out of things. Now, she'll have the trip and meet strange . . . meet interesting, I mean meet *new* people and . . ."

"Mary!" David fixed her with his eye. "You're not thinking of *My John!* I simply won't have you doing that and then getting disappointed. There has been coincidence enough in connection with him, so for heaven's sake, don't go making plans and . . ."

"Certainly not," said Mary with dignity and an expression of complete innocence. "I mean that this trip will be just what Faith needs at this time. It seems providential. There will be the President's reception and the Alumni Banquet and the Play and that will all be thrilling for her, not to speak of Commencement itself. We'll let her go in to Moreswell soon and get some new clothes. We could use a little of the college money, couldn't we? I want her to have *nice* things for once, and I've especially thought of a wide leghorn hat with a wreath of pink roses!"

She lay, looking past David toward the garden, immersed in some secret delight. David kissed her gently.

"A mere father can never comprehend the workings of a mother's heart," he said, and then, "And you're not too bitterly disappointed, Mary?"

"Not since I thought of Faith," she said.

And June came, all warm and tender like a lover's heart. The roses along the hedge, the honeysuckle over the front porch, the white lilies in the garden, the herb bed near the bees — everything sent out fragrance and balm into the soft air, while overhead, low white clouds drifted lingering as though they would droop to rest upon the scented earth.

On a certain morning the manse was early astir, for this was the anniversary of that fair and fateful day a year ago when Ninian and Lucy had first met. Now he was coming on a very special errand, and Lucy's own throbbing happiness communicated itself to the whole family. As a matter of fact she had been too excited the night before to go to sleep until long after midnight and so now had to be wakened. David did it in

characteristic fashion, using the poetic formula with his knock
which he had often employed since the girls were children:

> *"Get up, sweet slug-a-bed, and see*
> *The dew bespangling herb and tree!*
> *Each flower has wept and bow'd toward the east*
> *Above an hour since, yet you not drest;*
> *Nay! Not so much as out of bed*
> *When all the birds have matins said. . . ."*

"I'm awake, Father! Is it a pretty day?"

"Perfect. Better hurry though or you won't be on hand to
welcome your guest."

There was the sound of bare feet running across the floor and
the door opened a little, revealing Lucy in a ruffled nightgown,
her hair tumbled and curling about her face.

"Father," she said breathlessly, "I was just thinking last night,
when I'm so happy and excited over getting my ring, will there
be any big happiness *left* in me for my wedding?"

She looked so young, so innocent, so fair that a sharp mist
stung David's eyes. Then he kissed the tip of her nose.

"I'll tell you a secret," he said. "There is absolutely no limit
to the amount of happiness the heart can hold, so don't worry.
Only hurry," he added.

Faith laid the breakfast table on the back porch. The flies
were not bad in the early morning and besides Jeremy had made
a wonderful new paper brush which was quite artistic as well
as effective. Mary was up this morning with the rest and insisted upon making muffins. She noted that Faith's face was
unmarked by envy or strain. She was in excellent, even gay
spirits and in between necessary household conversation, spoke
of the coming trip. It *would* be exciting, she kept saying, to
buy two new dresses and a hat and shoes all at once and *wonder-*

ful to go on a real journey and be at the Commencement!

"If only you're not too disappointed at missing it, Mother," she said.

"Not since you can go. Really!" Mary answered.

And then Lucy appeared in the new pink gingham she had made herself with Mary's help, her hair for the first time tucked up with hairpins, a large bow at the top of her head and at the back of her neck.

"Am I all right?" she asked eagerly.

"Very nice," said Mary, curbing the outrageous praise upon her tongue, "and very grown-up looking, isn't she, Faith?"

"It's amazing," Faith answered, "what it's done to you to put up your hair. Oh, I hear them now. Run, Lucy."

The day was different from any other day that Ninian had been there. Before, even though they all knew of his feeling, there had been a certain shyness, a delicate hesitancy about him in the presence of the family. Now that was all gone. He kissed Mary; he even kissed Faith; he stood with his arm around Lucy looking down at her with such open, blazing love in his eyes that Mary and David, alone for a minute in the study after breakfast, gazed at each other and gave spontaneous if un-romantic utterance to their reaction.

"My gracious, David!"

"He's got it bad and he doesn't care who knows it now!"

And then, "Bless them!" said Mary.

"Even so!" said David.

The young people drove off at last to picnic again in Houston's Hollow and leave the family to endure the passage of time as best they might until they would see The Ring. For of course, Mary and Faith agreed, he would present it to her there. When the lovers returned at five, however, there was no sign of it. They seemed indeed, rather serious. Mary, whose heart was a harp of the winds for any air to set tingling where her children were concerned, was suddenly afraid something had gone wrong. After she and David were in bed she lay awake, still wondering.

"Davy, you don't think . . . I mean I felt sure he would give her the ring when they were on their picnic."

"Not in the daytime," he said sleepily. "Night is more romantic. That's when I gave you yours."

"Why, of course!" Mary exclaimed. "Why didn't I think of that? You're so comforting, Davy." And she turned over and went asleep at once.

It seemed many hours later when there was a knock on the bedroom door and Lucy's voice calling softly.

Mary roused in a second and snatched her wrapper from the bedpost.

"It's the children! Light the lamp, David. Come in!"

They entered, Lucy laughing and crying together, Ninian close, his dark eyes shining.

"Oh, Mother, I couldn't wait till morning to show you. Father, it's too wonderful to believe. *Look!*"

David held the lamp so they could see better. There it was on Lucy's slim finger, the dazzling, the beautiful, the incredible diamond! They were by turns speechless and extravagantly vocal, intoxicated by the wonder of it.

"And the way he gave it to me — Can i tell them, Ninian?"

"Of course, darling." The sweet word slipped out.

"You see he really *knew* he was in love with me that very first night he came when we were all singing on the back porch and we voted to get the ice cream. Do you remember? And Father was called to the country? Ninian *knew* as he was leaving and I stood at the edge of the porch watching him."

"The lamplight was behind her, you see, and she looked so lovely I thought I couldn't go."

"But he had to. So tonight we acted it all out just the same with him going across the lawn and looking around every few steps the way he did then, only this time . . . "

"I didn't leave!"

"He went clear to the gate. I thought he would never turn! Then all of a sudden he did and came running back and . . . and put the ring on my finger."

They stayed quite a while, Lucy sitting on the edge of the bed and Ninian on a chair close by, for Mary and Lucy couldn't look enough at the ring, and all that had been already said had to be repeated over and over. At last David glanced at his watch on the bedside table, clutched his robe about him and stood up.

"Good heavens," he said, "it's two o'clock, and tomorrow is the Sabbath and I have to preach two sermons! We must all get to our beds now and sleep if we can." He walked around to Ninian and grasped his hand.

"The ring is perfectly beautiful, my boy, but best of all we are happy and content that Lucy is to belong to you."

"Thank you," he said a little huskily, "thank you both for being willing to trust her to me."

The next morning dawned, as had many a June Sabbath in Ladykirk, with the early hush, the fresh air flowing over the gardens, the good housewives sweeping their sidewalks and then, at sound of the bell, the general exodus from all the houses toward the three churches. This morning there was one slight difference. Mr. Dilling did not come out to sit in one of the round armchairs at the side of the hotel and sun himself against the stone wall as was his custom.

David in the pulpit at five minutes to eleven watched the congregation enter and settle themselves as usual with the flutter of fans and collecting of hymnbooks. There were many small cries here and there also, for this was baptism day, and Colonel Harrison had whispered to him as he entered, "There's a good spring crop this year!"

Suddenly there was a slight stir and sound of raised voices in the vestibule and then in the midst of a stunned and breathless quiet, Minnie, carrying her lovely child, moved slowly up the aisle to the Masters' pew near the front where "the boys" were already settled. Beside her, dressed with meticulous care, his head high, one hand lifting his cane with a distinguished rhythm, walked Mr. Dilling.

David's heart all but stopped. While Minnie had met the Session successfully and he knew she was to be in church that day — the first since the baby's birth — he had never once dreamed that Dilling would come. He had never even thought of inviting him! Now, he was here, where he had never been before and probably never would be again, and how would the sermon seem to him? David's cheeks flushed red with embarrassment and anxiety; then he felt ashamed. Dilling had certainly not come *to hear him;* he had come solely to pay this his greatest gesture of respect to the woman and child who bore his name. It was the baptismal service itself, David thought, upon which he must concentrate, upon which he must pour out every beauty of rendition of which he was capable.

The order of service proceeded and at last it was time for the parents with their children to present themselves before the pulpit. They formed in a long half-circle with Colonel Harrison, as Elder, holding the pewter bowl of water. David saw at a glance that Minnie had taken her place hesitantly, humbly as it were, alone at one end. He decided to move to the opposite one and leave her child until the last. The words of grace were spoken; the opening prayers were said and then one by one, came the christenings! At last, with Colonel Harrison beside him, David stood before Minnie. For one hushed moment he remained silent, and then clearly, and with infinite tenderness his voice pronounced again the words of the ancient rite: *Victoria Dilling, child of the Covenant,* I baptize thee. . . . It was over. The parents went back to their places. Minnie rejoined

Mr. Dilling in the pew. Then the congregation rose to sing the baptismal hymn. David's eyes were fixed upon his old friend. He stood, holding the hymnbook in one trembling hand. His lips moved upon the words while one forefinger kept reaching up to remove stealthily a tear under each eye.

> By cool Siloam's shady rill
> How fair the lily grows;
> How sweet the breath beneath the hill
> Of Sharon's dewy rose!
>
> Lo, such the child whose early feet
> The paths of peace have trod;
> Whose secret heart with influence sweet
> Is upward drawn to God.

David, in summer weather, often greeted his flock at the church door below when the service was ended. This morning he waited with nervous eagerness until Mr. Dilling and Minnie would appear. When they did, Dilling gripped his hand hard.

"I was moved by your service, David, deeply moved," he said very low, then added, quizzically, "but don't get the idea I intend to make a practice of this!"

It was apparent that he meant to march straight ahead through the crowd now gathered sociably on the wide walk in front of the door; but this he was prevented from doing. He was surrounded, he and Minnie and the baby! When the people finally let them go, they walked off down the street, the child laughing over her mother's shoulder, Minnie's graceful walk slowed to the rhythm of the old man's cane. David watched them go. The final act of the drama had just been played. Although he was probably unaware of it, Mr. Dilling had at long last been accepted by the town.

The next weeks in the manse were full of preparation for the coming trip. It had been decided to use enough of the college money to fit the travelers out suitably, and now Faith had her new dresses and the rose-trimmed hat of Mary's dreams, and David, a much needed new suit. So on the sunny morning of their departure they presented — to the eyes of the family at least — an appearance of elegant sophistication. David came back when he was almost to the gate to give Mary another kiss, for in spite of her feigned brightness there was a deep wistfulness in her eyes impossible to conceal.

"I'm fine," she protested, "of course I am. We'll get on beautifully. Now have a good time. We'll be thinking about you on the great day! Good-bye! Good-bye!"

They were gone. Mary had not known until the last how greatly, how inordinately she had wanted to go. But she sat down now on the porch to work at her "Pretty Thoughts" box, determined to overcome what she termed her own selfishness. For once, however, this activity did not seem exactly inspiriting, so she finally put it aside and called up Jennie McLean and Mrs. Faraday to come that afternoon to tea.

In her bed at night, safe from all eyes, she wept a little. It had been so long since she and David had had a trip! Then in direct violation of his command she would let her thoughts turn very lightly to Faith in her wide leghorn hat, and *My John*. "Stranger things have happened," she repeated, confidently, "and if Faith just has an *interesting* time, nothing else will matter."

The travelers returned on Tuesday. There had been a thunderstorm that afternoon and the evening sky was alight with streamers of turquoise and gold, but no more bright than their faces. They had had such a wonderful, such a *beautiful* time! Over the supper table they poured out all the story, interrupting each other happily, or eagerly corroborating this and that. The wife of the President had taken Faith under her wing and seen to it that she had escorts for all the events. David had run into old classmates. . . . His face shed years as he talked.

"I didn't know I could enjoy anything as much as these last days," he said.

"And I didn't know it was *possible* to have as good a time as I did," Faith added, her usually reticent dimples now showing in full animation.

It was then Mary put her question.

"Did you meet *My John?*" she asked.

"Oh, indeed yes," David said earnestly. "He's a very fine person, brilliant, too. We had some good talks. By the way, he wanted to be remembered to you and to thank you very much for his mother's visit here. He said he was indebted to her for getting my book. He really put it very — " David's modesty made him hesitate — "very *kindly*," he finished.

"And how did you like him, Faith?"

Faith gave a small giggle and then sobered apologetically. "He's very nice. Only, you see, after Mrs. Jenkins' description I thought he would be young and awfully handsome, and he's really short and stout and bald and forty if he's a day, isn't he, Father?"

"Oh, at the least."

"Really?" said Mary, managing her tone well.

The talk flowed on. David must put his hood on now (since he had refused to do so before) and walk back and forth in the study while they all admired it and congratulated him to their hearts' content. It was late when they went upstairs and even then there seemed so much more to say.

"We'll tell all the rest tomorrow, Mother. You look tired now," Faith said.

Up in their own room David told Mary again how much he had missed her. "Every single minute I kept wishing you were with me! But since you couldn't go, I'm glad Faith did. Do you know, something happened to her out there!"

"Oh, *what?*" Mary breathed.

"Well, it's one of those indefinable things. I don't know whether it was that hat, or the dresses or the attention that did it, but she simply blossomed out. I couldn't believe my eyes, every time I looked at her. She really made quite an impression, Mary! My word, she surely did!"

"On any . . . anyone in particular?"

"Oh, I don't know about that. There was one young chap — from the History Department — who always seemed to be around, but that wasn't what I meant. I think out there she suddenly realized for the first time her full power as a woman — you know, that sort of thing. So I don't think you need have any fears about her future. She's got the talisman now. Like Lucy. Like *you*," he added tenderly.

"Oh, Davy!"

But she repeated his words over and over with sweet relish before she went to sleep. Perhaps this was enough. Perhaps now she wouldn't need to worry again, about Faith, ever. . . .

David was tired the next day and somehow he had picked up an annoying cold. He went down to see Mr. Dilling, however, and tell him all the news while the day was still young. With him he passed over the lighter elements and spoke honestly of his feeling about the degree.

"Of course," he added, "the college is a very small one. I shouldn't feel that it's such an honor and yet — it was rather a big moment for me."

Dilling was earnest. "You must never minimize it, David. You have a right to be proud. You earned that degree more than many a man who has received one from a larger college. I've even had a vicarious thrill out of it myself!"

When David left, Mr. Dilling made a few notes, then went

down to the office and called up the *Moreswell Recorder*. It was due to this that the Thursday's issue carried a neat article headed, *County Man Honored by Alma Mater; Ladykirk Minister Receives Degree*. It was there for all who ran to read.

A few days later David passing by on an errand, stopped at the post office to pick up the mail himself. Wes Shotwell took a long envelope from the box and slowly handed it out, his eyes meaningful.

"Well, R-Reverend, I g-guess mebbe havin' the degree is goin' to m-make some difference," he said.

David laughed. "Oh, I think I feel pretty much the same. Hat still fits and all that."

He turned to speak to someone behind him and did not look at the missive in his hand until he was on the street. Then he read in the upper corner: *Clerk of Session; Moreswell Presbyterian Church*.

David stopped dead in his tracks, staring at it. His body seemed to freeze, to grow hot, to become incapable of movement. Then mechanically his feet began to go forward, his lips spoke automatically to those he passed. He reached the manse gate, went up the walk and into the study. A great calmness had now settled upon him, a self-control bordering upon assurance. He sat down at his desk and looked hard at the letter. It had come. It was here in his very hand. After all the hopes, and the frustrations of the years, here apparently was the long, long looked-for *First Overture* from Moreswell!

Very carefully, slowly, he opened the letter. He thought he understood what had happened. That the visiting committee had been interested in him, he *knew*. But perhaps in calling a man of his age they had felt he should have a degree. Now that barrier was removed.

He spread out the sheet, glancing first at the signature. It was *John H. Griffith*, the older of the two men who had been

out last June! The one to whom he had felt especially drawn.
He read:

My dear Mr. Lyall:

Tonight as I record some Session business here at the church office I am moved to write you of my pleasure in your recent honor. I have already ordered a copy of your book. It has been my privilege to hear you preach more than once and I have greatly enjoyed your sermons. Perhaps it may not be amiss now to confess that I personally would have been happy to "sit under you," as the Scotch put it. However, the situation in which that would have been possible might not have proved congenial to you. The minister of our church here must be burdened with the duties not only of preacher and pastor, but of an executive as well. His days must, perforce, have in them much of what Walter Bagehot refers to as "irritable activity." With your quiet student's bent you are doubtless happier where you are. May I add my good wishes for continued literary work and congratulations again upon your degree . . . .
P.S. Our congregation has at last issued a call to a young man from the northern part of the state.

David folded the paper and put it back in the envelope; then he sat still, slowly smoothing the edges between his thumb and finger. It was all here, in the kindly letter: his gifts, his limitations, his great opportunity so narrowly missed. All here, and something else besides. His future too, was written between the lines.

At last with poignant finality, as a lover might put away a rose from a lost romance, he laid the letter in a secret drawer of the desk.

I'll not tell Mary just yet, he said to himself. I may never tell her.

The next week was a curiously disturbing one to David.

There was first of all the dull heaviness in his heart, in contrast to the lightness of the last few weeks, but in addition to this there was something wrong with the whole atmosphere! Not in the manse itself. Here everyone else was in unusually high spirits. Lucy had received word from Ninian that his father considered a year or two in the coal business good training for his son's future career in the steel industry, so it was possible he might actually begin his work in Kirkville! A possibility hailed with delight by all the family. No, the trouble, whatever it was, was in the town, and, David was forced to conclude, in some way, related to *him*.

When he went into the post office, a knot of men talking in low tones stopped suddenly and became elaborately interested in the great glass bottles of licorice set on the side shelf; when he went into Harrison's store, the Colonel came out from behind the counter and shook hands solemnly. While this was unusual, David imputed it at first to renewed congratulations. However, when the Colonel in weighing the coffee quoted, "Thy way not mine, O Lord, however dark it be," he was not so sure.

There was a vague, diffused attitude of gloom apparent in those he met as he went about his normal way. Or could it be censure? He pondered this possibility seriously, but could think of no glaring omission or commission that could be laid to his charge at the moment.

He said nothing of all this at home, fearing it might worry Mary, but by Friday he was not only uncomfortable, he was alarmed. As he came up the street that afternoon Mr. Wilson came out to his gate and leaned upon it as he often did at such times for a chat. Today, however, he spoke very low and with difficulty.

"I'm not gifted with easy expression," he said, "but I want you to know that the night you came to see me about — you know what I mean —and just sat talking about other things and even when you left, never reproached me, never even spoke of it — well, my soul was knit to yours that night. Sometimes we all put off saying what we feel and then regret it when it's too late. I just wanted to tell you."

David was now thoroughly frightened. *When it's too late!* What could that mean? In a flash he thought of his brief call on Dr. Faraday last week to get some medicine for his cold. The doctor had examined his chest, joking the while about the rare opportunities he had for doing so. Had he discovered something serious, something *fatal* which he had concealed from his patient but which the town by its own mysterious methods had discovered?

He went hastily up to the bedroom as soon as he reached home, caught up his small shaving mirror, carried it to the window and peered intently at his image. He did look pale. He ran a hand over his thin cheeks. He believed he had lost weight, too. He sat down on the edge of the bed with a sudden bitter fact facing him. He had lived too long in Ladykirk not to understand its moods. He realized now that this pervading melancholy which he had sensed for a week was the one usually related with *death*.

He came at last to his decision. Over the week-end he would call upon all his powers to act as usual. He remembered the line from old Euripedes, *To stand from fear set free, to breathe and wait.* Whether he could set fear aside was questionable, but at least he could "breathe and wait," the only way to conquer time. On Monday he would go back to Dr. Faraday and demand the truth. Anything was easier to bear than this uncertainty.

Early Saturday morning the telephone rang with violence. It was Aunt Betsy Wade saying she must see David that day, the matter being extremely urgent.

David, haggard after a sleepless night, answered somewhat shortly.

"I'm very busy today, Mrs. Wade, but I'll try to get over this afternoon if I can."

He walked heavily up the steps to the brick house at four, forcing a smile for Miss Miranda who ushered him in, her little dog at her heels. Aunt Betsy, in black silk and lace, sat in the big parlor as though this was an occasion.

"Be seated, Mr. Lyall. I have something of the greatest importance to discuss with you. Of course," eyeing him sharply, "I suppose you know you've set the whole town by the ears, first with your degree, for which I congratulate you, and now . . . this latest development."

She paused as though granting him a chance to speak. David had often wondered how much feeling Aunt Betsy really had. He decided now she was utterly devoid of it.

"It was Wes Shotwell started the whole thing," she went on. "He let it leak out that you had received a letter from the Moreswell church. They all think it must mean a *call*, and they're scared to death. Everybody's afraid to speak to you about it, since they got wind of it the way they did. That is . . . everybody but me. I decided today to take matters in my own hands."

David was looking at her stupidly, dazedly, trying to grasp the import of her words.

"Now, as I have pointed out to several who have been here to see me about it, the letter *may* have been about something else entirely. But it does look suspicious and the town is upset from end to end. Of course we've all known about the visiting committees from time to time through the years, but Wes Shotwell always passed the word along that no *letters* ever came after them. So, everybody relaxed."

An exclamation escaped David, but Aunt Betsy paid no heed to it nor to the sudden strange light in his eyes.

"I am free to confess that I am extremely agitated myself over the present situation, for I do not intend to have any young whippersnapper from the Seminary conducting my funeral service if I can help it! Now, will you answer me a straightforward question?"

"I'll . . . I'll try," David stammered.

Aunt Betsy leaned tensely forward. "As of this moment," she pronounced, "and to the best of your knowledge, do you intend to remain in Ladykirk?"

"Why . . . yes."

"Ah!" breathed Aunt Betsy. She leaned back in her chair with relief and began to wave her black fan. "That's settled then and I can go ahead with my plans. During these last days when everybody's been in such a stew I decided there was one thing more than any other that might keep you, and especially Mary, content where you are. So I am telling the Trustees at once to put a bathroom in the manse and *I'll pay for it!*"

That evening the June darkness fell softly upon Ladykirk. The field above the manse was ablaze with fireflies; the stars were bright, too, and there was a growing moon. If you listened carefully you could hear the Crick singing.

When the children finally dispersed after all the excited planning (during which the small storage room at the end of the upper hall had been pronounced perfect for Aunt Betsy's gift) David and Mary sat on the back porch alone, she in one of the high-backed rockers, he on the broad low railing. He told her then about the letter from Moreswell and tried to explain what he had read intuitively between the lines, but she could think of it only in connection with the bathroom! Her face showed blissful in the pale light.

David went on gently, trying to make his meaning more plain.

"I have a feeling that we'll always be here in Ladykirk, Mary. As long as we live. Will you mind?"

"Mind?" Mary echoed. "Why, I never really wanted to go anywhere else. Not for myself, that is. It was only for you and the children."

They sat for a little in silence, then he spoke again, looking off over the garden.

"I think now, after all the years, I'll put out of my mind forever any thought of . . . advancement. If I haven't the qualities for a big town minister, maybe I have the right ones for Ladykirk. I couldn't have taken my bees to Moreswell," he added whimsically.

"And," Mary said eagerly, "with your degree *and the bath-room*, it will make a difference here, won't it? Besides, it would have been hard to leave our old friends."

And then David brought forth from his heart the tender secret he had discovered in part while she had lain in the Valley of the Shadow and now again in these last strange days, interpreted to him by Aunt Betsy. They spoke of it in low tones of wonder. They knew now what they had never truly known before. They knew how much Ladykirk loved them.

When it was late, David grew concerned for her. "You must go on up at once," he said. "If you don't mind I'm going to have a turn under the stars before I follow you."

He had to be alone for a little, even from Mary, so he went out into the garden. The grass was moist with dew and the heliotrope was sweet upon the night. The hives were softly murmurous. Above, the golden, gibbous moon rode the reaches of the hills.

He had never known such peace. It was different from any passing elation or transitory content. He could even think now of the confident young man of dreams who had first come to the manse. He could remember without wistfulness or regret; for the old sense of inadequacy and failure had left him. He knew that he had done his best in the place to which it had pleased God to call him. While his feet had traveled the uneven flagstones of Ladykirk, his soul, too, had journeyed.

And so it would be now, on and on as the years passed.

His eyes brooded upon the little sleeping town; then he looked up, as though in dedication.

"And thus I'll take my pilgrimage," he said.

THE END

Date Due